D0387033

WOMEN AND THOMAS HARROW

WOMEN
AND
THOMAS HARROW

BY JOHN P. MARQUAND

LITTLE, BROWN AND COMPANY

Boston   Toronto

*Published simultaneously in Canada
by Little, Brown & Company (Canada) Limited*

PRINTED IN THE UNITED STATES OF AMERICA

*This book is gratefully dedicated
to my secretary, Dorothy Brisson,
because without her loyalty and interest
I would doubtless still be splitting infinitives
in the vicinity of Chapter Three.*

Contents

WOMEN AND THOMAS HARROW

I

The Name Was Spelled P-h-r-y-c-e When They Wove the Bayeux Tapestry

WALTER PRICE was talking about himself again, discoursing in detail on the distinguished and ancient history of the Price family. Tom Harrow had often heard Walter indulge himself before in egocentric reminiscence. Breakfast was almost over, and Tom Harrow was listening without being bored. In fact, he was not sure, because of his age and the erosion of time, whether or not he had ever before heard Walter on the subject of his very early forebears. This was not strange, because he had heard Walter on a great number of others, and for many years had only half listened. Given an adequate space of time, one could discount a number of things about Walter, but Tom Harrow still could not discount him personally. He knew that Walter had ability and he invariably respected Walter's powers of imagination. It was a pleasure to sit over a late breakfast and listen to Walter talk, because it was no longer necessary to give Walter full attention. He could think, as Walter's discourse progressed, that Walter must have overindulged in his old bad morning habit of sitting in a bathtub filled with cold water and drinking a jigger of straight gin.

Tom Harrow could recall distinctly the first time he had ever known Walter to indulge in this practice. This had been when Tom was living in an apartment on Lexington Avenue. It was summer and his wife, Rhoda, had gone to Watch Hill with their son, Hal; but it had been necessary for Tom to stay in town in order to pick the cast for a play, the name of which he could not recollect at the moment. It was a great many years ago, although even then his friendship with Walter Price had already burgeoned, but the whole scene was accurately dated because the gin which Walter had been drinking was still known as "bathtub gin." Walter had occupied Hal's tub, and Walter had not fitted into it accurately.

"Tom," he had heard Walter calling — and whenever Walter wanted anything his voice had the appeal of melodramatic urgency — "will you please come here quickly?"

He could remember the first thought that had run through his mind. Walter in those days frequently told of a crisis which he had faced while staying at the Hotel Biltmore in New York when he was working in an advisory capacity with the author of the play known as *Getting Gertie's Garter*. Walter had been very sure that the play was *Getting Gertie's Garter*, although it could have been *Up In Mabel's Room*, and Tom Harrow had already observed back in the bathtub gin days that Walter was becoming less and less accurate about plays and facts. Indeed, as of the present, Walter was beginning to move his early play-doctoring days to London, where he had helped Mr. Shaw with *Major Barbara* — a difficult move, since Walter's life span did not fit well with *Major Barbara*.

Back at the Biltmore, Walter had felt exhausted after hours of what he chose to call "close intellectual collision," and he had retired to the room supplied for him by the producer of *Up in Mabel's Room* or *Getting Gertie's Garter*, or whatever the confection might have been on which he had been working. The title did not really matter. The point was that Walter had plunged himself into a hot tub for purposes of relaxation, and there were fine large bathtubs in the Biltmore then, as perhaps there were still, but Walter only recollected the Biltmore as it had existed in the days contemporaneous with F. Scott Fitzgerald, whom Walter always oddly referred to as Fitzy.

Plunging into a hot bath for purposes of relaxation was a practice, he often explained, that had been taught him by his old colored mammy on the family plantation near Columbia, South Carolina — a lovely place, which General Sherman had spared after Walter's grandmother, then a mere slip of a girl, had inter-

4

ceded personally with the general. The plantation period had occurred long before Walter had begun moving himself and the whole Price family to their holdings at Halliday Hall in Hampshire, England — not that any of this concerned the bathtub. The point was that Walter in his warm bath had developed a habit of plunging almost beneath the water and then pushing himself upward against the back of the tub. Even in the twenties he had started putting on weight, because suddenly a suction developed between his shoulder blades so severe that any motion he made to extricate himself caused excruciating agony and his cries for assistance went unheeded, but finally nature asserted herself by abhorring the vacuum and thus he was released.

When Walter called on that distant day at Lexington Avenue, Tom hurried to Hal's bathroom fearing that Walter had been caught again, but it was morning and Walter was in cold water. It was Walter's old Scottish tutor, a direct descendant of Boswell, who had taught Walter to indulge in the rigors of a cold prandial bath. The pain, as the tutor had said, was worth the buttered scones, or words to that effect.

"Tom," Walter had said, "would you mind playing the good host and bringing me a bottle of gin to counter the chill? Gin and cold water of a morning give me my best thoughts. It was a trick I learned from my grandfather, Colonel Lamar, who served with Hood's Brigade before he acquired his large holdings in Nicaragua." That was certainly long before Walter had moved the Price family to Hampshire, but Walter had never given up a cold morning tub and gin. The practice set the wheels of the mind revolving, not that the wheels had ever needed lubrication, and ever afterwards Tom had seen to it personally that a fifth of gin was always placed in Walter's bathroom whenever Walter came to stay with him, professionally or socially.

Today at the breakfast table Walter's discourse on the early history of the Price family was not a bad topic for the late morning. Over the centuries, it seemed, the name Price, originally early Norman, had undergone considerable alteration.

"This fact first occurred to me when I was in the fifth form at Harrow," Walter Price said. "Those dear Edwardian days! I wish

5

you might have been able, Tom, to share with me the privilege of having attended Harrow."

Reluctantly Tom pulled his rambling thoughts together. A glance at his Spode coffeecup, at the mahogany of the breakfast table, and at the hot plates on the hunting board reminded him that he also had been occasionally to England.

"Now wait a minute," he said. "I thought you had gone to the Taliaferro School for Boys outside Columbia, South Carolina. You used to walk there barefoot from the old plantation, didn't you? The school was run by Colonel Taliaferro, a great Latinist, who had served with your grandfather Lamar under General Hood — or was I thinking of somebody else?"

Walter Price sighed patiently.

"That was considerably earlier, Tom," he said, "before my Uncle Roderick sent for me in South Africa. Uncle Roderick was one of Rhodes's protégés, you may remember. He started as Rhodes's office boy when he was eleven and a half. I'll have to tell you about Uncle Roderick sometime, Tom. He's a story himself — a true product of the old unregenerate days when England was Old England. May I have another cup of coffee? It's a beautiful George the Third coffeepot, Tom."

"Actually it's George the Second," Tom Harrow said.

"Of course it is," Walter Price answered. "And I remember now. You bought it after *Hero's Return*, didn't you? No wonder you could afford the piece, Tom. But I'm amazed that Rhoda didn't want it."

"She would have, if she'd remembered it," Tom Harrow said. "But she had switched by then to Early American silver. Go and call on her someday and let her show you the Reveres and Hurds I bought her."

"Dear me," Walter Price said, "I've seen them, Tom. I thought they were Presley's old family pieces."

There was no use pursuing the subject. Perhaps everything, even history, ceased being factually accurate after a term of years.

"Let's get back to your school days at Harrow," Tom said. "You must have been pretty old for Harrow, judging from what you told me about that Taliaferro School in Columbia."

6

"I've always admired your memory, Tom," Walter Price said, "but still you fall down sometimes on small details. What was it I ever told you about Taliaferro School in Columbia?"

"I don't suppose I'm as accurate as I used to be," Tom Harrow said, "but it seems to me that you told me once that in your first year in Taliaferro's School in Columbia, South Carolina, you got a young girl into trouble. I think you said that she had something to do with the Temperance Drink Bottling Company."

Walter blinked his eyes twice. There was no doubt that he had put on weight. In fact, his features hardly resembled those of the earlier Price that Tom Harrow had known once, but personality still persisted.

"We're getting off the subject," Walter said. "When was it I told you about Colonel Taliaferro's School?"

Although Walter Price had ceased to be useful long ago, if indeed he ever had been, Tom still enjoyed his company because neither seriously expected anything from the other — except that Walter would probably ask for a loan before his visit terminated.

"I'm glad you asked me that one," Tom Harrow said, "because I can remember the occasion exactly. It was in that apartment that Rhoda and I had on Lexington Avenue. You were sitting in Hal's bathtub drinking gin when you told about the Temperance Drink girl."

"I remember, now that you bring up the point," Walter said. "But please recollect that Southerners are more sexually precocious than Northerners, as a rule. Look what goes on in the West Indies, according to all accounts."

"Whose accounts?" Tom Harrow asked.

"Anyone's accounts," Walter Price said. "Frankly, I don't recall at the moment ever having got any girl in Columbia into trouble; and if I had, I do not think I would have mentioned it in Harold's bathtub because I would have remembered that Rhoda would not have liked it."

"Rhoda was at Watch Hill at the time," Tom said. "You had no reason to worry about Rhoda."

"If Rhoda had been less at Watch Hill," Walter Price said, "and more often in that dear old place of yours on Lexington

7

Avenue, and later on Park, Rhoda might be here this minute, mightn't she?"

Tom Harrow picked up the George the Second coffeepot. It had been with him on Lexington Avenue, but time was beginning to make it a less and less tangible object. He was only lately beginning to discover that one could reach an age when possessions could assume impermanence and lose intrinsic value as they mingled with associations.

"I don't think any trip to Watch Hill had much to do with anything," Tom Harrow said. "But let's get back to our primary subject."

"What subject?" Walter Price asked.

"The Price family," Tom Harrow said. "You were talking about the Price family, weren't you?"

"Was I being so egocentric?" Walter said.

"You were being informative," Tom Harrow said, "not egocentric, Walter."

Their glances met for a moment across the table.

"You grow increasingly dramatically constructive, Tom," Walter Price said. "I'm sure I don't know how I ever got on the subject of the Prices, but it is, quite impersonally, interesting. A Price came over from Normandy with William the Conqueror. I am told, although I cannot confirm it momentarily, that he is depicted riding at the rear of the Duke in the Bayeux tapestry."

"Did he wear a nose guard?" Tom Harrow asked.

"Strange you should mention that," Walter Price said. "I had almost forgotten nose guards, but I wore one when I played left half at Groton, just before I went to Yale."

"I thought you went to Harrow after your Uncle Roderick made money in the DeBeers Syndicate," Tom Harrow said.

Neither of them smiled since each was sufficiently considerate of the other to understand that revealed inaccuracy was not a laughing matter.

"I was popping in and out of several schools," Walter Price said, "directly before I went to Yale. It's hard to keep them straight, but I did wear one of those rubber nose guards at Groton. I distinctly remember the taste of it."

8

"How could you taste it if it was on your nose?" Tom Harrow asked.

"Part of it was in my mouth," Walter Price said. "You must be nearly old enough to have worn a nose guard yourself, even if you didn't go to Groton."

"Well, let's skip it," Tom said, "and tell me about the Price that came over with William the Conqueror."

Walter sipped his coffee.

"His name was Sieur Monsarratt de Phryce. P-h-r-y-c-e. They spelt it that way in those days. Phryce."

"Why did they stop spelling it that way?" Tom asked.

"The Phryce branch in England at the time of Charles the First changed it to Price after the beheading," Walter said, "but my own direct ancestors accompanied the young prince to France. The de Phryce château was only a few kilometers northwest of Versailles. I was entertained there when I was a young lieutenant in World War I. Did I never tell you about the Château de Phryce?"

"Not that I remember at the moment," Tom Harrow said. "But then, you've had a full life, Walter."

"I very seldom mention the Château de Phryce to anyone," Walter said. "It is painful to think about it, but General Pershing stopped there."

"Oh," Tom Harrow said, "if it's painful, don't feel you have to bring it up."

"It's quite all right, Tom," Walter Price said. "All that is painful was the ending of the château. It was completely destroyed with my dear cousins in it by the first shot of the Big Bertha, when the Germans were endeavoring to get the range of Paris. It isn't sensible, of course, that I should be so moved, after the obliteration of so many monuments; but none were so personal to me in quite the same way, Tom. After all, when one comes to think of it, the course of any life is marked by its series of small ruins, at least in the region of human relationships. But then, one must create ruin in order to develop. One can't stand still, can one?"

There was no doubt that occasionally Walter could exhibit a

9

flash of wisdom. It was true, what he had said about ruins of human relationships. People grew away from each other, tastes changed, and nothing was ever static.

"A good case in point might be my friendship with the Duke of Windsor," Walter Price said. "David was Prince of Wales at the time. We saw quite a lot of each other during World War I."

Walter was off again. It was impossible that Walter should feel that anything he said could be believed — or was it? Tom Harrow could not be sure because Walter was the only psychopathic liar he had ever known over a long period of time. It might be possible that Walter could contrive to believe the figments of his own imagination, since they all started on some small platform of fact — and no one was wholly accurate when he talked about himself. It might even be that the palpable falsehoods of Walter Price contained their own peculiar currencies of truth. They indicated a divine sort of discontent. When you thought of it this way, there was a magnificent element in Walter's battle against reality, and his prevarications became part of literary tradition.

Walter Price, when you came to think of it, was only doing to himself what the great Dumas had done to the real D'Artagnan in *The Three Musketeers,* but Walter Price was no Dumas. He was an agent who kept losing clients — a fat man in his sixties, with high blood pressure, traveling down to Ogunquit, Maine, to discuss the possible use of a client's play by a summer theatre; but he was doing the best he could and there was something heart-warming, almost gallant in the effort. The chances were a thousand to one that he had never met the Duke of Windsor, let alone the younger Prince of Wales, but there was still that thousandth chance. You might start to write off the Château de Phryce, but then there had been a Big Bertha.

In the last analysis there was a good deal to be said for that secondary school platitude about playing the game to the end. If you had been playing the game for a very long while, you became conditioned to it until you finally forgot embellishments and graces, and in the end facts were not so important as they used to be. Character in the end was about the only value left, and by disregarding fact, Walter Price had gained in character; yet he was meticulously reliable when it came to contracts and agreements — but then, he had to be.

Tom Harrow looked across the table to the window over the garden. Everything outside was fresh and delicately green because it was the end of May. The gentle pastel tints of the trees and bushes were a sign of renewal reminding him of a speech which his first producer, Arthur Higgins, had once made when presented with a silver tray by a grateful cast on the three hundredth performance of a play.

"This lovely gift," Arthur Higgins had said, "will stimulate me to rededicate myself anew." Although these awful words were not useful in themselves, they evoked anew a picture of Arthur Higgins, now deceased, which went to prove that the distillation of fact was all that mattered.

It was spring. Decoration Day was just around the corner, and it occurred to Tom Harrow that this year he must positively make a visit to the family lot in the Upper Hill Cemetery. He would stand there looking at his parents' graves and muse on the inescapable fact of mortality, which was one fact that could not distill itself; but he would not resolve to rededicate himself anew. It was too late, because you only dedicated yourself once in a life time, and there was no such thing as rededication. And the worst of it was that you never really knew that you had genuinely dedicated yourself until long after you had done it.

"There's more coffee and bacon if you want them, Walter," Tom Harrow said. "They are up there being kept at a constant temperature, like your friendship and mine. You are sure you don't want some more?"

"Oh, no thanks, Tom," Walter said, "and are you sure you don't mind my staying over tomorrow or the day after?"

"It will be a pleasure, Walter," Tom answered. "There will only be the family. But I hope you will excuse me for a while right now. I've got one or two things to do. I'm still worrying over finishing a third act, and I've got to call up Beechley in New York."

11

"I know that you and Ed are very close ever since the old Mort Sullivan days," Walter said, "but it does seem to me, quite frankly, that Ed has been slipping in the last few years."

It was hard to tell whether or not Walter had heard something. You never knew exactly when you were on solid ground with Walter Price.

"We are all slipping, I suppose," Tom said, "in our small, individual ways."

It was pleasant to realize that he was including himself in the slipping group only through courtesy, but the moment would arrive sometime and there could be no concealment.

"Are you sure Emily won't be bored if I stay?" Walter Price asked.

"You know very well Emily is never bored," Tom Harrow said. "That's the main reason why I married Emily."

"Oh, come now," Walter said, "there were lots of other reasons."

The worst of it was that reasons were like the lilacs outside the window — they burgeoned and bloomed triumphantly and then went to seed. Villon had said something along those lines. Villon was a very able poet.

"The capacity for not being bored was one of the main reasons," Tom said, "and someone, out of compassion, had to take her off the stage. But the point is that Emily is going to love your staying here awhile."

His glance traveled again around the dining room. The room and the whole house were the result of his having been director and producer as well as a playwright. It was inevitable that the place should have the perfection and the atmosphere of a stage set. Suddenly, because thoughts moved oddly sometimes, he found his mind writing stage directions:

The curtain rises on the Harrow dining room at a quarter before ten o'clock of a late May morning. The pale but glorious sunlight of a New England spring filters through window at L; through its small panes one glimpses dewy lilacs in bud and the fresh foliage of a copper beech. The dining room itself is austere New England of the early nineteenth century, as is ac-

12

curately indicated by its delicate moldings and the truly beauti-
ful mantelpiece at R. The wallpaper is authentic French pictorial,
showing the conventional scene of shipwrecked Ulysses en-
countering Nausicaa and her maidens. The furniture, Chippen-
dale, purchased in the great days of Christie's, is worthy of this
restrained and beautiful background, markedly the fine screen
concealing the pantry door, and the hunting board acquired from
an Irish castle. Hot plates for a comfortable breakfast stand on
its meticulously waxed surface. Obviously the owner of this
dining room has a sharp eye for detail. Seated, at the rising of
the curtain, one discovers WALTER PRICE, *corpulent, loquacious,*
in his mid-sixties; and his younger host, THOMAS HARROW,
director and playwright, turned fifty — a spare man, carefully
dressed, with an air about him showing that he is up from New
York and not indigenous to this expensively acquired background.
There is a sound of footsteps (the clattering of mules) on a stair-
case offstage at R. EMILY, *third wife of* THOMAS HARROW, *ash-*
blond and plumply late-thirtyish, in a gold brocade housecoat,
enters at R. Though it is only ten in the morning, she wears a
number of exceedingly heavy gold bracelets, a diamond-and-
sapphire clip, and three diamond rings. One gains the impression
that Emily carries as much as she possibly can on her person in
case things may become difficult again.

Tom Harrow had learned never to discount coincidence. He
could never remember whether the scenario had flashed through
his mind before or after he had heard Emily's mules on the stairs
outside. But there she was, entering at R, with the housecoat and
exactly the correct amount of jewelry, smelling of bath salts and
Chanel No. 5, and with her hair done in the new way that she
had picked up from that place in the sixties, just off Park Avenue,
run by that new little man about whom Rita had told her the
last time Rita or someone else had come East from Hollywood.

"Good morning, everybody," Emily said. "And it is a good
morning, isn't it?"

No one could have written a better entrance line. Tom pushed
back his chair, crossed to the right and kissed her lightly.

13

"Ummm, dearest," Emily said.

She had made the same humming noise the first time he had ever kissed her, and she still did it, and somehow the sound was never as perfunctory as it should have been.

"Walter and I were both wondering where you were, dear," Tom said. "We were hoping rather desperately that you would join us at breakfast — but better late than never."

"Oh, I would have, Tom," Emily said, "except I do know when to efface myself, don't I? I knew you and Walter wanted to have one of your good long talks. I can read all Tom's expressions now, Walter. The thing to notice is that teensy-weensy wrinkle just above Tom's nose. Whenever it deepens, I've done something wrong, and it deepened the last time I interrupted you and Walter, Tom, and why shouldn't it have? I was being selfish. Tom is possessive about his old friends, Walter, just the way he ought to be."

"Walter is staying for a few days, dear," Tom said.

"Oh, splendid," Emily said. "Then I will have a chance to see Walter, and so will Harold. Is Harold down yet?"

"No, not yet," Tom answered.

Emily seated herself at the foot of the table. Her brocade housecoat rustled discreetly, and her bracelets, as she put her elbows on the table, made a comfortable, solid sound.

"Stepmothers are always horrid, aren't they?" she said, and her brown eyes turned appealingly to Walter Price. Her ash-blond hair and her brown eyes were the combination, as Arthur Higgins had often said, that got Emily through the outer office, and they still were so beautiful that they frequently made one forget the beginnings of her double chin.

"I hate to be a prying stepmother, Tom," she said, "but Harold came in very late last night, and I don't see what there is for him to do in this poky little town. Not that it isn't a dear town."

"She means it's dear because I lived here once, Walter," Tom Harrow said, "and Emily's middle name is Loyalty. Emily Loyalty Harrow. She added it the moment she dropped her maiden name."

"Why, darling," Emily said, "you say the sweetest things some-

14

times, so unexpectedly, and you've never said that one to me before. He really hasn't, Walter. There's always something new every minute when you're the handmaiden to a genius."

"Yes, dear," Tom said. "Each day you must rededicate yourself anew, and let's not mind about Harold's late hours. Besides, it is very patient of him, and gracious, to be here with us."

"Darling," Emily said, "I adore having Harold, and you know I always have, ever since he first appeared in my life as a gangling, pouty little boy from Groton."

"Don't speak disparagingly of Groton, dear," Tom Harrow said. "It's one of Walter's alma maters."

"Oh," Emily said, "I never knew you went to Groton, Walter. You've never acted like a Grotonian. And coming from me, that's a compliment, darling."

"He went there," Tom said, "and he wore a nose guard."

Emily dissolved into soft laughter. Her laugh was still beguiling, and she usually knew when to use it.

"Oh dear," she said, "I never can tell when Tom is going to be funny. It still creeps up and pounces, just the way it did the first time I met him at dear old Arthur Higgins's apartment. Age cannot wither nor custom stale thy infinite variety."

"That's a very apt quotation, Emily," Walter Price said. "I've often applied it to Tom myself, but never out loud."

"She must have been browsing in the library, although the quotation is not quite correct," Tom said, "and stumbled over a loose Bartlett. And I have another one for you, dear. If you keep reading Bartlett, 'Get thee to a nunnery'—also William Shakespeare."

Emily laughed again.

"Darling," she said, "isn't this a nunnery enough — being away in this poky old house for the next three months or so? I don't mean that I don't love it, and that I don't love the creative improvements you've made on it. Sometimes I say to myself that it is one of your best stage arrangements. It's almost like a revival of *Berkeley Square*."

He had never been able to get over feeling a sharp surprise when Emily startled him. The experience was still like running into a door in the dark.

15

"That's a very valid observation, dear," he said, "and I know what you mean. But after all, we're both in the theatre, and if you've been in the theatre long enough I suppose you can't help becoming theatrical. I admit I'm theatrical, and Walter here is, too. Somehow you can't stop attitudinizing, even when you're at home."

"Oh, Tom," Emily said, "I didn't intend a single thing I said to be a criticism. I just love the whole house, and I know you do your best work here, and I know how you enjoy the atmosphere, and I'm beginning to enjoy it myself more and more each year — the cemetery and the streets and everything, and the small-town-boy-who-made-good part of it. But you will admit it is such a little puddle for such a big frog, dear, and you are big in *any* puddle."

There was no reason why Emily should have liked the house or the town, since she was unfitted for both by training and predilection. He was only irritated because she was obviously trying to solicit the sympathy of Walter Price. He wished that Emily would stop soliciting sympathy, but she always had — and from the most unlikely quarters.

"It isn't a puddle," he said; "it's an environment, my dear."

He was relieved when the pantry door opened, because Emily, once she started, always found it difficult to drop a subject. It was Alfred, the colored houseman, in his gray alpaca coat — a sign that it was morning. In the evening he wore a fresh white coat, and there was no reason why he should not have looked well on the wages that he and his wife were receiving as a couple. There were times when Emily expressed a suspicion that Ruth was not Alfred's wife, but if Ruth went where Alfred went, so far away from town, her adaptability overcame possible moral turpitude.

"Mr. Dodd asks if he might see you in the garden, Mr. Harrow," Alfred said.

The National Association for the Advancement of Colored People would have been delighted by Alfred's voice, which had no hint of Dixie in it. Alfred was a highly educated man for whom Tom Harrow felt a personal and professional respect.

16

If you wanted a scene in the White House, with a colored butler like the one who had appeared in a Sherwood war play, or if you wanted a gentle colored professor in a sequence of quiet social significance, there was no reason to look further. Alfred had a fine, high forehead, deep-set, sensitive eyes, and the delicate hands of an artist. It was incredible that what Emily said she had discovered could be true — that Alfred and Ruth daily used up a fifth of bourbon from the liquor closet and that Alfred made two surreptitious calls to New York each day so that he could play the numbers. On the whole, Tom Harrow condoned both these facts, because Emily never had been able to get on with servants — but Alfred and Ruth were able to understand her.

"Thank you, Alfred," he said, and he smiled affectionately at Emily and Walter Price. "I'm afraid I'll have to leave you two alone until lunchtime. There's the garden and then there are some calls to New York."

"Tom, dear," Emily said, "I wish you wouldn't force yourself into this routine. We've hardly settled in and we never seem to have any time to do anything together."

"I know, dear," Tom said. "I realize I'm always saying and hoping that I'll have some leisure on my hands here, and then duty obtrudes itself; but I'm sure, this year, that things will quiet down."

"I know you have to keep on paying alimony," Emily said, "to that Laura Hopedale, who doesn't need it, and besides, you support Harold and . . ."

Tom raised his hand deliberately. Emily never could learn the value of reticence or when it was time to stop if she had an interested audience, and possibly it paid her not to learn.

"Tell Walter the rest after I've gone, dear," he said. "Don't be hurt with me, but I think I know what else you're going to say."

He seldom needed to wonder what Emily was going to say. The unreality of the theatre world had descended heavily upon the breakfast scene. It was no wonder that people in the theatre found it hard to get on with outsiders and ended by clinging together in self-defense. Most of their lives were conducted in disproportionate make-believe, and dramatic effect was actually an unnatural phenomenon requiring years of cultivation. The gesture and the word that interested an audience across the footlights were peculiar deviations from ordinary life. A special talent was required to select such technicalities. No wonder the conversation in the dining room had been off the normal beat. No wonder the house was decorated with large, bold strokes, and no wonder he was not the man he used to be. He had lived so long with flamboyant personalities, had been obliged to cope so long with what was called artistic temperament, and had been compelled to deal so long and charmingly and patiently with actors' and actresses' stupidities, that of course his own character had changed.

II

It's Always Fair Weather, Even without a Stein, When Good Fellows Get Together

IT WAS not consoling to realize that he had been a ham actor in his sequence with Emily at the breakfast table, bidding for laughs and sympathy from a nonexistent audience. And now Jack, of Dodd's Arborists and Landscaping Service, was waiting for him in the garden. This fact in itself had its dramatic significance although it might be lacking in audience appeal. He and Jack Dodd, when in school together, had competed for the affections of the same girl, and he had often wondered what would have happened if Jack Dodd had not won the competition. It had been so long ago that they were now almost strangers, and yet you could not be wholly a stranger to anyone in a small town where you had once lived. The surface of the town had changed as much as he had; the business had once been called Dodd's Nursery. Now it was Dodd's Arborists and Landscaping Service, but the undertones were there. A new pickup truck labeled Dodd's Arborists and Landscaping Service stood in the driveway in front of the old stable, which had been turned into a garage many years before.

It would have been a desecration to change any part of the garden, which had been designed just after the house was built in the first decade of the 1800's. He had only tried, as he had with the house, to put it back in its original condition. Everyone, including members of the Garden Clubs of America, had called the final result a notable achievement, and, in spite of the professional advice he had received, he could give himself most of

19

the credit. He had always disliked a sloppy stage set and he was increasingly critical of the best stage designers. He had treated the weed-grown garden like a stage, yet with respect for the original architect, a Frenchman exiled by Napoleon, according to tradition. The summerhouse, or gazebo, not far from the crumbling brick wall, told more of that forgotten landscape artist than any of his box-bordered paths. Even in its ruined stage it had the spirit of the Regency and he knew from the moment he saw it that he must exercise great care in reconstruction. He had been uncompromisingly particular that nothing was planted that could not have grown there more than a few years after the sea-fight between the *Constitution* and the *Java*. It was the end of May and things would look better in a week or so, but spring would be gone by then. Now in the morning light the garden was full of hope, and though he was against pathetic fallacy, he could believe it was grateful to him for its renewal.

There was only one thing about it that marred his satisfaction — the remark that Emily had made about *Berkeley Square*. The reconstruction had been too meticulous, too self-consciously removed from the present. It was not a formal garden; instead it was a horticultural museum, and now the discovery appalled him. What was it in him that made him desire to recreate something that time had erased? Obviously his desire for self-expression represented some form of escape, but still he could not understand from what he was escaping. If the effort represented an intense desire for order, he could not understand the compulsion, because his life had been orderly — or had it? Perhaps he had been seeking peace of mind, although he should have known that doing over a house and garden was a childish way to achieve it.

Jack Dodd was standing on the yellow graveled walk almost in the center of the garden. There was something puzzling about his expression when Tom first saw him. You could not tell whether he approved or disapproved or whether he was simply making a mental financial estimate. His shoulders were bent forward and his face had a tanned, outdoor look. The pockets of his blue serge suit bulged with a Dodd catalogue and order blanks and there was a smear of lime dust on his left shoulder.

"Hello, Jack," Tom Harrow said.

"Hello, Tom," Jack Dodd said. "You're looking good."

There must have been some sort of reverse explanation of why he was pleased that Jack Dodd should call him Tom. It struck Tom Harrow that morning, as it had before, how curious it was that he could never be wholly at ease with Jack Dodd or with other of his contemporaries there in town, when he could deal with people in any other place in the world adroitly, affably, and without the slightest sense of strain. He had once tried to get things down to an easier basis by asking Jack Dodd into the house for a drink. He should have known that Jack would not have fitted into the setting, and Alfred, carrying a Georgian tray, had not helped. When Jack Dodd had asked for a shot of rye and some water as a chaser, Alfred had been obliged to go back for another glass suitable for a shot. There had been no rapprochement and no new basis.

Ironically, Tom Harrow could hear himself saying at dinner parties in the neighborhood of Park Avenue that the most useful thing that had ever befallen him was a public school education in a small New England town. And why was it he was grateful for this benefit? He was grateful because he could rub shoulders with people in every echelon of life, understand their problems and speak their language. And basically perhaps this concept was still true, except that the echelons had been changing since he was a schoolboy. What, he wondered that morning, did Jack Dodd actually think of him? There was a type of friendliness in Jack's glance, and curiosity, but also a broad indifference. Undoubtedly Jack Dodd was thinking that this Tom Harrow had picked up a lot of slick tricks and bad habits since the old days, and you had to watch things you did not understand.

"Well, it certainly is good to see you, Jack," Tom Harrow said. "How have things been all winter?"

"I can't complain, Tom," Jack Dodd said. "The snow hung on longer than usual, but it made up for the dry spring."

21

"I hope Malvina got through the winter all right," Tom Harrow said. He had nearly forgotten that expression, "getting through the winter," but its meaning had come back to him. Malvina was Jack Dodd's wife, and there was no reason whatsoever why he should not refer to her as Malvina, although when he did so to her face she very often became embarrassed and called him "Mr. Harrow."

"Malvina is all right, except for that hip of hers," Jack Dodd said. "It used to be called rheumatism, but now it's arthritis. It's getting so it's hard to keep up with these new names for diseases and flowers. Isn't that so, Tom?"

It seemed to Tom Harrow that Jack Dodd had stuck out his neck slightly more than usual by ending his speech with a question.

"I'm sorry to hear that, Jack," he said. "I was talking to a doctor in New York only the other day about arthritis and I understand they're coming up now with one of these new wonder drugs that's better than cortisone. I'll let you know when I hear some more about it."

"Thanks, Tom," Jack Dodd said, "I'd appreciate hearing. You look as though you'd come through the winter all right yourself. You didn't get that coat of tan sitting around New York."

"That's right," Tom Harrow said. "As a matter of fact, Emily and I took off for a while to the West Indies in March."

"Is that so?" Jack Dodd said. "The West Indies."

Sooner or later they would get down to business, but it would not look well to be brusque and, besides, at any cost Tom Harrow did not want to appear patronizing.

"How's that pretty daughter of yours getting along, Jack?" he asked. "What's her name? I'm getting worse and worse with names . . . Irene?"

There was a change in Jack Dodd's expression. You could not tell whether it was paternal pride or amusement, but the change was appreciable.

"Reenie's doing fine," Jack Dodd said. "You know, she started in at Mount Holyoke College."

"Is that so?" Tom Harrow said. "Well, that's fine."

22

He tried to evoke a mental picture of Irene, but she was only a name to him.

"But she's like her old man," Jack Dodd said, "no good at books, and she's back home now. Maybe Harold told you."

"Harold?" Tom Harrow said, and he was ashamed that his voice sounded sharp.

"He was over to the house last night," Jack Dodd said, "taking Irene to the pictures."

"I guess he came back late," Tom Harrow said, "after my bedtime, anyway. But that doesn't mean much. I always get sleepy here."

"The garden looks good, doesn't it?" Jack Dodd said. "Seems as if everything came through except a couple of the azaleas."

"That's right," Tom Harrow said. "I hope you're well enough fixed for help so you can take it over again this season, Jack. Aside from your knowing a lot more about it than I do, it would be nice seeing you around."

He was disturbed when the business talk was over. He could not understand, when Jack Dodd continued on the subject of Irene, whether Jack was amused or worried. He could not understand how Harold had met Irene Dodd. It was a piece of information, but he wished that he knew whether Jack Dodd had intended it as such. . . . At any rate, Dodd's Arborists and Landscaping Service agreed to take care of the garden.

The house stood on the town's main residential street on a ridge of high ground sloping gradually down to the river. It was one of a row of houses which had been built in the best McIntire tradition by the town's local shipwrights for the more prominent shipowners, in the days when the town had been a seaport. There was a marked similarity in the architecture of those houses, in cupola and cornice and in the arch of the doorways, and their interior plans were the same — the broad hall that stretched from the front door to the back, the two front parlors, the back parlor, and the dining room, the broad staircases and landings leading to the bedchambers on the second and third stories — but the finish of no two was alike. They had been

23

built pretentiously for large families. The plots of land on which they stood with their shade trees and gardens had run back to the stables and coach houses that represented a mode of living which no longer existed. There were very few people left in town who could afford any longer to keep up the houses on Johnson Street. In Tom Harrow's memory, several of them had fallen into a state of hideous disrepair, but their owners had clung to them so tenaciously that it was still difficult to buy a house in the row and it still meant something, even in a changing world, to live on this main street. In spite of increasing motor traffic, the row had a conspicuousness which must have been brash and arrogant when the houses were new, but which had been mellowed by time, without wholly disappearing. Johnson Street might become a thoroughfare of funeral and tourist homes eventually, but even then it would retain its dignity, and perhaps, it occurred to Tom Harrow, dignity in the end was all that mattered — and he wished very much that this fact had registered with him a number of years ago. Unfortunately, you seldom think of dignity at the appropriate period of life.

When the Saebury house on Johnson Street had come on the market, he had not hesitated to buy it at the asking price, even though he knew the decision was not practical. He knew he was indulging in a sort of pretentiousness which he should have outgrown after he had become inured to Broadway openings. He knew he was not fooling anyone when he came back and bought the Saebury house on Johnson Street. He did not belong there, but still he had not hesitated. It had been a gesture that was entirely personal. When Emily asked him why he had done it, he had produced the quotation about the weariest river winding somewhere safe to sea — but this was a superficial explanation. He had bought the house on Johnson Street because, instinctively, he had not wished to see it fall to pieces. He had bought it and restored it out of a sense of obligation; but if anyone had asked him obligation to what, he would not have been able to answer. The obligation was still upon him at the moment. He should not have left New York in late May — but there he was, because he had wanted to see the garden. He had no regrets for the impulse

24

when he walked from the garden around the house to the front door and saw the restored wood fence and the brick sidewalks of Johnson Street. He had no regrets, but he wished that he could fully understand his motivation. He was always accurate about the motivation of characters in a play, but he was seldom as successful in recognizing his own, and perhaps no one was ever wholly successful along these lines.

It was getting to be time to call New York but there was still a margin of leisure since nothing around him synchronized with New York. Ed Beechley was customarily in the office at 10:30, but it was safer to wait until eleven because Ed Beechley was one of those people who always believed that being late to the office and unavailable, indicated position, and Ed, like other people who had come up the hard way, was careful of position. Tom knew also that it would not be a good day for work, with Walter Price in the house. If he was to put finishing touches on the last act of the play on which he was working, he needed an interval of time unbroken by interruptions. It had always seemed to him that he could manage such a schedule after he had bought and renovated the house, and he was still sure that he would get things started, particularly if Emily should leave to visit someone, as she was very apt to do after a week or ten days of quiet. In the meanwhile, before calling up the Beechley office, he might walk downtown for the mail — not that he could not have sent someone — but he enjoyed the walk.

His hat and the key to the mailbox were both on the front-hall table and the shortest way to reach them was to walk up the steps of the front portico with its graceful Corinthian columns and push down the heavy brass latch of the Saebury front door. The door with its eight panels was fashioned from Santo Domingo mahogany that might have been carried north on one of the Saebury ships. It had been painted at some period but now the paint was off and the door had been rubbed and oiled. There had been no settling of sill or foundation in the Saebury house. The mahogany door swung inward as easily and quietly as it had for more than a hundred years, revealing the hall and stairway with its beautifully turned balusters. No amount of investigation had been

25

able to tell him who the designer of the house had been. He was certain it had not been McIntire. The stairs and the proportion of the hall did not have the McIntire touch. They were lighter and more spare, indicating as surely as print that the town had once been famous for its shipyards.

The unknown designer had no doubt been an artisan who had taken time off from the yards to draw the Saebury plans, but the instinct for space and proportion was the reflection of a definite personality. He had obviously been plagued by a series of intolerances, traces of which still remained in the Saebury hall. He had been intolerant of waste or clumsiness, and his honesty or his professional pride had made him intolerant of careless work. Beyond his conscientiousness had lain an appreciation of beauty, and with it, perhaps, a sense of revolt against his own environment — because the town must have been grim and cold in the days when the Saebury house had been conceived. The whole hall was a revolt and a craving for luxury which its builder had never known. It was easy to make these deductions, but something unspecified in the Saebury house showed that its builder's mind was a dawn-of-the-nineteenth-century mind, attuned to past difficulties which social historians might attempt to analyze but could not resurrect. Tom Harrow realized that if it were possible to meet the builder face to face they would not have understood each other. What one would have thought was remarkable, the other would have thought was natural. The creation of taste was based upon such obvious momentary desires that a simple mind did not have to analyze them. The builders of the new split-level ranch types that were sprouting up along the new highways doubtless were all obeying a modern impetus without being bothered by thought. The builder of the Saebury house would have been an unrewarding social contact, but there was no doubt that he had known his trade. Beneath the angle of the staircase, so much of which was waste space but all of which added to the sense of the hallway's ease and depth, came the dining room door, and the dining room door stood open. As Tom Harrow closed the front door, he could hear Emily's voice raised to its confidential, earnest note — a tone which indicated, even

26

before he overheard the words, that she was trying to tell her side of a difficulty to Walter Price, and trying also to enlist his support.

"He never told me a thing about it, Walter darling," she was saying. "He simply presented it as an accomplished fact; and now, here we are, uprooted merely because of a whim, and now after two years of building-up and tearing-down and living in a sort of madhouse, not really knowing where we were living, I honestly believe he's getting restless again. I honestly do believe so, Walter. It isn't as though he really had roots here. He only came here when he was fifteen, and just stayed awhile with his mother's sister, who must have been a very poky old spinster, according to her photographs. You know how sentimental Tom is. You can see her picture in the library. I do not believe that Tom was deliberately thoughtless when he moved me here without a by-your-leave. As a matter of fact, Tom has always been very sweet to me, right from the beginning. He was so desperately lonely, Walter, when we first met. He was so appealing — just like a little boy, and I think you, like everyone else, will say that his work has improved enormously. I will only say that Tom is forgetful, and of course he is enormously sensitive, Walter, actually to the point of emotional instability. But what I cannot understand is why, with his sensitivity, this place shouldn't give him the creeps in exactly the way it does me. I know the guest room is charming and everything's like the American Wing in the Metropolitan, but it still is creepy. It's all been cleaned and everything. It doesn't smell or anything, but I can't get over the feeling that lots of people have lived here and have had babies and everything. Somehow you don't have a sense of privacy — not nearly as much as you get in any apartment on Park Avenue, or even, say, in a cottage at Easthampton. Walter, I don't know if you've noticed, but there really isn't any room for bathrooms . . ."

The only reason he was eavesdropping was because it would have been needlessly embarrassing if they had heard him in the hall. There was nothing novel in any of Emily's remarks, all of which moved in the pattern of an old sequence. Her mind had a retentive quality that never permitted her to forget her obvious observations. In time, these formed tape-recordings that could be rewound and replayed by a chance word or observation; and he was quite sure that Emily did not know how frequently she repeated herself, and was unaware of her growing loquacity. It was not her fault that the old recording would start as soon as a particular thought struck her, and now she was on the subject of bathrooms.

"Of course there was plumbing in the house before Tom bought it," she was saying. "There was a zinc-lined bathtub in the servants' ell, and a family bathroom at the end of the upstairs hall that even Tom said was more interesting than that all-copper bathroom that was once exhibited in the Museum of Modern Art. Well, there just wasn't any space for more bathrooms, and Tom and the architect just had to dream up places so that the proportions of the bedrooms would not be disturbed. Now, I've always liked a good bathroom, and I don't like to be a contortionist getting in and out of a tub."

She paused and laughed in the informal tone she used when she was asking someone to share her little joke. He could remember that he had once been intrigued by Emily's laughter. Standing there detachedly in the hall, he could still recognize that it was attractive — but Emily was going on.

"Do you know where Tom's bathroom is?" she asked. "It's in a little niche called a prayer-closet! They thought more about prayer than about keeping clean, in Federalist America. That's only a joke, Walter. I've had my nose rubbed in Federalist America by now and I know that plumbing was not invented then, although they used to have it in Roman villas or what have you, and maybe Tom is right when I take up what he calls my Bath Routine, and when he says that the world might be better off if there were more praying and less plumbing. But when you come to think of it, Walter, India doesn't seem to be very well off, does it, where they have no plumbing at all and millions of prayer wheels and what have you?"

He had never heard the one about the prayer wheels before, but in any play that had a long run actors kept adding to their routine. He was wrong in fearing that Emily was moving off at a tangent. The prayer wheels were only a brief diversion.

"Tom is forever talking about motivation," she was saying, "and I suppose there was some motivation when he put *this* show on the road. But what do you suppose it was, Walter — to move here, when we had that lovely house on the dunes at East-hampton? I think in some ways he's full of free guilt because he didn't consult me the way he does about everything else. Do you suppose he was trying to escape from something? And if so — what? I really don't think he's looked at another woman since we were married, not that they don't keep looking at Tom — and they should, because he gets more and more attractive all the time; and that reducing and massage man who worked on him in the apartment three mornings a week all through the winter has honestly done wonders. I have had a thought that it is my predecessor that he was trying to escape from — Laura Hopedale, I mean. I don't blame his feeling bitter about her after the way she literally took him to the cleaners and then never offered to change the agreement, when I understand her Mr. Number 4 is worth literally trillions. Of course I didn't understand about these things, having only just come from Indiana — only a starry-eyed Hoosier girl, darling — when I first met Tom at dear old Arthur's. Tom was truly desperate, and you know, though he's miles older than I am, he does have that little-boy quality. . . . I don't see how so many men retain it after middle age — especially American men. I've never seen Frenchmen with wistful little-boy qualities, have you? Nor Englishmen, except young transplanted poet ones, who don't really count for any number of reasons. . . . Oh, dear me, where was I?"

Where was Emily, indeed? Off the rails on the curve of her own garrulity, but he had never heard her ask before where she was. It showed that Emily had lived so long that she, too, was beginning to forget, even though she was correctly miles younger than he. It was true that he had told her his troubles that night at Arthur Higgins's, but he was damned if he had told them in a little-boy way, or if he had a little-boy quality, either. It was too late to cough or make any sound in the hall by now, because if she were to know that he had overheard her it would only cause an unnecessarily difficult moment for them both. The point still was: where was Emily? Taken from the angle of their relationship, it was honestly quite a question.

"You were talking very charmingly and cogently," he heard Walter Price say, "about the immaturity of American men. I can agree with you completely. Having been educated in England and the Continent, after a carefree childhood in Columbia, South Carolina, I have the advantage of a very real perspective . . ."

"I know that I was talking about immaturity," Emily said, and her voice had assumed an unexpectedly compelling quality. She could stop anyone talking — even Walter Price — if she wanted to make a point. "But what was it that I was talking about before that?"

"About Tom's second wife, I think," Walter said, "and you were on the ever-painful subject of alimony. Between you and me, I disapproved of Laura from the first moment, and I did my best to warn Tom. I spoke to him in a very man-to-man way. Indeed, I went right to the mat about it, out of sheer affection. 'Why get married again?' I said. 'Isn't one experience enough? Why not follow the wiser precept of loving them and leaving them?' Now I had a great advantage over Tom, of course, of having followed for a lifetime a quite unattainable romance. I don't know whether I ever told you, Emily. . . ."

Obviously the time had arrived to create an interruption by a cough or a careless footstep, but Emily's voice cut in again.

"Of course I was just a little starry-eyed Hoosier girl," Emily was saying. Tom had tried to induce her to drop that phrase, but had never succeeded. In fact, lately she was using it more and more regularly. "But still I told Tom at the time not to put up with that agreement for a moment. Of course there weren't any grounds, or Tom didn't want to sue on grounds. He's so utterly frivolous sometimes and so beguilingly American, but thank goodness women don't have to conform to chivalry, do they? I know what a traumatic experience it was for Tom, facing marital difficulties a second time, and I think that a sensitive, artistic spirit like Tom's magnifies everything much more than we pedestrian people can realize. Do you know what I've often thought? I've often thought, thank heaven Tom isn't able to bear a child. He would distort the trauma out of all proportions. . . . But I really don't think he moved here to run *away* from Laura Hopedale. I think, on the contrary, he came here to run *after* someone —not a reality so much as a memory. It's Tom's incorrigibly romantic streak."

Her voice stopped. When Emily was on the stage, her timing had left much to be desired; but occasionally she knew when to stop, and this was a correct moment, when everything was hanging in dramatic balance, and even Walter Price's mind was off himself, which indicated a considerable achievement.

"I don't quite follow you, my dear," he said. "I've known Tom to pursue a number of projects very assiduously, but never a memory. What sort of memory?"

There was another pause. If he had been directing the scene himself, he would have insisted on this silent beat of time at just this point.

"I know it may sound fantastic," Emily said, "but every human being is fantastic in some department, isn't he? If you were to ask me, I think Tom's come here because of old memories of Rhoda."

Now and then Emily could still surprise him. Emily's monologues might continue by the hour. You might be fighting off drowsiness or the ultimate of boredom, when suddenly she would hit on something. It might be only the fabrication of a chain of inaccuracies, but Emily had her own qualities of perception. He was surprised to discover that he was startled simply because his first wife's name had been mentioned by his third wife, but then, perhaps if you had ever been closely associated with anyone, you might start at her name. You never could tell about memory. Take the memory of a horse, for instance, that caused him invariably to balk or shy at a certain turn on a riding trail simply because something had occurred there once that had shaken him . . . But Emily was speaking again.

"You see, I don't think he's ever lived-down Rhoda. Hasn't someone said, some poet or someone, that a first love is never over?"

31

Her voice dropped almost to a whisper, another effect which had been achieved by the teaching of Arthur Higgins, who had always had a weakness for the old Belasco school. But one should never discount techniques simply because they are timeworn, and Emily did not pause too long.

"I don't mean that he hasn't lived her down in a practical sense. Tom has always been a great liver-downer — the 'here today, gone tomorrow' school. An artist has to be, or else his sensitivity would kill him, and Tom is a creative artist, no matter how annoyed he gets when someone tells him so. Of course Tom is one of those people who would have been good at anything. Did you know he was positively brilliant in the war? Well, my only point is that a man who can turn his hand to anything must be a great liver-downer, but he hasn't ever got over Rhoda. Walter . . . it frightens me . . . just a little."

Arthur Higgins had worked hard on Emily. Arthur had undoubtedly thought, as others had, that anyone with her figure, combined with brown eyes and ash-blond hair, could develop a stage presence, given instruction — and the instruction had not been wholly wasted. You could believe Emily was frightened a little, and once again she did not pause long enough to risk an interruption.

"Walter . . ." Her voice was higher, but bravely controlled, eloquently pleading. "I wish you'd use your influence to get him to move somewhere else. There's something wrong about it all, Walter. His preoccupations here are somewhat weird, Walter, and I feel like a shadow. I'm subconsciously rejected, and it's very dreadful to be rejected by a memory. I never realized that it could be so dreadful. . . ."

Emily had the faculty of making many things difficult, and now she had done it again. It was now no longer possible to interrupt her discourse. To have done so would have trespassed on hospitality by embarrassing Walter Price. Also, as he had learned by now, any relationship, more especially one established between man and wife, was based in part on the uncatalogued facts one never faced or discussed, and Emily's habit of telling her most private troubles was beyond discussion. It was better to

32

pretend that Emily was the soul of discretion as she always said she was. It would now cause Emily needless pain and confusion if she were to find that he had been listening in the hall, and life was hard enough without deliberately causing pain. It was necessary to tiptoe softly to the front door and his admiration for the long-dead builders of the house increased with every furtive step.

The hall, as was customary in that ancient, brash era when the house was built, had been floored with native white pine. These broad boards had been protected for generations by various forms of carpeting, so that now, having been scraped and oiled, they were in excellent condition. Not a board creaked beneath his tread, but, if one had, it might not have mattered. Emily's voice had risen to a controlled but louder level.

"Walter, dear," she was saying, "you know what a respect Tom has always had for your opinion. He has a great many acquaintances, but not many friends, and you are a friend — a friend of both of us."

This was another expression that Emily had taken up recently — A Friend of Both of Us — and one could tell very readily what she meant. A Friend of Both of Us meant someone whom Emily could use conveniently in order to get her husband to do something that he might have been reluctant to do otherwise.

"All he needs is someone to get him interested in something new, Walter," she was saying. "You know how restless and questing Tom always is, and I don't think his play is doing well, either. He always shuts up like a clam when I ask him about his work. Work is a part of him he always insulates from me like a bamboo curtain, although darling Arthur used to say that I had a highly acute dramatic critical sense. Walter dear, I still have instinct even if he never tells me anything. He's worried about the play and I'll tell you something else, Walter. Between you and me, and I've never mentioned this to another soul, I think Tom is growing professionally afraid. You know that dreadful fear that comes over everyone in the theatre at some point, Walter — that sort of professional doubt — the discovery that he is just a little behind the tempo of today. Tom's wonderful. I know it, Walter — but then, there's Tennessee Williams. I just know there's some-

33

thing that worries Tom — something new he can't touch. I wish you could have seen his face at *The Cat on the Hot Tin Roof*. It was enigmatic, Walter, and sad, and I've never breathed this to another soul. What he needs is a change, Walter, and not living in a doll's house and questing back into the past. It's Rhoda, Walter, the memory of Rhoda that's making him uncertain; and if you could just speak to him, Walter . . ."

The gentle click of the front-door latch was not audible over Emily's voice.

He was on the steps again in that gentle May sun. He knew that his face was flushed, and it should not have been. He had only heard again what he had known already. He knew that Emily disliked the place and that for years she had let him down in subtle ways in order to build herself up, but something new had been added simply because of overhearing. Emily always came upon realities with glancing blows, juggling half-truths and quarter-truths. There was something to be said for her interpretation of Rhoda. There was some truth in the competitive fear but she should have known that one lived always with the fear that one might never write again. It was a common occupational disease, yet when you heard someone else say it, the shock was a little like hearing your own voice on a tape-recorder with tones you barely recognized, or suddenly seeing your face unexpectedly in a mirror. Such experiences always showed that there was a lot you did not know about yourself. At any rate, the old saying was true: nothing you ever overheard about yourself was ever favorable. How right the rule was never to listen at open doors, or closed ones, either.

III

It's Always Old Home Week in Any Old Home Town

HE HAD not intended to go to the office until after he had called downtown for the mail; but, once he had closed the front door, he found himself walking not toward the street but back past the cutting and vegetable garden to where the old coach house had stood. He had recognized, years ago, the utter futility of maintaining any serious working quarters in any house in which he lived. No matter what rules one might make against interruptions, they were always being broken; and, even if they were not, there was always something in the house to stimulate his curiosity — voices in the hall, the ring of the doorbell, or a crash of glass in the pantry. It was hard enough at best to concentrate, without having the extraneous appear suddenly to blot out some chain of thought; and also, in the house, there was a continuous battle between the sexes. Women, from his experience, preferred having a man beneath their thumbs, if such a thing was possible. It was true, of course, that most women — wives of lawyers, doctors, and businessmen — knew that they could not attain this desire; they watched resignedly when their men went downtown or to goodness knew where, and waited in the afternoon with growing curiosity and impatience if ever their husbands missed the 5:15; but there was no valid reason for writers, artists or composers to get away from home. Usually it was disloyal of them to think of such a thing, and uneconomical, and thoughtless.

It would have been difficult to count the number of times he had heard the wives of writers, artists, and composers say, at

35

some literary cocktail party after a third Martini, that one of the wonderful things about being married to a writer, artist, or composer was that you could share his work, or if not share it, at least watch the creative wheels go round, and this, though often trying, was fascinating in that it gave one a sense of worthwhileness to help, just a little bit, in those lonely, creative struggles. You never knew, you couldn't know, all that a writer, artist, or composer went through, unless you were actually married to him. Not even his mistress could know, not that any of their husbands had mistresses; but lots of other people's husbands did. Doubtless you knew some of the husbands to whom they were referring, and some of the gals, too, who appeared with them at first-night parties and things like that—but, let's face it, a mistress was different from a wife. She might be more attractive. One dared say she was — and why shouldn't she be, with nothing else to do but be clever and *simpática* for occasional, limited periods? Yet no matter how delightful she was, she could not have the same true interest in creative work that a wife had. She might be aware of the fun of it, but never of the pain. After all, men who had mistresses could not tell them *all* their troubles. At any rate, only a wife could understand the true difficulties and the pains of creation — that is, if she were the sort of wife who tried to understand.

It wasn't all peaches and cream being married to a writer, artist, or composer. They were naturally temperamental, and at some points surprisingly immature, with crotchets and vanities and little-boy habits that you would have thought they should have outgrown at grammar school. They were not even — let's face it — very good husbands from a conventional point of view. Sometimes they were so busy with creation that they could not remember that they were husbands. No matter how faithful he might be, a writer, artist, or composer did lead a double life, what with his copy paper, palette, or metronome, or whatever — but still it was the sort of life that an understanding wife could share, and it could be a fine adventure, and the best thing about it was companionship. He was always there and you could see and hear the wheels go round. It was a pleasure to listen to the typewriter in the study and, if there was a pause, to wonder whether one should interrupt and try to be of help or whether, if one did, one's head would almost literally be taken off. You never could tell which it would be if you were the wife of an artist, author, or composer — but this was part of the fascination. It was — let's face it — in spite of all the trouble he made, the cigarette burns on the rug, the aspirin and Bromo-Seltzer all over the bathroom and the glass rings on the furniture — it was still wonderful to have your man in the house and know where he was. Moreover, it was the way things ought to be, and anyone who was married to a writer, artist, or composer was silly and shortsighted not to give him a study, studio, or whatever, and keep him in the house instead of listening to suggestions that he move to an office outside with some blond secretary or model or singer or something. What was the use in being married to a creative man if you did not have him right there in the house?

Tom Harrow had heard it all and also he had tried working at home. He had tried it first in their apartment in the old and ungainly Lexington Avenue house where Rhoda and he had begun their married life. He had used one of the hall bedrooms for writing and, as Rhoda said herself, it was just a cubbyhole; but when he closed the door she made it a special point, on her word of honor, never to disturb him. If he had to leave the door open, in order to get some heat inside the room, it was his fault if Rhoda called to him or occasionally came in to give him a kiss when he was not typing. In retrospect, the hallroom study had not been so bad and surroundings were not important when you were in your twenties and in love. Then there was the study on Park Avenue in the cooperative duplex, and then the other study on Park Avenue in the other duplex which Laura Hopedale had decorated while in one of her beige-and-ivory moods. Nancy Mulford, now his secretary, had come in part-time to do letters and script typing at Park Avenue, on the days she was lent him by the Higgins office. But even before the end of the first Park Avenue duplex, he had had it — and he had rented an office of his own in a dingy building in the vicinity of Carnegie Hall.

The old coach house here, after it had been made over, was a pleasant office with an open fireplace and windows looking over the garden. Its location was one of its greatest assets: at the far end of the gravel drive, and a considerable distance from the garage and the couple's quarters. Fortunately Emily had not given up wearing high heels. In fact, she seemed to be under the impression that these made her different from the other tweedy women of this community into which she had been catapulted. He was careful every year to have fresh layers of gravel copiously poured upon the drive as well as on the path beyond the turn-around leading to the coach house, and consequently it was almost impossible for Emily to reach the place. In an effort of hers to do so, the previous summer, she had twisted her ankle severely and, as far as he knew, Emily had not attempted the trip again. Thus the coach house was free of interruptions; and there was another room for Miss Mulford, so that, when he wanted, he could be entirely alone.

His workroom impressed him that morning as at least one place that unself-consciously reflected his personality. The odds and ends of his past were around him, not placed in any studied balance, but with the sort of continuity that came with association. There were the Hogarth prints he bought in his last year at college. There was the desk he had bought in London the first time a play of his had been produced there. The armchair by the bookcase was an ugly Victorian interpolation that had come from his parents' house on Seventy-second Street. There were a few framed photographs on the wall that would have made no especial sense to anyone else — one of Jack Barrymore, and one of a general, signed, *Tom, with admiration — Arthur D. Whelk.* There was a photograph of his mother in an evening gown stiffly posed against an Italianate backdrop by a forgotten New York photographer, and a snapshot of his father in white tennis flannels and a yachting blazer with brass buttons. The main point about the room was that all its furnishings, including the clock on the mantel, marked some point in his past without obtruding on his thoughts.

The door to Miss Mulford's office was ajar and he could hear

38

the sound of her typewriter. His desk was bare except for the writing he had done the day before on yellow copy paper. The typing stopped and he heard Miss Mulford push back her chair.

"Good morning, Miss Mulford," he said — and he was glad to see her, because, like all the room, she was part of its continuity.

Like the furnishings, it had been a long while since Miss Mulford had demanded his full attention. She wore one of her severely tailored suits of gray worsted with a trace of ruffled white showing at the open neck. He had never known her to wear a piece of jewelry in the office. Her nails were unpainted and she had on only a dash of lipstick. It was often difficult to realize that she had been with him for about twenty-five years. Although there was no visible gray in her hair, there was no obvious tinting in it, either, and it made no startling contrast with her regular features. In fact, one could not tell whether she was forty-five or not and in the end the question had no importance. She was still the neat, quiet girl whom he had met in the Higgins office when he had called in 1928 to discuss the casting of his play *Hero's Return*, and, in spite of thirty years, her beauty was still apparent. The moment he had first seen her, he had known that she was a part of the theatre and that her aggressive simplicities were part of stage tradition. In the theatre, good secretaries drew an uncompromising line between themselves and actresses.

"Good morning," Miss Mulford said, and he saw that she was watching him with unusual care. "No one's brought the morning mail yet."

"I know," he said, "I thought I'd walk down and get it myself this morning, but the *New York Times* has been delivered, hasn't it?"

"Yes," Miss Mulford said, "but don't you think it would be just as well if someone on the place called for the mail regularly?"

"Yes," he said, "I suppose you've got a point there, but I rather like to go down and get it myself. I won't be away long."

"Don't forget that Mr. Beechley is waiting for you to call him about Hollywood."

He looked at the clock on the mantel.

"I'm not forgetting," he said. "He's probably not in the office yet."

"There are some more bills for you to look at."

"All right," he said. "Is there enough money in the New York account?"

"There isn't," she said. "There never has been, has there?"

"It's funny, isn't it?" he asked. "I keep putting money into that account, a little more each year, and yet there never is enough. But what about the housekeeping account?"

"That's down, too — so don't forget to call Mr. Beechley."

"Maybe I'd better go to Hollywood if they want me there," he said. "But then, there'd only be the income tax."

"Don't go," she said. "You've just got here."

"Yes," he said, "and maybe things will just settle down now. Guess who came in last night?"

"Who?" she asked.

"Walter Price."

"Oh," she said, "he isn't going to stay long, is he?"

"Only for a day or two," he said.

"Oh dear," she said, "he always makes you restless."

"I wish you'd been at breakfast this morning," he said. "He was telling about the Price Château, spelled with a Ph. Have you ever heard that one?"

"No," she said, "never about the Price Château."

"He met the Duke of Windsor there," he said, "but the whole thing was blown up by the Big Bertha in World War I. The château had the old Norman spelling, Phryce. It did not belong to the Price branch that came over to England with William the Conqueror. It belonged to the other branch and they retained the old family spelling."

"Maybe you'd better go and get the mail," she said, "if you're going to work this morning."

"Maybe," he said, "but I've just got a new idea. When I was talking to that man Dodd — he was here this morning, you know — in the garden. Did I ever tell you that we used to go to school together?"

"Yes," she said, "and you always call him Jack."

"That's right," he said. "It's pathetic, isn't it, clinging to a thing like that? Frankly, I'm tired of being pathetic."

"You're not pathetic, only restless," she said, "and you'd better go down and get the mail."

"Just let me make my point," he said. "The point is: once you get involved in the theatre, you can't seem to project yourself out into the rest of the world."

"Yes," she said, "I know."

"Oh," he said, "you know, do you? Have you ever tried to get away from being involved?"

"Yes," she said, "several times."

She had a good speaking voice. It would have been hard for her not to have picked up enunciation after all the scripts she had held through rehearsals, but there was nothing contrived in her speech. Nevertheless, he could not remember that she had ever sounded just as she had at that moment. It occurred to him that he had very seldom inquired about her private problems, but she had a right to her own life.

"I might have guessed at one or two," he said, "but I didn't know that there were several times."

"I'll get the bills ready," she said, "and there are still some letters you haven't answered."

"All right," he said. "I shouldn't have made that remark, but I was only trying to make a point. My point is that all of us keep dealing in unrealities until they finally get more real than reality. It was that way out in the garden."

He stopped because nothing he was saying had much coherence.

"I suppose everybody gets caught up in something sometime," he said — "that is, if you live at all." And he laughed. "First and last, I've certainly got myself caught up in a lot of things."

It was morning, but he was talking as he might have at the end of a long day. He was almost sure that the overheard conversation was what had cast a shadow over his thoughts. He felt uncertain, and uncertainty was a serious malady which invariably called up the fear that you were written out and finished. It did no good to tell himself that he had gone through the same mood often enough before. It was the penalty for creative talent, plus the knowledge that one only had oneself to thank for failure. He was facing loneliness again, and vanity — the worst of it all was vanity. He wanted reassurance, and he wondered what Miss Mulford was thinking. Was she thinking, too, that he was losing his grip?

"Yes," he said, "I've been in and out of a lot of things — and you always leave some of yourself behind. There used to be a time when I thought I could set the world on fire. I was under that impression the day I came into the Higgins office, do you remember?"

"Yes," she said, "you've got more sense now."

"Well, thanks a lot," he said. "And now I'd better go and get the mail, and before going I'll leave you with a quote from Ecclesiastes: 'Vanity of vanities, saith the Preacher . . . all is vanity.'"

He was pleased with his own voice, which spoke well for the rhythms of King Solomon.

"Oh, Mr. Harrow," Miss Mulford said, "there's one thing . . ."

He was half turned toward the door and he swung back sharply.

"Tell Alfred to lay out a new tweed coat for you," Miss Mulford said, "and do see that the one you're wearing gets pressed. You've been wearing the same coat for the last three days."

Emily was right that he was not really connected with the town. He was, like so many of his contemporaries, almost rootless except for business or profession. He and the rest of his generation had never lived in permanence. They had lived in the suburbs or in apartments during the winter, and the country places they bought they knew very well would be instantly sold by their heirs. There were no Old Home Weeks or old homes any more. If he had an old home at all, it was obviously New York, and New York itself had undergone such a metamorphosis that it was hard for him to reconstruct his old days there. The streets remained, but the buildings were evaporating. The Plaza was still there, and so was the entrance to the Central

Park Zoo with the balloon men and the peanut men, but where was the Murray Hill? Where was the Belmont? Where was the Ritz? The truth was, his life afforded few sites for landmarks. You lived for decades in New York, but the time inevitably arrived when you retreated to a small area of it. You finally could not adjust yourself to its constant changes. You were more aware of impermanence there than anywhere else in the world.

In everyone there was a lurking desire for permanence, and most of life was pursuit of it. He knew very well that his associations with the small town to which he had returned had been brief though poignant, and he knew very well that he did not seriously belong there. The town was changing, like everything else in the postwar world, but not hysterically. It still had elements of dignity. It still was a scene of his youth. Dock Street, which he had first remembered in the early days of the Model T Ford, was hideously crowded with arrogant, rainbow-hued cars lining each curb of the old business thoroughfare. The trolley cars that had operated when he had first known the town had disappeared. Except for the Dock Street Savings Bank, the façades of the shops along the street had all been altered in an aggressive way that reminded him of television make-up on the faces of certain superannuated actresses. The new plastic façades on Dock Street were as blatant as the cars when the May sunlight struck them, justifying the remark, which he had heard somewhere, that we were living in a jukebox civilization. In fact, all of Dock Street seemed to be dancing that morning to a modern jukebox record, luxuriating in its materialism and in the pseudo-sophisticated displays in its shop-windows. In the show business one had necessarily to develop an eye for change, but he was forced to admit that the rising tide of new gadgets for sale on the old street was beginning to confuse him. All you could perceive was that everything was on the verge of change which would eventually be reflected in every facet of life and thought. He wished to goodness that he could gauge the trend, which was vaguely reminiscent, of course, of the upsurge of 1929, but no trend was ever identical with another.

43

Nevertheless, the town was still reassuring. The present was only a garish coat of paint over older buildings whose façades and shapes were scarcely altered by new blends of color. He wished that Dock Street could be translated to the stage, and in his thoughts he had occasionally attempted to do so, but he had never found a way to present its subtleties to an audience — that sense of being partly old and partly young. The youth that came with spring, for instance, was apparent in the elm trees that had survived hurricanes and disease, and yet the trees themselves were very old.

Everyone knew about everyone else on Dock Street, and everyone knew where everyone else fitted in the elastic but undeviating social order. He knew very well that he did not belong in Clyde, but that knowledge in itself gave him a sense of identification. The gray slacks and the tweed coat that he wore that morning were things he would never have worn in New York. They were not the costume of the local citizenry, either, but they suited his category. He was the nephew of Miss Edith Fowler who had lived on Locust Street, the nephew whom she had taken in, the one who went through the last two years of high school here and who had been around town off and on later visiting his aunt, and who had married the Browne girl — Rhoda Browne; not one of the regular Brownes, but the daughter of the Browne who had once had the Ford agency. He was the Thomas Harrow who had written plays that had been produced on Broadway, and who had bought the Saebury house and fixed it up. He walked with his shoulders set exactly as he should have to maintain this part, in the military manner that he had picked up in his first week or so in the Pentagon during the last war. Emily had said that morning that he could have been good at anything. Generalities are never correct, but he had learned to walk and to talk like a soldier, and a little of it did not hurt on Dock Street.

While thoughts like these moved through his mind aimlessly, he was still able to appreciate everything that went on around him. His interest in people and places had never lagged, and his instinct for caricature was as good as his memory for names and faces. Just in front of the Dock Street Savings Bank he recognized Mr. Everett Wilkins — not that this was a remarkable feat, because Mr. Wilkins was vice-president of the bank, waiting in quiet confidence for its president, Henry Baines, to retire; trustee of the Public Library; on the directors' board of Smith, Hawley; president of the West End Burying Ground. These offices all had a local value which were incomprehensible beyond the town limits, but Tom Harrow understood them, and also knew that if he had lived in town all his life he would never have attained these positions.

"Well, hello, Everett," he said. "It's nice to have this glimpse of you."

"Why, hello, Tom," Mr. Wilkins said.

Bankers of the Chase or the First National in New York made honest if clumsy efforts to be broad-gauged, but such efforts would not have been desirable on Dock Street. The clear, pinkish face of Everett Wilkins was cool and intelligent. He wore an old Leghorn straw hat and a blue serge suit, the trousers of which were more shiny than the coat because inside the bank he wore a black alpaca jacket.

"You've come back early this spring, Tom," Mr. Wilkins said.

"Yes," Tom Harrow said. "We did move up earlier this year, Everett, but it's very impressive that you should remember my comings and goings."

Mr. Wilkins smiled with what a columnist might have called a cracker-barrel smile.

"At the bank we keep track of customers," he said. "As soon as I saw your last deposit, I said to myself: Tom Harrow is back in town and he's going to make more improvements on the Sae-bury house, or else he's moving his account from New York, and that couldn't be possible, could it?"

Tom Harrow smiled. He never had been able to understand why business at certain levels had to be conducted in terms of badinage, or why money, when the subject was first introduced, should be a joke.

45

"No," he said. "You might need some extra help if I increased my account that much. I hope you've had a good winter, and that Mrs. Wilkins is well."

He could not recollect the first name of Everett Wilkins's wife, although she had once been a friend of Rhoda's back there in the past; but on the whole it was better not to remember her first name because he did not want Everett Wilkins to think that he was overanxious to improve their relationship.

"We had a very good winter, thanks," Everett Wilkins said. "In fact, so good that Mrs. Wilkins and I were able to realize a dream we've always cherished — to take a two weeks' winter cruise on a Grace Line boat in the Caribbean. I heard that you and Mrs. Harrow were down there yourselves. It's quite a place, isn't it, the Caribbean? As long as you were down there I guess you and Mrs. Harrow had a good winter, too."

"Oh, yes," Tom Harrow said, "except that we were on the West Coast more than I like."

"Working on a new play, I guess, aren't you?" Mr. Wilkins said.

"Yes, in a mild way," Tom Harrow said. "We can't sit around and do nothing, can we, Everett?"

"We certainly can't," Everett Wilkins said. "Well, I've got to be moving. Is there anything we can do for you at the bank?"

"Not at the moment, thanks," Tom Harrow said. "It's nice to have seen you. How's Mr. Baines?"

There was a transient sharpness in Everett Wilkins's eyes, but it faded very quickly.

"Never better," Mr. Wilkins said. "He'd appreciate it if you came in and shook hands with him sometime, Tom. He was looking over your account only the other day. He remembers all about you."

It was hard to tell whether or not there was an edge to Everett Wilkins's voice. Small-town values were refined and difficult.

"He doesn't look a day older than he did when we were kids," Tom Harrow said. "I certainly will come in and pay him my respects, Everett."

He had just finished speaking when a strange thing happened, one of those irrational things that you always wonder about

46

later, that move out of the sequence of events. He was just about to nod to Everett Wilkins and walk on when he saw a girl walking toward them up Dock Street, and for an instant he had the illusion that she was part of memory, because her figure and posture and her walk reminded him of another day on Dock Street. Very few women walked gracefully. Even on the stage they had to be taught how to put one foot in front of the other; but the stride of the girl moving toward them was natural, matching the folds of the inexpensive polo coat she was wearing and falling into perfect tune with her head and shoulders. Her head was bare, her hair was a copper-chestnut, and in spite of her still being some distance away from them, he saw that the bone structure of her face was not unlike the face of Kit Cornell.

"What a very striking girl," he said. "And she walks well, too, no hip sway, nothing. She just walks."

Everett Wilkins's look of surprise made him realize that by evening everyone would know that he had come to Dock Street to look at girls.

"What girl?" Everett Wilkins asked.

Tom had gone too far, but it was too late to stop.

"The only one worth looking at," Tom Harrow said. "The one in the polo coat."

"Oh," Everett Wilkins said, "she walks in a sort of a sliding way, doesn't she? But she looks kind of plain to me."

"She wouldn't, with another dress and another hairdo," Tom Harrow said. "Look at her bone structure."

"Bone structure?" Everett Wilkins said. "I'm afraid I don't quite follow you."

By evening everyone would know that Tom had been discussing bone structure on Dock Street, but it was too late to stop.

"The cheekbones and the molding of the jaw," he said. "It's a beautiful face. You'd see it if she had another hairdo."

"Well, I suppose you ought to know, Tom," Everett Wilkins said, "just the way I know good mortgages."

He stopped because the girl was too near them to allow further discussion; Tom Harrow was embarrassed by the clumsy silence that followed, and yet the quality in the silence in it-

47

self was a part of memory. . . . He was standing on Dock Street again, and it was spring with the same sun and the same tone of sunlight.

"God damn," he was saying, "that's a pretty girl." . . .

She was still walking toward them and Everett Wilkins raised his antiquated straw hat.

" 'Morning, Irene," he said. The girl nodded and smiled. She must have known they had been talking about her, but she looked more interested in both of them than in what they were saying. Tom Harrow was highly conscious of the glance she gave him. She had blue-gray eyes. He was glad he was still not too old to be attracted by a pretty face. He would never be too old. She looked at him in a questioning sort of a way, just as he must have looked at her, but of course their reasons were different.

"Good morning, Mr. Wilkins," she said.

She had not changed her pace. She walked past them unhurriedly and it would have been ridiculous if they had still gazed at her without speaking.

"I don't know what you see in her," Everett said. "Frankly, she looks kind of skinny and peaked to me, Tom, but then maybe I don't understand women."

"Irene . . ." Tom Harrow said. "What's her last name?"

"Why, Dodd," Everett Wilkins said. "She's Jack Dodd's oldest girl. She's been at college somewhere. Mount Holyoke or somewhere. But I hear she's been dropped or something."

Now that he had seen Jack Dodd's daughter, he could understand why Harold had come home late the previous evening and he could completely applaud Harold's good taste, but at the same time he felt no wistfulness, no twinge of envy and no regret that he was no longer Harold's age. He was not moved by the girl herself — only by memory.

The girl's voice lingered with him, modulated, confident and unself-conscious. "Good morning, Mr. Wilkins" was all she had said, but he was not thinking of the voice of Irene Dodd. He was thinking, instead, of that constantly written scene of fiction and drama, the scene now stereotyped in Hollywood, of boy-meets-girl. In spite of all the times such scenes had been written and rewritten, the essence of them was evasive. At some time or other almost everyone on Dock Street, or anywhere else, for that matter, had played that scene, but always without knowing until later that he had played it. You could not rededicate yourself. Dedication could be done only once. And there never could be consciousness in that sort of dedication. There was a scene in *Richard Feverel*, and Beatrix walking down the stairs in *Esmond*, and the gawky grace of one of Arnold Bennett's heroines. These approached what he was thinking of, without being wholly satisfying. They reminded him, like the Dodd girl, of something in one's life that had never completely been put into words and something that could happen only once.

He had been Henry Esmond and Richard Feverel himself once, when he had first seen Rhoda Browne on Dock Street. He had thought the whole thing was forgotten, but then, no one ever completely forgets anything. Irene on Dock Street had not looked like Rhoda Browne. Rhoda had been better-looking, in spite of the impossible clothes of the period. There had only been the voice, the walk, the self-confidence and the restiveness. But now it was time to get to the post office and go back and call New York, and it was not time to think of melodies that boys and girls once sang on the beach at night. He had been able to sing "Mandalay" himself once, and some of the words were appropriate. . . . Long ago and far away . . . There ain't no buses running from the Bank to Mandalay. . . . There were no buses going back to Dock Street, either, and it was time to get the mail.

IV

He Meant It When He Said, "God Bless and Keep You, Thomas"

IT OCCURRED to him, as he crossed Dock to Walter's Drugstore and proceeded down Bay Street toward the post office, that he was walking under the umbrella of consciousness, which he recalled from his college reading of Bishop Berkeley's philosophy. He had never returned to those pages to refresh his memory and now doubted that he ever would, but he still thought he had the whole thing straight. It was the Bishop's contention, if he remembered rightly, that nothing could provably exist which was not within the immediate radius of an individual's senses. Frequently this concept had given him considerable consolation. By its logic, for example, as he walked down Bay Street, Rhoda Browne, Laura Hopedale, Emily, Walter Price, Harold, and a lot of other people including Mr. Beechley in New York, were merely figments of the imagination and Bay Street alone was demonstrably real. For some reason difficult to explain, Bay Street had been the point from which the commercial impetus of the modern town had emanated. The first chain stores had opened on Bay street. Warren's Toggery Shop had been the first men's store to handle nationally advertised sporting regalia. The Bijou Theatre opposite the venerable Congregational Church had been the first motion picture house in town. Pendle's Notion Store, having changed its name to Chez Nanette, had been the first store in town to produce a window display of girdles and brassières, and right next to the old First Congregational Church. Tom Harrow had once walked each morning the length of Bay Street to reach high school and the street had given him many ideas. For instance, he had never seen a brassière until he encountered one in the window of Chez Nanette, and his knowledge of the Bible had been derived initially from Mr. Naughton's Bible class at the First Congregational Church. A swinging sign had been placed in front of the church ending with the name of its present minister, Ernest W. Godfrey. A narrow strip of lawn separated the church from Chez Nanette on one side; an identical strip on the other side separated the church from a candy shop; but Sam's Liquor Store (another first on the street, having been the town's first package store after Repeal) was at a legal distance. Upon the strips of lawn were two identical billboards facing the advertisements of the Bijou Theatre across the street. This morning the church was advertising Mr. Ernest W. Godfrey's sermon topic for the next Sunday. The topic was, "How Happy Are You Inside?" and the Bijou Theatre feature across the way was entitled *Love, Honor, and Oh Baby*. Tom Harrow read the signs just as he had reached the package store and it was a coincidence that he should meet Mr. Ernest W. Godfrey at almost that same moment.

"Well, well," Mr. Godfrey said. "Welcome back home, stranger."

The breezy greeting made Tom Harrow wonder what Mr. Naughton would think if his spirit still lingered by the old church door. Mr. Ernest W. Godfrey's face had not a cracker-barrel but a quizzical expression, and it was too young to have many lines on it. In fact, he was not much older than Harold and his hair was done in a crew cut. There were heavy, crepe-rubber soles on his low shoes and he, too, was in gray flannels and a brown tweed coat. He was also vigorously smoking a straight-stemmed, straight-grain pipe. Trollope and Barchester Towers were no longer in the picture.

"Well, hello," Tom Harrow said. "Am I blocking your way to the package store?"

It was just the sort of joke that anyone who was in there pitching should appreciate, and Ernest Godfrey laughed.

"Seriously, sir," he said, "I can shake a pretty mean Martini, if you would care to come to the parsonage and try one some afternoon. There are a lot of things that I should like to get together with you about." He waved a hand toward the church. "Seriously, we're both in show business, Mr. Harrow."

"I suppose that's one way of putting it," Tom Harrow said.

He looked at Mr. Godfrey more attentively now that his train of thought had been broken. As far as he could remember, he had met the young man only once before.

"But then, perhaps my line is more in the area of entertainment than yours," he said.

Mr. Godfrey shook his head decisively.

"Well, now, I wouldn't be quite so sure of that," he said. "It always seems to me there is a kind of message in any good play — and in my experience, anyway, entertainment helps the message."

Everyone was always interesting if you looked at him in a certain way. Mr. Godfrey's obviousness was illumined by an enthusiasm and that would be destroyed by time. Mr. Godfrey made him remember his own somewhat hysterical discoveries of the obvious and the turbulence of his own enthusiasms. It seemed hardly credible but still it was barely possible that he had looked like Mr. Godfrey once.

"You mean it pays to sugar-coat the pill?" he said.

Mr. Godfrey shook his head again.

"Oh no," he said, "not seriously, but how about the New Testament? The parables are entertaining, aren't they?"

"Maybe you're right," Tom Harrow said, "but they were never presented to me in quite that way."

"I know what you mean," Mr. Godfrey said. "Black leather on the Bible and all that sort of thing. You've got to sell religion, don't you agree, Mr. Harrow?"

Tom Harrow glanced at the theatre sign across the street and at the two-tone cars and at the liquor store and at Chez Nanette.

"We've got to face competition like everybody else," Mr. Godfrey said. "Have you got enough time on your hands so you could step inside the church for a moment? I'd like you to see the swell new paint job we did this winter, incidentally, and we'll be out of the noise there, and we might embroider on this salesmanship topic for a while. It's been on my mind."

He waved his hand toward the church invitingly, and Tom Harrow nodded. It was a new experience and he had never avoided experience.

"All right," Tom Harrow said, "but if I go inside there with you, don't try to convert me. Just remember you're young and I'm a hardened sinner, will you?"

"Right," Mr. Godfrey said, "not a conversion in a carload, sir."

He took a key from his pocket and opened the wide church door.

The noises of the street died away to a murmur when the heavy door had closed behind them. In their place there was silence and the musty odor of pew cushions and hymnals. The interior was puritanically but theatrically impressive. Light flooded it without adornment impartially emphasizing the box pews, the carpeted aisles and the fluted columns supporting the balcony, and the tall pulpit with its double staircases. The vacancy around them made him feel very much alone, and, as he stood in the aisle looking at the pulpit, he forgot for a moment that the latest incumbent of the First Congregational Church was with him, until Mr. Godfrey spoke.

"It's a pretty big house for one man to play to, isn't it?"

Although the remark was characteristic of some of Mr. Godfrey's others, it was appropriate. It was a big house, indeed, a fragile monument in perishable wood, and yet there was eternity in the white light and the white woodwork. There was a defiance in the simplicity, a breaking-away from imagery and tradition that had itself become traditional. He felt closer to truth there than he ever had at Notre Dame or Chartres. The thing that was called the New England conscience was in the cool silence, not reproof, but conscience. He and Rhoda Browne had been married at the foot of that pulpit, but there was no rebuke, only a feeling that the cards were on the table, although that was not the religious way to put it.

"I use the small room under the pulpit for writing and think-ing in warm weather," Mr. Godfrey said.

Tom Harrow followed Mr. Godfrey without speaking.

There were some places that were better skipped, and the room beneath the pulpit was one of them. He had not seen it since the day he and Rhoda were married. "How Happy Are You Inside?" he remembered was the sermon topic for next Sunday. He did not feel happy inside. He could almost hear again the low, wheezy tones of the organ that had played when he had stood there waiting.

The small room itself, built directly beneath the pulpit, with its single window cut in the rear wall of the church revealing unimproved back yards beyond the lot, was so startlingly un-changed that his last time in it might have been yesterday. The room was the place where, ever since the church was built, ministers had donned their black gowns, and then had waited until the moment arrived to march out the small door and ascend the pulpit steps. It could have been furnished by a Ladies' Auxiliary shortly before the outbreak of the Civil War. At least the horsehair sofa and the two horsehair armchairs were Gothic rather than General Grant. The Boston rocker was older, but all those four pieces were indestructible, and the horsehair still shone like new in the light that was dim and gray because of the single window's unwashed exterior. The pen rack and the iron inkwell, on the writing table that held the parish record book, had seemingly not moved an iota. The reddish carpet tacked down to cover the flooring had not faded. The glass in the mahogany veneer mirror above the writing table had the same smoky opaqueness as when it had reflected his wavering image in the last moments when he had waited for the strains of the wedding march. He could almost believe that Mr. Naughton was back there with him and Mort Sullivan, who had been best man. Tom Harrow pulled himself together. Given the time and place, he thought, it could be completely possible to believe in any doctrine of original, not to mention homemade, sin and of retribution. Instinctively he glanced in the mirror above the table and saw that he was fifty-four and

54

not twenty-four. He was gray at the temples. His eyes were harder. His mouth was firmer; it had to be. But in the surface of ancient glass backed by its half-oxidized quicksilver, he could see traces of the young Tom Harrow waiting on the verge of his first great decision and wondering, as he wondered now, exactly how he had got there.

"The last time I was here beneath this pulpit," he said to Mr. Godfrey, "was when I was waiting to get married."

"That's funny," Mr. Godfrey said, "I would have thought that you had been married in New York."

It was time to get things straight with Mr. Godfrey.

"New York was my third time," he said. "I was referring to the first time. It occurred here on the low platform in front of the pulpit. She was what I think you might call a local girl and she wanted to get out of town. We may both be in the show business, Mr. Godfrey, but you preachers seem able to work out your marital problems — with the exception of an occasional choir singer — better than actors and playwrights. I'm not going to mention actresses."

It may have been a good idea that Mr. Godfrey had been called by the First Congregational, but at the same time, his easy laugh was startling when delivered beneath the pulpit.

"Now, Mr. Harrow," he said, "please don't act as though you think I'd be shocked. I haven't been in this game as long as I might, but I've been in it long enough to know that every single one of us has his own problem and his own method of motivation as well as his own particular means of adjustment, and his own particular subconscious mind."

"I suppose you're right," Tom Harrow said, "although it doesn't seem to me that anybody knows very much about the subconscious. I am interested that you refer to your calling as a game, Mr. Godfrey."

He had written dialogue so long that the problems of measure and compression of words often obtruded themselves in an ordinary conversation and he was aware that this was happening now. He and Mr. Godfrey were playing a scene, and the

55

scene and its values and the horsehair furnishings as a background all meant more to him while they were talking.

"Maybe 'game' is a colloquial word for the ministry," he heard Mr. Godfrey say, "but it strikes me as about time that a little informality got into ministry. Only last week when I was thinking along these lines I happened to pull the *American College Dictionary* off my shelf so I could get the word 'minister' redefined. It's funny how all of us deal with words without ever getting together on their meanings, and that wouldn't be a bad sermon topic, come to think of it. Forgive me, will you, while I pull out the little black book and jot it down?"

It was a fair piece of business as done by Mr. Godfrey. First he pulled from his tweed coat a massive pair of horn-rimmed spectacles of a design which Tom Harrow had thought was indigenous only to the West Coast. The spectacles changed Mr. Godfrey. Combined with his crew cut, they made him resemble a skin-diver. It was a bit that was worth remembering; and so was the black notebook and the ball-point pen.

"When you get ideas, catch 'em," Mr. Godfrey said. "That's what one of the profs used to say back on campus. That's how I got my idea for this Sunday's sermon."

It was time to break the continuity. Too long a speech never went well out in front. Tom Harrow coughed softly. It was time to break the speech.

"You mean, 'How Happy Are You Inside?'" he asked.

"That's it," Mr. Godfrey said. "I like to personalize topics. However, I guess I'm a point or two off the beam and we were sailing another course. Let me see, where was I?"

Like Emily back at the house, he needed a gyroscopic compass, but then, the older you got, the less sure you were of latitudes and longitudes.

"You were taking down your *American College Dictionary,*" Tom Harrow said, "in order to refresh your memory of the definition of a minister, and not a bad thing to do at all, I'd say, for anyone in your game."

Mr. Godfrey laughed. With the horn-rimmed spectacles, the laugh was also an effective bit.

"I knew the first time I saw you, Mr. Harrow," he said, "that you would have the lovely sense of humor which sparkles in your plays. Well, I wanted to look up the word 'minister,' not the noun, but the intransitive verb. Wait, I can give you the direct quote."

The black book came out again, confirming the old rule that you could always successfully do the same thing about twice.

"Here it is. Definition number seven, verb intransitive. 'To give service, care or aid. Attend, as to wants, necessities, etc.' Well, there I am, and that's what I'm here for, Mr. Harrow."

Tom Harrow thought of the last time he was in this room, and the associations were so vivid that it was difficult to give his whole attention to Mr. Godfrey. He was not really listening; instead, his attention was focused on the silence of the church outside, and subconsciously at least he was waiting for the organ to strike up its commanding notes.

"Say," Mr. Godfrey said, "I've been so intrigued by our conversation that I must have forgot to ask you to sit down. Pardon the inhospitality and have a seat. Or maybe in my position I ought to say, have a pew. I suggest the rocker instead of the horsehair ones."

"Why, thanks," Tom Harrow said.

The Boston rocker groaned arthritically and its instability fitted with his mood. Mr. Godfrey, carefully pulling up his gray slacks to preserve the creases, perched himself on one of the Gothic chairs. It was as though Mr. Godfrey were not quite sitting down and not quite standing up and at any moment he might do one or the other. As it was, he was almost doing both. He was a long way from the aging and gentle Mr. Naughton who, as Tom Harrow recalled, had entertained him in that room with nothing but earnest silence. The room had been so still, in fact, that you could hear the rustling of the wedding guests above the muted organ notes. Perhaps Mr. Naughton had believed that those last minutes should best be spent in meditation, although he might have known that meditation was too late.

"Now my idea," Mr. Godfrey said, "is that the modern church

57

ought to be a sort of spiritual service station where people can get the impetus to dedicate themselves anew."

Tom pushed out his legs hastily to catch his balance.

"Do you really think it's possible, Mr. Godfrey, to dedicate yourself anew?"

Mr. Godfrey laughed and rubbed his hands together.

"Why, say," he said, "if it weren't so, I wouldn't be out here in my coveralls with First Congregational embroidered on the back. You ought to drive up to the pumps sometime and try my octane, Mr. Harrow — some of Godfrey's special. But, seriously, you've got to be on your toes these days to service all the new models of psychological cars coming to the pumps."

Tom Harrow was only half listening. He was thinking that his image of Mr. Naughton had never been so clear, but there was no doubt that Mr. Godfrey had a point. The spirit which had raised the spire of the First Congregational had been militant and not gently somnolent like Mr. Naughton, and yet he would have preferred Mr. Naughton's company.

Now that Mr. Godfrey was started, it was like listening to Emily in that little further effort was required. Mr. Godfrey, perched on the Gothic chair, had rested his elbows on his knees, cupped his chin in the palms of his hands and stared bemused across the small room.

"This ministry business is more of an eye-opener than you'd think," he said. "Say, I wish I could write, and of course I could if I ever had the leisure. I owe a little time to Mrs. Godfrey and our children, but if I could write, believe me, I could tell a mouthful about psychological interrelationships. That line of mine about new modern psychological cars driving into the filling station has more significance than I thought when I first turned it off. I wish I had more time to write and more time for quiet meditation. Frankly, the way things are going, there's no place I can get away by myself, what with Mrs. Godfrey and the children. Actually, when I put on my thinking cap, I like to crawl in here below the pulpit, but it's mighty cold in winter, that is, weekdays."

Tom experienced a faint surge of relief. A second or so before he had been almost positive that Mr. Godfrey was going to come up with an idea for a play or an offer of collaboration.

"Isn't there any way of heating this room?" he asked.

"Not unless you heat the whole church along with it," Mr. Godfrey said. "I'm an idealist; but I'm practical, and I couldn't ask for that."

Tom Harrow smiled his most sympathetic smile and half closed his eyes. He was enjoying this conversation with Mr. Godfrey, partially, and the best of it was he could think his own thoughts. It may have been that Mr. Godfrey's prof on campus had taught him to phrase things simply. You simply could not make too many points at once, and the filling station and the new model cars represented an effort that impinged upon everyone's daily life. He had a vision, himself, of two-toned cars with blended upholstery and plastic instrument panels to match— shocking pinks and baby blues and chartreuse and violets.

"Yes, sir," Mr. Godfrey said, "this stress and strain of modern civilization creates some pretty mixed-up people. It's a wonder to me sometimes how some men and women in this town can put up with each other the way they do, but a lot of them can't afford not to. No wonder that a lot of folks need a new spark plug or a turn or two on their distributors now and then, or a realignment of the wheels. No wonder the treads don't wear the same on everybody's tires. We were speaking of that sermon topic, weren't we? 'How Happy Are You Inside?' It gave me a real thrill when I discovered it caught your attention, Mr. Harrow."

Mr. Godfrey's voice had broken his train of thought and Tom Harrow moved uneasily.

"Now that you mention it," he said, "I don't know exactly why it did attract my attention. Maybe because it was such an obvious question."

"You got that, did you?" Mr. Godfrey said. "Well, that makes me feel happy inside myself, because I deliberately wanted it to be obvious."

Mr. Godfrey nodded brightly and sat up straighter.

"You've got to hit them where they belong. That's another

59

thing my prof said when we were back on campus. I wanted to hit on something that everyone thinks about at some point. Don't you think about how happy you are inside, Mr. Harrow?"

"I used to," Tom Harrow said, "but lately I've put the question out of my mind. I seem to have learned pretty well to know exactly how I'm going to feel inside each day without thinking about it."

Mr. Godfrey's forehead wrinkled.

"Now that sounds fine," he said, "but I don't quite get it. You mean by what you say that you are always happy inside?"

"No, no," Tom Harrow answered. "I only said I know how I'm going to feel. If you want my opinion, I have a deep suspicion of anyone who always feels happy inside, as you put it."

"You mean there must be something wrong with him?" Mr. Godfrey asked.

"Either that," Tom Harrow said, "or he hasn't learned much from living. And if we want to get personal, let me ask you the topic question: How happy are you inside?"

Mr. Godfrey was silent for a moment.

"Pardon me," he said, "while I do a little soul-searching."

The small room was beautifully quiet, and once again Tom had the impression of the silent church outside, and then the illusion of people waiting, and then he had the memory again of the muted organ.

"No," Mr. Godfrey said. "Naturally I am not always. And you're right, it would be euphoria or something like that, wouldn't it? I am not recommending feeling happy inside all the time. I am merely recommending making the effort. I am merely recommending being at peace, at peace with the world and God."

It had taken a very long time, but there He was and Tom Harrow was very glad of it. The mention of God had brought back the memory of Mr. Naughton. It was safe to assume that Mr. Naughton had not studied social anthropology at the Harvard Summer School; but at the same time, Mr. Naughton had mentioned the name of the Divinity more frequently and more convincingly than Mr. Godfrey. On that day when he and

Mr. Naughton had sat in silence, prosperity had reached a new plateau similar to the more fantastic one which was unwinding itself now outside on Bay Street. It had seemed that automobiles would never be brighter or larger, that electronics and automation had reached an acme of perfection, that girls could never conveniently show more of themselves than in those days, but how wrong those convictions had been. In retrospect, times were quiet before the crash and before Roosevelt and it was easier to mention God.

Mr. Naughton was looking in the mirror above the writing table, adjusting his academic gown.

"God bless you and keep you, Thomas," he said. "I shall go first, then you and your friend." He was referring, of course, to Mort Sullivan. Then music had entered the pulpit room. The organ was playing the wedding march.

V

And Some Day the Nation May Honor You, Too — Just Like Your Dear Old Pop

IN RECENT years, Emily had become more and more frequently right until she was rapidly reaching the situation, which Tom Harrow had observed in several other women, of knowing she was right even when proved wrong. Of the other women he had known who had developed this propensity, three had played leading parts on Broadway and one was the only daughter of the senior partner of a New York law firm who had inherited a very large fortune under her father's will. Though all these people were very different, this single character trait gave them all a serene expression which was almost a family resemblance. In the last few years Emily herself was becoming noticeably serene, even to the point of occasionally delivering homilies, and Tom Harrow had observed that lately her lips were habitually bent into the same half smile that he had observed on contented psychiatrists.

This, however, was somewhat beside the point. The point was that Emily had been partially correct regarding several of the things he had overheard her say that morning. She had been almost right when she had said that he did not have enough association with the town to make such a production of it. She had been right, although he did not know where Emily had picked up the facts of his family history because he was sure that he had not told Emily any of them. Emily had always said frankly that she was bored by stale reminiscence about people whom she had never known and would not have understood;

62

and when he came right down to it, he did not know much about his mother's family, the Fowlers, either, except that it was respectable and that his grandfather, Thomas Fowler, had once been a judge in the district court and that his Aunt Edith Fowler had lived in a Victorian house on Locust Street, an aggressive-looking house of the late Currier and Ives vintage which had been sold and demolished long ago.

He could not forget its draftiness or the golden oak staircase or the bronze Nubian slave on the newel post holding a taper designed for gas light. He could remember the other gas fixtures, too, and the gas lamp that stood on the flat mission desk in the library, a room which still bore faint imprints of his vanished grandfather. It was strange how firmly insignificant detail could persist when so much that was vital could evaporate, or perhaps no detail was insignificant when handled artistically. At any rate, one of the eccentrically useless things he could remember most clearly was the tube that connected the gas desk lamp with the small gas spigot projecting from the library baseboard. The flexible tube covered with green cloth had twisted in a sinuous, tropical way across the Brussels carpet.

Only a year or so ago while they were motoring through Florida, Emily had insisted that they stop the Cadillac at a snake farm because she had seen a sign advertising kumquat jam. She did not mind if there were snakes. She had been looking and looking all the way up from Fort Lauderdale for kumquat jam, and while she was buying it, Tom Harrow watched the snake pit. The rattlers, relieved of their venom, had been resting in postures of extreme lassitude, curved like that gas hose in his Grandfather Fowler's library. Aunt Edith had always referred to him as "Grandfather Fowler" or "the Judge," and there was veneration in both titles.

"If your Grandfather Fowler were alive," his Aunt Edith had told him once, "I think he would offer you a gold watch if you were to promise not to smoke until you were twenty-one."

And perhaps — who knows? — Aunt Edith might have been right, although there was no present way of telling.

"The Judge had that sofa upholstered the year before he

died," his Aunt Edith had said once. "That is why I drape the shawl over it, so the fabric won't wear down."

Why had he never asked more about the Fowlers? The answer was that the problems of puberty were enough in themselves so that one accepted one's parents' parents as static facts until it was too late. It was too late now to learn anything about the Fowlers, too late to learn anything about Aunt Edith, too, or why she disapproved of his mother. The Fowlers, all except his Aunt Edith, had vanished with gaslight and the hand-cranked Locomobiles before he was sixteen. Save for a voice or a gesture, they were academic now — except for his father. Tom's self-consciousness regarding his father was with him still. His father was a drunkard and one might as well let it go at that, except his father had been a valuable influence in a purely negative way. The memory, vague though it was, had always made him careful about liquor; but then, there were plenty of other examples from which to profit on Park Avenue, Broadway or points west.

"Your Grandfather Fowler, the Judge," his Aunt Edith once said, "never permitted anything in the house, and I hope you won't, either."

Well, his grandfather was gone and so was the house on Locust Street, but academic questions remained which he could consider on a sleepless night. Which people were the more disagreeable, for instance — those who said at the drop of a hat that they never permitted anything in the house, or those who could not leave it alone? The couldn't-leave-it-alones probably won the contest because sterling character was bound to command respect. That great Civil War cavalryman, for instance, the plumed and bearded Confederate general, J. E. B. Stuart, when dying of an abdominal wound, inflicted at a Virginia crossroad, had refused a shot of brandy to assuage his pain because he had promised his mother never to take a drop. It was seriously impossible not to respect and admire such consistency. At the age of twelve, when his father, in spite of opiates administered by Dr. Crocker, emerged early one evening from his bedroom and fell down the stairs in a brownstone house on Seventy-second

Street, Tom, too, had promised his mother that he would never touch a drop. Unlike General Stuart, he had broken the vow in his freshman year at college. He could not recall what justification he gave himself, but his reason probably was included in one of that dashing general's favorite songs, "If you want to have a good time, jine the Cavalry." It was hard at the age of eighteen not to conform to environment. He had never experienced much free guilt about that promise, even the morning after, and he had never sworn again never to touch another drop. Nevertheless, the deterring memory was with him, including his father's handsome, pale face, whose features he had inherited himself, and Dr. Crocker's amber, goatee beard. The age of bearded doctors had been waning but had not wholly ceased when he had seen his father fall down the stairs in the house on Seventy-second Street.

Goodness knew, he had seen enough of the same thing since. If a fringe of useless ineffectuals was present in any area of endeavor, he often thought that there were more in entertainment fields than elsewhere. You were forever encountering them, forever feeling sorry and giving assistance when common sense told you it was money down the drain; but invariably these people had charm. Ironically enough, some of the most delightful individuals he had ever known had been gamblers, drunkards and liars. In general, it was advisable to beware of charm.

Later that evening, after Tom had made his transient promise to his mother, his father had never been so fascinating. As happened with most inebriates, the headlong plunge down the stairway — he confided to Tom later that he thought he was diving off the high board at the Lake Placid Club — did no great physical harm to Mr. Roger Harrow. He ended up with only a slight cut over the temple, and the shake-up had a sobering effect. As Dr. Crocker, who had many human traits, said when he applied a piece of adhesive tape to the cut, complete relaxation had done it and that the Lord usually took care of drunken men and fools.

Roger Harrow, or Roggie, as the group who came to the house

65

for Wednesday night poker used to call him, could snap back very quickly. Besides charm, those people generally possessed oxlike constitutions. No headache, no hangover, a cold shower and there he was; the color was back in his face and the adhesive patch made him look distinguished. He even looked well in those queer starched collars of the period exemplified by the drawings of Leyendecker. He had put on a short, dark coat, a pearl-gray waistcoat, and striped, diplomatic trousers, a costume not conspicuous at that time.

"Mary, dear," he said to Tom's mother as he bent and kissed her hand, and it was too late now to discover where he had discovered the trick of heel-clicking and hand-kissing which he always practiced when he was sorry, "what can I say? Absolutely nothing."

"Oh, Roger," she began, but he raised his hand and stopped her.

"One moment, my love, my sweet," he said. "There is one thing I must add, merely as a grace note. It is what the telephone girls say when they give you a wrong number — Excuse it, please. And may I add, my only love, that I have never seen you look more adorable?"

"Oh, Roger," she said again, but he raised his hand a second time.

"Please, sweet," he said, "I am ready to receive the well-merited lecture, but first may I embroider on that final thought of mine for one more mere second? Can you guess what I'm going to say? One guess, and a kiss if you can't."

And then he kissed her gently.

A son's loyalty to his mother was unnecessary to remind him that she was very pretty with her dark hair done in a psyche knot and her cheeks flushed and her brown eyes still shining from her tears. There was always that hope that it would never occur again.

"Oh, Roger," she said, "you're rumpling everything." But then, it was never going to happen again.

"And now," he said, "I shall continue with my thought. There was only one time when you have looked more adorable than

66

now and that was when I first saw you on the sidewalk of that God-damned town, when you were standing in front of your God-damned house and when I rammed that old Olds of mine into the elm tree instead of getting to Bar Harbor."

"Roger," she said, "don't swear in front of Tommy."

Roger Harrow smiled. There were smiles and smiles, and Tom had seen them all. His father's had a genuine, outgiving quality, a smile that made headwaiters love him and captains ask about him years after his demise.

"My sweet," he said, "I stand corrected."

If he had been an actor, he might have been good. He had that measured quality which veterans mentioned when speaking of Gillette, and his charm might have projected itself out front like the charm of Arliss.

"Let us say that very odd town," he said, "and that fantastical house, my sweet. If it had not been built of wood, it could have come right out of Malory."

She smiled and the tension in the room was gone.

"You didn't think it was fantastical after you hit that tree," she said.

He raised his eyebrows and touched the adhesive on his forehead.

"There was the concussion and you were there," he said. "Anyway, you were glad to get away."

"Even after what happened to it, it was a beautiful motor car," she said.

"But it wasn't the same afterwards," he answered, "neither it nor I, and it wouldn't have happened if I hadn't been looking at you. Your hat was almost a sunbonnet."

Then he smiled at Tom, and, after all, anxiety to appear well and to win admiration was an integral part of parenthood.

"Mary," he said, "I have a strangely virtuous feeling from sole to scalp and it's Saturday night and I don't think it would do a bit of harm if Tom and I were to step out to the Avenue and hail a taxi. I don't believe Tom's ever seen Broadway after dark."

Then he went on at once, not waiting for any answer.

67

"I'd like to take him out to see the lights just once. How about it, Tom? I could do with a bite to eat and we might go to Jack's and I promise to be back by eleven, dear. It's time Tom and I did something together. He's growing up, you know."

It was curious to remember that his mother answered promptly.

"Why, I think it would be lovely, dear," she said. "Tom, run and get your hat and coat."

It was another age, of course. The pre-twentieth-century flavor was there; but looking backwards one saw there was a more significant and pronounced cleavage from the present than any question of manners. It may have been that gaiety was harder to come by now, even in New York. The bright lights, the neon signs, the meretricious marble of motion-picture houses, and the dime-a-dance pavilions had not spread like a tide over every country town. There was only one place then like Broadway. "Don't blame it all on Broadway," they used to sing, "you've got yourself to blame." There were the great hotels, the Astor and the Knickerbocker. The street was an American symbol and there were still white ties and tails and opera hats, and there was also another quality that had disappeared long ago, the quality of a frontier town, on Broadway. There was generous spending and there was vulgarity on a large scale. It was a braver street, or perhaps it only looked so to a boy.

It was hard to remember that everything had been new once. There was a time when hansom cabs must have been novel to a particular generation, and it would have been hard to imagine that anything would ever be more modern than the taxi which stopped for them on the Avenue when Mr. Harrow raised his Malacca walking stick. The taxicab which they entered that night was painted a dignified black, and it was not necessary to bend double in order to climb inside or to hurl oneself in backwards as one did at present. The roof was high enough to accommodate Mr. Harrow's black bowler hat and the eager pulsation of the engine gave an anticipation of coming speed long before the gears began grinding jovially. There was no doubt any longer that motor cars were there to stay on that balmy

April night. There were even self-starters instead of cranks.

"Drive us through the Park," his father said, "and then down to Broadway, slowly, so that we can see the lights, and then please stop at Jack's."

Tom Harrow was a New York boy. He attended Gregory's on East Sixty-fifth, a fashionable boys' day school in those days, and he knew his way around certain areas of the city. He had been, like all his generation, to the circus at Madison Square Garden, and to see the mummies in the Metropolitan Museum, and to the Bronx Zoo. He had been to matinees and to luncheon at Delmonico's and the Plaza. He had seen the lights of Broadway in the dusk, but never late at night. He had never noticed the glow that they made in the sky. The devices of the moving advertisements were as crude as the flickering silent films in the motion-picture houses, and yet he was sure that the lights were brighter than they ever had been since.

"It's about time," his father said. "I should take you around a little, Tom. Only the other day I was talking to your Uncle George about you."

He felt a quiver of apprehension, but it was only slight; and, besides, his Uncle George had nothing to do with Broadway.

"George says you should go to boarding school, and I suppose you should. Of course neither George nor I did, but George points out that nowadays coming from a good boarding school is a very considerable help when entering college, and your Uncle George, I must say, is a specialist in those things."

His father laughed without malice. "George knows how to do the right thing, and I must say he's been very kind to me about furniture and finances and everything. I think George is right about boarding school—Groton, Pomfret, St. Mark's."

But he had not been seriously interested in education. Tom knew instinctively that his father's fall down the stairs had put them temporarily on an entirely equal basis.

"Say," he said, "I never knew you had an Oldsmobile, or that you ran it into a tree or that was how you met Ma."

His father's laugh was an invitation to share in a store of jovial thoughts.

69

"I had your same difficulty once," he said. "Parents should be legally compelled to give at least an antiseptic summary of their pasts to their children instead of taking it for granted that their lives are open books — but when should one begin? Certainly not when a child is mewling and puking in his nurse's arms, as you did more than appeared necessary — not that I had any previous firsthand experience with infants."

Mr. Harrow laughed again. The taxi was threading its way through Central Park along the old carriage road that curved in a delightful contrast to Manhattan's other streets. The taxi's headlights, which might very well have been acetylene and not electric, unrolled a changing scroll of trees and shrubbery and rock. It was still a period when riding in an automobile presented delicious novelty.

"In fact, I've finally grown so accustomed to you, Tom, that it amazes me that you do not know all about me, not to mention your dear mother and your Aunt Edith and that charming though provincial town from which they hail. Well, well, its umbrageous streets once formed, and doubtless do still, a quaint interlude in the thoroughfare that extends from New York City to Bar Harbor, Maine, and I trust that horses are not as startled now as they were by motor cars when I collided with the tree. It was a choice between the tree and a horse drawing a buggy driven by an unpleasant man who looked like General Grant, and then there was your beautiful mother on the sidewalk. Naturally I chose the tree and the damn Olds didn't stop."

"But why were you going to Bar Harbor?" Tom Harrow asked.

They were approaching Columbus Circle and the evening sky was aglow with the lights from Broadway.

"Why was I going to Bar Harbor?" Mr. Harrow said. "What an amazing question — or is it? I was going, of course, to visit my dear father, your grandfather, who was about to purchase me a junior partnership in the financial house downtown with which I still have the pleasure of working. Seasoned bonds. You must remind me to take you down there and introduce you

70

around the office so that you may listen to the tickers, but don't buy stocks, Tom, only seasoned bonds."

"I didn't know you ever lived in Bar Harbor," Tom said.

"Well, well," Mr. Harrow said, "I never did in actuality, but my father, your dear grandfather, used to rent a cottage there after my dear mother died. There was gossip, although as your Uncle George would say, entirely unsubstantiated, that he was interested in a Mrs. Coventry, who resided during summers in that quaint village known as Northeast Harbor. Well, well, this is a mere aside. We had more money then. We might have still if your dear grandfather had not become engrossed in mining stocks. Mrs. Coventry came from Colorado, but that is neither here nor there, except that seasoned bonds are generally more reliable. Well, here is Broadway. By gad, it's always a magic street."

There was nothing like old Broadway any more. There had been a graciousness about the city that had vanished. The horses that were still not supplanted by motor trucks were less obtrusive than the automobiles of another generation. The street cleaners, with their brooms and shovels and their galvanized ash cans on wheels, kept the asphalt neat and there were no rows of cars to clog the streets. Litter was taken care of efficiently by the whitewings, since the day of packaged goods was only dawning. Tom could never remember in his youth swirls and eddies of newspapers, of cigarette cartons and chewing gum and candy wrappers. Even the noise of old New York had a magic quality that now was lost. It was an antique conglomeration of human voices, police whistles, the clanging bells of street cars and of motor horns operated by rubber bulbs, the clop-clop of horses and finally, the comfortable and solid roar of the elevated on Sixth Avenue. Broadway and its side streets were bright then with the golden light of old Edison incandescent lamps as yet unadulterated by colored glass, and not affected at all by neon signs. There was an expansive radiance that made everything like the Emerald City of Oz. All theatres had numbers that flashed above their marquees so that the proper vehicles might be promptly delivered to the carriage trade. The wonder of it all never left Tom's mind. It was with him still as a sort of driving force, despite all later transmutations.

Of course this New York, according to present standards, was as dated as a set of books by Richard Harding Davis and yet as handsome as the deckle-edged editions of the ephemeral novels that were turned out at the beginning of the century. Sociologists might say that the inequities of wealth were appalling, that the slums were beyond description, and that there was callous cruelty in place of social consciousness — but he had been too young to know. If not a better town, New York was more comprehensible and more magnificent. "Edwardian" might have been another way to put it — a word that had not been invented then. The food and hospitality at Jack's were Edwardian, with its welcoming doors in the shadow of the Sixth Avenue elevated, and reminiscences of Jack's existed in London still. Perhaps the ghosts of Jack's had returned across the sea and still haunted Simpson's on the Strand. The past was visible in London, never shouldered into oblivion by the present as hastily and remorselessly as was the New York past.

There was a captain named Ben standing inside the door at Jack's. From the pleasure he displayed, he obviously approved of Mr. Harrow.

"Tom," Mr. Harrow said, "I'm particularly glad that Ben is on duty tonight because I want you to shake Ben's hand. Ben has been a great comfort to me on many occasions."

"And it's always been a pleasure, Mr. Harrow," the captain said. "And a pleasure to meet the young man. But we can't have minors in the room with the bar."

"A pity," Mr. Harrow said, "to be so far away from the source of supply, but any place will do."

It was quiet at Jack's that night, since the hour was well before the theatre closings.

"Some oysters, I think," his father said, "as long as they are still in season; and, for myself, a double Manhattan cocktail, and follow it with another in ten minutes. We won't be long here, I'm afraid. Tom must get his beauty sleep."

"Are you sure you ought to have one of those things again?" Tom asked.

"Oh, certainly," Mr. Harrow said. "Ben is really a delightful fellow. Don't you think he has an honest face?"

"He looked pretty tough to me," Tom said.

"It's merely poor Ben's nose," he said. "You see, he forms the apex of the flying wedge."

"What's the flying wedge?" Tom asked.

"A mass formation of waiters," his father said, "intended to evict unruly patrons. They move at a signal. Right out the door —no fuss or anything, but it sometimes is rough on the number-one man. Well, it's delightful you're here, Tom, and here's looking at you."

Ben had come back with the double Manhattan. His father swallowed it quickly.

"There," he said. "Thank you, Ben. The tail of the dog that bit you. It's delightful to have you with me, Tom. Your company reminds me of a little song. Wait, Ben, don't go away yet. I wonder if you've ever heard it."

"What song is that, sir?" Ben asked.

"Just a snatch, a jingle," Mr. Harrow said. "Would you care to have me render it?"

"As long as it's not too loud and it isn't too funny, sir," Ben said. "As you know, singing often causes trouble because other patrons may want to sing."

"This will only take a minute," Mr. Harrow said, "and I rather think you'll enjoy it because it's peculiarly apposite to the occasion.

> "Stay in there punching, sonny,
>   Don't let your heart fall plop,
>   Some day the nation will honor you, too,
>   As it's honored your dear old pop."

He sang the snatch melodiously, and he might not have been bad in a vaudeville turn.

"Thank you, Mr. Harrow," Ben said. "That was a lovely song. Would the young man like a Welsh rarebit?"

It was a lovely song as it was sung that night, and it was strange what an effect incongruity might occasionally have upon future resolves and actions. That night had always meant a great deal to Tom Harrow. He wanted to be in there punching, and the lights of Broadway were what made him wish the wish — but he never was fool enough to want to be like his dear old pop.

You were surrounded by a dangerous sense of permanency when you were young, by a conviction that people and institutions would never change. He should have asked his father more questions that night when Mr. Harrow had brought up the subject on that ride along Broadway. That evening with his father back in 1916 was one of the few they had ever spent together. The influenza epidemic reached New York two years later. His father came down with it first and then his mother caught the virus. He was at boarding school in Massachusetts at the time and word had been sent that he was not to go home because of possible contagion. People died very swiftly in 1918. His parents were both gone before he knew they were ill. The Rector was the one who told him, in one of those sad set scenes once so popular with Victorian novelists. There was something strong and set about the Rector's speeches, as though he were reciting a service from the *Book of Common Prayer*. Transportation had been arranged, and his uncle, Mr. George Harrow, would be waiting at the Grand Central Station, and Uncle George had been very kind. The meeting was mainly memorable through his uncle's display of extra kindness. If his Uncle George had been the sort of person of whom one asked questions, Tom might have found out about his family from his Uncle George.

"Tom," he had said, "we'll have to do the best we can together. Your father was a most delightful man." And his Aunt Mabel had been very kind. He had only seen the house on Seventy-second Street once again. When he returned from school for the spring vacation, everything was gone — the shadow of his father and mother, the legend of his grandfather in Bar Harbor and the lady from Denver, Colorado. They were gone, all the familiar faces, except occasionally his Uncle George and his

74

Aunt Mabel and his cousins. Everything, in fact, had evaporated into a small trust fund. It appeared that his father had never practiced what he preached about the seasoned bonds.

It was impossible any longer to ascertain how much of a problem he may have been to his Aunt Mabel and his Uncle George, but he could not have been much trouble because the George Harrows were adroit at avoiding burdens. His Aunt Mabel had often pointed out to him what an enormous amount of thought and attention his uncle had given the trust fund and his educational future. There were some people, she often said, who did not understand his Uncle George, because of his uncle's retiring modesty. There were even some people who felt that his uncle was financially selfish, whereas nothing could have been more wrong. The truth was that for years his Uncle George had been in failing health and under his doctor's orders never to put himself under strain; but Uncle George was always doing kind little things for people. She could not imagine how gossip got around that she and his uncle were rich when the truth was that they were not even well-to-do. It had been necessary, obviously, to maintain a standard of living equal to that of his uncle's law partners. They had to keep up a house in the East Sixties and the children had to go to the right schools, but they also had not wasted capital like some people she might mention.

She knew very well that a number of people had said that they should have had Tom live with them after his tragic bereavement. His uncle had been deeply troubled for several weeks over just what was the right thing to do and no one had any right to say that financial aspects in any way affected his uncle's ultimate decision. It was true that the income from the small sum that could be salvaged from a nearly bankrupt estate was not in the least sufficient to pay for an expensive private boarding school, and also the very large though hidden expenses that would have been incurred if Tom became a member of the George Harrow household. But absolutely no one had given the question of expense more than a passing thought. She wanted Tom to realize this, and she was certain that Tom did, although sometimes

75

she did feel that he was just a little neglectful of his uncle after all his Uncle George had done for him. But then, the younger generation never could understand the difficulties of the old — the bringing-up of children, the struggle to make both ends meet, and, finally, the effort to be a worthy example, because example always was more important than precept.

Of course they would have taken Tom in if the step had been advisable. They had only waited until they could consult with his Aunt Edith. After all, his mother's older sister's feelings might have been very much hurt if she had not been given a chance to help. When his dear Aunt Edith offered to have him come live with her, Tom would have been very touched if he could have known how carefully his Uncle George had weighed the pros and cons before making an affirmative decision. He kept saying, often in the middle of the night, that he wanted to do what was best for Tom, and she was sure that Tom had known it even though Tom had been quite neglectful of his uncle; but she knew very well that this was attributable to the carelessness of the young and not due to any small-minded resentment.

Living in New York admittedly had its benefits and advantages, but Tom had already been brought up in New York in a manner which was much more extravagant than it should have been, and change was always wholesome for a growing boy, and that quaint house of his Aunt Edith's would give him lots of room. Also to be considered was the uniform excellence of New England public schools. The money which would be saved there could be put back in the Fund so that a sum would finally be available to pay his expenses through college, with perhaps a tiny bit left over for him to do what he wished with when he was twenty-one and the trust had expired. His uncle had been right; there had been a tiny bit left over. It had been very generous of his Aunt Edith not to ask payment for his board but his Aunt Edith had been very lonely in a big house and was much more comfortably off than she appeared to be. You could never tell about people in small towns who did not have to maintain standards according to conventions. She might in the very end leave Tom a little something that was considerably more than anyone might expect; and if his uncle had taken the usual commission for administering the fund, she was sure Tom would have wanted it that way for his own self-respect.

Tom had heard this rationalization from his Aunt Mabel more often than he cared to recollect. There had always been a musty monotony about it derived doubtless from his aunt's having been a musty, monotonous old woman whose thoughts had been concentrated for years on trying to maintain what she called a position. His Aunt Mabel was one of that small army of the insecure upper middle class who had honestly thought that complete disaster would shower down if the rug were pulled out from under their positions. Well, it was different now. Even the Cadillacs were not so secure as they used to be. When it came to his Aunt Mabel, he knew her apologia by heart and he could remember distinctly the last time he had heard her recite it.

It had been in the winter of 1933, the year when his third play was running on Broadway and when serious evaluations were beginning to be made regarding his Contribution to the American Theatre. It was a Sunday in February, at the time when the banks were crashing but before citizens had learned, as they did in the Roosevelt March inaugural, that the only thing to fear was fear itself. Because of ignorance Tom had not been afraid, that Sunday morning, and Rhoda wore the new mink coat he had bought her for Christmas. He was not afraid, but he had sense enough to be disturbed at the way things were going — and beyond being disturbed, he was intensely interested. At least the Great Depression had not been a dull time through which to live.

He had not wanted to go to his aunt's for Sunday luncheon, but Rhoda had made him go. She had said that he had not been to see his Aunt Mabel for over a year. He had answered that his aunt had begun asking him to Sunday luncheons only after a piece had been written about him by Mr. Brooks Atkinson in the theatre section of the Sunday *Times*.

"I don't see why you want to go," he said to Rhoda. "I don't

77

owe her anything. She was always dull and now she's beginning to be sorry for herself. I don't know why Uncle George ever married her."

"Oh Tom," Rhoda said, "she isn't nearly as bad as you think. She's rather sweet, really. At least I think she's sweet."

"Exactly why?" he asked her. Rhoda pursed her lips for a moment, but it never took her long to find an answer.

"Well, she's always reassuring," she said. "I guess because she makes me realize that you have a conventional background. There aren't ever any sword-swallowers or gag artists or nymphomaniacs or anything at your Aunt Mabel's."

"You mean she isn't Bohemian," Tom said, "and you're afraid we're going to get Bohemian?"

"I'm not afraid," Rhoda said. "I suppose I'm a little stuffy, myself, and you do have a sense of order, yourself. You don't like cigarette ashes sprayed all over the rugs and white circles all over the tables.

"You mean show business keeps coming into the home. Is that what you mean?" he asked her.

"Well," she said, "sort of, sometimes. And now that we have Hal — well, you know what I mean."

"Yes, I know partly," he said. "But I wish you wouldn't keep lumping everybody into one category. Do you think I'm Bohemian?"

"Oh, darling," Rhoda said, "no, no, and promise me you won't be."

She could never seem to understand, and perhaps no woman could, that people do not readily change from one personality to another.

"I'll work on it," he told her, "as long as you don't forget you're a pretty extravagant girl and want a lot of things."

"I know it, dear," she said. "I know I'm extravagant and I suppose I'm always worrying about Hal."

He was very seldom annoyed with her — because he was in love with her.

"What makes you worry about Hal?" he asked.

78

"I wish he had a bigger nursery," Rhoda said, "and we ought to think seriously about renting a place in the country."

Child rearing was a subject that he had never been fully able to understand. It was always just beyond his horizon of comprehension, never to be grasped any more than he could grasp the theory of integral calculus.

Although the hundred days of the New Deal had not quite yet occurred, one had a very definite sense that events were moving into a period of drastic change, but he could say one thing for his Aunt Mabel Harrow. She was still maintaining her position. At Uncle George's death, dear though all associations had been to her, she had known enough not to continue in the brownstone house in the Sixties, where she would have rattled around now that both her children were married and so, naturally, engrossed in lives of their own. His dear Uncle George had always said that she had possessed an excellent head for business. She had sold the house before the market break in 1929, just when there was a heavy demand for New York real estate, and she had rented her present apartment in one of those new buildings on Park Avenue, in the upper Fifties, which was not a cooperative. The apartment did not have the atmosphere of the dear old brownstone house, but she still had the things she loved the best around her — her portraits of the Morton family, for instance. (She had been born a Morton, one of the Poughkeepsie Mortons.) She had also kept the furniture from the drawing room and from his dear uncle's library, and also some of his dear uncle's more important first editions. As Uncle George had always said, sound and seasoned first editions held their value. Thus the apartment, though it was so high up that it made her a little dizzy to look out of the windows, had the original family atmosphere. It still gave her a sense of keeping up her position, and a part of the position was a solid family luncheon of roast beef and Yorkshire pudding. She supposed that Tom and dear Rhoda, being very gay, would have preferred pheasant and champagne, but still, Tom would remember his Uncle George's old roast-beef custom.

He was in the aura of the custom when he and Rhoda entered Apartment 10 B and stepped into the area poetically termed "a foyer." The maid was new, but she wore the same frilled apron that his aunt had always insisted that a parlormaid should wear. The apron and the pedestrian odor of roast beef made him momentarily adolescent. It was a pity that only sights and sounds could be translated to the stage. Today the aroma of a roast was no longer pedestrian. This Sunday luncheon was in the days before World War II was followed by an era of national abundance, days which had made standing rib roasts rare and almost strange. His Aunt Mabel and, to his surprise, his cousin Louise were in the living room. Louise's husband, Guthrie Hyde, was away in Chicago on business. His aunt had put on weight, which did not convey the same rebuke among the elderly that it does today, and a five-pound box of caramels was still a suitable gift to bring one's hostess. Her dress was new and beautiful but it was the same beige-colored satin that Tom had always associated with his Sundays at Uncle George's — almost the color of the caramel sauce you could pour on your Sunday vanilla ice cream if you did not like chocolate.

"Dear children," his Aunt Mabel said, "how delightful of you to come, and so promptly, too. It shows you remember what your uncle always said, don't you, Tom, that time, tide and rare roast beef wait for no man."

He wanted to say that the same was also true with death and taxes but Rhoda would not have liked it.

"Please don't get up, Aunt Mabel," Rhoda said, and she kissed her aunt-in-law's cheek.

"Thank you, dear," his aunt said, "my chair is somewhat cushiony for popping up and down as I should. It is a present from Louise and Guthrie."

Tom moved toward her with dignified respect. He had watched enough actors to know how to cross from L to R in a drawing room as though it were a stage, and he knew also how to kiss a cheek with gay and debonair aplomb.

"Dear Tom," his aunt said, "you look so distinguished, more and more like your Uncle George each year, but still a little . . ."

Her voice died into a pregnant sort of silence.

"You don't mean dissipated, do you?" Tom said, and he was immediately sorry he had said it because Rhoda did not like it.

"Oh, Tom," Rhoda said, "I wish you wouldn't keep having the idea on your mind that you're an old roué. I know what you mean, Aunt Mabel, it's the theatre. Theatre people never go to bed — that is, at times."

"I'm glad you made that qualification, dear," Tom Harrow said, "because they do go to bed, and often with the most unexpected people — especially in summer stock."

That had been quite a line for the pre-Repeal and the pre-Roosevelt era, and he would have enjoyed it more if Rhoda had not been there.

"Oh, Tom," Rhoda said, "don't always try to be too funny! It's the drawing room dialogue he keeps writing, Aunt Mabel — dialogue, dialogue, dialogue, and always changing lines."

At any rate, Louise laughed, reminding him that she was beginning to look more and more like her mother, confirming that old-fashioned maxim that before proposing to a beautiful girl one should take a good look at her mother.

"Now I know why that play of yours is so killing," she said. "Does he always think of such excruciating things to say every minute, Rhoda?"

"Only every other minute," Tom said.

"Anyway, I just loved the play," Louise said, "and it was so cute of you, Tom, to give us first-night tickets. I told Guthrie that you wouldn't mind at all if I were to ask you. It's so hard to get Guthrie to take the initiative. Anway, Tom, it was cute."

"It was wonderful having you there," Tom said, "as long as you didn't sit on your hands."

"What do you mean by that, Tom?" his Aunt Mabel said. "Louise never sits on her hands."

"I'm sure she doesn't," he said, "no nice girl should, ever, and Louise has always been a nice girl."

There was no reason why he should not enjoy himself even though Rhoda might have something to say about it later, and Louise laughed and laughed.

"It's just a theatrical expression, Mother," Louise said. "Isn't it fun having someone famous in the family, let alone a playwright? Tom means he likes people to applaud, don't you, Tom?"

"That's exactly it," Tom Harrow said. "Rhoda and I and Harold have to live entirely on applause."

He had never said a truer word and he hoped that Rhoda was listening.

"And simply the most excruciating part of it all," Louise said, "was when the butler came in with a tray of glasses in the third act and slipped on the rug. Honestly, Tom, I thought I was going to die, it was all so natural."

"He slipped at just the right minute," Tom said, "when people from Bernardsville were wondering whether they could catch the last train."

"That's true, you know," Rhoda said. "Tom does think of things like that, even when everything seems natural."

"I suppose every profession is exacting," his Aunt Mabel said, "at least it was that way about the law. Your dear uncle never forgot anything, but he did say when he left the office he never took it home with him at night. But speaking of a butler and trays, I was telling Louise that I thought we might have a little something to celebrate our family reunion. There was quite a little something in the cellar at Sixty-second Street."

When he was young and endowed with the ambition and self-confidence that came from lack of self-knowledge, he had never dreamed of using malice either as a weapon or a pain killer. Besides, he had been gay in those days and the delicious euphoria surrounded him that he had seen attack other three-hit playwrights. Uncle George had been able to leave a little something in every department, but he did not envy his uncle.

"Well," he said, "thank goodness there was something in the cellar. I could do with a drink."

It was not malicious to be amused by the look that his Aunt Mabel cast toward Louise. His aunt had always been waiting for dipsomania. For years she had a fixed belief that he would never turn out well; and now, glad though she doubtless was that he was being successful, even to the extent of making a position for himself among peculiar people, there was still his unstable background.

"I should like a rather large drink, Louise," he said, and he smiled at his aunt. "The tail of the dog that bit me."

"Oh, Tom," Rhoda said. "He's only trying to be funny again, Aunt Mabel. He hardly ever takes anything."

Old people could never change their patterns. If that luncheon, which was one of the last of the sort he had attended, was different from those that preceded it, the fault was his and not his aunt's. He was the one who had changed. Aunt Mabel was going into her old routine, as precise in her patter as a well-seasoned vaudeville actress — not that Aunt Mabel's act was vaudeville. She was justifying herself again, and he preferred people who struggled silently with the pangs of conscience. It would have been much better if she had simply said that she and his uncle had always felt a qualm of guilt because they had done so little for him when he needed help. Yet Rhoda listened with apparent interest to that redundant tape-recording.

"Tom, dear," Aunt Mabel said, "how has your dear Aunt Edith's health been lately?"

The question was the opening gambit of the game that often started after Sunday lunch.

"I think she's frailer than she was the last time you inquired," he said.

He was not so ironically amused by the question as he had been previously. He was astonished that his voice had assumed a cutting edge, but Aunt Mabel had not noticed.

"I am sure you are doing everything for her comfort," she said, "exactly as you should. I am sure you have not forgotten how much you owe her."

"No," he said. "Aunt Edith is in a class by herself. I don't feel grateful to everybody." He hoped that he had not been rude, but he wanted her to realize that she was not priority number one.

"I'm so happy," she said, "that it all turned out happily, just as your dear uncle knew it would. It was so much better for you not to be competing with other children, just as your uncle said it would be."

"Yes," he said, "I might have fallen in love with Louise and that should not have happened."

Louise tittered and he smiled at Rhoda.

"I was susceptible in those days," he said, "but I am sure Louise and I would have handled ourselves correctly."

His aunt had never been able to understand lightness of touch.

"It's so interesting that you should have mentioned that, Tom dear," she said, "because your dear uncle mentioned the same possibility once. He always thought of everything."

"Yes," Tom said, "I think he did. You know, I'm afraid I never appreciated him as much as I should have."

Rhoda looked at him again, but his aunt was very gracious. "Don't reproach yourself, dear," she said. "We all always wish we could have done more after someone goes. And it was hard for many people to understand the real extent of your uncle's kindness because he had innate modesty. He would be so proud of you if he were here now. Do you know what he said once, Tom?"

It was time to be grave and proper.

"No," he said. "I'd have remembered if you'd told me, Aunt Mabel."

"Well, it's another thing to treasure," his aunt said, "and to put in your memory box. Your dear uncle said, quite suddenly one evening — and it wasn't like him to say anything suddenly — 'Mabel,' he said, 'I honestly think Tom has got a lot from living with his maiden aunt and enjoying the benefits of a free New England education. It's the sort of experience that makes for quality.' And then he made another remark that I've often pondered over."

"I hope you'll tell me what it was," Tom said.

"Well, I've often pondered over it," his aunt said. "He said quite suddenly, 'I wish I might have had the privilege — that was the word, 'privilege' — 'of a New England boyhood.' That's another thing to remember, don't you think so, Tom?"

"Yes," he answered. "Uncle George must have been reading *The Story of a Bad Boy* by Thomas Bailey Aldrich."

His aunt shook her head. "No," she said, "your Uncle George

84

never did care for fiction. When he had time to read, it was always Beveridge's *Life of John Marshall*."

It was time to go, and it was delightful to see that Rhoda had picked up her gloves and purse. The last speech made a good curtain for some sort of act, and indeed the whole conversation had its own dramatic proportion. It represented a part of his life that was over, far away and long ago. He owed no loyalty or duty to anyone in that act, except to his Aunt Edith Fowler.

VI

There's an Awful Lot of Knowledge One Never Learns in College — or in a Judge's Library

HE WAS well along through fifteen, and fifteen was not one of his favorite ages, when the Model T Ford that used to meet the train in those days drove him with his suitcase to the Fowler house to spend two years of a small-town boyhood. He had been there only once before on a visit with his mother and he had been too young then to have retained a coherent picture. Now the ornately shingled, gingerbread building, with Japanese maples and umbrella trees in front of it, gave him a deep feeling of loneliness when he paid the driver and walked up the steps and pulled the doorbell. There was no electricity in the house. His Aunt Edith did not believe in it because electric wires might cause fires if rats should gnaw them. It was still the gaslight era, in the Fowler house, plus kerosene table lamps.

His Aunt Edith never believed in keeping people, even book agents, waiting at the door; she opened it at once and she kissed him in a dutiful manner. The uncompromising steel structure of her corset proved that there had always been something about her of iron women and wooden ships.

Speaking of Thomas Bailey Aldrich and his *Story of a Bad Boy* — or speaking of *Tom Sawyer* for that matter, even though this work was based upon a different regionalism — what had become of the conventional spinster? Where was she now, indeed? Popular though she had been in Victorian and Edwardian literature, she was now swept away with other myths destroyed by two world wars. Where was the prototype of the

86

kind Miss Nutter who used to feed her young relative hot drops in the family homestead in Portsmouth, New Hampshire? Where were the modern models of self-effacing, religiously inclined, unmarried sisters who appeared when needed to take care of their handsomer sisters' offspring or who, when not so engaged, ministered to the querulous wants of aging fathers and mothers, and even great-aunts and uncles, and also of unemployed or maladjusted brothers? It was disturbing to discover, on mature reflection, that there were no modern models. They had disappeared with the sound of horses' hoofs and the rattle of iron-rimmed wheels on cobblestones. They had vanished with the lamplighter and the hand-cranked telephone once impaled upon the wall of the side entry, with the kitchen coffee mill whose merry noise once aroused one in the morning, simultaneously with the ruder sounds of the chore man shaking down the coals of the furnace. There were plastic telephones now with colors to match every décor. There were heating units governed by electronic devices; and street lights, multiplied recently to combat juvenile delinquency, now turned themselves on and off by remote control; but there were no spinsters any longer — or if they did exist, they seldom admitted their condition. Society, effectively assisted by the late Sigmund Freud and the whole psychiatric profession, had no longer much respect for the once honorable guild of spinsterhood. The girls had been laughed off the stage long ago. Faced by pitiless pictures of the subconscious, they now made frantic and pathetic efforts to conceal the solitudes of their existence, lurking in beauty parlors, going on safari, becoming interior decorators or hard-boiled businesswomen, leading dedicated lives that were more useful and a whale of a lot more interesting than looking after a bunch of snot-nosed children as their sillier sisters had who were basically girls who could not say "No." Middle-aged spinsters were not respectable any more, now that health and happiness magazines were on sale on every drugstore counter. Nice girls always got married young and there was something queer if they didn't, and having an affair or a series of affairs was no honest solution of the problem but merely a further indication of emotional maladjustment. There was some-

87

thing wrong, in modern life, with any woman in her middle thirties who had not at least tried a year or two of marriage, and the poor girls knew it very well because they had been told so by friends, admirers and family physicians. If they weren't married, they were frigid or, if not frigid, promiscuous in a nymphomaniacal manner; and it did no good, either, to stay at home and keep house for Mom and Pops, when modern medical science now knew very well what *that* meant. It meant that they had ugly and immature habits of dependency in the Oedipus region, or at the very best it meant that they did not have the courage to cut the umbilical cord and live.

What, Tom Harrow often wondered, would his Aunt Edith have thought if she had known all the things that were wrong with her and had recognized the sinister motivations that had made her stay at home and look after her father until it was too late for any knights to come riding? What would she have said if she had been told that her deeds of sacrifice were as much a defense mechanism as were her impervious corsets reinforced with modern flexible steel which science had proven more reliable than whalebone? He was sure she would have been very angry, and her temper had not always been equable. He was also rather sure that she would have been right to be angry, because there had been such a thing as duty, once, in smaller fields than at present, and public opinion had once not so easily condoned evasions of sacrifice as it did today, particularly on the part of women. There were no Aunt Ediths any longer who consistently gave and asked for little back. She was a figure now in an album of family photographs. They had been beings apart, and yet he had depended on her presence even while he discounted it. There was no one like her any more. The only person, he sometimes thought, who remotely resembled his Aunt Edith at present was Miss Mulford, his secretary. It startled him occasionally to discover that in many ways their relationship was much the same as his had been with his Aunt Edith. Miss Mulford wished many of the same things of him, such as punctuality, industry and neatness. It was not wholly an impossible thought that the Aunt Ediths of yesterday had turned into the Miss Mulfords of today.

His Aunt Edith, as far as he could recall, had kissed him only three times; first, on the morning she received him into the Fowler house; second, on the day he had left for college; and finally, on the day when he told her that he was engaged to Rhoda Browne. The embarrassed affection that had prompted these three lapses from normalcy made them unforgettable. Once she had revealed a partial explanation for her behavior — not complete, but interesting. It happened when he had given her a bowl of goldfish for Christmas, and tears had come into her eyes when she saw them in the snowy light of Christmas morning beneath the small tree on the Judge's desk in the library. They were pale, plebeian goldfishes swimming around a submerged Norman castle decorated by a few leaden-weighted strands of aquatic flora.

"Why, Thomas!" she said. "Why, Thomas!"

He could tell more by her inflection than her expression that she was pleased.

"They aren't much," he said. "I wish they had been fantails, Aunt Edith."

"The thought counts very much more than the animal," she said, "and I've always wanted a goldfish, ever since I was a child; but pets made your grandfather very nervous, and I could not have bought one later because it would have been frivolous — I mean going into the five-and-ten-cent store and asking for a goldfish. It could not have helped causing talk."

"What sort of talk?" he asked.

"Nothing unpleasant," she said, "but it would have been peculiar when the word got around that I had bought a goldfish for no particular reason. But I always did want a goldfish."

This was what older people often said about Christmas presents, but he was sure she had meant what she said.

"Hello," she said to the goldfish. "Hello, my pretty darlings."

It was more than she had ever said to the kitchen cat, called

Bellamy. She always treated Bellamy correctly, but she always made Mike Gorman, the choreman, drown Bellamy's kittens promptly, and she had never relented even when they had six toes and mittens.

"We must be firm, Thomas," she had told him once, "or one moment of weakness will lead to another. And the birds must be considered."

There were always all sorts of things to be balanced and watched about the house and grounds, constant crises that demanded judgment: an attic leak, or the sudden discovery of a hornets' nest on the window outside the laundry ell. She prided herself on being a good housekeeper, but she would never turn her hand to cooking. This was up to Marie, the French Canadian maid-of-all-work, but she could tell Marie exactly how everything must be done. She was hard on Bellamy, the cat, but she was sentimental about the goldfish.

"We must do everything we possibly can to prevent Bellamy from eating them," she said. "Look at the little darlings. I could almost kiss you for your thoughtfulness in giving them to me, Thomas," she said, "but as you know very well, I do not believe in kissing, particularly young boys."

Sentiment as it existed for him in that late Victorian mansion, when it did not appear in a heavily framed engraving in the front hall entitled *The Love Letter* and another engraving in the parlor entitled *The Sister's Kiss,* was derived from sources fully and hilariously treated by authors of the school of Fielding and Casanova. On thinking back — and there were always doubts and regrets when dealing with hindsight — he might have been much kinder to Marie. But it had not occurred to him at that time that sex had to start somewhere — and besides, he was involved in other problems of adjustment.

"I think," his Aunt Edith had once said at supper, "that Marie is spoiling you." At suppertime the golden oak dining room possessed a spurious, baronial quality. The gas chandelier above the table was lighted at suppertime by a long instrument that both held a lighted wax taper and turned on the gas. The gaslight was dim and cold against the imitation Cordova leather wallpaper. The mirrors built into the massive sideboard reflected back the fan-shaped gas flames as though they came from a very long distance. The heavy plush portières that had suffered from use since the Judge's time absorbed such an enormous portion of the light that the moosehead above the sideboard — the Judge had shot this trophy in his early days in Maine — assumed a weird sort of liveliness. Tom always associated the dining room with coolness in summer and draftiness in winter. No matter how much Marie might heat the blue-and-white Canton plates, they were always as cold as the pressed-glass water pitcher.

Years later in a comedy he had written, called *Give Back the Time*, he had attempted to reconstruct that room as a set for the second act, and he was surprised at his capacity for almost total recall. But the set never had the proper atmosphere. The truth was you could not reconstruct the past.

"How do you mean she's spoiling me?" he asked.

His aunt smiled. At supper she always wore one of her handsome evening dresses that Miss Mayhew, the dressmaker, made over each year directly after the spring cleaning, and often her garnet necklace and her garnet brooch, but never the earrings from her mother's jewelry.

"I always used to have great difficulty in getting Marie to bake a pie," she said, "and now she bakes them continually so that you may have a piece of pie when you get home from school."

"I'm glad she does," he said. "She makes fine pies."

He could use his age and his preoccupations as an excuse, but he should have known what was coming; and the confrontation was still one of those incidents in life that one struggled to put behind one, with no success at all because they were too close to the mainspring of motivation to be entirely forgotten. He was awakened, and he never knew what time it was, except that the light of the waning moon was coming through the windows of the back spare room that his aunt had given him. What must have awakened him first was some intuition that made him aware before he opened his eyes that he was not alone in the

91

spare room, and he had been absolutely right. There was moonlight enough to see that someone was standing beside his bed and he knew it was Marie even before she spoke. She was a heavy girl and he could recognize her build and posture although he had never seen her in a cotton nightgown.

"Hey," he said, "what goes on?"

He was a long way from Casanova. In fact, he was a long way from any Kinsey report up there in the back spare room.

"Don't talk so loud," Marie said. "Are you crazy?"

There was no reason not to talk in an ordinary tone, since his Aunt Edith slept in the corner front room of the house with a large number of closed doors between them.

"Is that so?" he said. "Who says I'm crazy?"

"Well, don't talk so crazy, then," Marie said. "It's only me, Tommy, and I thought maybe you was lonely, because I was feeling lonely — the moon and all."

"Well, it's a funny time to be lonely," he said, "right in the middle of the night."

"It ain't so funny, Tommy," she said, "with the moon and all. I bet you was lonely laying here thinking about girls."

She put her hand on his head and rumpled his hair.

"Hey," he said, "quit mussing me up."

"Say," she said, "you're funny. I think you're funny."

"Cut it out," he said. "What's there so funny?"

"You ain't very polite, Tommy," she said. "You ain't even asked me to get into bed with you. That's no way for a boy to behave."

"Listen, Marie," he said, "stop kidding me. I want to go to sleep."

"Ain't you ever had anything to do with girls?" Marie asked. "Say, I bet you ain't."

Even though she was absolutely right, it was not a time for truth.

"Oh, you go on, Marie," he said. "I've had a lot to do with girls."

"Then don't you like me, Tommy?" she said. "Come on, I can show you a lot more about girls than those stuck-up high-school kids who don't know nothing about nothing. It's time you was getting wise to yourself, dearie."

It must have been only at that moment that he realized that he was face to face with the unknown. It was true, he suddenly realized, that time was marching on, and it was time for him to get wise to a lot of things, but he did not want to get wise to them with Marie, and, thinking of it in retrospect, this was her fault, not his. He could never blame himself for repulsing her.

"Listen," he said, "I'm wise to everything, Marie. I know all about girls."

"Well, say," Marie said, and she giggled, "I won't believe that until you show me. Come on and show me, Tommy."

He was glad that he had been tactful. He had always been fond of Marie, and she had been the first woman in his life.

"Well, thanks, Marie," he said, "but how about some other time? I've got a lot of schoolwork tomorrow. Thanks, Marie."

There was one thing he had to say for Marie. She was not angry. In fact, she laughed, and not at him exactly; she was only laughing.

"Well, good night," she said. "You're a nice kid, Tom," and she kissed him and that was all there was, except his glimpse behind the curtain of things. Somehow, although there had been nothing more, that superficial scene had taught him a lot about Marie, and about life, by indirection. He had always had the gift of seeing behind the curtain. He had often wished that there were more women like Marie.

Sometimes when there was nothing better to do in the night, when he and Rhoda could not sleep, they occasionally talked in the dark about the town where they had each lived briefly. It was interesting how their points of view would differ. He was the one who could remember people best and who could tell anecdotes, including that one about Marie, and what he had heard about older days and older manners. He was the one who had total recall, though time had mellowed the rough parts of

93

his memory. He wanted to remember those days and they had been valuable to him, whereas Rhoda had wanted to forget. She had not seen the appeal of the place, but only its limitations. She had never wholly recovered from the fear which she had as a young girl that she might be compelled to stay there forever. She invariably spoke with gratitude of her escape, which she owed entirely to him. She had been restless and impatient with the town, and she had never got on well with his Aunt Edith, but he could never blame Rhoda for this. His Aunt Edith was an acquired habit — and she had never approved of Rhoda. This had not been Rhoda's fault entirely, because Aunt Edith was instinctively disapproving and she had always blamed Rhoda for the precipitous way in which everything had occurred.

"I daresay she's a very sweet girl," she told him once, "although I know nothing whatsoever of her parents, because, quite frankly, the Brownes are not the sort of people who would be apt to cross my path. I daresay Rhoda is sweet, and I will admit cheerfully that she exhibits towards you an extreme sort of possessive devotion, but try though I may, Thomas, I never can quite allay suspicion that she threw herself at you in a manner which would not have been tolerated in my time. Also I understand what I am speaking of, having once had an admirer myself. The courtship was protracted, nor was it disagreeable because of its long duration. It was many months before he reached the point of having an interview with my father, the Judge — a privilege which I did not think I had the right to deny him after taking into account his attentiveness over such a long period. I admit that when the occasion of the interview was reached time had solved many problems, because I had come to know him so well that I no longer had any ardent desire to become his partner for life. This, I think, is one of the advantages of the protracted courtships which were conventional in my young girlhood. The World War, I admit, has of course changed matters, and the hysteria which surrounded those trying days has projected itself unpleasantly into present manners. I hope you will excuse this digression, Thomas, for I have never approved of reminiscing over affairs of the heart. I only bring up my own experience to explain why I cannot help feeling your courtship with Rhoda was precipitated unduly, as indeed was your father's of your mother. I can only wish that you had allowed time to be somewhat more the arbiter than either of you did permit, although I have no reason whatsoever to believe that Rhoda is not a sweet girl, and will not become, in time, a better housekeeper and a more experienced mother." There had been no reason, ever, to expect that Rhoda and Aunt Edith would understand each other.

He recalled the last time that the three of them had been together in the Fowler house. It was when his aunt had been ailing, before her last illness. Coming from New York and going to the Fowler house, Rhoda had always said quite frankly, gave her the heebie-jeebies — the same sort of reaction she had experienced when as a child she read back volumes of a set of bound copies of *Harper's Young People*. The house was, as Tom himself had often admitted, an architectural impossibility that exhibited the extremes of an era of bad taste. Of course Tom had his obligations to his Aunt Edith, and so Rhoda, being his wife, was glad to come on flying visits, but that fixed idea of his aunt's that they should occupy the three-quarters, black-walnut bed in the rear spare room, simply because it had been his room once for two years, was honestly preposterous. It was true that it was far enough away so that they could mix a Martini before supper without causing undue excitement, but he had to admit that the mattress was like a washboard; and the bathroom still had a zinc bathtub and a stained-glass window.

"Tom," she said, on the last night they had ever spent in the Fowler house, "move over here. I wish I had wool socks on because my feet are frozen. It's that back entry on the way to the bathroom, and I will not use the bedroom crockery. Tom, dear, I don't know how you stood it. I honestly can't understand."

She could not, and why should she have? "Everyone to his own taste," though a tiresome motto, at the same time was true. She simply had not seen what he had. It had never been Rhoda's gift to project her imagination behind façades.

It may very well have been that Tom had always known that

he would inevitably leave that *galère* only too soon, whereas Rhoda never had thought she would. Anyone who had suffered from claustrophobia, even restless houseflies of a summer's day, found it difficult to observe the beauty of environment. He must always have been aware of a sense of destiny during the two years he had lived in the Judge's house. Subconsciously he must have realized their precious quality. Somehow he had recognized the values around him because his character had been set.

Once when Rhoda told him that those two years with his Aunt Edith, desperately unpleasant though they must have been for a boy who had previously attended a fashionable school, had done a great deal to mold his character and had taught him his neatness and industry, he had not argued. His years with his Aunt Edith had done more to train his character than any subsequent experience. It was tantalizing that he never could discover exactly why, because they had been dull years, without a glowing moment of triumph or excitement.

Yet on sleepless nights they were the years his mind moved back to most often. For instance, he would be back again in the Judge's library, and somehow it would always be snowing or sleeting outside and there was comfort in the minute staccato sounds of ice particles against the window panes.

The Judge must have faced, like many another self-made man, severe discipline and feelings of inferiority in his youth, combined with an intense desire for self-expression. It was odd that although the house had been sold to wreckers years ago the strength of the Judge's personality lingered in its decoration. It was now only a fascinating air castle and not an heirloom that could be passed on. Its unanswered questions could be treasured only by a single survivor now. Had the entrance hall, for instance, with its hideous yellow fireplace and fake inglenook, warmed the Judge's heart when he returned there from his chambers? Tom could only depend on a single remark of his Aunt Edith's left for him to treasure.

"The Judge always said," she had told him once, "that this hallway is baronial. He had always desired such a hallway after reading Scott's *Marmion* in his childhood. And he always used to add, 'Wax it, Edith. Wax brings out the beauty of the golden wood.'"

She had seen that it was waxed until her last illness. But she only dusted, never waxed, the library floor, because the Judge had once slipped on the Oriental rug before the library door, because of excessive waxing. Tom could still hear the gentle tapping of sleet on the library windowpanes as though ghosts were tossing the sands of time against them, and genial warmth always rose from the hot-air register behind the Judge's desk. The library, being directly over the furnace, was the warmest room in the house; yet his Aunt Edith with her embroidery sat by preference in the cold front parlor, by the artificial gas fire, which she never lighted except in emergencies because gas was expensive.

"Your mother and I were never accustomed to enter the library," she had told him once, "unless we were invited by the Judge. The Judge made it clear that the library was a man's room, and so it is. On a damp day there is still the odor of his cigar smoke, and I am sorry to say, though Marie and I clean it faithfully and dust the books twice annually, there is still the odor of something worse. When Court was in session, the Judge occasionally entertained visiting lawyers in the library and he then thought it necessary to offer them a glass of Kentucky whiskey. The Judge never drank himself in company, and in private as he explained to me once, only because of a nervous affliction. At the time of his death there were eight bottles of Kentucky whiskey in the cupboard directly below his shelves of Legislative Acts, and there still remains a slight odor of whiskey. Marie mentioned it only last year. Your father asked the Judge for your mother's hand in the library."

In such a game of retrospection, it was impossible to gauge the degree of seriousness with which his aunt had been speaking, but a sort of irony did remain — something that was sweet and infinitely gentle, the sort of strange balance that existed between love and laughter. She must have loved the Judge whose ghost still wandered through the memory of his house, and particularly in the library, and she had been right. There was the ghost

97

of the odor of cigar smoke, not the best Havana, either. There had been no one to disturb Tom there. He could sit by the hour in the Judge's leather chair that made flatulent sounds whenever you settled yourself, and instead of doing his high school reading, could examine the Judge's libido. The library became his first theatre of the imagination, and he realized later that the only true reality in the world existed there — the reality of appeal of mind to mind.

He learned more about women from the library than he ever did from Marie. The personality of the Judge was kinder and more genial in the library than elsewhere. When you examined the books in the golden-oak bookshelves, there were splits in the façade and traces of human frailty. It took time to detect these rifts. It was necessary first to face the lawbooks, some of which stood on every shelf like a masonry curtain protecting the inner bailey of a fortress. It was necessary to look in lower cupboards and to take down the state statutes to understand the Judge fully.

The library had been a gentleman's library, consisting primarily of solid leather-bound sets, all of them lubricated annually by Aunt Edith. A gentleman's library, as the Judge very well understood, comprised the British poets, the works of Bulwer-Lytton, the Waverley Novels, Dickens and Thackeray, Austen and the Brontë sisters and Trollope. Given these, there was space for a few deviations of fancy. Tacitus, perhaps, and Gibbon, and a set of Grote's *History of Greece*, Green's *Short History of the English People*, Macaulay's *History of England*, and Boswell's *Johnson*. Because the Judge was American, Parkman's *Montcalm and Wolfe* was with the histories, and Prescott's *Conquest of Mexico* and Motley's *Rise of the Dutch Republic*. Then, as a dash of erudition, a set of Goethe — which appeared never to have been touched — and a set of Molière and Racine next to several volumes of the *Variorum Shakespeare*. Tom got his first taste of the theatre on that shelf, and his first love for reading French. He often wondered where the Judge had bought those books, so massive and so conventional, and his Aunt Edith had once given him a partial answer.

"Many of the volumes," she told him once, "particularly the more handsome ones, were acquired from the estate of a deceased client which was in partial bankruptcy when the Judge acted as its administrator. The Judge was anxious that his children be exposed to proper literature. He frequently read aloud to us portions of Dickens in the North parlor, and once I saw a tear in his eye when Barkus was passing on."

Judging from the almost mint condition of these volumes, it was safe to conclude that neither the deceased owner of the embarrassed estate nor the Judge had turned to them frequently, but his Aunt Edith said once that she had read them nearly all.

"I mean the ones that the Judge left exposed for perusal," she said. "Of course I covered each, on reading, with a folded wrapper of brown paper in order to preserve the exterior, and I trust you will do the same, Thomas."

He did not always do so. He was a fast reader and that dangerous facility threw him too closely into the bookshelf world to make him think of protective covers. Molière, he always thought, drew him to the theatre more than Shakespeare ever had. He remembered having told Rhoda once that there was a modernity and a compulsion and a sparkle in the Molière dialogue that Shakespeare had never captured. He must have been very much in love with Rhoda when he told her that.

"Tom, darling," she said, "I wish you wouldn't feel you had to be so radical in front of me, because I'm not one of those people at those theatrical Sunday nights. Now give me a kiss quickly and stop trying to be odd. You know that Shakespeare is a greater playwright than Molière. You said that he knew everything. I heard you say so the other night to Walter Hampden, darling."

"Maybe he knew too much," he had told her. "Maybe I don't go much for Shakespearian actors. You always have to be so polite to Shakespearian actors that you get to thinking that they are Shakespeare."

But it never did any good to argue with Rhoda, or any other woman, either. It took time to make an estimate of the books the Judge had really enjoyed. These were in the lower cupboards, presumably to be protected from perusal by his daughters. A large part of the *Comédie Humaine* was there, and so was *War and Peace* and *Anna Karénina* and the maladjusted *Madame Bovary* and *Salammbô,* this one a French paperback, and an almost complete set of the romances of Dumas. It was surprising how often he found flecks of cigar ash between their pages. It was only months later that he found the other books, when he had thought of looking behind the *Legislative Acts.* There he had found standing guiltily sideways the *Memoirs* of Casanova, Burton's *Arabian Nights,* Suetonius, three plays by Plautus, Balzac's *Droll Stories,* an odd volume in a very limited edition entitled *Kama Sutra, or Love Practices of the Hindus,* Rabelais, Boccaccio, and Chaucer's *Canterbury Tales.* He might never have appreciated Chaucer if that volume had not lurked behind the *Legislative Acts.*

There was no wonder that he learned a lot about women, there in the Judge's library, in his lonely years during the long, hard winters. There was many a time when he was so engrossed with the way women behaved on the printed page and what they might be up to next that he often tiptoed downstairs in the small hours of the morning and lighted the Judge's table lamp. Twice his aunt had interrupted him, standing in the doorway in the heavy Jaeger wool wrapper which she had inherited from the Judge, with her hair tight in curlpapers. She had never once asked what he was reading. It may have been unmentioned experience with the Judge, or possibly her own literary perusals, that had stopped her.

"Thomas," was all she had ever said, "you must not study so hard or else you will overstrain your eyes and have to be fitted for glasses."

You had to study hard, and strain your eyes and reflex emotions besides, if you were to understand about the women in the Judge's library. And all he had to help him in the beginning were those obscure hints of Marie's; but his reading taught him what she meant, and incidentally it was generally more brightly stated. Yet he still did not understand all about women. They had delighted him in the Judge's library and they delighted him today, disparate though they were, and confusing. If he had never written in college an exhaustive disquisition on the women of polite and impolite literature, he was nevertheless fully equipped to do so after his time in the Judge's library.

The difficulty in any such effort was to set an arbitrary standard of values by which the women in the Judge's library could be classified. One could take Scheherazade in the *Arabian Nights*. She was not, according to standards under which he was brought up, a good girl. She was not only glad to suffer at the hands of an embittered sultan a fate worse than death for a thousand and one nights, instead of throwing herself off a castle tower as Rebecca had threatened in *Ivanhoe*, but she had also contrived to tell the Sultan a series of absorbing if immoral stories, and she had appeared to enjoy it all. In spite of her habit pattern, Tom had ended by thinking of her as a very nice girl and even on occasions wished that he might have been the Sultan. Then there was Madame Bovary. She was a flighty young woman, but who would not have been, after associating with that dull doctor? Besides she received her just deserts as had Mr. Tolstoy's Anna. Tom regretted the just deserts partly because later in Hollywood he so often heard them brought up, although few of the participants in the story conferences there had read more than a synopsis of any of those works.

Then there were the naughty girls who took everything they could without ever throwing their hearts over the jumps — or only for a very material reason. Becky Sharp was a classic example, as was Beatrix Esmond, and Cleopatra was designing. Then there were King Lear's daughters, and why go further than Goneril? They, too, most of them, received their just deserts. Then there were the very wicked women, including Lady Macbeth, and Miladi in *The Three Musketeers*, and Jeanne de LaMotte Valois. These were all people who made one shudder, though later he sometimes also wished that he might have met them. Then there were the girls who went wrong, who could not seem to help it, particularly in the pages of Charles Dickens. Finally, in his classification, came the good girls, not the grisettes or the farmers' or the shopkeepers' daughters — who could never be expected to help what they did when they met a handsome young gentleman — but the Jane Austen girls, and the more impulsive but still correct Brontë girls.

It was not a bad training to review this gallery of literary portraits in the Judge's library, and very early his acquaintanceship made him aware of a disturbing fact.

Somehow the Balzac girls, the Brontë girls, the Tolstoy and the Dickens girls, and all the rest, never seemed wholly to resemble girls he met. He could understand that there were differences in period or in historic culture, but there was something more elusive still. It was seldom, in fact almost never, that the behavior patterns of living women coincided with those on printed pages.

It was no help to go back to high school after a session in the Judge's study and to glance across the rows of desks to the space where a girl named Malvina Frith, the first girl with whom he had ever fallen in love, was sitting. He would have done better to have gazed at her, bemused, watching the north light from the classroom window give luster to Malvina's reddish hair and add an incomprehensible piquancy to her unpowdered retroussé nose, without connecting Malvina with *The Ordeal of Richard Feverel*. She did not behave in the Meredith manner when he finally got up courage to ask her to go for a walk to look for wild flowers one afternoon in May. She did not behave like a Balzac or a Charles Lever girl, either. There was always a fearful inaccuracy about falling in love.

Come to think of it, Malvina Frith, whose father had been in the hardware business, might not have appealed to Mr. Meredith. Her nose, which had been irresistible across Room A in high school, had freckles on it. Due to their search for wild flowers, she was perspiring so freely that the undersleeves of her blue cotton dress were moist and her posture was no longer so agile and graceful as it had seemed to be when they had brushed past each other in the high school corridors all winter. Actually, though small, she was a rather dumpy girl, and she was more direct than anyone in Thackeray. Fielding might have understood her better, but she did not have the eighteenth-century touch. Her moment and her setting belonged to her alone, and she could never be removed from either.

"It certainly took you a long time to get around to it," she said.

"Around to asking you to go for a walk?" he asked. "I don't see why that's getting around to much."

"Don't be so dumb, and don't talk like you were in a book," Malvina said. "Haven't you been looking at me all winter, and not getting around to doing anything, and haven't I done all I could?"

"I don't see that you did much," he said.

"You can't in school, can you, dumbness?" Malvina said. "I did all I could and I kept bumping against you outside in the hall."

"Did you?" he asked. "I didn't know it was on purpose."

"The trouble with you," she said, "is that you read too many books and people who read too many books never know what is what outside of books — at least that's how it seems to me."

It was what you might call intuitive. It went to show that character was character and he should have treasured what Malvina had said a long, long time ago.

"Well," he said, "I'm glad you did it on purpose. I think that's swell, Malvina."

She laughed, not the way one of the Judge's girls would have laughed, but in a ripply way.

"Maybe you'd have got it if you'd been a football player or something," she said, "you dumb thing, you. Anyway, I'm glad you started doing something. Gosh, it's been awful waiting and kind of wondering — and you haven't done much yet."

He took her hand. It was pudgy and her fingers were blunt and soft, but he thought of these aspects only later. He took her hand and he raised it to his lips.

"Gosh," she said, "you did that like someone in a book or somewhere. Gosh, I bet you read more books than any boy in school."

She drew closer to him. It was the first time that he had ever thought of converting desire into creation.

"I guess it's all right to neck here," she said. "Let's go to it, Tom."

She sighed in a noisy, unliterary way after their first clumsy embrace.

"Now won't that stop you reading books?" she asked. "Gee, it's great to kiss a boy — not just any boy like in post office, but a boy you feel about the way I've been feeling about you across the room all winter. Let's do it again, and now it's May, we can go necking all the time."

"Malvina," he asked her, "do I neck better than Jack Dodd?"

It was not a question that any man should have asked, but at least it did not come out of George Eliot.

"To hell with him," Malvina said. "You're the handsomest and the smartest and the best-necking boy in school."

He could see now that he had been different from all the others. He could see now why Malvina herself, with all her wiles and wishes, could not wholly erase that difference in a close embrace. Both of them had tried, and everybody had recognized that Malvina was his best girl all through his senior year in high school. All through life he had been prone to kiss the wrong girl and to say the wrong thing to her at the wrong time and place. He could only add that he was used to being wrong by now, and it was time to get out of the stream of consciousness and walk on the solid shore. In his opinion, streams of consciousness never did get anybody to any place where they ever should have gone.

VII

After All, He Couldn't Take It with Him

HE HAD walked downtown to get the mail and not to discuss
abstractions beneath the pulpit of the First Congregational
Church with Mr. Godfrey. He wished that events and people
were not constantly overlapping, because there should be a time
and a place for everything. There should be; but somehow he
had never found it.

"It's been a real pleasure," Mr. Godfrey said, "sitting here,
kicking ideas around."

Mr. Godfrey had opened the door and the church with its cool
white silence was over them.

"God bless you, Thomas," Mr. Naughton had said the last time
that he had passed through that door to face the church, and
that had been quite a while ago. There was still that gateway to
remembrance. He was walking again over the reddish carpet
toward the low raised platform in front of the pulpit, and
beneath the carpet the same pine boards that had complained
before creaked beneath his weight. The noise again brought back
a sensation of apprehension. That was one of the things that his
art or profession, or whatever it was you chose to call it, had
taught him: the ambivalent curse of being able to be a part of
things, and yet to stand away from them untouched.

He knew as soon as he stood on the brick sidewalk of Bay
Street that he had emerged from the stream of consciousness.
He stood there feeling a little like a swimmer on a river's bank
with the water still moist about him. The post office, an oversized

gift from the Roosevelt administration, stood diagonally across the street. He was back in the present, where Providence had placed him, and he was, thank heaven, still able to live in and appreciate it. He was acutely aware of everything around him, yet he was still outside it. He had to be, because he had been born to live and look.

Why was it that post offices always smelled the same and always put one in the same anticipatory mood, which could not be conveyed across the footlights, as he knew, because he had attempted it? It was the sense of the unknown that did the trick, of course — the unknown that lurked behind the glass façades of the private boxes and behind the bars of the delivery windows.

"There's a registered special delivery waiting for you, Mr. Harrow," the clerk said. "We telephoned the house and they said you were walking down for the mail."

"Well, thanks," Tom Harrow said.

A registered special delivery meant that someone wanted something, but then, everyone was always wanting something. The exquisite bond of the envelope seemed like a violent effort to compensate for the undistinguished names of the law partners printed on its surface.

"Thank you very much," he said to the clerk, and he dropped the letter into the side pocket of his coat. He had a very good idea of what it would say, and there was no reason whatsoever for him to read it.

He realized, as he was walking up the drive again to his office in the carriage house, that he had gone through a good deal of experience since he had left the drive, in a purely vicarious way. In fact, he had gone through so much that it was harder than usual to know what he really felt or what he pretended to feel. He was sure that the letter in his pocket was no surprise because it was like the second shoe dropping, and he was glad that it had dropped. He was sure that the house was less substantial than it had been.

He found himself thinking of an evening he had once spent at the Casino in Monte Carlo. Once when he and Rhoda had spent a winter on the Riviera, when a winter on the Riviera was almost a must for intelligentsia, they had gone to Monte Carlo, and for once he had been as hot as a pistol. For a while there was no wrong in him as far as the columns and numbers went, and he had a complete awareness of his temporary power; and he knew that the croupiers themselves must have witnessed the same phenomenon before. It came from the unknown, something just beyond the borderline of fact. It did not last long, that run of his, but ever afterwards he knew how a confirmed gambler felt. He had never forgotten the impression that those minutes had made on Rhoda. She was wearing her green dress and the emerald he had bought her at Cartier's, solitary and beautifully conspicuous on its delicate gold chain. When that heap of counters was passed to him, so fast and in such quantity across the table, she could not understand what under the sun had happened to him, and he was sure that she had not shared his sense of temporary power. It was not only the gaming table, either, that exhilarated him. It was being married to the best-dressed and prettiest woman in that overdecorated room. He could also believe that the size of his winnings had made Rhoda forget some of her inhibitions, but he was wrong about that. Whether on the Corniche drive or the Saw Mill River Parkway, Rhoda hardly ever lost her balance.

"Tom," she said, and there was beautiful incredulity in her voice, "pick it all up and take it to the cashier. You know you can't go on like this forever."

"What?" he said. "Right in the middle of the run?" He had not done what she had said, and he was glad he had not, but the chips only marked what was inside him, the measure of a hitherto unexperienced emotion. He could feel a new knowledge of life and he knew that it was something he would never lose, but the counters that evening had never even appeared like financial symbols, although they had been wholly real to Rhoda.

"Oh, Tom," she said, when everything was over, "you could have given me my emerald for nothing if you had only stopped."

The idea of this financial parallel had startled him, but no doubt she had been right.

"I never wanted to get that thing for you for nothing," he said.

"That isn't the point at all. I wanted to give you something that meant something."

"Oh, Tom," she said, "why didn't you stop?"

"Darling," he said, "it wasn't those chips on the table. Don't you see it was the thing itself?"

The point was that he had had the thing for the moment, and that Rhoda had never understood.

His workroom was no different. He had been young, but not so young that he could not remember the peculiar phrase, "back to normalcy" coined by President Warren G. Harding. In all his adult life the room in which he worked had always been normalcy; and he did not realize, until he was back, how far he had deviated in his short walk.

Miss Mulford was sitting at his worktable as she did sometimes when he was out. Once long ago she had apologized for doing so and he had told her not to be silly. She was reading a typescript which he recognized immediately as the third draft of the third act of the play on which he was working. He was pleased that she was doing so, because it showed that the play might have interested her.

She put down the manuscript and stood up.

"Don't start to apologize," he said. "I've told you to sit there when I'm out. As a matter of fact, so long as you're there, you'd better sit right down again."

She laughed.

"I can't get over the feeling that it is a deviation," she said.

"I know," he said. "And if you look in the upper right-hand drawer, you'll find a case of my Egyptian cigarettes, and you may take one, because it will be more in character."

She laughed again. "You mean that sergeant in the war play, who kept smoking the general's cigars?"

"Yes," he said. "You're right on the beam this morning. Have a cigarette and keep up the old tradition."

Occasionally it was startling to realize that Miss Mulford understood him better than any other woman ever had and that he had spent more time in her company than with any other woman, and the best part was that he did not know much about her. All he had to know was that he liked her and could trust her and he hoped that she liked him or at any rate the job.

"How do you like that new third act?" he asked. "Not that you have to stick your neck out if you don't want to."

"I don't mind," she said, and she lighted one of the Egyptian cigarettes, and she looked more ageless than ever. "I've never known you to sulk or to hold it against me when I've been frank about anything you've written."

"Why, thanks," he said. "I've always tried to get along without a whipping boy."

"Or girl," Miss Mulford said.

He sat down in one of the armchairs.

"Toss me over a cigarette," he said. "I wouldn't be too sure about the girls. There must be at least two or three around who feel they have been severely flagellated on my account."

"All I know," she said, "is that I've never been one. It could be that you're not very good at whipping."

"Maybe you're right," he said. "But then, there is another angle. Maybe you've been a whipping girl for years and just don't know it."

"Oh, I'd know it," she said.

"I wouldn't be too sure," he said. "The bright way of looking at things nowadays is that we — none of us — know what we're doing really, because all of our motivations arise from unknown compulsions and even when we know what we are doing we do not know what we want."

"If you mean that nobody knows everything, I suppose you're right," she said. "But I think the third act draft is all right now. I always like the way you can pull things together when you have to. Please don't think I'm being loyal or trying to cheer you up. I know that's what you always think."

He had always disliked the highly developed ego of writers, but he had his own. In fact, in the end, it was all that any so-called creative artist possessed.

"You mean you think Old White-Fang is not going to be pulled down by the wolf pack, at least for this next season?"

"No," she said, "not this time, especially if you could get your mind off other things and finish the third act. It shouldn't take more than a few hours. The casting ought to start by August in this sort of play, I think."

"Well, it's good to know there's someone left on the team," he said. "Madame thinks I'm slipping."

"She didn't tell you that, did she?" she asked.

"Oh, no," he said. "I heard her telling Walter Price in the hall this morning."

"You shouldn't listen at doors," she said. "When I first came here to work, the word was that you were on the way out. Besides, she hasn't read it, has she?"

"No," he said. "It doesn't do much good to show Madame a script because she always reacts to it exactly like Higgins. He entirely molded her character long before I came along — not that maybe it was such a bad idea."

"Then I wouldn't worry as long as she hasn't read it," Miss Mulford said. "I wish you'd think about getting some time to finish it today."

"That's right," he said. "Maybe I can finish with it this afternoon, but it's too late this morning. I don't know what happened to the morning."

"Neither do I, now that you mention it," Miss Mulford said.

"It seems as though I've been all over Robin Hood's barn this morning," he said. "It seems to me that one thing after another has happened. It's been a world of fantasy this morning, like flying across the ocean against the sun. By the way, the sun isn't over the yardarm, is it?"

"No," Miss Mulford said. "It's only a quarter to twelve. Besides, you won't finish the third act if you have a drink before lunch."

"That doesn't necessarily follow," he said.

"It does, usually, and besides, you've got to call up Mr. Beechley. He said it was very important, and he ought to be in his office now. And besides, I've got to go over the mail."

"Have I forgotten anything else?" he asked.

"No," she said, "but it's been a long time since you've asked for a drink before twelve o'clock. Has anything serious happened?"

"Toss me another cigarette," he said.

"You haven't finished the one you're smoking," she said.

"You needn't be so obvious at this time in the morning," he answered. "I want a new cigarette because I've always found a new one is like a New Year's resolution. It wipes the slate, moderately."

"You might as well admit," she said, "that something is the matter."

"All right," he said. He took the registered special delivery letter from his pocket. "Never mind the rest of the mail but just read this one and tell me what it says." He stood up and handed it to her and sat down again.

There was an art in making a casual gesture interesting to an audience, but he was sick and tired of dramatization just then — real or artificial. And when you faced facts, you had to face them.

"Are you sure you shouldn't read it yourself?" she asked. "It's marked 'personal.'"

"You read it," he said. "You know I don't like legal letters."

She took the paper cutter from his table and slit the envelope.

"It isn't good for you to pass on letters like this," she said.

"Now please," he said, "I know my behavior is immature. It used to be un-adult, and now it's immature, and God knows what they're going to pick out of Roget for next year. Of course I'm being immature. You know, when I was in the First Congregational Church this morning, I discovered that I knew quite a good deal about myself in bright, feverish flashes."

She stopped opening the envelope.

"What were you doing in the First Congregational Church?" she asked.

"Just talking to the pastor," he said. "Go ahead and read it and give me a synopsis."

There was a moment's pause after she had read the letter. There was no sex, but there was loyalty. She had always been a very nice girl.

"You've always said it's just as well to brace yourself," she said. "Well, maybe it wasn't such a bad idea, about my giving you a drink. It might help you with the synopsis."

"I'll hear the synopsis first," he said.

"All right," she said, "but I hate to be the one who hurts you."

"It's kind of you to say that," he said. "Remember I can take it, and go ahead."

"All right," she said. "They want three hundred and fifty thousand dollars ten days from yesterday or else they will sell out your securities — the collateral on the loan, you know, for that musical you produced, *Porthos of Paris.*"

The feeling in the pit of his stomach was not unknown to him. The last time he had experienced such a sensation was when he had climbed down the cargo net off a beach near Oran in North Africa, without previous combat training. He was too old for combat and he knew nothing about war except what he had learned from casual literary research. Yet he was a lieutenant colonel, not that lieutenant colonels weren't worth a dime a dozen when they had first started passing around commissions.

It was ridiculous to feel the same way now because a New York bank was about to sell his collateral. He had been aware for several months that the market had been sliding off and his securities were mainly common stocks. It was ridiculous to feel so strongly, even when the sum represented four fifths of his savings. It was also ridiculous, at that moment, to allow his mind to dwell on how Emily would react to the news. There was no doubt that she would be furious and personally offended; but then, it was his money — not hers.

"All right," he said. "Madame is the one who is going to be sorry, but you're in the clear. Don't forget you told me that musical would be a flop. Let's neither of us mind it."

"And there's the other bank loan," she said.

It was not a time to lose his dignity, at least not in front of Miss Mulford.

"That's right," he said, "but that one is only seventy grand, on my personal note. Don't bring up trivia at the moment — not that I won't hear about that note as soon as they sell me out down the Street."

Truthfully, he had forgotten about the other note. It required all his self-control not to get a scratch pad and juggle with figures. If it was called, the house would have to go, and so would the apartment in town. He could see the auction booklet in front of him already, "including the collection of Mr. Thomas Harrow."

Just as the full picture was impinging upon his consciousness, Miss Mulford began to cry. He had known her to do so only once before, when she had skipped a whole page of a play script and had discovered it only after she had put it in the mail; and the rarity of her weeping, compared to that of other women in his life, made him unduly sensitive. The only thing to do, he told himself, was to go out of the room and let them cry, because crying was a bid for attention — except that there was no reason for Miss Mulford to make that bid.

"Stop it," he said. "It's my funeral, not yours."

While he watched her, she gave what is known in directions as a stifled sob.

"It was so needless," she said, "to take such a big piece of it."

"Yes, my dear," he said. "I should have realized that musicals are more expensive than they used to be. This is no longer the day for what they used to call an extravaganza. Madame is going to cry — but honestly, you don't have to."

Miss Mulford rose and went into her own room. He hoped and expected that she would close the door until she could control herself, but he was wrong. She had only gone to get some Kleenex.

"To think a Louis Treize soldier could do that to you!" she said. "I'm sorry. It's just so unnecessary, that's all."

"If you're referring to dear old Porthos, he was a turkey," he said, "but I still think Bethel did a good job setting the ballads to music."

"Oh, no, he didn't," she said. "And I told you no one living would care about any of the Three Musketeers."

113

"Please don't go on telling me," he said, "because Madame will tell me, too, as soon as she gets the news. . . . No one can be always right."

He could still believe, even if the show had closed at the end of two weeks, that it was the customers' fault, not his.

"You know what the idea was — a *Beggar's Opera* satire on life today; and I still say it had sound dramatic values — Paris, the Louvre, inn courtyards, whores, thieves, rags and tatters, the noblesse, the clergy, and then the voice of a great man running all through it. The loves of a great man to exciting music, and Porthos actually was a great bighearted man."

"He wasn't, at the Winter Garden," she said.

"I know," he answered. "I know very well that I'm not a Hammerstein now, and I know it wasn't *South Pacific,* and I know I shouldn't have tried to make a million dollars. Besides, we're not finished yet." He smiled. He had talked himself into feeling better. "Don't forget the picture rights. It will make a better film than stage show. They're screaming for musicals around Culver City, and don't forget Ed Beechley wants me to call him and he's just in from the Coast."

He smiled again. He had succeeded in talking himself out of disbelief, and there was no reason why he should not have, because he had become expert over the last twenty years at maintaining confidence. He had always had to stand by himself in all that period, when all the chips were down. He did not have to be infallible, but he had to have confidence, and once one lost it, one was gone. He believed for the moment that it was not the fault of the book but of the composer, together with bad direction, that his effort at a musical comedy was ruined. The idea had been basically sound.

"Get me the Beechley office. He'll be there now," he said.

He believed, as he watched her call Long Distance, that she had forgotten about the picture rights — a silly thing to do, because picture rights had averted a lot of wrecks in his experience.

"I want to make a call to New York City, please," he heard her saying.

It was her cool, polite and precise telephone voice, but it had

114

a different timbre. It never paid to depend too much on any-one, because in the end you were always out there alone. If you depended, you became suspicious. You listened for details. . . . There was not the conviction that there should have been in her voice when she made that call. . . . A few sentences from the reviews passed through his mind. The production had been "pre-tentious" and "perfunctory." The badinage, which had amused him at the time he had written it, had been "bad Rostand." But in *Cyrano* there had been room for pretentiousness and mecha-nized slapstick, because there had been warmth and humor and sentiment. It had never occurred to him until that instant that he might really have been imitating Rostand. In the end you always began repeating yourself, or repeating someone else. In the end the sands in the hourglass ran out, depositing themselves in a small and undramatic heap of rubble, and in the end there was absolutely nothing left on top.

"What's holding up the call?" he asked. "Are the circuits busy?"

"They're ringing now," she said. . . . "Mr. Beechley, please? Mr. Harrow calling for Mr. Beechley . . ." And she handed him the telephone.

He sat down in front of his worktable.

"Hello," he said, "is that you, Ed?"

It could not have been anyone else, because he could hear the wheeze in Ed Beechley's voice showing that Ed, who had never been careful with his weight, must have moved rapidly to get to the telephone.

"Well, well, Tommy," Ed Beechley said. "How are things up there? Is there still any desire under the elms?"

Ed had been his agent ever since Mort Sullivan had died and they had been associated long enough so that he could judge Ed by his voice as accurately as he could Miss Mulford. He knew when Ed was going to be tactful by a certain clearing of the throat. He could tell when Ed was going to give hard advice by the slowing of the tempo. He could tell when Ed was going to prevaricate by a sudden gay spurt of humor, not that Ed was not always honest when you laid it on the line. As Ed put it, why throw emery dust into the gears? The truth was, there were a lot of people in the theatre who honestly did not want to know the truth and who lived on the belief that what you did not know would not hurt you. It was a world of diplomacy and implication, and Tom Harrow had moved through it so long that he had become as pliable as a willow wand. Rhoda had told him so once, after overhearing some statements he had made at a Sunday night party. She never had been able to understand that it was unpardonable to hurt anyone's feelings in the theatre unless it was absolutely necessary.

"Frankly, Ed," he said, "the elm trees up here are literally dripping with desire. It's all I can do to remember my age up here. I wish O'Neill could have seen them."

"Well," Ed said, "Emily's all right, isn't she?"

"Oh, Emily's fine," he said, "uprooted but gallant, the way she always is when she moves out of Sutton Place."

The mistake was that he had called up Ed. Ed should have been paying for the call, and it was time to get down to business.

"It was nice of you to want me to call you, Ed," Tom said, "on your first day back from the coast. I had rather hoped to hear from you out there."

There was a pause that would not have been perceptible to a stranger, but it registered accurately with Tom Harrow.

"You know how it is out there, Tommy. Talk about cats on a tin roof — what with the TV and everything, nobody can keep his mind calm out there any more. I've got quite a lot of thoughts for you, fella, but I know how you feel about the telephone."

"I'm sorry I've never been able to get over how I feel about the telephone," Tom said.

Ed gave an appreciative chuckle.

"There you go," he said. "Everybody's funny about money in some area, but what about business deductions? We're talking business, aren't we?"

"It would be nice to know," Tom said. "Are we?"

There was an infinitesimal pause.

"And even if we weren't," Ed said, "you're talking to your agent, and you're in the eighty-five per cent bracket, aren't you?"

"Not as far as I know," Tom said. "Not after we went to the cleaners on that musical."

"Oh," Ed said, "do you mean to say you're up there desiring under the elms and beating your head against the *Porthos of Paris?* Well, don't worry."

The title, which had seemed so merry once, made Tom wince, but Ed's voice was running on. "I always loved that title, with its alliteration. And Doré has got it, too. You know, they're gradually going nuts about the whole idea — that is, Doré and Egbert."

"Who is Egbert?" Tom asked.

"I thought of course you knew him, Tommy. I'm referring to Egbert Rhinestein. Egbert's the newest, most brilliant independent director and producer out there, with real Texas money behind him."

"As long as it's Texas money," Tom said, "and not funny money."

"It's real, all right," Ed said, "right out of the ground in barrels. It's occurred to me, during my visits to the Coast, that Texans sometimes don't know what to do with money. But Egbert knows. He has that De Mille sense of grandeur and he wants something big — crowds, streets, costumes and music. He's all the time thinking wide-screen."

Tom could not help feeling more cheerful as he thought of Mr. De Mille.

"Well, that sounds pretty good, and I'm glad he's interested," he said, "and I'd just as soon let Egbert do it all himself, and not go out there. I want to put on the new play."

"Of course you want to, Tommy," Ed Beechley said, "and there isn't anything as immediate as all that."

Tom Harrow straightened up and he saw Miss Mulford watching him.

"How do you mean, not immediate?" he asked.

"It's only at the simmering stage," Ed said. "You know it takes quite a while out there, Tommy, to get anything as subtle and, well — statuesque as *Porthos of Paris* to impinge."

"You mean nobody gives a damn for it?" Tom Harrow asked.

117

"Oh, no," Ed Beechley said. "Doré and Egbert are both slowly but surely going nuts over it."

Tom Harrow spoke so quickly that he interrupted the even flow of Ed Beechley's speech.

"Are they ready to bid against each other?"

There was a longer pause. It could only mean that Ed Beechley was being obliged to pull himself together.

"Frankly, it hasn't reached the negotiation stage yet, Tommy," he said, "but I know they're basically both nuts about it. It's only simmering, but haven't I told you that it's a real piece of property?"

Tom Harrow sighed. He felt like an explorer who, after struggling through the entangling vines of the jungle, has finally reached the hidden river.

"Good," he said. "Now tell me this. "Does anybody out there really seriously give a damn about that flop, or don't they?"

Another pause reminded Tom Harrow that Ed Beechley was tenderhearted.

"Now you put it that way, Tommy," Ed Beechley said, "I would say that the interest, at the moment, is negative."

"Well, thanks, Ed," Tom Harrow said. "That's the information I wanted."

There was concern in Ed Beechley's voice. "I don't quite understand what's worrying you, Tommy," he said. "Is it the bank loan?"

"Yes," Tom said, "that's what's worrying me."

Ed Beechley laughed.

"Tommy," he said, "I love the way you always get mixed up about money. I was with you — remember? — when you put up five hundred thousand for collateral. Why should they be worried?"

He wished that he might see Ed's expression. It always had a slapstick quality when Ed was wrong.

"Maybe you haven't noticed," Tom said, "the market's been going down. And there's an item I had forgotten myself. There are capital gains on all that stock. They've called it, Ed."

"God," Ed said. "You mean they're cleaning you out?"

"Approximately," he answered. "It's a funny feeling, Ed."

There was no doubt any longer that he and Ed were friends.

"I'll get a plane this afternoon, Tommy, and you meet me at the airport," Ed said.

"Oh, no," Tom Harrow said. "Don't bother about that, Ed. I suppose in the end I'll need a lawyer to go over facts and figures, but never mind it now."

"God, Tommy," Ed said, "I know how you worked for that money."

His arm was cramped. It was a relief to set down the telephone.

"Ed gets more and more long-winded all the time," he said. "Don't say anything. I guess you get the story, and I should say the sun is definitely over the yardarm. How about being a good girl and getting us each a drink?"

The Scotch-and-water she had given him was stronger than usual. It was surprising, after the first sinking feeling he had experienced, how little he seemed to care. There would be regrets and wonderings, later, why he had ever done this and that; but they would be like the backwash that followed any crisis; and he was not aware of them as yet. Instead, a feeling of relief centered around the idea that he had heard the worst.

"Thanks," he said, and he took a careful swallow from his glass. "Let all this be a lesson to you, Miss Mulford."

"Everything here has always been," she said.

"Well," he said, "sit down and take your drink. I don't know whether that remark of yours was kind or not."

"I didn't mean it that way," she said. "I only meant that you've taught me a lot."

He was alarmed to see that her eyes had filled with tears again, because his own self-pity was somewhere just around the corner.

"But still, I haven't taught you all I might have," he said. "But remember not to forget this lesson: Don't start getting interested in large sums of money."

He took another swallow of his drink, and as usual he could see pieces of his thought in dialogue.

"It is gratifying, isn't it, to believe that our elected rulers and representatives in the last decade were as keenly alive to the danger of the rich as the late Karl Marx once was? They're doing the best they can to stop new people from getting rich and occasionally they try, in halfhearted ways, to whittle down the ones who are. Now please don't think I'm being bitter about this for a single moment, Miss Mulford. A wise and kind government has done its level best to keep me from the troubles in which I find myself involved. There is the graduated income tax, the justest form of tax ever imposed on man, in that he who earns the most pays the most, and I believe that there was a judge not so long ago who stated that it is every citizen's duty to pay as high, not as low, an income tax as possible."

"Did he? When?" Miss Mulford asked.

He was startled by her interruption.

"I don't know when," he said, "but the thought is in keeping with our times. Then there is the inheritance tax, and the state income tax, and the gift tax. Of course all of these things are beneficial in that they conspire more and more to prevent any wage or salary earner thinking of making money — and after all, why should we?"

"Would you like it if I sweetened your drink a little?" Miss Mulford asked.

Miss Mulford was the only person left with whom he could share his intellectual excursions. Rhoda had listened once, but she had not always been an intelligent listener. Laura Hopedale was never good at following abstract thought; and Emily, he had learned, seldom listened to anyone except herself. Miss Mulford listened because she was paid to do so, but at the same time, she might have learned rather to enjoy it.

"That's thoughtful of you, as always," he said. "Just a very little and I'll be over being loquacious very soon. I don't want you for a moment to think that I am criticizing our economic way of life, because I've learned very succinctly, only this morning, exactly how unhappy the profit motive can make one. There's only one difficulty about these benign, restrictive measures.

They tend to make you a little wistful when you come into contact with the rich — and you can't avoid them always."

He paused to taste his reinforced whiskey.

"You see," he said, "I've had the misfortune to be thrown with a number of wealthy persons, not only in the theatre, but also in the area of what we might call established wealth. My first wife used to make friends with these people. You see, we were an interesting, intellectual couple who didn't get drunk or disorderly, and they began asking us around to all sorts of places, like Palm Beach; but never mind. I'm not a Marxist, but occasionally they did elicit a spirit of social envy. Occasionally I would start thinking how such dull people could make money. I should have known that money-making has more to do with emotional stability than with intellect. Then another great misfortune befell me."

He lowered his voice. Miss Mulford was listening; you had to have an audience.

"I had a Broadway hit in the autumn of 1928, and another in '30 and another in '33, and in '34 I had a very big Hollywood contract. Granted these last were depression years, still they hadn't got around to doing much about the income tax. I made quite a pile of money. And, as I say, some friends of my first wife's took a friendly interest. You see, I was writing reasonably light comedy, but the main point was that I bought a sound list of stocks at the bottom of the market. . . . Don't worry, I'm almost through."

"I was only looking at the time," she said, "because Alfred will be coming with the tray."

"What? Is it as late as that?" he asked.

"It's getting on toward half past twelve," she said. "But what happened then?"

He would have to stop. Emily and Walter Price would be expecting him for lunch and a cocktail on the terrace.

"And I forgot to tell you," Miss Mulford said, "that Harold wanted to see you, and I told him to come over any time after half past twelve — but I hope you'll go on with what happened."

He could guess Hal's subject would be money and as long as Rhoda had given him custody, which was one of those unanticipated things that Rhoda did sometimes, he was financially responsible.

"I'm glad I've held your interest," he said. "There isn't much more except that I wish I had that money now — and it was well invested, too. It's better for me not to think what it would be worth today, but most of it went into my settlement with Rhoda, which was perfectly correct. She was always afraid of being poor — and Hopedale of course still draws alimony."

"I know," she said.

"It's a little ironical, under the circumstances," he said, "to recall that both of them are now married to very wealthy men. But then, I have never cared much about money, even as a symbol. Unfortunately, it came so easily in the beginning that it gave me the bad habit of believing that I could get some more at any time."

He stopped, arrested by recalling the phrase in that overheard conversation of Emily's about his having "a little-boy quality." He could not help it if he instinctively dressed well and still had a trace of the outmoded Scott Fitzgerald youthfulness, but he did not have a little-boy quality. He may have been a product of the Twenties, but his thinking had not stopped with bathtub gin or the *American Mercury*. It was true that he could not write a piece like *Death of a Salesman* or *A Streetcar Named Desire*, but by the same token, neither Miller nor Williams could have written his own last play which had closed a year before, after two years on Broadway.

"It's impossible not to be spoiled," he said, "if you achieve any sort of artistic success. You're like a college freshman at his first cocktail party. It's impossible to stop with one Martini unless you have character. It would have been better if I hadn't had a success so young. Maybe there ought to be a law against college experimental theatres. Well, I had to talk to someone; and I know you're paid to listen, but thanks."

"I'd do it for nothing most of the time," Miss Mulford said.

"Now listen," he said, "let's get this straight. I enjoy it, but you

122

must get over this spirit of dedication." He smiled at her and he was acutely conscious that his smile was theatrical. "There's nothing really valid to be upset about. There isn't any plot in it. An old man in his fifties, who has let himself get into a lot of unnecessary trouble, all at once discovers that he's going to lose his lifetime savings. This doesn't mean that he isn't going to eat, or that the little wife will have to scrub floors to support him. It doesn't mean that his earning power is gone. It doesn't even mean that he's going to be without a motor car. Who cares about an old guy in that situation? He isn't Miller's salesman. There's nothing poignant about him except for just one small thing — and maybe you'd better give me one more small drink."

"You won't be able to work this afternoon," she said.

"Thanks for reminding me," he said. "And I am going to work this afternoon."

He thought the conversation was over, and it should have been.

"What's the one small thing?" she asked.

He stared into his glass before he answered.

"When you get a kick in the pants like this," he said, "if you have any sense, you know you've deserved it, and you begin wondering what you could have done differently. You begin wishing you could have the whole film played back. You'd like to know what started the trouble that got you where you are, but you can never watch the reel again. You can see little pieces, but you can't feel them as you did once. You can't live life over, and for God's sake, don't ever try."

He wondered why he had never spoken such thoughts out loud before. He was still wondering when Miss Mulford spoke again.

"I know what you mean," she said, "about not being able to live life over."

It was characteristic, in such a relationship, that in spite of all the years they had been together he should have known surprisingly little of her outside life. She had not wanted him to know, and if she had, the relationship would have changed. Her background was as good as his and her education, he had often thought, was considerably superior, but he could not have mixed successfully with her friends and family. He had always considered it his duty to respect her other life, but it had never worried him that she knew all about his. Her saying that she knew what he meant about not living life over marked one of those rare times in their years together when she was thinking of herself and not of him.

"Are you thinking of that boy friend you had ten years ago?" he asked.

"Yes," she said. "But as you would say, you can't do it over again. I just wanted you to know I know exactly what you mean."

He had only seen the man once, one evening in the city when her friend had called at the office to take her to the theatre. He had been an awkward man in his late thirties, with dark hair receding at the temples and very dark brown eyes. He had looked thin and nervous, probably because Miss Mulford had obviously instructed him to wait downstairs by the elevators. His blue serge suit did not fit him.

"You can't live it over and I'm glad he didn't take you away," he said. "You see, I don't know what I'd do without you. I've said that to a good many women, but I've never meant it so completely as I do when I say it to you. And now let's change the subject, shall we?"

"Yes," she said, "let's."

"And I've got another suggestion," he said. "Suppose you call up the house and tell Alfred to say I'm busy and have him bring my lunch out here with yours."

"Madame isn't going to like it," she said.

"Don't worry about that," he said. "I just don't feel like going in there for lunch."

There was a knock on the door and she stood up quickly.

"Oh," she said, "that's Harold. I'll let him in; and I'll order lunch sent over in half an hour."

"You'd better bring the Scotch and another glass," he said.

The incident was over. The time lapse had not been so great, but he had been through a good deal, and he was right about one thing. It did not make a good script — even in synopsis form.

124

VIII

Don't Change a Barrel on Niagara Fall

EVER since Harold as a little boy was brought down at cocktail time by one of a series of governesses to say good night to Mummy and Daddy, everybody including Rhoda had always said that Harold was the image of his father. It was sidesplitting to see him assume the postures and expressions of his father; and when it came to features, they had the same florid skin that tanned beautifully, the same eyes and forehead, and the same left-sided way of smiling. All of this may have been true, and it was natural that little boys should attempt to imitate their fathers; but still it had always seemed to Tom, when he had seen his son running toward him across the beach or across the drive at boarding school, that Rhoda was the one who had left her mark. Harold's sudden brightening of expression that was never time-worn was Rhoda's. And so was the color of the eyes — or a series of colors that could vacillate according to mood like flames in an open fire. And there were other subtle resemblances, each small in itself, but together capable of making him remember Rhoda through a glass seen darkly.

"Hi, Nance," he heard Harold say.

He had never dreamed of calling Miss Mulford by her first name, but if he had done so, he would certainly have called her Nancy and not Nance; but it sounded correct coming from Harold.

"Your father was saying he'd like to have a drink with you," Miss Mulford said, "but don't let him have too much. He wants to work this afternoon."

"Well, well," Harold said, "so that's what you've been doing with him, drinking Scotch while Madame and that old Price are waiting for him on the terrace. Jesus, Nance, have you seriously ever listened to Price?"

Harold was a man now, and there was no reason not to feel a sense of achievement. There might be points about him that were better changed, but things had not gone so badly, in spite of the maladjustments that came from a severed home. He was a man, and it was possible not only to take pride in him but to envy him. He had passed the mark of maladroitnesses and he was nearly past the age of arrogance and conceit. There were aspects in the trying present that produced certain latent advantages. The boy had completed his years as a Naval officer only a week or so before, finishing one of those Dr. Faustus-like compacts that youth made with the armed services, and the hitch had done him good. In fact, Tom Harrow found himself wishing that the opportunity had existed for him also. It might have stopped his precocity when he was Harold's age. When he was Harold's age, he had finished the play that Arthur Higgins had taken. It was better to let success like that come later; but then, perhaps if you waited too long it might never arrive at all.

The Navy had left its own peculiar young officer's stamp on Harold — a combination of authority and respect, watchfulness and patience. It was an attitude with which Tom Harrow had never been entirely at home, which he had respected ever since North Africa. Harold was almost Annapolis — almost, but there was no substitute for the Annapolis patina.

"Sit down and pour yourself a drink," Tom Harrow said, "and make me a very small one. Please sit down. When you stand up you make me think I've joined a Joint Civilian Orientation Course."

Harold laughed. It was the laugh he had inherited from Rhoda.

"Is it really still as bad as that?" he asked.

"Yes," Tom Harrow said, "but I rather enjoy it. It's nice to see you on board, Harold, to use a nautical expression, if time-worn."

"Maybe I haven't made it clear enough to you," Harold said, "how glad I am to be on board." His hand that held his glass was large and competent. He had inherited his mother's rather long fingers. His voice was easy and, thank heaven, it was not an actor's voice. "You know, I'm beginning to like this place. When you bought it I thought you were out of your head. You weren't. It's the first time I ever felt that you and I belonged anywhere."

There were times when it was rewarding to have a son and their very unexpectedness made such occasions stand out in a jewel-like way. Now and then you felt such a keen gratitude having had a son that instead of counting costs and interruptions, conscience would bring up the question of whether the reward was not too great for the casual hours expended in parenthood. This was one of those moments. He knew that it would not last and that it would be succeeded by grief or exasperation, but the moment was still there.

"I appreciate your saying that," Tom said. "It means quite a lot when your child understands what you're doing, and tells you so. You'll know what I mean someday."

He was watching for that Annapolis manner that both flattered and implicitly acknowledged the correctness of a commanding officer, but instead, Harold (and it was Rhoda's idea, not his, to name him Harold) had a shy, embarrassed look. He picked up his glass and rotated the scotch and water in it in an annoyingly expert manner. There was no ice in the glass and the rotation could not cool the drink.

"You know," Hal said, "there's another thing about this place. I hope you won't get mad if I mention it. Promise me you won't get mad."

It was a conversational gambit that disturbed Tom Harrow more than any other. It was another of those vestiges of the nursery that must have come from the time when Rhoda used to tell Hal he must not do that or he would make his father angry.

"Listen," Tom said, "you ought to know by now that I don't get mad without a reason. You're two inches taller than I am and if I started anything, you could throw me out the window. Well, just get it through your head that I'm not anything to be afraid of, physically, mentally or morally."

When he saw that Hal was smiling it meant the chances still were that Hal had grown up after all.

"I'm not afraid of you," Hal said. "Let's get this straight, Pops. You know you've got a quick temper. Everybody says so."

"I suppose you picked up that Pops business overseas," Tom Harrow said. "Who says I have a bad temper?"

"Why, everybody says so, Pops," Hal said.

Tom Harrow nodded toward Miss Mulford's closed door.

"Suppose you step in there and ask Miss Mulford," he said. "She's the one who ought to know."

Hal laughed. It was a relaxed laugh that seemed to diminish their age differential.

"Who? Nance?" he said. "Why, Nance wouldn't be reliable."

"What was it you were going to say," Tom said, "that you thought might make me mad?"

"Oh, that," Hal said. "I was just going to say that when you bought this place, Pops, and began fixing it up like a Jo Mielziner stage set, I was afraid it was going to be a sort of literary shrine or something. And the funny thing about it — it ought to be, but it isn't. I don't know how it is, but everyone around town is natural about you. There isn't any of this Mr. Harrow, the playwright, business. I'm not a great man's son here, and boy do I enjoy it!"

In spite of experience, one never could tell exactly how one would react to any remark. He should have been pleased by what Hal had said, but instead he was disturbed.

"You ought to get over the vestiges of childhood," he said. "Don't let them cling to you in a Wordsworthian way. You ought to have sense enough to know by this time that you're not a great man's son. You ought to know I'm not as good as that."

"The hell you're not," Hal said. "Just because that musical was a flop doesn't mean a thing."

For a moment it was like playing over the reel again in a lonely projection room.

"Let's face it, Hal," he said, "there was a time when I might have been good, but I've never been, not really."

It was pleasant to observe that Hal was a loyal boy.

"Say, you're in a sort of a low mood this morning, aren't you?" Hal said.

"I wouldn't call it low exactly," Tom Harrow said. "I've just been facing a few home truths this morning and I have never known them to give anyone euphoria. Don't let me give you an inferiority complex. I repeat: I might have been good once, but I never have been really."

"That isn't what they say in drama courses," Hal said. "You're the great American playwright, now that O'Neill is dead. That's what they say in the drama courses. As a matter of fact, they even say it in the Navy."

"In the Navy?" Tom repeated. "Not really in the Navy."

He was thinking of Walter Price and of the value of a psychological lie. It was better to feel that you were good instead of facing facts. It was the only true road to survival, and he was following it instinctively; but he did wish that he could make Harold understand.

"Everybody knows who you are," Hal said.

Tom Harrow wished that the conversation did not disturb him.

"Everybody knows how famous he feels inside himself," he said. "As a matter of fact, that's going to be the subject of next Sunday's sermon at the First Congregational Church. The topic is going to be, 'How Happy Are You Inside?'"

"How do you get around and find out things like that?" Hal asked. "I never do."

It was the way your mind worked and if Hal's mind worked on different lines, it was probably just as well. It was simple enough to say that he happened to see Mr. Godfrey when he was going for the mail.

"He took me inside the church," he said, "to the little room beneath the pulpit where he customarily sits and thinks. I hadn't been there for a long while. I hadn't been there, as a matter of fact, since I married your mother and I couldn't notice very much change."

He made the last remark only to make things sound easier. As always, there was an air of restraint when Rhoda came into their conversation.

"Say," Hal said, "that reminds me why I'm here. My mother called up this morning." His voice was elaborately careless, as it always was when he spoke of Rhoda, and it was impossible to tell, when he referred to her as "my mother," whether he was being thoughtful or intended a mild reproof. "She called up when you were down there in the church, I guess, learning how you felt inside."

He felt the muscles of his shoulders tauten. The reaction was purely instinctive and so was the new care with which he spoke.

"She didn't want to speak to me, did she?"

"Oh, no," Hal said, and his voice was elaborately carefree, "nothing like that, Pops. She wanted to speak to me, and Emily answered the telephone. They still don't get on well, do they?"

"I don't know why they shouldn't," Tom said. "They both have been faced by the same tough problem. How is your mother?"

He laughed, although the laugh was unnecessary.

"Oh, she's fine," he said. "She's motoring with Presley in his new Bentley — you know the way Presley is about motoring. If he gets a new car, nothing relaxes him more than driving it five or six hundred miles a day, and his new Bentley is quite a car if I do say so. Its instrument panel is made of real inlaid wood. The factory only turns out about a dozen of those Bentleys every year and you know how Presley reacts to a thing like that. You know Presley."

Tom Harrow cleared his throat.

"As a matter of fact, I don't know Presley so very well," he said. "You see, he appeared in the picture very seldom and was kept away from me after one or two rather formal meetings. On the whole, I should almost say that I don't know

130

Presley, but I'm glad he can afford to have a good time with Bentleys."

"I've often thought you'd get quite a laugh out of Presley," Hal said. "I imagine you'd say he's kind of naive, but at the same time, seriously, he means well."

Tom Harrow laughed and the internal tension had left him.

"You've got to be simple and mean well," he said, "to acquire that kind of money. And you've got to have something else, I don't know what it is, but maybe you've come somewhere near it when you say it relaxes him to drive five or six hundred miles in a day. I wonder how your mother likes it. She always used to be exhausted when we drove from New York to Boston. But then, of course I never went in for Bentleys."

"Gosh," Hal said, "you have a funny way of putting things. Hearing you is almost as good as a show."

He had to be as good as a show. Hal's laughter all at once had the gratifying sound of an appreciative audience.

"What's so funny now?" Tom asked.

"About my mother," Hal said. "She says she doesn't care how many miles she drives as long as it's a Bentley and as long as Presley's driving."

It was better instead of answering to keep a straight face or to be only silently amused. That last remark of Hal's was not a bad description of everything that Rhoda had wanted, and now Rhoda had it. There was Presley and there was the Bentley with a real wooden inlaid instrument panel. It was hard to think of a better picture of solidity in a changing world.

"They're stopping at the Wellington Manor House," Hal said. "They're going to stay for three days because Presley likes the golf course there."

The thing was too true to life to seem completely real. There was a sort of inartistic coincidence in it that was associated only with the ineptitudes of daily life and never with the stage. Only that morning he had stood by the pulpit facing the aisle of the First Congregational Church with the ghostly music of the wedding march ringing in his ears and tomorrow Rhoda would be at the Wellington Manor House where they had spent

131

the first night of their honeymoon because it had been too late to get train connections to Niagara Falls.

"It's funny," he said, "why they should pick the Wellington Manor House. It's one of those places that I understand has been running down lately."

"It's because Presley likes the golf," Hal said. "It seems the course is very well kept up and they have a colored pro."

"A colored pro?" Tom Harrow said. "How does he fit into the picture?"

"It's the way Presley is," Hal said. "He's very serious about taking a liberal stand. He admits the service in the hotel is not what it used to be, but it does have a golf course with a colored pro."

"That's an interesting point," Tom Harrow said. "I shouldn't dare to quarrel with it. Well, I hope your mother enjoys it there."

In spite of himself he was thinking of that first time. Both he and Rhoda had been very nervous then, but the situation had been different.

"Rhoda," he had said, "why don't you go up and get ready for bed and I'll stay down here and play billiards for a while?"

"You never told me that you knew how to play billiards," Rhoda said.

"Oh, I've played a little now and then," he said.

"But whom do you know to play billiards with here?" Rhoda asked. "You said you haven't seen anybody you know."

"I'll play billiards with the marker, Rhoda," he said. "There's always a man in every billiard room in every hotel who is called the marker."

"Oh," Rhoda said, "as long as you know how to play billiards well enough to play with the marker, Tom."

As a matter of fact, he had not played billiards that evening.

"By the way," Hal said, "my mother sent you a message."

The words moved him out of his reverie and suddenly reminded him vividly of a song:

> Don't change a barrel on Niagara Fall,
> Stick to one girl or no girl at all.

"Oh," he said, "she sent me a message?"

"Yes," Hal said. "That's what I came out to tell you. My mother wonders if you would motor up alone — she emphasized the word 'alone' — to the Wellington Manor House tomorrow afternoon to see her."

"Good God," Tom Harrow said, "what for?"

"She didn't say. She just said it was important."

"But not at the Wellington Manor House," he said. "She certainly couldn't have wanted to see me there."

He saw that Hal looked puzzled, which showed that Rhoda had not indulged in any reminiscences regarding the first night of their honeymoon any more than he had.

"She wants me to call her back," Hal said. "She says it's very important or she wouldn't dream of asking you."

"Didn't she say why?" Tom asked.

"She only said she couldn't say why over the telephone," Hal said.

"My God," he said, "that's queer after what she used to say over the telephone."

"She wants me to call her back," Hal said, "and tell her whether you'll go up there. You'll tell her 'Yes,' won't you? You've got to be civilized."

"Oh, yes, tell her 'yes,'" he said.

He tried to say it easily. In fact, he had always tried to be what Rhoda had liked to call "civilized" about the whole divorce. It was the fashion in those days to be civilized about such matters, and he had been influenced for years by tolerance. He had heard it said so often that he was sure that he believed it — that the artistic demands made on creative or interpretive artists caused them to be different in their private lives from brokers, bankers, wool merchants and lawyers. It was necessary to live more fully and love more freely than might be customary on a more humdrum plateau, and this was confirmed by statistics supplied by his professional associates. Tolerance was the watchword, and how could one create the illusion of reality or interpret life unless one lived? Nevertheless, he could not avoid a sense of uneasiness.

133

"Why don't you drive up with me?" he asked. "It would make it a whole lot easier."

He was aware, as soon as he spoke, of the implied cowardice in his request. After all, he had never been afraid of Rhoda, and it could not be that he was afraid of reality.

"No," Hal said. "She specifically said that she wanted to see you alone."

"All right," he said, "all right." And then Alfred came in with a tray.

"Say," Hal said, "why all that food? Are you having lunch out here with Nance?"

"Yes," he said, "I want to be quiet. I'm trying to finish the third act of this play."

"Gosh," Hal said, "does that mean I've got to go back there by myself and listen to Emily and that cornball?"

This new word from the bright lexicon of youth was a suitable way of describing Walter Price in the eyes of youth, but at the same time, it demonstrated a lack of charity that could be overcome only by living.

"I suppose he is a cornball," Tom said, "but perhaps your base of judgment is not broad enough to enable you to condone cornballs like Walter."

His remark was not reproof. Actually he felt somewhat sorry that his own base was so broad that he knew he was telling the truth. There was something wrong perhaps in being able to have a kindly thought for everyone.

"I wouldn't mind him so much," Hal said, "if he didn't think he was fooling me when he isn't telling the truth — which is practically all the time."

It was not fair to Walter Price and it was beyond the dictates of convention to discuss him in front of Alfred, who was arranging the dishes on the worktable, but he was rather sure that Alfred would have been intelligent about Walter Price.

"You see, Hal," Tom said, "I don't believe anybody ever tells the whole truth and nothing but the truth about anything, because the process is very painful. We start with a few basic

134

facts and we shift them around and minimize or exaggerate them in our own different ways. Alfred, will you tell Miss Mulford, please, that our lunch is ready?"

"Yes, sir," Alfred said, "and Mrs. Harrow wanted me to tell you that Mr. and Mrs. Bramhall are coming to dinner, so that you'll be back in time to dress."

"Well, well," Tom said, "just exactly when did this news break?"

In spite of all his seekings, he had very seldom discovered anything approaching continuity. There was no doubt that Emily understood how he felt about the Bramhalls, because he had told her definitely on several occasions, and thus he was almost positive that Emily's asking the Bramhalls to dinner could not be construed as a friendly act. It did not help the situation, either, to feel that Alfred understood what was passing through his mind.

"Mrs. Bramhall, she called up," Alfred said, "and asked you and Mrs. Harrow there to dinner, I guess." Alfred smiled in the sympathetic manner of man talking to man. "Mrs. Harrow thought you'd prefer it better this way. She said you never liked the cooking there, sir."

It invariably happened that any servants he employed became too interested and too familiar after a term of years, and this was what was happening to Alfred — and there was no use blaming Emily, who would only say that he was the one who spoiled servants.

"All right," he said. "Don't forget to lay out my evening clothes, Alfred, and a starched shirt and my pearl studs, not a soft shirt, and please tell Miss Mulford lunch is here."

"Say," Hal said, "you're getting pretty shirty, aren't you?"

There was still a moment when Tom could be himself and he availed himself of the moment.

"God," he said, "the Bramhalls." And then he thought of something else. "I hear you took Irene Dodd to the movies last night."

It was pleasant to observe that someone besides himself could be startled.

135

"You hear everything, don't you?" Hal said. "How did you hear about that one?"

"You can't do anything here that doesn't get around," Tom said. "Everybody knows whom you took to the movies last night and everybody knows what time you took her home. Don't let it worry you — you were saying this is a friendly town."

"Well, it isn't anybody's business," Hal said, "not basically."

The thing to do was to think about other people and then you did not have to think about yourself.

"You'd be surprised," he said, "how everything gradually gets to be everybody's business, including the things you don't think ought to be."

"Well, I don't see how it matters if I go out to the movies with a girl," Hal said.

"Listen," Tom said, "Irene's a pretty girl. She was pointed out to me down on Dock Street this morning, and it only squares the circle."

"Squares what circle?" Hal asked.

There were times when everything fitted into place and it was about time now that something did.

"You see, I was deeply devoted to Irene's mother when I was about sixteen," he said. "Her name was Malvina Frith and she used to know exactly what she wanted back in those days."

"Gosh," Hal said, "you never told me that."

"The occasion never arose," he said, "and I never was a kiss-and-tell boy, and now you'd better go to lunch or else Emily will think that you and I have been talking about her. You know how Emily is."

It was like closing a lid. Miss Mulford was back, and the show was over.

He had learned the discipline of writing in the school of practical theatre. Once upon a time, when he was very young, he had labored under the delusion that a play script, when submitted to the producer, was a product demanding only minor changes. This may have been so once on an older Broadway. According to the reminiscences of older playwrights, there was

136

a time when shows had their first nights in New York without having been previously dragged for weeks through a series of tryout towns, but things were different now.

The truth was that a play was now written on the road much more completely than in a playwright's study. In fact, plays were getting to be as malleable as a sculptor's art wax. Why, indeed, attempt a final draft when you knew what was bound to happen in New Haven or Wilmington or Boston? In the end, after you got to the hotel suite, not Scotch or bourbon or aspirin or benzedrine or tomato juice could wholly drown the question of why anyone had ever thought the play would be any good in the first place. Something would have to be done immediately because, in polite language, the play needed working over. If you could keep your head when all about you — that was the essence of modern playwriting when the show was on the road getting pulled together and set for Broadway. It was no longer necessary for Tom Harrow to write when the spirit moved him, having been obliged too often to write any time, anywhere, sick or well, sad or happy, when the show was on the road; and in the process he had developed concentration.

After lunch his mind moved immediately from one compartment to another, shutting out thoughts of investment lists and lawyers. His draft of the third act was more complete than he had remembered and he was no longer worried about the second act curtain. In fact, his judgment assured him that the second act was a skillful piece of work. He realized by now that no other form of writing was so irrevocably framed by limits of time and space. With the third act, it was necessary to remember the weariness of the audience, and besides the artistic limitations, there were costs and the stagehands' union.

Now that his mind was on these variables, the problems on which he was working had become more real than the immediacy of his own life. For a while he was in a silent world, oblivious to the passage of time, forgetful of everything except the problems, but he was neither shocked nor annoyed when Miss Mulford interrupted him. He had learned on the road never to show impatience at interruption. Besides, Miss Mulford

137

must have been standing by his worktable for an appreciable length of time without speaking.

"Yes," he said, "what is it?"

"I hate to interrupt you," she said, "but it's half past four, Mr. Harrow."

He could see as he looked out of the window that the light on the leaves of the trees had changed and that the sun was lower than it had been when he had first started working, but the time lapse did not upset him because he had grown accustomed to making such adjustments. When one's mind was pulled suddenly from one place to another, the only way to manage things was to be relaxed.

"Half past four?" he said. "I'd forgotten I'd let myself in for anything."

"It's the high-school paper," she said. "You made the appointment with them yesterday."

"Oh, yes," he said. "Yes, I remember now."

"I thought of sending them away," she said, "but I was afraid you wouldn't have liked it."

"I am glad you didn't," he said. "I think I have it finished anyway."

IX

I'm Glad You Asked That Question

IT WAS not because he wanted publicity, in fact, he had always disliked it, but he was invariably kind to the press, and particularly to editors of school and college publications, having been a high-school editor once himself. In fact, a part of the reel was playing back again. When the three adolescents, two boys and a girl, came into the room, he could understand their desperate desire to appear casual, and the efforts that must have been made at dress, and the whispered conversation that must have taken place outside as to who was going to ask what questions.

"Hello," he said. "Come in and sit down."

He knew how to put them at their ease. The main thing was to be kind but never condescending.

"It's nice you people want to interview me," he said. "I'm pretty well through here for the day, so don't feel in a hurry and I'll try to tell you anything you want. But how about telling me who you are first." He smiled, but it would not have done to smile too broadly. "That is, if it isn't a secret."

They laughed and at least he had learned to understand every gradation of mirth.

The sight of them gave him no sense of nostalgia. The feeling that he experienced was of complete relief that he would never be their age again. He would undoubtedly deteriorate physically, losing teeth, hair and money, but he would never be that age again. He had already lost his money and, as he had already confessed to himself that day, he was not as good as he might have been. Something had slipped somewhere, but he would never be that age again. He would never have to struggle for assurance or die a thousand microscopic deaths or live a hundred unrequited loves. He would never have to wonder again, gazing at his image in the bathroom mirror, whether or not he was growing to resemble a little more each day Van Johnson or Gregory Peck or whoever the moving picture stars were in his youth whom, at the moment, he was delighted he had forgotten. He would never have to worry again as to whether he would have acne forever. He would never have to go out for any teams again. He would never again have to fill out the coupon, enclose a dollar and wait anxiously for the postman to bring him a brochure on sex in an inconspicuous wrapping. He would never again have to debate whether the girls would like him better if he sprinkled himself with shaving lotion or if he compromised on glossy hair tonic.

He could experience no desire for repetition as he watched the young girl, barelegged in bobby socks, pleated skirt and deliberately taut sweater, and the boys in their loafers, plaid socks, dungarees and sport shirts, uneasily squirming in their chairs. The two boys looked at the girl. Her orange-red lipstick made a clashing contrast with the sallowness of her complexion, and her hair needed washing. She would never be a front-row Rockette. She had to be an interesting girl.

"My name's Evangeline Krumbough," she said.

"Well," he said, "it's a great pleasure to meet you, Evangeline. Somehow I've always got on well with girls named Evangeline."

It was the boys' turn next. It was the freckled boy wearing steel-rimmed glasses who finally spoke.

"I am Ted Williams," he said, "Chairman of the Editorial Board — no relation to the ballplayer."

"Well, it's nice you're in here pitching," Tom Harrow said, and everybody laughed.

"My name's Tommy Scalponi," the third boy said. "We deeply appreciate your kindness in allowing the *Lectern* to interview you, Mr. Harrow. We are planning this to be the feature article in the *Lectern's* Commencement Number."

It was possible to consider the scene on two levels, either guilelessly amusing or introspectively serious. It would have been easy enough to smile at the editorial delegation from the *Lectern;* he could remember things about himself which he had forgotten when he looked at their faces.

"I am very pleased you want to put an interview with me into the Commencement Number," he said.

It was a fatuous remark which made him hope that they were too young to realize it. There had been too many interviews, too many questions, too many candid camera shots, but one of life's mottos was to be always affable with the press.

"It was our idea, Mr. Harrow," the freckle-faced boy named Ted Williams said, "that it would be kind of inspirational for the graduating class if you could just tell us something about your early theatrical career — what got you started doing it and sort of other junk like that. You see, I don't suppose it would occur to you, but it's kind of inspirational, Mr. Harrow, to think that you went to this same school yourself, and besides, we're pretty theatre-minded back at school, aren't we, Eva?"

Perhaps the hours they had listened to muted soap operas while they studied gave the younger generation a glibness that had been lacking in his youth.

"Yes, that certainly is so, Ted," Evangeline Krumbough answered, and he could see that it was quite a moment for Evangeline. "We have an enthusiastic theatrical group at the high school, comprising the sophomore, junior and senior classes." Eva paused and drew in her breath before she could continue. "This season we gave a production of *Lady Windermere's Fan.*"

"Did you?" he heard himself answering. "That's a very interesting play. Back in my time there used to be an organization called the Footlights Club, but we never got much further than *Charley's Aunt* and *Officer 666* — slapstick, you know, not art."

He was unhappy to see they were not quite with him.

"Is that so?" It was the boy called Tommy Scalponi speaking. "Did you happen to play in either of those productions, Mr. Harrow? I mean, *Charley's Aunt* or *Officer 666?*"

"As a matter of fact, I did have some small part in *Officer 666*," Tom Harrow said.

"Ted, boy," Tommy Scalponi said, "make a note, will you? We'll look it up in the *Gazette* files in the library. Is that where you got your inspiration, Mr. Harrow, for starting writing for the stage?"

"Well, no," he said. "To be frank, I am pretty much of a ham actor."

"But at the same time, Mr. Harrow," Ted Williams said, "you direct plays sometimes, don't you?"

"That's different," he said.

"Just to start the ball rolling," Tommy Scalponi said, "when did the urge of writing plays strike you?"

Exactly when did anyone ever start wanting to do anything? Desires and half-born wishes sprang from too many vague unfulfillments to set them into any mathematical relationship. It might very well have been the electric lights on Broadway on that single night his father had taken him to Jack's.

"It's a little hard to tell," he said. "Everyone finds himself pushed into things by circumstances. As a matter of fact, my family sent me to a boys' camp one summer when I was about thirteen. The man who ran the camp was named Grimsbee." They were hastily writing in their notebooks, except Evangeline, who stared at him fixedly. "He was the benevolent despot type and he had a curious way of gesturing with his hands, and a string of phrases. He would always start by saying, 'What I want most is to have everybody —' and then he would always end, 'Now I hope you boys have followed my line of thinking.'"

They had all stopped writing and there was nothing like an audience. "You get to imitating someone like that. After about a month, on Award Night, our tent gave a Grimsbee play. I was the one who wrote it." He could remember it very clearly now. "It was the first time I ever heard words that I had written spoken by someone else and received by a group of people. There is nothing exactly like it. You can write a book and people will read it, but you don't hear them laugh."

If he had not been working that afternoon, he would not

142

have gone on so far; but as it was, he had momentarily forgotten his interlocutors.

"There's nothing like it except drug addiction," he said. "There's nothing more, well, naked than writing a play. If you write a book and the critics pan it, you can comfort yourself by believing that you are a misunderstood genius, but when most of an audience walks out on you after the first act, it's your own fault, and it's one of the worst in the realm of human experience."

"Did you ever have it happen to you, Mr. Harrow?" The girl had asked the question.

"Oh, yes," he said, "of course."

"But I bet it hasn't happened many times."

"Often enough so that I know how it feels," he said. "You have to have intestinal fortitude in the theatre — most of the time."

"You said the same thing once, didn't you, Mr. Harrow, in the introduction you wrote for the Modern Library collection of your plays?"

It was the bright one, Tommy Scalponi, who had asked the question.

"So you took the trouble to read that?" he asked. "Well, everyone repeats himself."

"Would you tell us, Mr. Harrow," Ted Williams asked, and the light glinted sharply from his spectacles, "what was your first successful play, and what was the date?"

"*Hero's Return*," he said. "I remember Mr. Arthur Higgins, who produced it, gave me a thousand dollars cash advance, an unusually high advance in those days, because he thought that I had promise. Maybe I had, in those days. It opened in the autumn of 1928 and it ran all through the next spring. I was lucky. It was my first try on Broadway."

He was lucky. He had married Rhoda that autumn. He could remember sitting beside her on that first night, before the first curtain.

"You must have been awfully excited," Evangeline Krumbough said.

143

"I suppose I was," he said, "but I felt sick to my stomach first."

"And your next play was *Little Liar*, wasn't it, about the man and his conscience? Say, that was quite a play, Mr. Harrow."

It had been and perhaps it still was quite a play.

"That's right," he said, "*Little Liar*."

When he repeated the title, he could see the curtain rising again on its first act. He could remember the long sessions and the interviews in the Higgins office when they were looking for an ingenue. Arthur Higgins was never a careless producer. When he came to *Little Liar*, he exhibited flair and courage, and besides, perhaps he had thought of a brilliant way to cut down on production costs. It had an ingenue part, a word which Tom disliked as much as he did a lot of the theatre jargon. Helen Hayes would have been a natural selection, but Arthur Higgins had wanted a new girl. Laura Hopedale had been the ingenue, a Drama League girl with no previous experience, and Tom's having picked her out had made him realize that he had casting ability himself and that a flair for the offbeat could succeed. Arthur Higgins, who was dealing with the values of an older theatre, had only seen that she was shy and rather plain and too precise when she read the lines. He had not seen the sensitivity or the malleable intelligence that finally put Hopedale in the class of Hayes and Cornell.

"Mr. Harrow, could you tell us how you first started writing plays — aside from the skit at the camp, I mean?"

He was surprised how far his mind had wandered off the track, but his voice was easy when he answered.

"I got pushed by degrees. When I was at college there was a sort of local boy-and-girl thing called the Play Club. Then I was in a summer theatre and I met a Mr. Walter Price there who was working in the old Sullivan and Herrick dramatic agency in New York. It's interesting, now we're on the subject, that Mr. Price is right here in the house spending a few days with me. Well, he got me a job at Sullivan and Herrick's, and the only way to know the theatre is to be in the theatre. During my three years in Sullivan and Herrick, I wrote my first play. You've got to get a touch of grease paint," he laughed, "and grease paint doesn't rub off as fast as lipstick."

It would be quite a day for the *Lectern,* he thought, if Walter Price were to start talking, but he was the one they wanted, not Walter Price.

"Mr. Harrow, do you write every day or when the spirit moves you?"

He found himself laughing as though they were old friends.

"These days," he said, "I write whenever my wife and the tax collectors let me."

"Are you writing on anything now, Mr. Harrow?"

"Oh, yes," he said, "I'm working on a play, but I won't tell you what it's about. I've always found it bad luck to talk about anything I'm writing."

There was a moment's heavy silence.

"Well," Evangeline Krumbough began, "it's really been awfully kind of you, Mr. Harrow, to give us all this time, and we certainly appreciate it . . ."

She drew in her breath hastily so that she could continue with her speech, but she never did finish with it. There was a slamming of a door, and there was Emily.

X

If Change Would Not Keep Changing

THEY all stood up as she crossed the room and he hoped that Miss Krumbough and Williams and Scalponi had not observed, as he had, that Emily was annoyed and was making very little effort not to show it. A tight new curl and the fresh lacquer-luster in her blond hair indicated that she had been out from under the dryer only very recently. She was slightly out of breath from negotiating the gravel path in her high heels and her breathlessness gave her face an unduly reddish tinge. The editors of the *Lectern* stared, and Emily was still something to stare at in a small town. It was true that she had put on weight. As Emily had said herself, it was neurotic fat. When she was nervous she simply could not restrain herself from nibbling. Nevertheless her tight girdle partially dispelled the impression of *embonpoint*, and she still had her stage posture and she was making the typical Arthur Higgins entrance, with just the right sway of hips. Her light gray gabardine suit, tailored by Dior, had a smartness that was deceptively ascetic, and it served to bring out her best features — the wide brown eyes, the dimple on her cheek. The Dior suit, too, was a suitable setting for the jewelry, and its severity partially dissipated the impression of being overbraceleted with tangible property that Emily gave when in a housecoat. Her diamond and ruby clip made in a modernistic gold swirl and the matching earrings and the oversized link bracelet and the gigantic star sapphire in her ring were only barely overelaborate against the Dior backdrop. They only gave her a freshness that was not rural, that was accentuated by a touch of Guerlain.

146

"My dear," he said, "what happy concatenation of circumstances brings you here?"

She only looked good-naturedly put-out. It was her color, not her expression, that betrayed her annoyance.

"I wish you'd stop them putting more and more pebbly gravel on the path," she said, "it's like something on the bottom of a fish tank. I don't see how you keep your footing on it. I turned my ankle twice."

"If you'd only wear country shoes," he said, "you could cope with the gravel better. This is pretty rural here, my dear; in fact, almost country."

"Almost?" Emily said, and she laughed in a way that indicated that she was a perpetually good-natured person whose patience was being tried. "Isn't this really country?"

There were times when he was still diverted and amused by Emily.

"My sweet," he said, "you ought to know this isn't on the farm, even if it isn't Westchester County. As you've so often said, you're still just a Hoosier girl at heart."

"Tom," she said, "you do sink ankle-deep in that round slippery gravel, and you know it. But let's not quibble in front of company. . . . I'm sorry, darling, I'm afraid I've interrupted you."

Yet as she looked at the *Lectern* editorial board, she did not appear very sorry.

"This is a part of the *Lectern* editorial board," he said. "They've been good enough to stop in and interview me."

"The *Lectern*?" Emily said. "What's the *Lectern*?"

"You really ought to get around more, dear," he answered. "The *Lectern* is the high-school paper and they're putting their finishing touches on the Commencement Number."

"Oh," Emily said. "We've been wondering what's been keeping you all afternoon."

"We were just going," Evangeline Krumbough said. "You've been ever so kind, and we mustn't keep you any longer, Mr. Harrow."

"Don't go," Tom Harrow said. "I'm glad Mrs. Harrow's dropped

147

in so that you can meet her. This is Evangeline Krumbough, my dear. This is Ted Williams — but no relation to the ballplayer — and this is Tommy Scalponi, who, I predict, will make the Phi Beta Kappa when he gets to college."

"Oh, how do you do?" Emily said.

"How do you do, ma'am," Tommy Scalponi said. "Well, thanks a lot, Mr. Harrow, and good-by."

Emily was silent for a moment, and then she sighed.

"Jesus H. Mahogany Christ," she said.

She sank down in a chair and he thought as he watched her that there was hardly an actress anywhere who could ever sit down naturally.

"Why the initial?" he asked.

"Jesus H. Mahogany Christ," Emily said again. "Tom, darling, can't you find some more interesting and dignified way of pandering to your vanity, darling, than showing off before three high-school adolescents?"

There was truth to her impeachment. He had been showing off.

"You can't be disagreeable to three poor kids, Emily," he said.

"And my God," Emily said, "you remembered all their names. Honestly, darling, don't you see how you are beginning to behave here? It's getting to be just a little too good to be true — or, to put it another way, and to use one of your favorite words — isn't it almost on the verge of being corny?"

"Perhaps," he said. "I wouldn't be a bit surprised. I've been coming apart at the seams all day, but you didn't come out here all this way to ask me that specific question, did you?"

He lighted a cigarette, but he did not offer one to Emily because Arthur Higgins had told her long ago that cigarettes were bad for the voice. Some cynic had once said that you never really could find out what any woman was like until you married her, and then it was too late. He was trying to recall what Emily had been like. He could only remember that she had

148

been good-natured and gay; but as for the rest of it, reality had obscured illusion.

"Tom, darling," Emily said, "I know you can't help it because I know it's the stock-and-trade of every artist, but I do wish at least in the late afternoon you could stop having yourself continually on your mind and recollect at least with half of yourself that other people, too, have problems."

Again there was no doubt that loquacity was growing on her and every year her methods of expression were becoming more involved.

"Now, Emily," he said, "I haven't had time to be thoughtless. I've been out here working."

Emily laughed lightly.

"I know," she said. "Alfred said you were too busy to come in to lunch. Oh, hello, Mulford."

Miss Mulford had opened the door of her office.

"Good afternoon, Mrs. Harrow," she said. "I just wanted to ask you, Mr. Harrow, if you want me any longer today."

"Oh, no," he said, "I don't think so" — and he handed her the penciled pages he had written — "as long as you can get these typed first thing in the morning."

There was silence after Miss Mulford closed her door — the heavy, self-conscious silence that ensued when someone had interrupted a quarrel.

"I have told you," he said, "that I wish you wouldn't call her Mulford."

Emily laughed again in her airiest manner.

"That's right," she said. "I remember now. It sounds patronizing when I call her Mulford, and I remember now that you didn't like it when I started to call her Nancy, and I remember that she's been with you for years and years, longer than I have, but please don't say that I haven't tried to make her like me. I've done the best I could with what I think is a very anomalous position, darling. I don't mean that there's anything that can be helped, and I'm not blaming anyone at all — and why should I, because I know in many funny little ways that I am an outsider, especially in the area of your workroom or studio, or whatever you call it, darling."

Emily must have always enjoyed the sound of her own voice, but lately she was beginning to enjoy her own balancing of words. It would have been fruitless to interrupt her, but one could always play a guessing game as to what was coming next.

"I am only saying, darling," Emily said, "that it's a little hard to accept the truth that there is someone like Nancy Mulford who is so much more integrated in many ways than I am into your life and who knows so many sides of you that are deliberately concealed from me, somebody who knows so much more about your business affairs than I, for example. But I don't mean to be disagreeable, darling, and I'm sorry that I inadvertently called her Mulford, but I don't think I hurt her feelings. I couldn't; I'm not important enough. You see, Nancy Mulford and I know where we both stand, darling."

"Well, that's fine," he said. "If I may be allowed to get a word in edgewise today —"

"Oh, darling," she said, "you're so irrepressibly funny when you talk about getting a word in edgewise, as if everybody doesn't listen to you and simply hang on everything you say. That is, everybody except Walter Price, and he's your friend and not my friend, darling. Walter's the one who won't let anyone get a word in edgewise. My God, darling, that's why I came out here, just in self-defense. A refugee from verbosity. Tom, just what is it that strikes you as funny now?"

"That phrase of yours," he said, "a refugee from verbosity."

Emily shook her head in a careful balance between tolerance and irritation.

"Seriously, Tom," she said, "you're not implying that I talk too much? I wish to goodness that you wouldn't always be so logical in such a superior and masculine way. There isn't any need for it. Goodness knows that you're brighter than I and people like to listen to you more than to a poor little girl from the Midwest, who started to try to be an actress and who, just when she knew that she couldn't make the grade, was rescued from failure inadvertently."

"I wouldn't say inadvertently, my dear," he said. "As far as I can remember, I gave the matter a lot of serious thought. Why don't you take off your shoes and see if there's any of that round gravel in them?"

"Oh, Tom, you do get off the subject in the funniest ways," she said.

"Maybe if you'd tell me what the subject was, I wouldn't get off it," he told her.

"Oh, Tom," she said, "you say the funniest things sometimes. Please don't ask me again why I came out here, because it isn't very polite or gracious, is it, and I know there's a sort of Polynesian tribal taboo about this place, what with you and Miss Mulford — and don't forget I called her Miss Mulford — and the family photographs and everything? I still did come out here, didn't I?"

Her voice was controlled but sharper, and something told him that she was ceasing to be part of a production.

"Yes, my dear, you're here; you made it," he said.

"But you don't know why I'm here, do you?"

"It doesn't matter why, as long as you're here," he said. "And Emily, if I may say so, and if I may get in a word edgewise, you are looking especially lovely this afternoon."

"Oh, Tom," she said, and her voice broke "please don't say that."

"Why, Emily," he said, "I meant it as a compliment."

"God damn you and your God-damned compliments," she said. "I have been lonely as hell all day and you don't love me any more."

When she finished, she began to cry. He was used to Emily's crying in a number of different ways, and this was the poor-little-Hoosier-girl way that had no artistic point of reference. She was crying for something they both had lost and momentarily he shared her desperate unhappiness. He crushed his cigarette in an ash tray and crossed the room to where she was sitting and knelt beside her chair, quite aware of what he did because he had directed such crossovers frequently enough. He could almost hear himself telling someone else to take it more slowly, to give it time, but he shared her grief because he had long ago faced the truth that had made her cry.

"Now, Emily," he said, "don't get your face all undone. I love you as much as I love anyone."

The devastating thing was that his speech was absolutely true, and when he saw her looking at him through the tears that had already puffed her cheeks, he knew that they were alone there, clasped together by a hideous loneliness that shocked him so deeply that he could think of nothing more to say, and Emily was the one who spoke first.

"Go into Mulford's room," she said, "and get some Kleenex. She's the kind who must keep Kleenex somewhere."

Miss Mulford's office was impeccable. Her typewriter was collapsed into the secretary desk; the loose papers were in folders. The only trace of her that remained, now that she had gone home, appeared in the books on the window sill in front of the desk, Fowler's *Modern English Usage*, the *Concise Oxford Dictionary*, *Who's Who in America* and the *Columbia Encylopedia*. He found the Kleenex tissues in the desk's upper left hand drawer and he brought the entire box out to Emily, a crude gesture perhaps, but he did not want to make the trip twice.

"There," he said.

But Emily still was weeping.

Where had everything gone, he was thinking — love and skill and wish to live and everything? The thought, as Emily sobbed, filled him close to panic. It was like the ending of the whole strange day. Where in hell had everything gone? Where, for that matter, did anything go?

The late Dr. Albert Einstein, or others vaguely in the Einstein category, had advanced the theory that time, being immaterial, was indestructible — and perhaps it was. Perhaps everything that ever happened still existed on a sight and sound track in interstellar space. There was that star, three thousand light-years away from the planet upon which he was situated. If one could only make one's way to it like a hero in science fiction, and be equipped with a suitably powerful telescope trained upon the earth, one would not be witnessing a contemporary scene, but earlier and archaic recordings, such as the geometric civilization in Athens or the Minoan eccentricities of Crete. Yet, granted that the past was indestructible, exactly where was it now? Was it in good order, in keeping with theories of relativity? He did not believe it was. The past in his experience was in a tangled mess like ticker tape, unwinding from the staccato recording machines and pouring in sinuous coils into wastebaskets that stood beside them. The past was twisted and slithered. Instead of being instructive and nostalgic, it interfered with the definitiveness of the present, forever impeding and very seldom helping present logic or decision. That was what the past was doing to him now. The past that he and Emily had spent together was snarled around them, no less tangible because it was invisible. It did not help the situation in the least to know that he did not want any of the ticker tape or that he regretted most of it.

"Emily," he said, and he touched her radiant head gently because of the indestructible recollections — and her hair had an unfamiliar tactile quality, the latest contribution of forward-moving beauticians. There had been no lacquer finish when he had first met her. Emily had been Emily, happier, younger, with an unsophistication that no Arden's Maine Chance could conjure back. "Emily, dear, stop being actively unhappy," he said. "You and I have both lived long enough to know that active unhappiness doesn't resolve anything. It's only going to make you have to do your whole face over, dear, and believe me, it really was lovely when you came in."

"Don't try to be so damned diplomatic polite," Emily said, and she choked back a sob, "and don't pat me. I've always hated head patters; it's so tentative."

"I wouldn't say I've ever been quite in that class, my dear," he said.

"I never said you were," she answered. "Oh, Tom, why can't you love me the way you used to when you used to say that you

loved me more than you loved Hopedale? I know she was a bitch
to you twenty different ways at once, but still you did use to say
you loved me better."

He laughed, and he sat down on the arm of her chair and took
her hand. It was something that she could still make him laugh.

"My dear," he said, "I still love you better than I loved Hopedale, and don't forget that I also told you that I love you as much
as I do anyone. It isn't our fault that love has varying values.
We can't help things like that, Emily — and besides, there's always affection."

"Hand me another Kleenex," Emily said. "You haven't been affectionate for years."

"Now, Emily," he said, "I don't know that I've ever been what
you would call affectionate, even in my most unforgetful moments. I'm talking about affection, dear, as a general state of
mind."

"I never did expect you to love me as much as you loved the
first one," Emily said.

He handed her another Kleenex. Her remark served to throw
them together more effectively than any other which he could
imagine. The vanished memories and the people and the possibilities and the might-have-beens, left them unbelievably alone.

"Emily, dear," he said, "let's not get off the beam. There's a
whole lot to affection, and I know I've neglected you, and I
know you don't like it here and that coming here has been a
self-indulgence on my part. Please stop being unhappy. Listen,
I've got a surprise for you."

"A surprise?" she asked. "What surprise?"

She blew her nose and tossed the Kleenex toward the open
fireplace. It did not reach there. As long as he had known her,
Emily had been tossing olive stones and crumpled notes toward fireplaces. At least Emily was no longer sorry for herself.

"Oh, Tom," she said, "I hope you're not going to build a greenhouse or anything. Tom, dear, promise me it isn't going to be a
greenhouse."

He stood up and smiled down at her with a sense of considerable achievement.

"No, it isn't," he said. "I'm going to send this whole show to the warehouse, Emily."

"Tom," she said, "are you talking about our life together? Do you mean you're asking for a divorce?"

"Now what under the sun put that thought into your head?" he asked. "I was just using a professional expression. When a show doesn't work, you send the property to the warehouse and all the backdrops and everything. Well, dear, I know you haven't been happy here, and maybe this whole effort has been sentimental and preposterous. Anyhow, I'm going to put up the whole place for sale. That's all I mean about the warehouse."

"Why, darling!" Emily said. "Darling! Then perhaps we can go back to Easthampton again."

It was reassuring to be able to estimate again with accuracy which way her mind would work.

"Well," he said, "we'll have to see how things turn out before I get pushing on the old treadmill at Easthampton again."

"Why, Tom," she said, "you know you always loved it there in spite of yourself."

Why was it, when women knew that men were against something, they always said they liked it in spite of themselves? Easthampton, he was thinking, was much like the environment here that he was preparing to leave. The aura of the stage had arrived there early. The late John Drew had once sunned himself in the then primitive solarium of the men's part of the bathing pavilion. The late Augustus Thomas had written plays in its neighborhood. The Barrymores had appeared there at odd moments; and as a final proof of validity, the hucksters now trod assiduously upon the heels of art. Everyone who loved the old town said it was more attractive than Southampton. But then, one should remember that Easthampton had More to Start With. When John Drew had first seen that village, it had still been dreaming of its past, the simple, homespun past when it had been a semiprosperous whaling and fishing village that America's great god of literature, Melville, would have understood. Queequeg, his harpooner, might once have walked Easthampton's streets, as well as the ghost of the author of *Home*

Sweet Home, who had once penned his lyric there. Easthampton had More to Start With than Southampton, and even the hucksters knew it. In spite of all the new shops and of all the new parvenus who annually pressed their way in with their new Jaguars, Easthampton still had More to Start With.

It had what were now called "the Dear Old Things," that were now preserved with a revered fetishism that was basically moving. There was the Village Green, with the Dear Old Pond, in which perhaps they had once ducked dear, old scolding women. There was not in the world, even in England, a more lovely village green. Then there was the Dear Old Windmill, with its hand-made wood machinery, rather well preserved in spite of time. Then there was the Dear Old Cemetery, where those Dear Old People who had once ground corn in the Dear Old Windmill were now laid to rest. The dead never, never would have dreamed of with what loving care the hucksters and the huckstresses and an occasional contributor to the *New Yorker* magazine, and the theatre folk, were to snip the grasses of their dear old graves with their quaintly carved inscriptions which a huckster or a huckstress might sometimes quote over the Martinis. The living knew now that it was their manifest destiny to fight against signboards, night clubs and the encroachment of chain stores. Even the weariest huckster, just off the copy desk of Batten, Barton, Durstine and Osborn, and in Easthampton for a week end with his boss, knew that modernity must never impinge on the dear old things that made Easthampton, excepting always the Jaguars, the Cadillacs, the matched irons and the laminated woods which in their way were a modern expression of loving art that exactly paralleled the Dear Old Things.

"I know," he said, "you are right, Emily. I did love Easthampton in spite of myself. I suppose I had better face the fact, Emily, now that it is too late to change, that I am partially a huckster at heart."

"Darling," she said, "please don't get on the subject of hucksters again. It always made me frightfully nervous when you started huckstering everything and saying our cabaña was located on Hucksters' Row."

"I agree with you," he said. "After all, John Drew liked Easthampton and *Home Sweet Home* was written there. I admit we shouldn't have moved away."

"Tom," she said, "please don't start getting difficult. Without wishing to rub it in, this does go to show that I was right about one thing, wasn't I? Just one little drop of rightness; just one teeny, weeny little thing?"

"What teeny, weeny little thing?" he asked.

She smiled at him and gave his hand a loving, reproving pat. It might have been a more definite pat than she had intended due to the extra flagellation caused by her bracelets and her ring.

"I told you, didn't I," she said, "that I knew what would happen when you sprung this place on me, darling — and I do understand the restiveness in artistic temperaments. Arthur always said I did. I always said, didn't I, that buying this place and making a big antique shop of it would be just like another play? I always said that, just as soon as you got it fixed the way you wanted it, you'd grow tired of it. I don't like to be right all the time, dear, and I know very well that you are right when you occasionally say that rightness does not go hand-in-hand with femininity. But I was right about this, wasn't I? I did tell you exactly what would happen, didn't I?"

He glanced down at her hand resting over his. From the very first time he had met her, he had recognized that her hands were overlarge for the rest of her, but now Emily had grown up to them. Her hand looked surprisingly young considering her age — no wrinkles, no enlargement of her finger joints, and with beautiful enameling on the nails.

"Yes," he said, "I do recall that you made that point on several occasions, Emily."

"Well, don't say it in such a cross way," she said. "It spoils all the fun of knowing you don't know everything. I knew you'd get just as bored with everything around here as I am, and those

157

high-school children were pretty nearly the last straw. . . . Tom, there isn't anything that is worrying you, is there?"

Her voice was sharper, reminding him that Emily could be perceptive at the most unexpected times. He realized as soon as she asked the question that it was time to give her the exact reason for his putting the place on the market. He would have to tell her eventually. It was time, but he drew away from inevitability. He had had enough that day, although he was ashamed of the hesitation.

"Nothing's the matter particularly," he said. "Maybe I'm feeling a little tired. I've been waltzing around with the third act. Maybe I'm not as resilient as I used to be."

Her voice was still sharp.

"Isn't it going well?" she asked.

Where had everything gone? he was thinking again. Where in hell had everything gone? He should not have been suspicious. He should not have harbored the idea that she might be hoping that his work was not going well. He wished that he had not heard that morning's conversation.

"As a matter of fact, I'm not worried about it any more," he said.

"But you were before, weren't you?" she said. "Why didn't you tell me, dear?" She laughed briefly but disarmingly. "What's the use in being married to the Dean of American Playwrights and everything, if he can't let you just a teeny, weeny bit behind the scenes and if he won't tell you when he's worried, and won't let you share even a little in his work?"

She always was at her worst when she was in the teeny, weeny stage, but it was a time to repress impatience, and he was still sorry for her — for them both, with a dry sort of self-pity. Instead of answering, he patted her head again.

"There," he said, "maybe I should have been a patter."

Emily shook her head, but her plaintiveness was gone.

"Dear old Arthur," she said. "Arthur liked my critical judgment; he used to say he depended on it."

It was no time to explain to Emily that any girl was a good critic when she was also an old man's darling.

"Now, Emily," he said, "haven't you had enough good news for one day? It's dangerous to want everything."

"You mean about selling all this?" she said.

"Yes, and about being right all along," he said. "Let's not forget the right part."

"Tom," she said, "don't be horrid. Don't spoil everything."

"I'm not being horrid," he said. "Honestly, you were dead right, Emily."

Her face brightened, and the traces of her tears were negligible.

"If you only knew how sweet you are when you admit something," she said, "maybe you'd admit a whole lot more." Her hand closed over his. "Pull me up and let's go back to the house. Alfred gave you the word, didn't he, about the Bramhalls coming to dinner? And Dick always dresses, you know."

"I know," he said, "but I still haven't got it quite clear how the Bramhalls came into the picture."

"It was one of those times," Emily said, "one of those damned-if-you-do, damned-if-you-don't times, darling. Marion called up and almost insisted that we go there, and you know how sensitive Marion is. Of course they're not as interesting as some of our more glamorous friends. And you know how hard it is when Marion starts insisting, because you've mentioned it yourself, and I know how really fond you are of the Bramhalls, even though you do call them the flotsam from your first marriage. Well, I knew, darling, that you'd simply explode if I accepted, because I do know something of the writing mind, if only through osmosis. I knew you'd blow your top if you had to drive twenty miles at the end of a working day. So I explained this to Marion and asked them to come here instead. I apologize, but there wasn't anything else to do. You've known the Bramhalls so long; in some ways I think they are our nicest friends."

"Yes, it was the only thing to do," he said, "and of course I like them, but I wish they weren't such neutralists."

"Neutralists?" she said.

"About Rhoda," he said. "They've been such perfect corkers — ambassadors of good will, I mean. They've always loved Rhoda, and they've always loved me, and they're going to keep on loving us both, no matter what. And I've never seen them but Marion doesn't make that speech, even if you feed her only one weak drink. They're such perfect corkers that I can't even be rude to them because they'd go and tell Rhoda."

"Why, Tom," she said, "I never knew you felt that way about them. I always thought you simply adored the Bramhalls."

"Maybe I only feel so temporarily," he said. "Maybe I don't feel like making an effort tonight. Maybe I don't want to move into someone else's world."

"But that's what you always say you like to do," she said, "move into someone else's world. You often say it is all that keeps you going."

"Yes," he said, "that's so, but still it's an effort sometimes."

"It won't be any effort at all tonight, not with Walter here," Emily said. "He gets more and more loquacious. He positively rambles. Come on, let's get going."

It was not necessary to pull Emily out of her chair. She still had coordination.

"I'll be over in about half an hour," he said. "There are just one or two things I've got to look over in my third act, but if I'm not back in half an hour, maybe you'd better send for me. And don't be lonely, Emily."

"All right," she said. "I don't feel that way any more. You're the one who looks lonely."

"Why, Emily," he said, "it's always lonely, writing, and I'm pretty used to it by now."

"Well," Emily said, "don't get too lonely. And mind, only half an hour. You know how nervous they get in the kitchen if everybody's not on time."

There was a more solid sort of silence in the room after Emily was gone that reminded him of the silence of a dimly lighted house after the last of an audience had left a theatre. There was still the consciousness of recent excitement, of noise and voices long after the audience was gone. There was still the echo of Emily's voice and the imprint of her personality. There was no

160

doubt that Emily was becoming increasingly what the world called a character. The bounce and the ebullience of the little Hoosier girl was growing rather than diminishing. It was a quality that reminded him of the magic rubber ball. He should have told her the whole story. He knew that it was dangerous to put things off when it came to Emily, or any other woman. They always interpreted delay as a sign of weakness, and usually they were right.

The quiet had a deeper quality when he took the Kleenex back to Miss Mulford's office. He picked up the folder from her desk containing his penciled pages, took out his ring of keys, and opened the locked drawer of the letter file and found the investment list in the securities folder. It was an act that had always demanded an effort, because he was congenitally bad with figures. He sighed as he put the play folder and the investment list on his writing table. The securities, with their book value in one column and their current market value in another, were like a complicated equation which he knew before he started that he had not the skill to solve. The neat pages, as he turned them, made an ominous, rattling sound in the silence, reminiscent of the noise of rain on a shed roof. And after all, it was a matter for the lawyers, and the bank had warned him at the time of the loan that the collateral offered no great margin.

It was a matter for the lawyers, but his draft of the third act was different. He was surprised, as he read his penciled pages, how well he had written in spite of all that had occurred to disturb him. There were always pitfalls that the most experienced writer could not avoid — of easy effects that led to sloppiness, and also the constant danger of repetition; but he was sure that nothing that he had done was bad. In fact, he believed that the problems of the third act that had vexed him for the last six weeks were solved in the draft that he was reading; and there was even a spontaneity in the lines that reminded him of some of his earlier work, although it was not the same sort of spontaneity. Professionally, he knew very well, no one stood still. Work either went up or down, but he was sure that what he had before him was nothing of which to be ashamed. Still, the spontaneity which pleased him also disturbed him. Its lightness and what he hoped might be its brilliance, had the echo of an earlier time — the echo of the boundless confidence of youth. The spirit of the earlier Harrow was in it without the crudeness or the carelessness. He wished that he might get some of the crudeness back and that he might recapture his old, boisterous quality, but it was gone of course, lost in years of rehearsal and rewriting. As he was feeling now, he would willingly have traded the competence that time had given him for the old self-confidence that had once almost been like a gambler's intuition. If you had it, nothing could go wrong. And where had it gone, he wondered. He was back where he had started earlier that afternoon. Where in hell had everything gone?

XI

There's Something I Ought to Tell You, Emily

IN THE days before air travel had become a popular means of locomotion, he and Rhoda had sailed to France each winter for several years, after he had purchased a perfectly impossible house at Antibes. They had gone to the French Riviera during the last months of the bright assurance of the Twenties that had submerged so rapidly into the social consciousness of the Roosevelt era. There had been a brief moment, after his first play had been a hit on Broadway, when taxes were still too low to siphon off all earnings, so that the prospect of increasing affluence had seemed rational. There were no caustic remarks among the intelligentsia during those brief years if a writer or artist chose to buy or rent an interesting place on the Riviera. Even some of the theatre's greatest liberals had enjoyed the Riviera then, but the climate had changed by 1937 when he sold the Antibes house for half of what he had paid for it. On the whole, it would have been nearly as profitable to have given it to Rhoda, and she might have owned it still if old associations would not have been disturbing. Indeed, he often found himself thinking affectionately of old pre-war Antibes, before it was saturated with trippers, and before its roads were jammed with English, French, German and Italian motor vehicles.

There were always guests stopping at their villa, most of whom, as Rhoda said, exerted a bad influence on him. Yet Rhoda herself sometimes admitted that it was fun at Antibes, and sometimes she even forgot to worry about Antibes's lack of solidity, and heaven knew, in retrospect, that it had not been very stable. As Rhoda had said more than once — when they were safe in their small suite on the old *Aquitania*—expensive though she knew it was, and uselessly so since neither of them was a good sailor, it was fun to get away. It might not be good for Harold, in spite of the chance the winter gave him to make French his true second language, but still it was fun to get away; and if Antibes was not a constructive sort of change, it surely was a change.

The *Aquitania* still remained in his memory as a fine symbol of a vanished world. It had been wholly different from the *Elizabeth* and the *Mary*. For one thing, in spite of all its comfort, the *Aquitania* had given the impression of being a ship, and he had always had the feeling of going on a voyage. There was also a sense of irrevocable commitment, the illusion that you might not return, or, if you did, that things would never be quite the same again.

If he was not mistaken, ships in those days customarily sailed at midnight, and once the *Aquitania* was under way his last glimpse of New York was a large and magic panorama of lighted buildings, never so beautiful or so poignant as when one sailed at midnight. He was separated from the city once the ship was under way, no longer a part of it, and merely not being so made him wish vaguely that he might be back. There was always regret, now that New York belonged to him no longer. It had been a long while since he had thought much of the *Aquitania*, but now the same sense of impending change was back with him as he walked toward the house. Although he still owned it, it was no longer his, and he saw it in a new proportion because his emotions and immature visions were no longer involved in it; the house had never seemed so beautiful.

He could regret that the place would belong to someone else and that it would doubtless sell for half of the money that he had put in it, but this regret was tempered by the conviction that nothing he did in a business way had ever turned out as expected. In spite of mixed emotions, he was able to view the lawns, the shrubbery, the fenestration, the cornice, and the cupola of that graceful Federalist dwelling nearly with the eyes of a stranger. It seemed to him that he had never been so lightly involved with anything else that he had ever done.

The small front parlor was finished and the marble-topped table from the Judge's sitting room, and the iron plant-stand from the Judge's house helped, like the horsehair sofa, to break down formality. The large sitting room, too was finished. He had been careful that none of its furnishings had been too violently restored and he had spent a long while searching for a well-worn Oriental rug. The place looked easy. The sofa and chairs by the fireplace had a used look. He had not needed an interior decorator, nor a stage designer, to achieve what he desired. This effect was now enhanced by the corpulent and aging figure of Walter Price, dozing in the wing chair by the sitting room fire, with a battered play script half open beside him. You always needed life to make a room alive. He could not blame himself for admiring the whole setting, and he found himself mentally writing stage directions again, as he had in the dining room that morning.

"Oh, Walter," he said, "I'm sorry to arouse you. You looked so comfortable, but perhaps we both should do something about getting ready for dinner. Dick and Marion Bramhall are coming over."

Walter straightened himself slowly and blinked his bleary eyes.

"Dear me," he said, "I must have dozed off. It's an old habit of mine, as you may remember — the habit of the old trouper and the old soldier. Snatch a catnap while you can. One of my favorite mottos."

"I'm glad you snatched it here" Tom said. "It's just what the room needed — a touch of informality. Do you remember the old Belasco days, when the curtain rose on an empty stage, with nothing but a cat asleep in the old inglenook? And then the cat would rise and stretch, just the way you're stretching now, except that it was a cat. Was it Belasco, or who was it who thought of that?"

Walter Price smiled.

"Dear old Tom," he said. "I was thinking only this morning that there is no one else so beautifully endowed with your powers of reminiscence. I am familiar with the one about the cat, but I do not believe it was Belasco's idea. Actually, as I cudgel my brains, I think I invented the cat technique myself when I was property man for a horror play. *When the Clock Strikes*, or something of the sort. I distinctly remember the opening scene called for a cat stretching. It was I who conceived the idea of placing our cat in a small box one hour before curtain. By removing him and placing him on stage just one half-minute before the curtain was rung up, the cat would always be stretching before the fire. There was always applause. I'm very sure I invented that technique."

He had not, and doubtless both of them knew it. He was obviously quoting from some theatrical memoir, although Tom Harrow could not remember the exact one at the moment.

"Yes, Tom," Walter said, "I frankly attribute my present mental alertness and my powers of memory to my having cultivated the habit of snatching a sleeping minute at odd intervals. I invariably wake like a flash, as I did just now, revivified. You know, it might not do you harm to practice that same relaxation. You look drawn and tired this afternoon — unnecessarily tense. There's nothing on your mind, is there?"

The question made Tom nervous, since Walter Price very seldom noticed anything except himself.

"Well, I do have a few things on my mind, Walter," he said. "I've been working on the third act most of the day and maybe I overdid it."

"I'm afraid you're not very happy about it," Walter said.

He understood that Walter's curiosity had sprung from what Emily had said in the dining room that morning. The difficulty of success was that even one's best friends were seldom averse to the prospect of eventual failure.

"If you want to know," Tom said, "I've never been happy when I'm writing, Walter, and I suspect anyone who says he is."

"Perhaps you are right," Walter said, "but I believe dear old George used to be happy while in the throes of composition."

"Dear old George Who?" Tom Harrow asked.

"Why, dear old George Bernard Shaw, of course," Walter said. "You remember, naturally, how dear old George depended on my advice during his last years. But perhaps you did not know that we had reached a first-name basis? Believe me, not everybody called him George."

"I'll bet they didn't," Tom Harrow said. "You certainly have something there, Walter."

"Ah, memories, memories," Walter Price said. "Who did you say was coming to dinner?"

"Dick and Marion Bramhall," Tom Harrow said. "You remember them, don't you? Rhoda and I met them that winter we were at Palm Beach before we bought the Antibes villa."

"Yes," Walter said, "indeed I do remember."

It was time to be walking up the stairway to its nearly perfect landing, with its fine old clock, the product of a Hingham, Massachusetts, clockmaker, and then up the left of the landing to the so-called "flying staircases" to dress for dinner. It was time and high time, as he knew after having lived so long with the dogma that the show must go on. It was time, as common sense told him, to tell Emily of his financial ruin, and his conscience also told him that he had been a moral coward not to have given Emily this briefing in the reconstructed coach house. What was it that had made him hesitate? Was it his annoyance because Emily had called Miss Mulford, Mulford — or was it due to the high heels and the petulance of Emily's manner, which he realized now had given him a hopeless feeling of encirclement? He was obliged to doubt these reasons. In the end he had been a moral coward, lacking intestinal fortitude. Truthfully, he had put off the moment because he had feared Emily's tears and her recriminative anger. Truthfully, he had the American man's dread of the potentialities of the American woman, that was instilled in the American male, beginning with his schoolmarm. It was time to pull together the vestiges of manhood left him from this hurly-burly, but he was still reluctant. Though his conscience and the fine old staircase of the Saebury house were beckoning, he felt an old call from the past. Although it was true that Walter Price was boring him to extinction, habit told him that there were no friends like old friends.

"Well, Walter," he said, "you look perfectly all right as you are, and this dinner party is not your funeral, but I've got to change because Dick Bramhall invariably dresses for dinner."

His tone lacked complete conviction. Walter did not look all right as he was, and Emily would be waiting upstairs, reproachfully if nothing else, to have him zip her up, and zipping Emily was growing to be more of a problem annually.

"Dear old Tom," Walter said, "you never did like dinner parties."

"No, I never did, dear old Walter," Tom Harrow said, "and from what I gather from indirection, if not from intimacy, your dear old friend, dear old George, didn't like them, either. It's pretty tough writing all day and then sitting down with an unrehearsed cast and talking dialogue all night."

"If I may say so," Walter said, "your dialogue grows more succinct and crisper every year — but how about you and me having a little drinkie, Tom, before you go upstairs? We've hardly had a moment together. How about a little drinkie, just for old times' sake?"

At least Walter had not said "for auld lang syne." It was a bad idea to have a drink before the dinner cocktails, but then, Walter was his guest, and it was only courteous to have a drink with Walter, but he could not fool himself about the underlying reasons for his courtesy. He was a moral coward. He wished to delay telling Emily the bad news.

"All right," he said, "I'll get Alfred to make us a Martini apiece. Alfred isn't bad with Martinis."

"I'm delighted you fall in with my mood, Tom," Walter said, "and that gin you left in my bathroom is smooth and delicious. May I be so bold as to make a suggestion? Almost no vermouth, and let us hold that thought."

Tom Harrow crossed the room to an authentic petit-point bell pull and rang it. The bell pull, he was happy to remember, had been one of the architect's ideas, not his, and it operated by electricity. After ringing it, he remembered that Alfred was averse to answering the summons of a bell, perhaps because of some directive from the National Association for the Advancement of Colored People, and so he was not surprised that there was a considerable interval before Alfred, in his alpaca coat, appeared.

"Alfred," Tom said, and he used almost the same smile that he employed when he had to say "No" to talented but middle-aged actresses, "I know how busy you must be, but even if the table will not be quite so perfect, do you think you could find time to stir one Martini for Mr. Price and myself — the best gin, and almost no vermouth?"

"Yes, sir. Directly, sir," Alfred said.

It was a response that demonstrated that he was popular with servants because he respected their routine. Emily, he was thinking, never respected anyone's routine, including his own. When he drank the Martini, his heart felt warm toward Walter. After all, there were no friends like old friends, but there was more to it than that. The Martini had created a change of mood. He felt a new confidence in his capacity. Through the sitting room window, where the lilacs were budding and where the reddish shoots of the peonies soon would turn to green, the late sunlight was mellow, gilding the Chinese shapes of the azaleas. There was no house like an old New England house, sparse and graceful, and he had saved it — not any architect. He had taken the burden and the heat of the day, and he still was able to take more because he was the master of his fate.

"Walter," he said, "those delightful Bramhalls will be upon us before we know it. But don't you move, you look perfectly all right."

The gracious Saebury staircase was no longer formidable. It gave him no feeling of effort or reluctance, and there was another good thing about that crisp, dry Martini. He was now fully prepared to tell Emily the bad news, and delightfully enough, the announcement would not be time-consuming because very shortly now, the Bramhalls would be arriving. The show would be on the road. On the whole, it was delightful that Emily had asked the Bramhalls.

169

His bedroom, with its controversial bath, was in the rear of the main part of the house, and a door connected it with Emily's larger room and her bath-dressing-room that looked over Johnson Street. When the house had finally been remodeled and adequately furnished, a magazine of the *House and Garden* school had sent a writer and a photographer to do the Harrow house. Of course it was good publicity, if you were seeking publicity, but Tom Harrow had refused to let them go upstairs. He had always felt that those snooping photographs of bedrooms, boudoirs, with their chaise longues and conveniently arranged closets, were an indecent invasion of privacy and an indecent exposure of convention. He was not going to have *Life, Look, House and Garden* or any other magazine taking photographs of his wardrobe. The living quarters of his house were private and he had insisted that they be comfortable, regardless of the authenticity; but those fine rooms, with their fireplaces and their excellent woodwork, had demanded formal furniture. His own bedroom was larger than any he had ever previously occupied — large enough so that it was a considerable walk to the curly maple bureau where he kept the gold-backed military brushes that the cast of his first play had given him — large enough for a writing desk and an armchair with a good reading light in case he wanted to work late in the evening, and for a radio and record player. This was an idea of his that was not successful because music, when he wanted it, invariably disturbed Emily, who was a fitful sleeper. Out of sentiment, he had hung in his room two steel engravings from the Judge's house, not caring whether they clashed with the authentic reproduction wallpaper. It was sad to think that he was just beginning to grow accustomed to the room, now that necessity would make him leave it, but that interlude with Walter Price had moved him off the track of self-pity.

The door connecting with Emily's bedroom was open. Emily enjoyed calling through open doors while dressing for dinner and she always said there was no reason why dinner dressing should not be a companionate act. She wanted advice regarding what to wear and some of her best thoughts came to her when she was pulling on stockings and picking out proper shoes.

"Where under the sun have you been, Tom?" she called.

"Just downstairs," he answered, "having a drink with Walter."

He saw that his dinner coat, socks, evening shoes, pleated shirt — everything — were all laid out upon his bed, proving that Alfred, among his other skills, was an excellent valet.

"You should have waited until the Bramhalls came," she said. "Please hurry, Tom. You know how rude it is to keep people waiting."

Then he thought of Harold.

"Where's Harold?" he asked. "Harold's coming to dinner, isn't he?"

"Oh, yes," she said. "Harold's in his room, I think. Please hurry, Tom."

Her voice had a curiously muffled sound.

"Tom," she called, "please come here a minute. I'm stuck, and I don't want to rip anything."

Many of Emily's most attractive dresses had become too tight for her, but she never would have them let out because of her inherent vein of stubbornness. She believed that they were an incentive to diet, and she was sure that eventually she would work into them again, as she was working into one now, her green and gold taffeta, which was too elaborate for the Bramhalls.

As she stood in the middle of her room, her helplessness had a pathos that aroused his protective instinct. Her head was covered by the upper part of the taffeta dress. Its flaring skirt was only midway to where it should be, and her arms still waved above her head while she wriggled carefully so as not to rip anything.

"Pull it down slowly, Tom," she said. "It isn't really funny."

"I'm sorry," he said, "but I'd try something else. It's beautiful, but it's too small, Emily."

"It isn't when it gets on," Emily said, "and it's the way Dior makes these things. He makes them like a strait jacket. Now zip it slowly, Tom, and let me draw my breath in, and don't get it caught on the slip. I don't know why Dior is so careless with his zippers."

She was out of breath when the dress was zipped, but this time her breathlessness gave the illusion that she was a young girl at her first dance. There was every reason when he saw her then, to know why he should have been as attracted to her as he had been when he had first met her.

"Darling," she said, "would you be a perfect saint and open the slipper closet and get me my gold sandals on the third shelf? At least my feet haven't got a middle-aged spread."

As a matter of fact, her feet had only recently begun to look too small for the rest of her.

"I'm going to wear the gold necklace with the little diamonds —the one you gave me on our last anniversary, in case you've forgotten, darling."

He had not forgotten the necklace, or the bill from Cartier's, and now that she had mentioned it, the bill from Cartier's reminded him that neither of them would be around Cartier's so much as formerly.

"Tom," she said, "please hurry. Why, you haven't started to shave or anything."

Would it, after all, not be better to await another opportunity, to cultivate a more propitious, more sentimental moment? Emily was right, time was marching on, and he must dress very hurriedly indeed if he were to be down in time to meet the Bramhalls. The morning might be better, or later in the evening when the company was gone — but he knew the reason behind his hesitation. There was a contemptible species of fear inside him. There had been too many scenes with too many women, the gentlest of whom were usually the worst fishwives when aroused. Emily was putting on the necklace, seated in front of her dressing-table mirror, looking rather like a Renoir. It was always hard to tell what drove one to a decision. It might have been the necklace, or it might have been the way she applied her lipstick, or one of a dozen other reasons that made him believe that his manhood and his self-respect hung in the balance if he did not tell her.

"Emily," he said, "I guess there's something I ought to tell you, and I'd better tell you now."

Things were always easier when you walked up the line. Her face staring into the mirror showed him that she had recognized that something was serious, and she had never been able to cultivate the guile to hide her thoughts or emotions. He believed that her first reaction was fear, but she had never been a timid girl. She wheeled around immediately and her eyes met his for a moment, the same beautiful eyes that could not fail to hold any man's attention. Her voice changed, like his own. It was high and steady, without dramatic affectation.

"Is this so tough," she asked, "that you have to tell it now?"

"Yes," he said, "and I'm afraid it's going to be hard on you, Emily. I got a pretty tough piece of news this morning."

She had never been a good actress, but in real life she was eloquently convincing. There was stillness in Emily's disorderly bedroom. She was always leaving her shoes and mules exactly where she had stepped out of them, and tossing her clothes indiscriminately over bed and chairs; and at dinner dressing time, there was always a snarl of nylons on the floor. This disorder added to the suspense and drama that they both were facing.

"All right," she said, "what is the news, Tom?"

He knew her so well that he recognized that she never had been the girl to pick up the pieces.

"Well," he said, "it's about that musical I tried to put on. The one about Porthos and the Musketeers, in case you don't remember."

"In case I don't remember," she said, and gave a mellow laugh. "In case I don't remember the fortune you put into it, and then all the extra money when they changed the costumes and sets at the last minute. You never should have done it, and I've always told you so. And I told you right from the beginning that the thing had no future. I told you and I told you that no one ever goes to a costume musical. Did I or did I not tell you?"

Her voice was ironical, as it always was when she had been correct.

"Yes," he said, "and you told me the same thing about *The King and I.*"

She laughed again.

"Well, this one wasn't *The King and I,*" she said. "I always told you it was the kiss of death, didn't I, when you started being the big producer instead of scribbling on your copy paper? I always told you that playwriting and business did not mix, and Arthur always said so, too. Did you ever hear of G.B.S. producing musicals about Paris?"

"All right," he said, "just so long as you don't start calling him dear old George."

"There you go being flippant," she said. "All right, you lost your shirt going into musical comedy, but we've known that already, haven't we? Well, what about it now?"

"I suppose I should have been franker with you," he said. "It's the bank. I put up everything from the safe deposit box to secure a loan."

He could see that finally she saw what was coming. He heard her draw a sharp breath as she pulled herself up from her seat before the dressing table.

"Do you mean," she said, "that you underwrote that thing all yourself? Do you mean you didn't get Hollywood to help you, or play safe selling pieces of it? Oh my God, Tom, I told you to sell pieces."

"Emily," he said, "you were absolutely right, but there's no use going backwards, and I'm very, very sorry."

It was time to get the thing over. He hated the humiliation of telling her, and she had been absolutely right.

"I guess you'd better get the rest of it," he told her. "The market's dropped. The bank is selling all the securities. There's only about enough to pay the loan after taxes. There it is, Emily."

There it really was. The reality had not struck him so forcibly when Miss Mulford had begun to cry, but stark reality was on Emily's frozen features.

"Oh, my God!" she said. "You mean you're cleaned out?"

There was nothing to do, he was thinking, but take it. Humiliating and personally painful though the scene might be, he was still withdrawn from it. It was his instinct that still made him assess the values. He stood there both being and seeing himself.

"That's the usual way of putting it," he said: "cleaned out."

"So that's why you were going to sell this place," Emily said. "Oh, my God!"

"That's right," he said, "and I'm afraid it isn't all, Em."

He did not know why he had called her "Em," because he had not done so for years, except that he could not help feeling sorry for her.

"I don't like this any more than you, my dear," he said. "I also have an unsecured loan for seventy thousand dollars. They'll be after me, too, and that will take the house and furniture here and the apartment in New York, I'm afraid."

"Afraid?" she said. "Oh, my God, afraid! What about the picture rights?"

"I called up Ed this morning," he said. "No one's interested. I'm sorry, Em."

"So that's why you didn't dare come to the house for lunch," she said. "Don't stand there with that smirk saying you're sorry!"

"All right," he said, "I guess that wraps it up, Em. I don't blame your feeling the way you do, but we'd better pull ourselves together. After all, we're not going to starve. There are royalties and some motion-picture payments, and I've about got the new play finished."

There was no change in her expression. He heard her draw a deep breath.

"The new play . . ." she said. "Why don't you be a man and face it? You know just as well as I do that it won't get anywhere. Don't you ever read the notices? You've been repeating yourself for the last five years."

There was always instinct, including that of self-preservation. Writers and slack-wire artists eventually reached approximately the same ending. You were gone once you lost faith in skill, and writers and slack-wire artists, too, knew that they could not go on forever. The contempt in her face was what made him react at last more than anything she had said.

175

"All right, Em," he said. "Here we are on the beach with the Bramhalls coming. I know it's tough, but you shouldn't have married me for my money."

When he saw her face flush, he knew that he had dished out as much as he had taken.

"Now that's funny," she said. "Very, very funny — after Hopedale had just taken you to the cleaners. Very, very funny — when you used to say I was the only one who could help and understand you. I married you because I thought you were a man, with a career ahead of you. I thought you could be somebody I could admire, with a great name in the theatre — and what did I get?"

She laughed. It was a laugh straight from the old school, and there was no stopping Emily once she had started.

"And what did I get?" she said. "It's about time someone told you — a conceited, washed-out, middle-aged has-been, and not even much of a lover. My God, why didn't I see the fallacy in all the lousy plays you wrote? Why didn't I know you were a conceited literary prostitute, who only cared about money? And don't smirk at me! You're the person who made me depend on money and ruin my ideals, simply by association. You and your limousines and your antique furniture, your trips abroad. You're the one who made me soft and made me put on weight just out of sheer nervousness. Why didn't you tell me you didn't care for art and that you had the soul of a stockbroker?"

"Emily," he said, "that's about enough for now."

"Oh," she said, "it is, is it? Who ever told you you could produce a play? Well, I suppose you had to, when you realized you were slipping artistically; but all you've ever been able to do successfully is spend money, money, money. I've watched your self-indulgence, your pouring money into this house, trying to bolster up your crumbling, pathetic ego. Well, it doesn't make any difference now, because you're on the beach, as you have said; and it isn't even pathetic. Do you hear me? You're absolutely through!"

"Yes," he said, "I hear you, and you're a ham actress if there ever was one. Now put some powder on your face and go down-stairs."

"And what do you know about acting?" she said. "Tom Harrow, the great director. Tom Harrow, the superannuated show-off, going to the war with a picture crew. Oh, my God! I don't know how I've stood it. No wonder Rhoda walked out; no wonder Hopedale couldn't take it!"

"Emily," he said, "that will be enough for now." And he walked into his own room and slammed the door, but even so he could still hear her voice dimly addressing the unseen audience.

He had not expected sympathy or commiseration from her, but neither had he thought she would be able to play so accurately on his emotions. The evidence of deterioration in their relationship shocked him, combined with his memories of having been drawn to her once. He had been a fool to marry her, of course, after the Hopedale episode, but there had been gaiety and good nature and forgiveness once. Now there was only débris, after that explosion. He could see her point of view and at that moment he could sympathize, but he was shocked to discover that he was more distressed than he should have been and it was no help to tell himself that the picture she had drawn of him was spitefully distorted. He could not get away from a new belief that there was nothing left.

XII

Bread upon the Girls

THE reflection of his face in the bathroom mirror was blank and pale and there was a slight tremor to his hands when he fixed his shirt studs. Once there had been everything, he was thinking. The only thing to do was get such thoughts out of his mind. He was standing before the full-length mirror attached to the back of his wardrobe, straightening his tie and giving a final tug and a pat to the folds of his dinner coat, when he heard the inevitable voices downstairs, and then he opened his own door to the hallway. The thing to remember was that the show must go on. Even if you fell flat on your face, the show must go on. Then Emily's voice in the hall told him that she realized it, too.

"Oh, you two dears," he heard Emily say, "it's so sweet of you to have come all this way! Tom is dying to see you, and he will be down in just a minute. We're having cocktails in the library. Harold will barkeep until Tom comes down. You know how Tom is, absent-minded and always putting off dressing until the last moment."

There was invariably a delayed action and aftermath to unpleasantness, and now he could feel it sweep over him. Emily's voice had been responsible for it — her gay voice, full of cordial warmth that had been so appealing to him once. Her voice and the emanations of her personality down there in the hall aroused in him unreasoning anger, but then, the anger was a help. It flowed through him like a stimulating wonder drug, changing his attitude toward all that Emily had said. It aroused in him memories of the hero-worship of an earlier Emily that had touched him once so deeply, and with that worship there had been a helplessness continually appealing to his protection. There was nothing like helplessness and blond beauty to create appeal. Emily had seldom been right in those days, and there had never been a woman more anxious to marry an eligible older man, and by God, she had managed it. She had found him off balance and had kept him off balance. Anger was beneficial, given the proper time and place, and the beauty of it was that his wrath was cool and controlled. He smiled as brightly as Emily when he walked downstairs to the library.

Hal was at the table with the drinks and Alfred was passing appetizers, which the Bramhalls had refused, but it was different with Emily and Walter. In the first seconds of his entrance he saw that Harold had put on a dinner coat, presumably without having been told, and although the coat was tight for him because his shoulders had broadened during his time in the service, it fitted adequately, and Harold looked very well with the lawbooks from the Judge's library behind him, startlingly like his mother. All the diverse threads of personalities became wound together in a pre-dinner way when he entered. As he had often said, there were few greater ordeals than a conventional, semiformal dinner, demanding original conversation after you had been writing it all day. Emily gave him her most beaming smile, but her glance, he noticed, was worried. Her glance was telling him that she was already sorry for what had gone on upstairs, and Emily's fits of anger often smoothed out rapidly — but this evening he did not give a damn, nor did he give a further damn whether or not the Bramhalls knew that he and Emily had been quarreling.

"Oh, there you are, dear," Emily said, and if you wanted to analyze it, it was a hell of an obvious remark. Her glance was now pleading, but remembering what he had heard her say to Walter that morning, he ignored the overture. All he had to do was be himself.

"Hello, Marion dear," he said, as they embraced in the way that polite society now demanded of old friends of opposite sexes; and he thought, when he kissed her cheek, that she was putting on an extra layer of powder every year.

"Oh, Tom dear," Marion Bramhall said, "how wonderfully you look! I haven't seen you look so well in ages."

There was no time to recall the last age, but indeed, he and Marion had known each other for ages and ages and had made perfunctory conversation for ages and ages.

"It must be the country air," he said, "and the general bucolic atmosphere in which I live. Not that I am referring to you and Dick."

"Oh, we're bucolic too, this year," Marion said, "trimming hedges and setting out pansies and everything. It's given Dick a crick in the back. You must come to Bramma while the apple blossoms are still in bloom. There will be simply oceans of them this year. Do you remember when our yacht was named the *Bramma?*"

It was time to speak to Dick Bramhall and to forget the apple blossoms and the long departed yacht.

"Hello, Dick," he said. "It's wonderful to see you. It was a great thought of Em's to get us all together this way, and thanks a lot for motoring so far."

"It's wonderful to see you, Tommy," Dick Bramhall said. "Whenever I do, the journey's always worth while."

There was something about Dick Bramhall that was hard for him to understand, because of the different worlds in which they lived. Even through the veil of anger that still enshrouded him, Dick's speech both disturbed and moved him, because he knew that Dick had meant every word of it, and it was one of the few wholly honest expressions he had heard all day, not contrived, but exactly what it was, demanding no analysis. Dick had honestly meant that the journey was worth while, but the honesty was disturbing. It was still hard to see why Dick Bramhall should like him when they had never had much in common with each other.

"Dick," he said, "you're a damn nice guy."

He always spoke lines with Dick and Dick Bramhall never did. Dick's face resembled the others that stared from the financial pages of the *New York Times;* there was the same assurance of success, but there was also a subtle difference between Dick's and other photographic faces — a look of contentment, something wholly different from complacency, and the bewildering thing to Tom Harrow was that it was impossible to tell exactly what Dick had to be contented about, aside from finance.

"What can I get you to drink, Pops?" Harold asked.

He smiled at Harold.

"Make it a double Martini," he said. "I've got to catch up with the rest of you, and you remember how I want them, almost no vermouth."

He saw that Emily, who was standing beside Walter Price, was watching him, and he did not give a damn.

"Alfred," he said, "I don't know what's been planned in the way of wine, but if it isn't champagne, we'll have champagne."

"Darling," Emily said, "we're having roast beef."

It was a pleasure to show Emily that she was not always right.

"Let's not forget," he said, "that champagne goes with anything."

It might be interesting to think that when the champagne down in the cellar was used up, there might never be any more, and when he smiled at Emily, he was sure that the same thought had crossed her mind.

Harold handed him his cocktail and Dick Bramhall stared at it admiringly.

"That's about as pale as they come, isn't it?" he asked. "That's what they call an 'in and out,' isn't it?"

"Yes," Tom answered, "in the drinking, not in the hunting sense."

"If anybody fell off a horse into that," Marion Bramhall said, "he'd just stay in. There couldn't be any out."

"I didn't know you'd christened your place," Tom Harrow said. "Did I get it right? Is it called Bramma?"

"That's it," Dick said, "pronounced as in grammar. You get the significance, don't you?"

Dick's simplicity was disturbing because you never could be sure how simple he really was.

"Let me see if I can guess," Tom said. "Bram is for Bramhall; and Ma is for Marion. Am I right or am I right?"

"You got it," Dick said, "first crack out of the box, Tommy. You think it's simple, don't you?"

"Well," Tom said, "maybe it's a little simple, Dick, and Marion just reminded me that you had a boat called that once."

"I like the name," Dick said, "because you don't need a classical dictionary or anything."

You never could be quite sure whether Dick was serious or not, not after a double in-and-out Martini.

"That's right," Tom said, "only it sounds more like a yacht than a place."

"That's right," Dick said, "it does sound more like a yacht."

"Tom," Marion Bramhall said, "don't get him thinking about yachts, or else he'll buy another."

"I wish he would," Tom said. "I'm right down to my last one, personally. Hal, get moving and take the orders and get me another of those in-and-outs."

"Now, Tom," Marion Bramhall said, "if you ever get into another one of those, you never *will* get out."

"You watch me," Tom Harrow said. "If I've got in and out of two marriages, I can get out of a second double Martini, even at my age, dear."

There was a slightly offbeat silence, but Emily spoke promptly.

"Tom, darling," she said, "dinner will be ready any minute."

What annoyed him particularly was that he knew that Emily was less worried about the effect the double Martini might have on him than she was about the Bramhalls; and he was not taking any more from Emily, not any more at all. Moreover, the intensity of his anger had made the first Martini negligible.

"Have you ever noticed," he said, "that at some point when you want a cocktail, somebody's wife is always saying that dinner is just about to be ready? And then if it is ready, she says you can take it in with you. I don't like to take it in with me. Cocktails should be encapsulated. They should not go in to dinner outside you. Stir them cheerfully, Harold."

He listened to himself carefully while he was speaking. His syllables were accurate, but not exaggeratedly so. The first drink had been of no help and he was grateful for the other.

"I'm going to tell you something that I said to Dick about you the first time we met you — oh, years and years ago, wasn't it, Tom?" Marion Bramhall said. "At Palm Beach. And you don't look a day older, Tom, only more distinguished."

Her words put him in a warm and kindly mood toward everyone, excepting always Emily.

"I wish you'd come around more often, Marion," he said, "and tell me that every time."

"You don't have to," Dick said. "Everybody tells Tommy that."

"Well, anyway," Marion said, and he found himself thinking that the bluish rinse in her gray hair gave it a look not unlike the sunlight striking the Gulf Stream off Palm Beach when the weather was rough, "everyone was in quite a tizzy, asking everybody else if they had met the playwright, Mr. Harrow, and his perfectly lovely wife. And Prince Boris, that Russian who is always all over coconut oil at the Bath and Tennis Club, said he had met you often, and of course he hadn't, and of course he wasn't a prince. Well, anyway — no, thank you, Hal, I don't think I'll have another one."

She smiled sweetly. He had nearly forgotten that Marion was a talker, too. He would not need to talk to anybody during dinner, and after dinner Walter Price would take over. There was a real sector of usefulness in the world for talkers, and often they conjured up memories. He could see Palm Beach again and he could smell the sun-tan lotions at the Bath and Tennis Club, a different scent from Antibes, peculiarly but not unpleasantly American. It might be that Americans, because of their enlightened inflationary prosperity, were developing a national body odor. It was an interesting thought, but a mere parenthesis, because he had to follow Marion Bramhall as she made her point.

"Well, anyway," Marion was saying, "and please don't interrupt me, Dick. Dick always says I sound like someone in a Ring Lardner story when I've had a Martini, but I don't, do I? Well, anyway, when we met you and Rhoda, we clicked just like that, didn't we, and we always have ever since, haven't we? And I don't think any other four people in the world could have had more fun than we — well, used to have, on the yacht and things like that. Well, anyway, I said to Dick, you were the only man I had ever known who could use long words gracefully, in a rhythm like other words — just the way you used 'encapsulate' just now. When Dick uses a word like that, it's out of those old business reports of his. It isn't living language, and I adore living language."

"Tom, dear," Emily called, "here's Alfred looking very nervous. And it is roast beef, so why doesn't everyone take their drinks in with them?"

It was exasperating and typical of Emily, who was always listening and never hearing.

"No," he said, "don't let's take them in. Turn down an empty glass — not original with me, but with the *Rubáiyát*." And he found himself repeating the sentence in loud, sonorous tones: "Turn down an empty glass."

If he was not an actor, and he was very grateful that he was not, he still could not help picking up from actors the quality of compelling attention. Everyone listened as he repeated those last words, and he had forgotten, until the repetition, that they were hardly cheerful. He stood quietly while everyone filed into the dining room until he heard Emily giving directions for the seating. It was time for him to move and, like a courteous host, to pull out Marion Bramhall's chair, but he lingered, listening to the voices. The library was still again with the silence that could only emanate from a wall of books, and his Martini glass was empty in his hand. It was not bad symbolism. The glass in his own life had been full with a fullness he once thought would last forever, and now in another minute he would be asking himself again where it had all gone, and it would be fatal if he asked himself that again. He tossed the glass into the library fireplace. At least he had achieved one thing; he had not taken it in with him.

He could think and talk regardless of his thoughts. The conditioning of a hundred dinner parties made the meal run smoothly. Emily respected him at dinners, because he had taught her what she knew about the amenities of a well-set table. He could still recall with a twinge of pain her ideas of a good meal and of a proper selection of dishes during the first months of their marriage. They had been derived from recipes in women's magazines and from colored advertisements sponsored by mayonnaise and mustard companies. If he had known Emily's taste for salads, he might never have married her at all; but she had listened to him in those days, and now the table was beautiful, the roast beef rare, the brown potatoes and the string beans perfect, the lettuce and water cress salad meticulously stirred, and the Bel Paese cheese exactly right. It was the couple, of course, but Emily had given the orders, and it was Emily who had ordered the three-pronged forks and the rattail spoons and the pistol-handled knives. It was Emily who had ordered the Crown Derby china. At least he had taught her a respect for possessions and the Crown Derby and the George the Second candlesticks and the George the Second bowl with its flower arrangement might all fetch more than he had paid for them when they went on sale in New York. The table was beautiful and mannered, but he could regard it, like the house, as a phase in his life that was over, and would there be any more phases? He was glad for the double Martinis, since it was not necessary to search for an answer to the question. And the champagne was very dry — a '47 vintage.

"A delightful wine year," he heard Walter say to Emily and Richard at the other end of the table, "what I would call an amusing year. As I may have told you, winetasting has always been my pet diversion, ever since I convalesced from my wound near Bordeaux during World War I. At that time I could do a very creditable blindfold act with the clarets. In fact, one evening at that dear old restaurant, the Chapon Fin, while dining very informally with, if I may say so, several of the outstanding wine-growers of the district . . ."

The '47 vintage, if amusing, was so cold and good that it rebuked him for the Martinis in the library. You ought to respect wine and not allow your senses to be dulled by gin. When he had been with Rhoda at Antibes, he would have been outraged at the thought of a Martini. When was it he had taken them up? It was the war, of course, and nobody in America, or in Palm Beach, any longer seriously cared about wine and food.

Plain living and high thinking could have been significant substitutes, but it occurred to him, just as Alfred was refilling his glass, that there was neither plain living nor high living in America. Instead, national life was approaching an average that expressed itself in gastronomical and in spiritual mediocrity, and he had always hated mediocrity. At least the dining room and the table, and the champagne, though representing set conventions, were hardly in that realm; but they, too, would all soon be engulfed in the wave of the commonplace. The house, no doubt, would eventually house tourists or a dental clinic. No one could escape from convention for long, not even James Joyce. It was advisable to accept the mores of one's time, no matter if they shifted. It was better to be in tune, like Dick Bramhall, with the beat of marching music.

He must have been speaking while he was thinking because he found himself smiling at Marion Bramhall.

"Tell me," he asked her, "have you seen Rhoda lately?"

It was the gin plus the champagne that had released his subconscious enough to make him ask, but Marion was not embarrassed. If she was nothing else, as she always said, she was a tolerant, noninquisitive person who realized that, just because a lot of her friends could not make the wonderful go of marriage that she and Dick had achieved, there was no reason to take sides or be a voice of experience. On the contrary, it was more imperative than ever to be more friendly and gentler with these unfortunates, while being more grateful than ever that everything had been so wonderful between her and Dick. Oh, naturally, there had been troubles (what married couple did not have difficulties?), but she and Dick had been fortunate enough to worry through theirs. That name of their place in New Hampshire, Bramma, was an example in a nutshell of how she and Dick worked things out. By that she meant that Bramhall came first and Ma came second — most of the time, but not all of the time. She would not say she was a feminist or anything like that, but now and then she did have to put her foot down. She could not even tell how she and Dick had contrived to make a go of their marriage. All she could say was that associations seemed to grow

186

and maybe that was all there was to a happy marriage. However, there had been enough friction, thank goodness, now and then, to cause her never to be censorious, but only very, very understanding about others. Tom saw her looking at him now in a very understanding way, as a friend and counselor should — a friend of both, of course.

"Yes, Tom," she said, "Dick and I still see as much as we possibly can of Rhoda — of them — just as we try to see as much as we can of you and Emily."

"Yes," Tom said, "You don't need to explain, Marion. I appreciate your and Dick's position, and you've both been wonderful."

"Tom, I'm so glad you think so," Marion said, "and you do understand, don't you, that Dick and I love each of you for your own characters, of course, just as much as we ever did when things were the way they used to be."

The candlelight was reflected on her blue-gray hair.

"Of course I understand, Marion," he said. "You and Dick have been swell."

"Oh," she said, "that's sweet of you to say, but Dick and I haven't done anything, really, except just love the people we love."

The conversation had reached dead center, and he felt powerless to turn the wheel of talk.

"I know how much Rhoda used to love you and Dick, Marion," he said. "Well, how is Rhoda?"

Marion paused with that judicial impartiality characteristic of friends of severed couples.

"She's looking beautiful, Tom," she said, "but not so — how shall I say it? — happily comfortable as Emily."

He glanced at her, but her eyes were guileless and her expression sympathetic, exactly the right expression for one who understood that there were two sides to every question.

"I'm glad she hasn't changed," he said. "Rhoda was always beautiful, and she never was the comfortable type, at least not with me very often, but I can't blame her."

"I know you can't, dear," Marion Bramhall said, "and I'm going to tell you something that may be talking out of school. Rhoda

187

knows you've never blamed her, and I think that's made her very happy."

"All right," he said, "just so long as it doesn't make her comfortably happy. Does she still wear the emerald I gave her? I hope she does sometimes."

"Yes," Marion said. "Let me see — yes, I'm sure she does sometimes."

"I used to try to compete in those days," he said, "but you can't compete with oil wells. And there's a difference between me and an oil well. I don't get a tax allowance for depletion. Rhoda noticed things like depletion."

Mrs. Bramhall raised her blue-gray eyebrows.

"I think that's being a little hard on Rhoda, dear," she said. "I know what you mean, and Dick and I have always understood your point of view, and how wonderfully generous you were about Rhoda, but we also understand Rhoda's side, too. Rhoda was always concerned with security, and I do think she was once a little immature, the way she used to worry, but she isn't worried now."

"Well," Tom said, "that's fine. Rhoda always knew what she wanted."

Marion Bramhall nodded slowly and judicially, the tolerant mediator who had seen so many forms of human frailty that criticism vanished, giving place to great compassion.

"Yes, she did and does," she said, "and I suppose that was a little of the reason for what went wrong between you. Rhoda always knew so definitely what she wanted, and you never did know for sure; and you never do quite now, do you, dear? Dick and I were talking it over only the other day. It isn't a criticism, only a comment, made because Dick and I love you, and that restiveness of yours, that never being sure, is what has kept your talent so wonderful and youthful."

He was weary of talent, and he wished that he might never have to listen again about it from people who could not know what it meant. He wanted to be alone, but he could not be alone. Alfred was refilling his glass, and after all, there was nothing like good champagne. It was occasionally called the beverage of the parvenu, an artificially charged wine that had none of the subtle strength of a fine Burgundy — but neither had Burgundy the gaiety, the power of partially restoring youth or of resurrecting memory. It was the champagne, of course, that made him say what he did, although he did not feel the slightest trace of intoxication.

"I don't know whether you're right or not," he said, "but I do know I always wanted Rhoda."

Immediately he realized that it was a gauche piece of self-revelation, and the Bramhalls, on their drive back home, would analyze that true confession. The first love was always the best love, that happily adjusted couple would be saying — and it could be they were right.

"Let's skip it, Marion," he said. "I shouldn't have said that, and please remember I was speaking in the past tense. I said I wanted Rhoda; that doesn't mean I want her now."

She smiled at him with an old friend's understanding.

"Of course you don't," she said, "not with Emily. Dick and I were just saying, driving over, how beautifully things had worked out with you and Emily. We were concerned at first, not knowing Emily. We didn't realize that she has just the restful charm you need and that lovely, buoyant good-nature that makes her so good for you."

He glanced toward Emily at the end of the table at just the moment that Emily looked toward him, and she smiled timidly and he raised his glass to her.

"We're saying very wonderful things about you, my dear," he said, and turned back to Marion Bramhall. "I think you're right," he said. "On the whole, Emily has been good for me. You can tell these things, can't you, just by looking? For instance, it's obvious that you've been good for Dick."

"Oh, dear," she said, "I hope I have, but not all that Dick deserves."

"No one ever does get all he deserves," he said. "The game isn't rigged that way."

"Oh, Tom," she said, "don't be ironical."

"I'm sorry," he said, "but I don't know whether anybody is

189

meant to get back all he gives, and maybe it isn't right to expect it. It's fine if it happens, of course."

"But, Tom," she said. He had forgotten how much she loved earnest, interesting conversation. "What about casting your bread upon the waters?"

He laughed. He did not feel in the least like a serious conversation, not on the surface, anyway; but underneath his thoughts were somber and it was necessary to keep on with the champagne in order to be good company.

"In my experience," he said, "every time I have tried to cast it on the water, some girl has got in the way. Come to think of it, my whole life has been devoted to casting bread upon the girls."

"Oh, Tom," she said, "you say such incorrigible, naughty things! I hope that Rhoda — oh dear, I mean Emily of course — I hope that Emily keeps a notebook and jots them down."

"If she did," he said, "it might be very good for Emily."

Marion called across the table. It was obviously time for her to talk to Walter Price before she and Emily moved into the other room.

"Dick," she called, "did you hear what Tom said? He said that he's spent all his life casting bread upon the girls."

For a split second Dick Bramhall's face was a blank, but then he laughed as uproariously as though it had been a Shavian line out of *My Fair Lady*.

"He says every time he tries to cast his bread upon the water, some gal gets in the way," Marion Bramhall said, but Dick had already got it.

As a matter of fact, it was possible to go on with it, now that the conversation was general.

"It's like Marineland in Florida," Tom said. "Did I ever take you there in your childhood, Hal? Or maybe it wasn't built in your childhood?"

"All right," Dick Bramhall said, "why is it like Marineland?"

"At feeding time," Tom said, "you can't see the loaves for the fishes. There's a man who comes up with a pailful of food and every time he tries to throw it on the water, a dolphin jumps up, or maybe it's a porpoise. The point is, nothing ever gets cast upon the water."

"Don't you think you're getting a little mixed up, darling?" Emily said.

"No, my sweet," he called to her down the table. "I mix my drinks, but never metaphors."

Hal was on his left and now all effort was over, because he could talk to Hal.

"Hal," he said, "you've been a good boy tonight. Thanks for mixing the drinks, and thanks for not going out."

"Oh, that's all right," Hal said. "My mother wouldn't have liked it if I'd walked out on the Bramhalls. Of course I had to miss tossing a French roll at your old schoolmate's daughter."

"That makes a rather nice rhyme, doesn't it?" Tom said. "Cast your bread upon the water, you're bound to hit a schoolmate's daughter."

"I don't see how you do it," Hal said.

"Do what?"

"Get along with everybody," Hal said, "and seem to have a damn good time. Get along with Mrs. Bramhall, for instance."

"It just takes time, boy," Tom said, "and intestinal fortitude. Maybe she'll ask you to call her Aunt Marion before they take off for home. I wonder why Emily doesn't move. Damn it, she always talks and never ends these things."

"Well, my mother does like Mrs. Bramhall," Hal said.

"Of course your mother likes her," Tom said. "Marion's the securest woman I know."

He glanced at Marion. Her tanned shoulder was now turned toward him and she was talking securely with Walter Price. Tom had a twinge of conscience about what he had said, for criticizing a guest broke a law of hospitality that was as old as the conventions in Frazer's *Golden Bough*.

"I don't seem to get anywhere with her," Hal said. "There doesn't seem to be any place to start. Maybe it's my extreme youth."

"I wouldn't let it worry you," Tom said. On the surface he was feeling cheerful and the somber mood had retired further into

191

the background. "It saves an enormous lot of trouble if you don't get anywhere with married women, and the worst of it is, it's usually pretty easy to get somewhere."

"Say," Hal said, "you're in pretty good form tonight. The play must have gone well or something."

"Boy," Tom said, "you can only do the best you can. Even when you're running out of the chips, you'd better toss in as many as you can. I wish Emily would get up. By God, she did it! There she goes."

"Tom," Emily called in her merry voice, "shall we all go in together, or do you want your brandy and coffee here?"

"We'll stay here for a little while," Tom said, "only to maintain a shred of convention."

"Well, don't drink brandy indefinitely," Emily said, and he saw that she was looking at him pleadingly. "Just bear in mind that women are people."

"My dear," Tom said, "I have given that proposition a lot of thought for years and years, and there's a chance that you may be right."

He could tell that he had hurt her by the way her eyes widened, but no one else had noticed. Everyone laughed and Emily joined the laughter.

"Emily," Marion Bramhall said, "is he always like a walking play?"

"Always," Tom said, "when he isn't flat on his face and when it isn't a musical."

It stung him, the expression "a walking play," because it was not such a bad summing-up. He thought, as the men sat down again and drew their chairs nearer, that all that was left to him might very well be a few light lines; that all of what critics called significance was gone, if there had been any. He felt like an empty glass, which, when hit, might give forth a melodious note, but which still held nothing. But then, what was significance? He was tired of the word. He was thinking of a statement attributed to O'Neill, that all drama must be tragic. O'Neill probably never would have been so didactic, but Tom could understand what was meant, and now he was playing tragedy.

192

"Brandy, sir?" Alfred asked.

"Yes, thanks," he said. "You'd better change your mind and try some, Dick. It's London Dock, 1906. I bought four cases of it once. It's the only intelligent thing I've ever done with money."

"Dear old Tommy," Walter said.

It annoyed him when Walter called him "dear old Tommy," but he smiled, and there was no need to answer, because Walter was talking to Dick Bramhall.

"Tommy's and my friendship is not quite so old as this brandy," Walter was saying, "but I love to think it is as sound, mellow, and honest. I don't know whether I told you, Mr. Bramhall, how I first encountered Tom. It was at a summer stock theatre, just at the very dawn of the movement, and Tommy was just a college boy, but I've always had an eye for stature. It has always given me pleasure to recall that I was one of the first to recognize greatness in dear old Eugene. I had casually stopped off for the night in Provincetown, and there was dear old Eugene."

"Eugene who?" Richard Bramhall asked.

"Oh, I beg pardon," Walter Price said, "it was absent-minded of me. Eugene O'Neill, of course. Those were the days of brilliant, literate theatre. Tommy would be very angry were I to compare him with Eugene, and the divergence of their works makes comparison impossible, but one cannot avoid feeling the lion's paw."

"Wait a minute," Tom Harrow said, "what's that again?"

"The lion's paw," Walter Price said, "but maybe that is a bad word for it. Let me rather say sense for impact, and you do have a sense for impact, Tommy."

"Hal," Tom Harrow said, "pass Mr. Price the brandy."

The brandy was unnecessary. When Walter was in a certain condition, he was apt to recount his experiences in discovering genius, and over the years there were several occasions when he had discovered Harrow, and the wording was always the same.

"I sensed it," Walter said, "the instant the curtain rose on that skit of Tommy's in that horrible rustic theatre. The seats had been sheer torture, but when the curtain rose I might have been ensconced on foam rubber. I sensed stature and I turned to dear

193

old Arthur Higgins. I have forgotten why Arthur was there, and it honestly does not matter, but I can remember what I said to Arthur as though it were yesterday. 'Arthur,' I said, 'here is God's latest gift.'"

There was moisture in Walter's eyes, and no doubt he believed that he had said it.

"And I said the same thing to Eugene later in the week," Walter said. "'Eugene,' I said, 'I'm never going to lose sight of Tommy,' and from that day to this, I haven't ever, have I, Tommy?"

Tom Harrow stood up.

"You're damned well right you haven't," he said. "Well, let's go in and see the girls."

He led the way across the hall, opening the door to the large sitting room with its worn Oriental carpet, and stood while the others walked past him, wishing that he did not so frequently see life in terms of theatrical dimension. Granted that theatre, if it was good, was a distillation of life, the two were not interchangeable. There was always exaggeration in the theatre, and necessarily insincerities gave an illusion of truth. No living people were ever so good or so bad as those who spoke the lines.

He had been dealing all his life with the delicate fabrics of make-believe. His mind could touch them as the fingers of a connoisseur could touch the glazes of Chinese porcelain and judge their weights and values, but he was weary of exaggeration. For years there was always someone to laugh dutifully when he exercised his wit, but in the end, unless you were a moron, you had to know yourself. There was always someone as fulsome as Walter Price and a few more intelligently so, but he could weigh the exaggeration, and it was as cloying that evening as the champagne. He had drunk too much of it, and yet, like the champagne, it was buoyant to the spirit.

Never in the world had Walter Price said to Arthur Higgins that he saw stature in that summer theatre; but there had been stature of a sort. There was always the parable of the talents in authors he had known. Some buried them, some used them, but could anyone really help what he did about talent? Talent was a variable, merging on one side into skill and approaching genius on the other, changing from day to day, from year to year, in quality and content. You could not cultivate talent like hothouse lettuce or keep it sterile like a commercial orchid. Talent was one of the most indefinable things in the world, and closest in the world to God. There it was and there it wasn't and there it was again.

You could ask the same question about it that the county fair gambler used to pose when he placed the walnut shell over the pea in the shell game: "Where is the little joker now?" The little joker was not around at present. The Martinis and champagne and brandy had not conjured him up, but there had been something once. Then he heard Emily calling to him in the patient, cheery voice every good American wife must use when publicly addressing a recalcitrant husband, and he had the impression that this might be the second time she had called him.

"Tom," she called, "what are you thinking about, standing there all alone?"

"I was thinking," he said, "where's the little joker now?"

"What?" she asked, and the question made him aware that perhaps the drinks were catching up with him.

"It doesn't matter," he said. "He must be up somebody else's sleeve by now, not mine."

He saw Emily glance at the Bramhalls, soliciting their understanding, and there was no reason whatsoever for her to solicit anything from the Bramhalls.

"Well, why don't you join us?" Emily said. "We're lonely over here."

"I'm just about to, my sweet," he said. "I was just admiring the composition, and there's only one thing lacking in the picture. Hal, ask Alfred to bring in the drinks. Maybe you'd better get out there and help, in case Alfred's getting tired."

"Aye, aye, sir," Hal said, and he sounded nearly like regular Navy.

Then, while he was still standing in the doorway, he saw that Emily was crossing the room toward him, and her dress had the reproving swish of the evening dress of a good American wife who realized that it was just a little too late to keep on being tolerant.

"Tom," she whispered, and her whisper also had a reproving swish, "please come over here; we've all had enough to drink. Walter is sound asleep."

He put his hands in the side pockets of his dinner coat and gazed at Emily steadily.

"Lucky Walter," he said, "so long as he doesn't snore."

He was thinking, poor Emily; she had bet wrong, and there was nowhere else to go.

"Tom," she whispered, "please."

"Yes," he said, "yes, Emily." After all, the Bramhalls were there, friends to both of them and friends to Rhoda and friends to Presley, and there was nothing so unpardonable as rudeness to a guest. "Yes, my dear," he said.

It was true; Walter was sound asleep in the same chair he had been sleeping in very late that afternoon. For a moment Walter looked like a preview of the brave world of tomorrow, and, in spite of all precautions, Tom felt a twinge of fear. Ten years from now, would he be like Walter? He smiled at Mrs. Bramhall in his most disarming way.

"We were just having a domestic conversation about Walter," he said. "My idea is not to chivvy him as long as he doesn't snore."

"That's perfect," Marion answered. "Do you know what I was just whispering to Dick? I was just whispering that something delightful always happens at Tom's."

"But Price was right," Dick said, "you have got stature, Tom."

"Thanks for saying that, Dick," he said.

"Now, next time," Dick said, "next time you and Emily have positively got to come up to Bramma."

"We will," Tom said, "we'd love to, Dick." And he felt himself emerging from the world of make-believe.

"Marion," Dick Bramhall said, "I guess we'd better think about shoving off. Henry's driving us, and you know how Henry gets when he stays out too late."

"Oh, dear," Marion said, "yes, I'd forgotten about Henry. We've got to go. Tom, kiss me good night."

It was over, and, as he often felt at the end of a dinner party, he had been through a miniature life cycle, and, thank God, it was over.

"I think they had a good time," Emily said, "don't you, Tom?"

"Yes," he said, "I think so."

"Well," she said, "I'm going up to bed. Aren't you, Tom?"

"No," he said. "Hal's gone after drinks. I want another drink."

"Oh, Tom," she said, "you know how you'll feel in the morning. Tom, please stop being cross — and I'm sorry for what I said."

"Let's not have a post-mortem," he said. "Poor little Em. Now run upstairs to bed. Here comes Hal with the drinks."

"Good night, dear," Emily said. "Good night, Hal, you've been a real lifesaver."

She was still walking up the stairs when Tom nodded to the library.

"Bring the tray in there, Hal," he said, "and let Walter sleep, and give me a Scotch-and-soda."

"Be careful, or you'll tie one on," Hal said.

When he sat down in the leather armchair owned once by the Judge, the glass in his hand felt heavy and he felt tired.

"Never mix whiskey, gin, and champagne," he said. "It's funny, isn't it, how I always do the wrong thing? But don't you do it, boy. Never you mix whiskey, gin, and champagne; and now let's skip it. Did you telephone your mother? Did you tell her I'd be over tomorrow afternoon?"

"Yes," Hal said. "I told her you'd be over about four."

"You drive me over, will you?"

"I told you," Hal said, "that she wants to see you alone."

"Never mix whiskey, gin, and champagne," Tom said. "But how can you help it? You have to take everything as it comes, and some things are whiskey, and others are gin, and others champagne. Well, it'll be nice to see her again, just for a change, I mean."

"I wish you'd tell me sometime," Hal said, "what happened between you and my mother. No one ever tells a kid those things."

"Listen," Tom said, "nobody ever tells anybody else much of anything. You'd better go wake up Price now and get him on his feet and upstairs, and don't let him get in here. That's a good boy, Hal."

The library lights were soft and the room was almost as silent as the library had been in the Judge's house. All his worst thoughts were returning, but he had to face them eventually. All the disconnected questions were coming back. Where was the little joker now? Where had everything gone? And once again he knew that he had once had everything. People like himself could not help but be aware of it. He knew that he had once had something, if not everything, when he first met Rhoda Browne, and that was a long way from anywhere — and the funny part of it was, he needn't have met her; but that was true with almost everything. You needn't have done almost everything you did, but you could never separate the need-not from the want-to of the moment.

XIII

The Play Might Get to Broadway — and Never Mind the Girls

THERE was always a beginning to everything, which was not as trite as it sounded, considering how a lot of playwrights he had known could hash up a beginning. He had been interviewed by members of the press and by staff writers for periodicals far more frequently than he cared to remember. There was, he perceived, after the first flush of his success, a horrid similarity in journalistic thought. They actually always asked about the same things as those recent adolescents from the *Lectern*, and he had spent endless hours saying the same things brightly. One of the oldest chestnuts was the inevitable question of what had started him writing plays, and this was a silly question. You started writing plays because you had to do something. He could have phrased a better question. When did he first have the knowledge that he had a gift of quality not possessed by anybody else?

He first had an idea regarding quality in his sophomore year at college, which was an archaic period, now that it was becoming difficult for him to realize that any moment in the past had once been a new and glittering present. There were still surface trolleys in his sophomore year, and he still could remember the crackling of blue sparks that came from the overhead wires, but trolleys were nearing extinction now. There had been people then who jacked up their cars during the winter months because of the wear-and-tear of unplowed city and suburban streets. True, there was prohibition, but there were several reputable college bootleggers, much less aggressive than present purveyors of Scotch and bourbon. Believe it or not, the radio was in its infancy and there were even individuals who used earphones and crystal sets. In the gay and roaring twenties, as they called them now, there was still a veneer of good manners and the last dim echo of Edwardianism. He should have known that even in the Coolidge era the world was breaking away from its old security, but of course he had been too young to care.

Motion pictures were still silent in his sophomore year at college, and there were only vague reports of sound, which one received with incredulity. You could sit in a moving-picture house in those days and see restful, silent, flickering film, and hear only the playing of a piano that followed the pictorial mood. Now it was voices, voices, voices — coming out of radios, out of TV's, out of public and private address systems — until he was beginning to develop a detestation for human speech. How different it had been when the motion pictures were muted, and how infinitely desirable! And when you were tired of the film, there would be trick dogs or a juggling act or illustrated songs. Time was marching on, and how time had marched! Nobody played a piano in a movie house any more, except occasionally in the Museum of Modern Art to the tittering sophistication of young people who did not know what Theda Bara and Francis X. Bushman had meant to the youth of another more charming era.

And there had been private charities in those days. There were living then people who were even so backward as to possess what was called a "sense of social obligation" and what is now generally termed "free social guilt." There were efforts, pathetic and abortive in view of the enormously intelligent efforts of the present, to bring culture, good behavior and good fellowship into the less privileged areas of our cities. And from such efforts sprang an institution known as a "settlement house," a term now becoming as obsolescent as the trolley car. But in his sophomore year, settlement houses still possessed a novel social significance and also a note of social hope.

Doubtless settlement houses still existed in underprivileged neighborhoods, but the emphasis was changed and the social workers who once staffed them had moved long ago into fields where their enthusiasms could blossom into something more closely approaching a Messiah complex. The spirit of philanthropy had now assumed a professionalism which had only existed in rudimentary forms during his sophomore year at college. Doubtless there were still volunteers who ventured to be big brothers and to organize basketball games and dances, calculated to tempt children off the streets, but guidance clinics and marriage counsel clinics were taking the place of mere entertainment. Back in his sophomore year, a number of his contemporaries gave up one or two evenings a week to help out in settlement houses, and one of them was Garrison Wilkes, who also rowed number five on the second crew and played basketball in the winter.

Garry, as his friends called him in those days, was already developing qualities of leadership that carried him far up in the WPA and eventually to important posts in foreign aid. From his earlier years he had evinced an intense desire to help other people and this had always struck Tom Harrow as an admirable attribute. Yet at the risk of being critical (and there was nothing so devastating or so useless as nonconstructive criticism), it was apparent now that it had never occurred to Garrison Wilkes that anyone might have different desires and drives from his own, and this gave him a fine assurance that led to qualities of leadership.

"Now, fellows," Garrison used to say, and it never sounded embarrassing when Garrison addressed a group as "fellows," "it will do you good and give you a fine feeling inside to do something for other people, and fellows, we need more help down at Fellowship House. There's a fine group of boys and girls there who want fun and exercise as much as you and I, and every Tuesday night is entertainment night at Fellowship House. Who's going to get on the entertainment team? How about it, Tommy?"

In the light of the present there was an element of pathos in that appeal. It contained none of the resounding words that one heard so often later, such as "underprivilege" or "inequity." It was only a suggestion that one should share something, and Tom Harrow would have gone much earlier to an entertainment night

201

at Fellowship House if it had not happened that every time Garrison Wilkes appealed to his better nature there was something else he had to do.

"How about it, Tommy?" Garrison kept saying. "You'll get a real thrill out of it if you think up a skit or something. It doesn't take much to entertain those kids, and you'll get a real thrill out of it, Tommy. Say, you can be the life of the party — just an imitation or any kind of a skit."

One of Tom's greatest troubles had always been that he could not say "No" indefinitely, and eventually he found himself in Fellowship House on entertainment night.

He could remember the place distinctly. Years ago the large and shabby brick house on a shabby South End square must have been a prosperous, Victorian dwelling. The walnut woodwork and doors, and the parquet floor of the big front parlor that could be made into a schoolroom, a game room or gymnasium, was still in fair condition. He could remember the unwashed atmosphere, the lack of ventilation and the suspicious faces of the neighborhood boys and girls. He was standing beside a piano, and it was the first time he had ever wondered in this particular way whether or not the journey was worth his while. It was the first time that he had experienced such a fervent wish that he might be anywhere else. Truthfully, he was afraid of those unwashed teenagers who were watching him.

Burt Hewitt was the boy who had been roped in to play the piano, and it was no help to Tom to observe that Burt was also nervous. Neither of them should have come and they had rehearsed for only half an hour what they were going to do; but it was too late now with Garrison Wilkes's voice ringing through the room.

"We have a real treat this evening, folks," Garrison Wilkes said, "and as long as we keep everything on a first-name basis at Fellowship House — this is Burt, who's going to accompany Tommy over here on the piano, but Tommy isn't going to sing. Tommy's going to do something else."

Then a girl's voice interrupted from somewhere in the middle of that watchful room.

"Gee," the girl's voice said, "I wish he'd do it to me."

He had never been able to explain why the indignant reddening of Garrison Wilkes's face should have amused him as much as it did. Then he discovered that he had taken over instead of Garrison Wilkes. For the first time in his life he knew what it was like to have the feel of an audience.

"Whoever made that remark is a very intelligent girl," he said, "and I hope she'll be waiting after the show."

He had never been a good actor in spite of his experience with the stage, but he could understand an actor's urge and ability to move outside himself.

"We are going to endeavor to give you," he said, "a short motion-picture show without a film, but only with sight and sound effects. It's about a poor but honest girl named Louise. Start the music going, Burt."

Stage sense was only instinctive and most of it included holding mass attention and forming a collective mood.

"On this particular evening," he was saying, "this poor but honest girl is sitting before the briskly burning logs in a humble cabin in the Kentucky mountains, watching as she wishes in the flames."

Burt did not do badly with the music. The chords were appropriate when he drew a matchbox from his pocket and lighted a single match. Do it wrong, and it would be nothing. Do it right, with just the proper elaboration, and you could get them. He knew before it came that the laughter would be right. It was the first time that he had ever dreamed of the delight that came of controlling mass reaction. He knew that the rest of what he was doing did not matter because they were all with him. The main thing was not to hold a mood too long, and the only point to the memory was that he knew that he was good and that not everyone could do what he was doing, evoking a girl out of a background of tin-pan music, moving up a halfbreed villain and an honest trapper, and finally bringing in the Canadian Mounted Police.

Considering the importance of what had happened to him, his sequence of recollection was surprisingly dim. In fact, he was unable to recall whether or not his admirer had waited for him after the show was over — probably not, considering that Garrison Wilkes was there. You could afford to lose money, children, women, and reputation as long as you did not lose belief in self. At least in the theatre this was so, and in that single evening he had been called into the theatre's service. There would be plenty of times when he would wish he had not been, but the addiction was already there.

There had been three of them there that night, Garrison, Burt and himself, thrown together without design; but their destinies must have already been written. Not one of the three of them could have turned out much differently from what they had, because of built-in qualities. The last he had heard of Garrison, Garrison had been trying to teach the principles of irrigation to a group of nomads in the vicinity of the River Tigris, who preferred to continue as nomads. When it came to Burt, he had always been one of those piano players whose rendering of nostalgic popular songs covered up his intellectual deficiency. They had met, not so long before, at a class reunion and their badges with their names on them had not been necessary, and Burt had played the piano at the drop of a hat and had kept on playing it until five in the morning.

"Say, Tommy," he had said, "do you remember how you panicked them at that Fellowship House? Come on over to the piano and let's put that act on again."

"Burt," he had answered, "I wouldn't mind, but I honestly don't remember it. It was quite a while ago."

There were some things that one should remember and some far better to forget.

Delightfully enough, Rhoda had never asked him how he had started writing plays. When he had first seen her, he was three years out of college, earning fifty dollars a week doing odd jobs in New York for the Sullivan and Herrick dramatic agency. There were still a few thousand dollars from his father's estate, enough for him to draw on occasionally to buy good clothes and to pay the dues of a New York club. He was at a crossing of the ways that summer, but he had finished the first draft of his first comedy, *Hero's Return*. Only a day or two before he met Rhoda, the Arthur Higgins office had taken the play and had paid him a thousand-dollar cash advance, and in spite of this, there was no way of knowing at the end of June 1928 that *Hero's Return* was going to hit the jackpot. He knew he was good, but he did not know how good, and neither did Rhoda Browne.

Rhoda was one girl at least who had never asked him how he started writing *Hero's Return*, or whether or not he wrote when the inspiration moved him. It was a relief that Rhoda, frankly, had never cared, because she was the kind of girl who accepted things from life without thinking or asking much about circumstances. But there was one question that she had often asked him, the beguiling question that one could only ask and answer when one was in love.

"Tommy," was the way her favorite question went, "what did you think when you first saw me that morning on Dock Street?"

"Why," he always told her, "when I saw you, my mind was a perfect blank, except I thought you looked lousy, Rhoda."

That was the sort of joke that could once bring the house down, given the suitable time and place. She had a way of smiling — and this was one of the first things that he had noticed about her — that gave her face mirth and expression without cracking it into pieces. There never had been anything perfunctory, up to the very last, when Rhoda smiled. There was something in this usual display of pleasure that had always appealed to him, as well as most other men; and he had seen a lot of smiles in his time.

Everyone, particularly women, unless the women were angry at him, had, it seemed, smiled at him ever since, but then, smiles were an American custom. Pictorially, everyone had to smile in America until finally, like President Eisenhower, they began laughing photogenically. Everyone had to smile in the American theatre or when the light bulbs flashed at the Stork or El Morocco, or whatever it was that light bulbs did when a Very Important agency was publicizing a moist yet kissproof lipstick, or a new dentifrice, or a foam-rubber mattress, or, best of all, one of those automobiles that were getting to be as flat as pancakes. Everybody except dentists explaining toothbrushes smiled at everything. They smiled when they applied paste to their teeth; they smiled when they finally realized that various nationally advertised ingredients could rid them of excess perspiration and body odor. They smiled when they were suffering from mal-de-mer on the rear decks of cruise ships. One had to smile, even though the Caribbean, the Mediterranean and the Aegean, where burning Sappho loved and sang, were usually as turbulent as the British Channel. You had to smile because everything, including electric toasters and diaper services, was so enlightened in America.

The smiling problem was difficult for a woman, who now had to smile in a prefabricated way, with an elaborate dental finish, and when she smiled, her freshly polished teeth had to be in a conventional dental juxtaposition; and her lips, freshly kissproofed with a lipstick that would not come off no matter how hard she tried, had to be entirely symmetrical. Also, any good American woman, housewife or mother, when she smiled, had to have exquisitely but informally plucked eyebrows, and at the same time she had to roll her eyes sideways in a roguish but not immodest manner. She had to be Pollyanna, the Glad Girl, even when she was in her girdle, or when the electrician came to fix the stove. It was immoral to admire a cross girl, and most cross girls knew it. But when Rhoda smiled, self-making pancakes did not matter, or vacuum cleaners — but why go on with it? Rhoda instinctively knew how to smile.

"You don't have to tell me how I looked," Rhoda used to say. "I didn't care how I looked."

"Oh yes, you did," he said.

"Only in a perfunctory way," Rhoda used to answer. "But what did you think? You know your mind never is a perfect blank."

It was a pleasure to try to recall what he had thought, though the effort made him sadder now, but it was still a pleasure.

"Well," he said, "I thought the old town wasn't what it used to be. And what did you think when you saw me?"

"Well, if you really want to know," Rhoda used to say, "I said to myself that here was someone who might save me from a fate worse than death. Don't be hurt, dear. You can't possibly understand because you've never been so mobile downwards, and besides, you looked perfectly beautiful, carelessly beautiful, I mean. You looked as though you'd won the game. It's funny, I've never seen you look exactly that way again, and you've won so many games."

There was every reason why he should have looked that way and perhaps one did look so only once, because there was always a first game which was different from all the others. He had finished his draft of *Hero's Return*, which must have been good because Mr. Arthur Higgins had paid out a one-thousand-dollar advance on it, and that was something that happened only once to anybody.

Mr. Mort Sullivan had handled the deal but he had been noncommittal about the script. Sullivan and Herrick, shortly before Tom had gone to work there, had moved their offices to the third floor of the Ledyard Building on Park Avenue in order to get Broadway out of his hair, as Mortimer used to say. It was the damnedest thing, he used to say, how young playwrights and even a number of intelligent producers could never distinguish a dramatic agency, solely devoted to handling the problems of playwrights, from a theatrical agency that handled actors, actresses, vaudeville turns and prestidigitators. If you were near Broadway — and he still missed looking across that street to Times Square — all the delightful people who were out of a job were always in your waiting room. It did no good to point out that the firm of Sullivan and Herrick was a dramatic agency. It always turned out that these delightful people — and there were more delightful people in the theatre district than anywhere else in the world — had dropped in just because Sullivan and Herrick was a dramatic agency. And Mort, who remembered them when, and was so successful handling plays, would know if there was a part for them in one of those new plays he was marketing and would put in a word for them just for old times' sake. There were no people in the world more time-consuming than actors and actresses when at liberty, and this was why he had finally made the move to the small office in the Ledyard Building on Park Avenue.

Actors and actresses, he had discovered after years of delightful associations with them, had developed an instinctive reluctance to move far from the theatre district, and only about half as many came to the Ledyard Building as used to come to the old shop off Times Square, and thus only half the time was consumed in brushing them off. He had tried, in decorating the new offices, to indicate in a tactful way that this was a literary dramatic agency. Mort Sullivan had not been able to bear the removal from the walls of his private office of autographed photographs of old friends and of old sets of old plays he had handled, but he had been very careful to make the outer reception room courteously uncomfortable. And here it had been Tom Harrow's duty to learn a lot about the theatre by being polite, but firm, when he told theatrical people who were at liberty that Mr. Sullivan was away that day, or was just about to leave in ten minutes to watch a tryout in Philadelphia. The theatre had been all around him day and night during those two years, with all its peculiarly intangible values.

You could have told immediately, when you entered his private office, that Mr. Mortimer Sullivan belonged to the theatre. Although he was only engaged in it by indirection, no one in his position could have wholly avoided its mannerisms. He had started years ago as an English instructor at Columbia, and then had become a minor dramatic critic on one of the New York evening papers that began disappearing so rapidly after World War I; and then he had been employed by Mr. Jack Herrick as a reader and general assistant in the agency, and he had saved enough to buy out the business at Mr. Herrick's death. But he always said he did not like the social side of the theatre; he tried to avoid it as carefully as he could, by having his house in New Rochelle and never going to first nights or to parties afterwards unless absolutely necessary, for, as he always said, this was a side of the business that he left to his assistant, Walter Price. It might very well have happened that his phobia against the stage would have put him out of it altogether if he had not been endowed with an exceptional sense of play construction and with an outstanding ability to assess potentialities in unknown writers.

"I am a man of letters," he used to say very frequently, "and not a play writer. I make my living out of them, but I should rather be found dead than be one."

He endeavored in his dress, also, to prove that he had only an indirect connection with the theatre. It had often seemed to Tom that Mr. Sullivan must have revisited in his spare time English classrooms at Columbia in order to get hints in dress that would make him look like an English Ph.D. living on an instructor's salary. He was as successful in his way as Mr. Belasco had been with his turn-around collar, but it never occurred to Mr. Sullivan that all these efforts to escape were in themselves theatrical. His attempts to look slovenly were an overelaboration, and his scholarly veneer was overdrawn. His hair was always too self-consciously unbrushed; his nickel-rimmed spectacles, that left metallic marks on the ridge of his nose, were an almost unobtainable piece of property, and once Tom had discovered him with the spectacles off examining his features in the mirror to assure himself that the spectacles had marked him. His blue suit was one of four that he had studiously allowed to grow frayed and shiny, and the spots on his lapels and waistcoat had a geometrical design. Best of all his properties, better than the scuffed shoes or his frayed shirts and ties, was his Phi Beta Kappa key. He must have gone to a number of pawnshops to have found a key that was worn to a ghost of its former self, a key that you would have thought a current of air would have blown from his gold-filled watch chain. And the strange part of it was that, besides having a good mind and a sense for drama, he also had a sense of humor. Yet he never understood that he was a character himself.

On the afternoon of the day when the Higgins office had paid the advance on *Hero's Return*, Mort Sullivan had called for Tom Harrow. It was toward the end of June and unseasonably hot, and since nobody in those days had heard of air-conditioning, the window overlooking Park Avenue was open, filling the space with sounds of traffic, and even in those days Park Avenue traffic was considerable.

Mort Sullivan had taken off his coat but not his waistcoat, presumably because of the Phi Beta Kappa key. He had been looking through a pile of manuscripts by unknown writers.

"Well, well, well," he said, "judging from your appearance, Walter Price has told you, hasn't he? And I suppose it's all over the office now. Well, it isn't every day the office boy makes good. I never told you, because I never like to be encouraging in such a hellish line as this, but I had a liking for that play. It almost surprised me. Do you know why?"

Whenever he was called into the private office, Tom could believe that he was having a college conference with a professor of creative writing, which was probably exactly what Mort Sullivan wanted him to think.

"No, sir," he said, "but I'd like to know."

"All right," Mr. Sullivan said, "the script surprised me because you've never looked to me like a playwright. You've never looked high thinking. Look at your clothes — they are tailor-made, aren't they? You ought to look that way after, not before a Broadway hit. You are in reverse sequence."

"It hasn't got to Broadway yet," Tom said. "Maybe it's just as well I've put the cart before the horse."

"Well, everyone's eccentric somewhere, I suppose," Mort Sullivan said. "I suppose you think I ought to go to a tailor instead of buying some thing off the rack. Well, I could, but I don't believe in looking too successful."

"Maybe it doesn't matter so much," Tom Harrow said, "if you are successful."

"Just the same," Mort Sullivan said, "you ought not to be as smart as you are and look like it. But don't let me inflate your ego."

"Anyway," Tom Harrow said, "I haven't got a Phi Beta Kappa key."

Mort Sullivan smiled.

"You know," he said, "you've got a good eye, haven't you? Let's leave it that way and tell me how it feels to have the Higgins office come over with a thousand dollars. The size of that advance is a compliment to you, you know."

The news was like a sudden inspired solution of a mathematical problem. It was a part of a chain reaction that had been developing for some time and the answer was inevitable, but his satisfaction was not conceit. It was the simple confirmation of the theorem that he was good, and there was no reason to conceal his satisfaction.

"Frankly," he said, "it makes me feel just fine."

There was no jealousy or regret in Mort's middle-aged face. Instead there was an almost parental look of friendly worry.

"Well," he said, "you look that way. I've been trying to put myself in your position, but I can't. Do you remember what the Greek father did when his son won the Olympic games?"

"No, sir, not at the moment," Tom Harrow said.

There was still a puzzled look in the agent's glance, a look of someone trying to be satisfied with a combination of unreconcilable factors.

"He prayed the gods that the punishment might be light."

Mortimer Sullivan had been his agent and his close friend until he had died seven years ago from a coronary accident, and unlike most agents, he had never refrained for business reasons from saying what he thought. That speech of his, punctuated by the warm June air and by the sounds of the internal combustion engines from Park Avenue, had traveled unnoticed for years, through memory like a sound wave, and now the echo returned, stronger than he would have expected.

"I wish it hadn't come so easy for you," he said. "Handling success is like handling liquor. It throws you when you don't have a chance to build up a tolerance. I wish you didn't look so much like a Shakespearian Golden Lad."

"Not too golden," Tom said, "not yet."

"No," Mort Sullivan said, "not yet, but I'm afraid you're going to be. I hope you don't think I'm being offensive."

"Oh, no," Tom said. "You only asked me how I was feeling, and I said I was feeling fine."

"Because it wouldn't be policy to offend an essentially valuable client," Mort Sullivan said. "You understand you are a client now, don't you? Not an employee, a client."

It was a fine day and Tom Harrow still felt fine.

"You mean you're firing me?" he asked.

"Only as an employee," Mort Sullivan said. "I don't pay smart boys to be playwrights; they pay me — and by the way, in this new relationship, you might as well call me Mort. And now, as a business gesture, I should like to ask you out to lunch. We could go to that speak-easy near West Fifty-second Street. The food there isn't bad, and we could have a drink to — what's the play's name again? I never could remember titles."

"*Hero's Return*," he answered, and Mort repeated the title after him.

"*Hero's Return*," he said. "Well, hero, I hope that you return all right."

Tom wished that he could have had lunch there. Even in those days, with all the Prohibition handicaps, the cocktails were excellent there, but instead he had an engagement with his Uncle George for lunch at his uncle's club on Fifth Avenue. The engagement, having been made ten days before, was something he could not break. Nevertheless, he still was feeling fine. He wore a very light gray felt hat when he stepped out on Park Avenue. It was strange to remember that it was possible in those days to carry a walking stick without causing any particular comment, but he had never used a walking stick except for the brief time it had taken to recover from a sprained ankle, an inadvertent accident that had occurred after coming home with Rhoda from the party after *Hero's Return*. The twisted ankle had been painful, and it was a strange coincidence that Rhoda had said almost the same thing that Mort had said.

"Well," she had said, "the hero's back home all right."

His luncheon engagement had been fixed for 1:30, the hour that his Uncle George usually selected when it was not necessary for him to return downtown for an afternoon appointment. There was ample time to walk uptown to the club, along Fifth Avenue, a more attractive street then, with finer shops and with a few of the great dwelling houses that had survived the novels of Edith Wharton; but then, any street would have looked well that day. There was truth in that apprehension of Mort Sul-

212

livan's, whom he could call Mort now that things had gone too easily for him. It was true in a way that he had superficially led an existence that could be termed, a few years later, one of overprivilege; and he would be criticized later for that easy beginning. It was true that he had gone to a fashionable boarding school until his uncle had seen that the money was running low. It was true, also, as his uncle had been careful to indicate, that those years at boarding school had given him valuable connections which had helped him get into a club at college. It was true that his Aunt Mabel and his Uncle George and other family connections and friends, like his father's cousins the Deerings and the Roswells, had been generous about school vacations. And he had invitations of his own when he got to college. It was also a fact, as his Aunt Mabel had often reminded him, that she and his Uncle George had been kind about getting him into the Metropolitan dances and onto the coming-out list; but this could not have been difficult, since eligible young men, and some not eligible at all, were eagerly welcomed at those parties, and also, he was always an extra young man for his cousin, Louise. Still, it always annoyed him when people, including liberal-minded critics, began harping on his gilt-edged youth as though there had not been many thousands of others and most of them better off. None of them ever seemed to remember that his had been a tragically lonely childhood, but it was over now. He was walking up Fifth Avenue to another of those luncheons with his Uncle George at the Carleton Club. As his Aunt Mabel had said, whenever he came to call and whenever he was asked to dinner when Louise needed an extra man, he must remember that his Uncle George would have done a great deal more for him if Uncle George were not very overtired and overworked by his partners downtown who, though brilliant, did have charming people's inconsiderateness.

"And Tom, dear," she often said, "you, too, are developing in charm."

But, by God, he had been considerate. He had danced for miles with Louise and Louise's friends, beginning with fat girls from Farmington and ending with plumper ones from Vassar.

He had done what he could, too, for Alvin, at college; and he had always been to call on his Aunt Mabel every time he was in New York, except when the Howland girl had asked him for week ends and had not wanted Louise to know about it. Somehow his Aunt Mabel always found out about these occasions, but she had always spoken about them in a patient, yet merry manner.

It was strange how vigorously one reacted to early impressions. The Carleton Club, he very well knew, was not much of a club as New York clubs went. Even in the Twenties, when it was in a highly solvent condition, it was already being said that its food and service grew mediocre like its membership. Nevertheless, Tom Harrow still had to pull himself together when he faced its solid doorway, still conscious of a sense of awe, and perhaps he had been right. The Carleton Club had been built at the turn of the century, when there must have been a general belief that all buildings would stand for eternity. It had the exterior of a Renaissance Roman palace, and an entrance hall to match. The doorman had been there when Tom Harrow had first appeared as a callow youth for luncheon with his uncle, and the doorman had a deep suspicion of all strangers. He stood behind his counter with the membership list in back of him and with pegs to mark the names of those present. He was writing on a pad when Tom Harrow entered and continued writing for some time while Tom gazed at the travertine marble hall, at the cavernous coatroom and at the red-carpeted staircase that led to the main rooms.

Tom Harrow found himself clearing his throat nervously.

"Is Mr. George Harrow in yet?" he asked.

The doorman, florid and white-haired, looked up.

"There isn't any Mr. Marlow a member of this club," he said.

He was positive the doorman had heard him the first time.

"Not Marlow," he said. "Mr. George Harrow."

"Oh, Mr. Harrow? Yes, he's in. Who wishes to see him?" the doorman asked, and he looked incredulous when Tom Harrow said his nephew.

"Quentin," he said to a boy in buttons — they still had boys in buttons at the Carleton Club in those days — "take the gentleman up to Mr. Harrow. And kindly leave your hat in the cloak-room; there's no place for hanging it upstairs."

No matter how well he did, he had always done something wrong in the Carleton Club. Chairs were always in the way. Glasses were always in just the right position to be pushed off the table.

His uncle, who was in the newspaper room, tossed down his paper at once and pushed himself up from his armchair when the boy in buttons spoke to him.

"Tom," he said, crossing the room, "this is a very real pleasure, and I have a surprise for you today."

Unlike most of the men of his age group at the Carleton Club, who were staring at them over the tops of their newspapers, his Uncle George had not lost his figure, although his hair was as white as the doorman's. He was dressed in a light blue flannel suit with a pin stripe, suitable for the time of the year, and a starched turn-over collar and dark blue tie. He was a handsome and distinguished man who looked to Tom like an aging copy of the only photograph he possessed of his own father. There was the same thin face, there were the same sharp features, the same keen eyes, and the same even, rather thin-lipped mouth, but the humor and carelessness that he had observed in his father's photograph was gone, and also some of the alertness. Uncle George was a measured, patient man who, however, would never quite make the first team of anything, but who had made the most of his capacities. His uncle's color was not good that afternoon, and he looked unusually tired.

"What surprise is it, Uncle George?"

Uncle George smiled indulgently, as he might have at Alvin or Louise. As his Aunt Mabel had often said, his Uncle George always thought of Tom as one of their own children, which was why he was so worried that he had not been able to do all for him that he might have wished.

"My doctor has given me a dispensation," he said, "in the form of a prescriptive, relaxing medicine, to be ingested with modera-tion before luncheon and dinner. I'm going to ask you to join me in taking it, but I am afraid it will not be a new experience for you, and that you and Alvin — and yes, even dear little Louise — are already familiar with it. The medicine, with proper seals and government releases, is now waiting for us in the old bar, where old Patrick, whom I fear your father used to know once, is waiting to dispense it."

Tom laughed. His uncle, as Tom had heard elder people say in his childhood, possessed the Harrow charm, and Tom knew that he possessed it, too.

"I won't guess to what you are referring," he said, "and don't tell me because I want to be surprised, but I hope you're feeling all right, Uncle George."

"Oh, yes," his uncle said, "it's only fatigue, the doctor says, and we've been busy in the office lately. This rising market is worrying when the responsibility of clients rests on your shoulders. And Tom, you're one of my favorite clients, and my dear nephew."

Uncle George had personal appeal, but after all, what was appeal? Something that concealed inadequacy, and it was startling to think perhaps that was why he himself had it. He was at a crossing of the ways that day with a guilty feeling that his problems should have worried him more.

"It's awfully kind of you to ask me up here to lunch, Uncle George," he said, "and to give me so much of your time. And you've always been very kind to me."

He was glad that his uncle had looked pleased and had slapped him on the shoulder.

"Tom," he said, "you've always been my favorite nephew."

Tom laughed again.

"I've got to be," he said, "as long as I'm the only one."

"Even if you weren't," his Uncle George said, "you would be. Patrick, two glasses of my medicine. This is my brother's, Mr. Roger Harrow's, son. You remember Mr. Roger, don't you, Patrick?"

"God bless me, yes," the old barkeeper said. "A fine gentleman, Mr. Roger."

There was a silence as they both listened to the echoes of that obituary, and then his uncle raised his glass.

216

"Tom," he said, "your good health."

"And yours, sir," Tom said, and he thought again that Uncle George's color was bad.

"Patrick," his uncle said, "if you have the luncheon card, we might order. Would you like clams, Tom? Clams are always in season. And then for me, eggs Benedict, Patrick, and please get the order up to the dining room right away. You see, the doctor has another suggestion, Tom. I have a nap upstairs here just after lunch."

"I hope you're feeling all right, sir," Tom Harrow said again.

"Oh, yes," his Uncle George said, "it's merely a matter of hypertension, which everyone must face given time, Tom, given time."

"I hope Alvin got through his year at law school all right," Tom said.

"Yes," his uncle said, "not brilliantly, but Alvin hasn't your quickness, Tom."

Then as Patrick left the bar to give his order to the dining room, his uncle's voice changed.

"I suppose you're still in that queer office, Tom," he said. "You know I've always disapproved of this theatre business. I wouldn't mind so much if there weren't a streak of instability in the family, and there's nothing stable about this theatre business."

"Well, I had to do something," Tom said. "The money's running out."

His uncle nodded and took a delicate sip from his glass of bonded rye whiskey.

"I don't mean for a moment that I don't respect your spirit of initiative and independence, but not in a theatrical agency. I don't mean to say I'm narrow-minded about a theatrical agency, but there's no future. You should have come to me, three years ago, instead of going to work there. You should be working at the Guaranty or the Chase, or some investment house downtown. It isn't stable, Tom."

Uncle George always spoke about stability, but Tom was feeling fine.

"You see, Tom," he said, "there's a factor that most young fel-

217

lows your age don't perceive. Your father never did, and I don't suppose I did very clearly once myself. A young fellow thinks there's plenty of time for everything because, with his lack of experience with time, he thinks that it moves slowly. This isn't so. It moves just as fast for you as it does for an old man like me. You may not know it, but you're in what are called the critical years, Tom, the years when you get your feet on the road which will lead you to success or failure. I suppose we all start wanting to be firemen or policemen, and without meaning to be personal, your summer theatre experience and then this theatrical agency is somewhat like that."

"Yes," Tom said, "I suppose it is." He was already able to perceive that work in any part of the theatre depended on a public whose probable reactions it was impossible to gauge, and you could measure thousands of failures against one success. This knowledge made him very reluctant to tell his uncle what had happened, but this was the time to tell him, before Patrick was back behind the bar. Tom was surprised that his uncle did not react to the news in the way he had believed he would.

"Well," he said, "so they gave you a thousand dollars? Well, I think that's very enterprising of you, Tom. I daresay they won't do anything about the play, but that's their problem. The main thing is that you have severed this agency connection and that is a step in the right direction. I tell you what I am going to do. I'm going to give you a letter to Matt Harris over at the Chase. The main thing is that you've got this theatre business out of your system and you've made a thousand dollars doing it. That's wonderful, Tom, and I think this calls for another small libation."

He was glad to have another and he could see his uncle's point, although it was exactly as though each of them addressed the other in a different language; and it was seldom worthwhile arguing about anything because arguments seldom changed a point of view.

"Another thing, Tom," Uncle George said, "Louise tells us that she hasn't seen you around anywhere lately, and that disturbs me a little. You've got to keep up with the right people, Tom."

"It's a little tough to do that and work at the same time, Uncle George," he said.

"I know, I know," his uncle answered, "I've found it so myself, long dinners and that sort of thing, and then the office in the morning. But, Tom, when you have a chance to see people, you ought to see them, and Louise and Alvin both say that lots of nice girls are trying to get hold of you all the time."

"That's so," Tom said, "they chase me all around town, Uncle George."

His uncle smiled and shook his head.

"Seriously, Tom," he said, "I wish you'd play around more with your own crowd."

"All right," he said, "I'll try to, Uncle George."

"That's right," his uncle said. "We've got to keep our feet on the ground, Tom."

"I agree, sir," Tom said. "Yes, I'll really try."

He knew by his uncle's expression that the words of advice were over and that they would discuss general topics during lunch, but Patrick was still not back and there was time for a summing-up.

"You see, Tom," his uncle said, "I wouldn't worry about you if I weren't fond of you. In case you haven't been told, you're very brilliant and very attractive, but don't let this make you lazy. Tom, if Louise hasn't seen you around, does that mean you've been seeing a lot of just one person?"

Tom felt his face grow warm and he realized that Louise and her mother had been talking.

"Well, perhaps," he said, "in a rather minor way. Well, yes, I've been seeing a good deal of Betty Howland lately."

Now that the name was out, he was amused by his uncle's respectful expression.

"Well, you know how to pick them, as they say," his uncle said.

"Well, I don't know," he answered, "but I will say she has your point of view, Uncle George. She wants to see me get ahead."

He stopped because Patrick was back and their luncheon was ready in the dining room. It did not occur to him then that it would be the last luncheon he would ever have with his Uncle George, or that after five that afternoon he would not see Betty Howland again for a long, long time.

Ever since high school, there had always been some girl on his mind, and, now that it was too late to profit by the knowledge, he could face the truth that he had never been made for celibacy. He must have always needed what the psychiatrists now called a "love object," and this was what Betty Howland had been once — a symbol in a relationship formula — ever since he had first danced with her at a coming-out party at the Hotel St. Regis. She was blond, tall and beautiful, and she was almost everything anyone could desire in a love object, always exquisite, with wealthy but kind and hospitable parents, and with an impression of untouchable aloofness with its own appeal because the impression was incorrect. It was also difficult to tell her exact degree of seriousness when she said she loved him, and it was fashionable then to talk lightly and philosophically about love.

"Tommy, dear," she said once, "do let's try to get it clear between us that love is a variable."

It had been late in the evening and they had been sitting together on a sofa in the parlor of the Howlands' Fifth Avenue apartment.

"Right at the moment," he said, "it seems pretty constant to me."

"Silly," Betty said, "it's a constant and at the same time it's a variable. For example, you're all over powder and lipstick, but that's not a constant condition."

"I'd like to make it that way," he said.

"Tommy, dear, that's sweet of you," she said, "but I'm afraid neither of us is very constant, and please don't try to prove anything right now, physically I mean, because I'm turning into a variable."

"I thought you flunked college mathematics," he said. "Where did you pick up that word 'variable'?"

"Seriously, Tommy, and please let's be serious for a minute. Seriously, I don't know how much I love you, because it shifts around."

She sighed and she was as beautiful when she was serious as when she was merry. Her blue eyes grew darker and her lips formed themselves into tragic little curves.

"Oh, Tommy," she said, "it discourages me because basically most of the time I love you."

"Don't be discouraged," he said, "because I know I love you, Betty." And he was almost positive he loved her. There was still a tragic sadness in the memory of their unsureness. It would have taken so little to have tipped the scales, but things either worked or they didn't, and there was no way to change the destiny, no matter how one tried.

"Sometimes when I love you most," she said, "an awful thing happens. Sometimes it doesn't seem real. It seems futile."

"How do you mean, futile?" he asked.

"Oh, I can't explain it," she said, "except that sometimes it seems everything with you and me wasn't ever meant to happen. Sometimes I get to thinking we're like the Maeterlinck people in the land of the unborn babies, and then I know it can't be real or serious."

"Why, that isn't so," he told her. "What you say makes it serious."

"Oh, Tommy, no," she said. "You know you seriously don't want to make money so that we could be married, and you said yourself you wouldn't live on an allowance from Father."

He was sorry that he could feel the truth in what she said. He could hear a voice inside him saying that it wasn't meant to be, but whenever the voice spoke, he wanted it to be.

"Believe me, Betty," he said, "I'm serious. What am I doing every night and week ends? I'm working on this play."

"I know, darling," she said, "and you're wonderful, but if you loved me, you'd go to work in Father's office, the way he asked you."

"It might get to Broadway," he said. "I might be good, you know."

"Oh, Tommy," she said, "let's not be dismal any more."

Betty was an expensive girl, which may have been what she was trying to say when she had spoken elliptically about unborn babies in Maeterlinck's *Blue Bird*. She married Harvey Griscombe, who later was master of a hunt in New Jersey, and Tom had sent her a George the Second coffeepot just to show her that he could, but he did not see her until a number of years later, when they met at the Stork Club.

"I meant to write you about the play," she said, "but I couldn't exactly get it down in words. I never dreamed it would come out the way it did. Maybe it's my fault that we're unborn babies, dear."

But that afternoon, after his luncheon with Uncle George, he had no idea of such an ending. It was pleasant, walking up Fifth Avenue just on the edge of a New York summer, and he thought of his Aunt Edith whom he had not seen for a long while. It would be possible to see her tomorrow if he wanted. In fact, anything was possible.

The Howlands' apartment faced the Central Park Reservoir where a light breeze was rippling the water. Axel, the Howlands' Swedish butler, let him in and his manners were an improvement over those of the doorman at the Carleton Club.

"Yes, Mr. Harrow," he said. "Miss Elizabeth has asked you to wait for her in the library."

He had never had the slightest intention until that moment of proposing to Betty Howland, yet suddenly he knew that he was going to do so, if only to show her that he was occasionally serious. The library, done in heavy, fumed oak in a style that was popular during the World War I era, had a Gothic quality that had never previously impressed him. The sets of books in varicolored leathers, all oiled and dusted, showing no mark of wear, blended beautifully with the gold velveteen curtains and with the masculine leather upholstered furniture. Neat piles of cloth material were heaped high on two straight-backed Spanish chairs, covers that would go over the furniture when the Howlands moved to Long Island. They were an orderly harbinger of change, but they disturbed him as he stood there waiting. He must have realized before Betty Howland entered the library that the pulse of his life was beating a new measure, and that balances were changing.

Yet when he saw her, he wanted her. One of the tragedies in his life had always been that he had wanted too many different things simultaneously. He had wanted to go to prize fights and to hear the handlers talking in the winner's dressing room. He had wanted to go to speak-easies, and, at the same time, he had wanted to play bridge at his club and to go to the best restaurants, and to bet on the races and to meet the prettiest girls. What would have happened if he had not been possessed of the restiveness of which Rhoda had always complained?

"Darling," Betty said, "kiss me. I was so surprised when you called up after lunch. Tom, has anything dreadful happened?"

He had never proposed to a girl before, not that he had not wanted to, but he had never before been in a position of having anything to offer. It was amusing to recall how many similar scenes he had later dealt with professionally. There were always proposals and avowals somewhere and he had always felt artistically that they should be simple, just as the result of any chain of circumstances possessed its own simplicity.

"Yes, something's happened," he said, "but I hope you won't think it's bad. I even hope you're going to like it."

"Why, Tom," she said, "you look so queer. What happened?"

"For one thing, I love you," he said.

"Yes," she said, "I know. We've been all over that before."

"Well," he said, "another thing. I want to ask you if you want to marry me, not hypothetically, but seriously."

He could sympathize with people's not wanting to face up to things because he had observed the same reluctance in himself, but he had seldom been so conscious of evasion as when he saw Betty's face.

"But why at five in the afternoon?" she said.

There was no trick to writing comedy if you had lived through enough of it.

"Well, dear," he said, "it's got to be at some time or other."

"Oh, Tommy," she said. "Why didn't you say it last night in a more informal way and when there would have been more of a background for fantasy? Darling, unfantastically — what could we get married on, for instance? You shouldn't bring these things up in the afternoon, on daylight saving time."

She was talking rapidly and he knew that she was worried about a lot of things and there was something highly poignant in her worry.

"They've taken my play," he said. "I didn't know it until this morning."

"Oh, sweet," she said, "how wonderful!" And she threw her arms around him. "Why didn't you tell me in the first place, instead of being so formal and stuffy and proposing and everything? Oh, sweet, now you won't have to worry about it any more."

"That's true for the moment," he said. "They're not going to try it until autumn."

"Tommy," she said, "it's simply wonderful, but what are you going to do now it's finished?"

"I guess I'll start another," he said. "I've got a few ideas."

"Another?" she said. "You mean you're going to keep doing them? You mean you're not going to do anything else?"

"Well," he said, "I've got a few ideas."

"Well, then," she said, "let's stop being serious before sundown, and I'm going to ring for Axel to get us some Scotch. Oh, darling, I never dreamed I'd love anyone who wrote a play, even variably."

"Betty," he said, "that isn't kind. I'm not going to write plays variably."

"Tommy," she said, "dear Tommy. I'm constant in certain ways, but Tommy, please, please let's not talk about it now."

He often wondered if she realized that they would never discuss the subject again. He was never entirely sure, and besides, most women were always believing that there would be another day. In the end, all that was ever left to a vanished episode was a certain amount of retrospection, and retrospection was always dangerous to handle. He could not recall being angry or even being surprised, which must have proved that his love, like hers, was a variable. There was only one thing very definite that remained from the experience. Any girl, in making up her mind, had to view a man from every angle that she could and he was a bad financial risk. It was her assumed knowledge of him and her casualness that hurt him most, and she should have known that things could not go on the way they had. It was time to be leaving town for awhile, but he did not tell her he was leaving. On the contrary, he had stayed for about an hour just as though nothing had occurred, and he had kissed her good-by and told her that he loved her, which was still true in some academic sense. Yet a resolution was forming in him which would affect some later aspects of his life. He would never put himself in a position to be treated casually again.

XIV

Good Night, Monte Cristo

HAVING dealt for most of his life with thoughts and motivations, he was not bad at constructing an imaginary scene. Over the years he had often diverted himself at odd moments by making a construction of what the Brownes had said when Rhoda had told them that he was coming to call to take her to the pictures the evening after he and she had met on Dock Street. He knew not only Rhoda but the Brownes so well that he hardly needed to draw upon imagination. As his Aunt Edith had said, when he had mentioned Rhoda Browne, she knew nothing whatsoever about them except that they attended the South Church and were strangers to everybody, and that Mr. Browne had come to town to manage the agency for the Ford Motor Company. She was sure that they amounted to nothing or she would have heard more about them.

"After all," she had said, "he's little more than an automobile salesman, and I think I know as well as you what automobile salesmen must be like, having read the way they talk in automobile advertisements. I am sure that the Judge would not have allowed an automobile salesman in his house, not that I believe he had to deal with them in his day."

There were many occasions on which he had wished that Mrs. Hudson Browne could have overheard his aunt's remark, but it was just as well she had not because each had always been frigidly patronizing to the other. His Aunt Edith, being the Judge's daughter, was descended from an old family which included in its tree a Colonial governor. In fact, if she had wanted, Aunt Edith could have been a Colonial Dame of America — not that this made any impression on Mrs. Browne.

As Mrs. Browne would have said, his Aunt Edith was not a Rhyelle of Baltimore, and Mrs. Browne had been Estelle Rhyelle of Baltimore, and even if you were only mildly interested, she could show you the photograph of the old Rhyelle mansion in whose ballroom she had been introduced to Baltimore society — a house which unfortunately had been torn down due to the enlargement of the city, and was now, like the Rhyelle fortune, a mere memory — the fortune having been dissipated by her careless brother at the horse races. Her brother had blown out his brains shortly after the dissipation and thus except for Mrs. Browne and Rhoda and the photograph, the Rhyelles of Baltimore were extinct.

Tom had never, in his saddest moments, derided Mrs. Browne. On the contrary, he had always listened with rapt attention to the histories of the Rhyelles of Baltimore, and had often asked questions to encourage Mrs. Browne, until on one occasion he had found Rhoda in tears. He had never intended to be unkind to Mrs. Browne, and, in fact, he had been fond of her and there was no doubt she had come from Baltimore; and there was no doubt she had married Hudson Browne, the son of a successful farmer in the vicinity of Salisbury, Maryland, who had received a college education and finally a legacy of fifty thousand dollars. There was no doubt about the legacy because Rhoda had once heard of it, but it had pretty well run out.

"Father," as Rhoda had often said, "should never have tried to be a businessman. It would have been so much better, wouldn't it, if he had tried harder and harder to do nothing?"

It was a good line and he had laughed at it.

"Don't," she said. "I'm not trying to be funny. You just don't understand. You never kept trying to be something and then failing, and trying and failing."

But, knowing Rhoda, he had understood enough to guess what the Brownes must have said before he came to call for her that first evening. The Brownes, when he had met Rhoda, had been living in one of those small and run-down houses on Harrison Street which now were rediscovered, their primitive quaintness fully restored by repainting and synthetic remodeling. However, Harrison Street did not amount to much in the days when Tom had met Rhoda, and the furnishings of the Brownes, battered from frequent movings, did not fit well into the small front parlor; the tapestried upholstered suite and the Brussels carpet clashed with the old woodwork and the wallpaper of the previous tenant. Still, the setting was perfect for what must have taken place. It would be late afternoon and Mr. Browne would have returned from the Ford agency, a florid, balding man in his late forties, in a sharply pressed brown double-breasted suit.

"What's there for supper tonight, Estelle?" he would have asked.

Mrs. Browne had been very pretty once and Tom was reasonably sure that Mr. Browne had married her because of beauty and not the Rhyelle name.

"He just thought I was another friend of Cynthia Ellis," Mrs. Browne had told Tom once. "Hudson never realized until later that I was Estelle Rhyelle."

She still had beautiful hands, and she still sat up very straight, and she still put on an afternoon dress of faded purplish silk that had the same faded quality as her hair, which she still wore in an outmoded pompadour.

"We're having soup and canned salmon and peas, Hudson," she must have said. "It's Friday, you know."

"Can't we have fresh fish, now we're near the ocean?" Mr. Browne asked. "Estie, do you remember those soft-shell crabs back in Baltimore?"

"Hudson," she said, "you have grime around your fingernails."

"It's the grease," Mr. Browne said. "The cars are greasy even in the showroom."

"That's all the more reason for you to keep clean," Mrs. Browne said. "The first thing I notice whenever I buy anything at the grocery is whether the man's hands are clean."

"My God, Estie," Mr. Browne said, "I'm not in the grocery business."

228

"Hudson," Mrs. Browne said, "please go upstairs — there's plenty of hot water — and scrub your hands with a nailbrush. Don't make me do everything about appearances, Hudson."

It must have been at just such a moment that Rhoda came into the room. He knew exactly how she was dressed because he had never fogotten the clothes she wore in those first days, and it was strange when he cast his mind back to realize how peculiar they would have looked in a later era. Their entertainment value was already being recognized in modern comedies that dealt with the roaring twenties. This was only a little later than the era of the skirt above the knee and the rolled stocking, and though skirts were a trifle longer, the spirit of exposure still prevailed. It could be said without danger of contradiction that women had never been more awkwardly or farcically dressed than they had been at the end of the Twenties, but when you were living in the age itself the impression was wholly different. There was also the vitality of youth, and anyone like Rhoda, looking like Rhoda, and being nineteen as Rhoda was then, would have looked wonderfully dressed in anything, or, for that matter, out of anything. He could still remember her pepper-and-salt ready-made coat and skirt, and her lisle stockings. She had no money for a silk pair then, except for evening and Sunday, and nylons lay unknown beyond the furthest horizons of the foreseeable future. She would have been wearing a bell-shaped hat, jammed like an inverted bucket over the boyish bob that the town's first hairdresser, who did not bother to call herself "Annette" or "Chez Marie" in those days, was currently offering the local youth. Aesthetically the effect must have been agonizing, and yet the whole effect had been more full of allure for him than anything he had seen since; but then, no woman had ever worn a hat with more verve than Rhoda in those days when hats were still part of a convention. She could rip off her hat in a seemingly slovenly manner and toss it on a chair or table, but her hair would seldom be rumpled in the process, or if it was, a shake of her head would bring it back in place. No one could put on a hat like Rhoda; there was no trouble, no standing in front of a mirror for feminine adjustments. She simply jammed it on and there it was, its angle perfect, setting forth her features in just the way its creator had planned. Yet perhaps hats had never mattered, because there was Rhoda's hair, reminiscent of Hepburn, but of course it was not Hepburn's, and the gloss and the vitality of the last years of her teens eventually left it. Its color was something he never could describe, not red, not gold, not auburn, and after all, when you saw it, description made no difference. When you first saw a girl you loved, she created an impression that nothing could ever change.

"How did you know right away that I had a good figure?" she asked him once.

And that was a difficult one to answer. With those clothes of hers, there had been no way of making an estimate regarding her figure visually except that her legs were long and spectacular; but somehow you knew all the answers without knowing how.

It was easy to imagine how she must have looked among the overstuffed upholstery, and fortunately he had given the Brownes better furniture later for their bungalow at Daytona Beach.

"Hello, Mother," Rhoda must have said, and there was a bell-like quality in her voice, reminding one of the Tennysonian line about echoes dying, dying. "Hello, Pa."

Often when he thought of the American male as a figure of fun, in the days before he was finalized by Lindsay and Crouse, Tom would picture Mr. Browne as ideal for the role.

"Back so soon, dear?" Mrs. Browne might have asked. "I thought you were going to do some typing practice after the school had closed."

"Well, I didn't," Rhoda said. "Some of the girls went out to get a soda, Mother."

"Rhoda, dear," Mrs. Browne must have said, "I do hope you're taking your shorthand and typing seriously," and she sighed in a repressed way that was always poignant. "I wish my own dear mother had thought of giving me typing and shorthand lessons, instead of harp lessons, and then I might be more useful than I am now. A girl can never tell, Rhoda, when it may be necessary for her to earn her own living honorably. Hudson, please put your paper down. Isn't it true what I've been telling Rhoda?"

"Yes," Mr. Browne said, "I think your mother's put it accurately, Rhoda. There are ups and downs in life."

Mrs. Browne would then have looked brighter. There was always a silver lining and no one could say that she had not always searched for it in a very gallant way.

"Besides, dear," she said, "your typing is only for this summer, because the agency for the Ford Company is bound to be a success and you'll be going to Wellesley College in the fall. Hudson, please put down your paper. Won't Rhoda be going to Wellesley in the fall?"

"Rhoda can go anywhere she wants in the fall."

Rhoda must have smiled. Unlike most girls her own age, she was not continually grinning and showing her even white teeth; she never had been a smily girl, which may have given her smile its value.

"Thanks, Pa," she said, "thanks a million."

When Mr. Browne smiled back at her, you could have seen from whom she had inherited the smile. In fact, smiling was about the only graceful thing the old man ever did. "Thanks a million" was a new phrase then and Mrs. Browne would have been quick to catch it.

"Where did you learn that expression, Rhoda dear?"

"Oh, from some of the girls at typing school, I guess."

"I wish so many common girls didn't take up typewriting," Mrs. Browne would have said.

"Mother, what time's supper? Can we have supper early?"

"Why, yes, dear, as long as this is Friday, but why do you want supper early, Rhoda?"

"Because a boy's going to call for me to take me to the 6:30 movie," Rhoda must have said. "It has to be 6:30 because you don't like me to go to the 8:30 show."

"A boy?"

"Why, yes, Mother, I guess you'd call him a boy."

"But I thought you were saying only yesterday that you hadn't met any boys around here that you'd be seen with," Mrs. Browne said.

"That was yesterday," Rhoda said. "I've met one now, and he's coming to take me to the half-past-six picture. I'll start helping with the supper, Mother, but I want to put on my green silk dress with the red dots on it."

At this point Mr. Browne must have put down his newspaper.

"Say," he said, "who is this boy, Rhoda?"

"I don't know exactly," Rhoda said. "I never saw him around here until today, but he says he has an aunt who lives here or something."

"Rhoda," her mother asked, "are you sure that he's a nice boy?"

"I don't know yet," Rhoda said, and she smiled again, "but maybe I will, after the picture show."

There was always one thing about Rhoda, she always told the truth when she was asked a question. Mr. Browne must have laughed, and it was hard to blame him because it was always difficult not to laugh when Rhoda wished it.

"I don't think that's humorous, Hudson," Mrs. Browne must have said. "Of course if he's a nice young man, I think it's very nice, but at the same time, dear, you are different from the girls at the typing school, and if he's a friend of theirs, I don't know. Where did you meet him, Rhoda?"

"Out on the main street," Rhoda said, "the one that's called Dock Street, just after I had that soda and was going back to do more typing."

"But how did you meet him, dear?" Mrs. Browne asked.

Rhoda must have smiled again.

"Why, I guess he picked me up. I guess that's what they call it, Mother."

"Hudson," Mrs. Browne said, "please let me speak. How could he have picked you up there in the street if you hadn't wanted him to?"

"Well, maybe I did want him to," Rhoda said.

232

Rhoda always did tell the truth when she was asked a question.

"But what did he do?" Mrs. Browne asked.

"Well, it was in front of the drugstore," Rhoda must have said, "when I was just coming out, and he smiled at me and took off his hat, a sort of city hat, and then he said hello. He didn't do anything else."

"Well, I'd say he did plenty," Mr. Browne could have said, "and I don't know as I like it, either."

"Hudson," Mrs. Browne said, "please. When he did that, what did you do, Rhoda?"

"Why, I smiled back and said hello, too," Rhoda said.

"Rhoda dear," Mrs. Browne said, "why did you do that?"

"I guess I sort of liked him," Rhoda said. "He's the only worthwhile-looking boy I've seen in this town, and besides, with all the other girls around, I didn't want them to think he was trying to pick me up. It would have been embarrassing, Mother."

"But Rhoda, your father and I don't know anything about him."

"Well, we don't know anything about anyone else, either," Rhoda said. "Mother, please don't go and spoil it all, and nothing ever happens at a half-past-six o'clock picture show. At least nothing has ever happened to me before, much, and I've been out to lots of places at three different high schools."

"Oh, Rhoda!" her mother said. "As though your father and I haven't wanted to give you everything! But you do say he's attractive?"

Mrs. Browne still could look for a silver lining.

"He's the only boy in this town who doesn't look like a crumb," Rhoda said.

(Out of all the imaginary dialogue this speech was certainly correct, because Rhoda herself had repeated it to him that same evening.)

"I wish you wouldn't use slang," Mrs. Browne said, "when I've tried so hard to teach you good vocabulary. I don't know the word, but I hope you mean he's nicely dressed and nice appearing."

233

"I wouldn't have said hello if he was a crumb," Rhoda said, "and he says he comes from New York City, and I think he's a college man."

"Young fellows are always showing off," Mr. Browne said, "and pretending to be something they're not in order to make a good impression."

"Did he tell you the name of his aunt or whoever it is he says he's visiting?" Mrs. Browne asked.

"Oh, Mother," Rhoda said, "I have to change my dress, and I can't stay answering questions."

"We're only being careful of our little girl," Mrs. Browne said, "aren't we, Hudson?"

"Yes, but let's not worry until we see him," Mr. Browne said. "If he doesn't add up, Rhoda will stay home."

Rhoda must have been annoyed, but it was always hard to gauge the degree because annoyance always made her cool instead of flustered.

"I've added him," Rhoda said. "Any girl's got to watch herself with a boy."

Her feet beat a swift clatter up the stairs, and Mrs. Browne sighed her eloquent, stifled sigh.

"Right in front of the drugstore," Mrs. Browne said, "and she smiled and said hello."

That June night was still a time of fantasy, and now it was impossible to discover where things began or where they ended. It was a relief to recall that Shakespeare himself had been confused under similar circumstances.

"Tell me, where is fancy bred," he had asked, "in the heart or in the head? How begot, how nourished?"

Nothing could be wholly accurate about that time, but his Aunt Edith had been unaffected by it, and his interview with his aunt was one he could draw from memory instead of imagination.

"I hope we're having supper early, Aunt Edith," he had said. "I'm taking a girl to the 6:30 picture show. She wouldn't go to the 8:30 one."

"Is she one of your old schoolmates, Thomas?" his aunt asked.

"No," he said, "they all seem to be married now — all the good ones."

"I'm very glad you outgrew so many," his aunt said. "But then, I've always trusted the Fowler heritage, in spite of your poor father's frivolity. If she isn't a schoolmate, who is she?"

"She's a new girl, I think," he said. "I happened to run into her on Dock Street when you sent me down for the afternoon mail."

"Were you introduced to her by running into her?" his aunt asked.

She was one of the few women he had known who was able to understand nearly everything from the basis of almost no appreciable experience.

"That's one way of putting it," he said. "We smiled at each other at almost the same time, and then we said hello."

His aunt was silent for a moment.

"Did she tell you her name?" she asked.

"Oh, yes," he said, "her name is Rhoda, Rhoda Browne."

His aunt had always possessed impeccable sources of local information. There was Marie, who was still in the kitchen, and who perhaps still loved him, and there was Mr. Gorman, who tended the grounds of four houses on Locust Street, and then there was the Monday Club.

"Where does she live?" she asked.

"On Harrison Street, at least I hope that's where," he said, "because I'm going there to call for her."

His aunt nodded slowly.

"That would be the daughter of Mr. Hudson Browne, who is the new manager of the Ford agency," she said. "A motor-car salesman's daughter . . . Did you say she was pretty, Thomas?"

"I don't remember if I said," he answered. "At any rate, she is."

"Well," his aunt said, "I hope she does not get you into trouble, Thomas."

Of course she should have hoped. To the end she had implied that Rhoda had made the play for him, and it was impressive

235

to recall on how many occasions his aunt had been correct, when by all the laws of averages she had no business to be correct about anything at all.

It was broad daylight still at 6:15 on Harrison Street, what with the institution of daylight saving and with June owning the longest day in the year, but at the same time you could feel the eventual approach of dusk, although this was a long way off. Voices of children playing in the yards of Harrison Street had a different quality from early morning voices, and there was a quiet and a peace that could no longer be recaptured. The streets were not full of traffic and strangers. The day, as occasionally happened in June, had been perfect, and the air around him was cleaner than that in any modern air-conditioned room. The fresh leaves of the trees were hanging motionless, and the sky had assumed a deeper hue, but it was still far from sunset. Harrison Street was for once like a Winslow Homer painting, with a charm that came from spirit as well as fact. In the next few months, while he was writing the draft of his second play, his thoughts were on Harrison Street for hours and hours. He could amuse himself when alone by picturing the houses in the row where Rhoda lived, house by house, down to the peonies and Oriental poppies in the yards, but nothing was ever the same as it had been that evening.

The house, like his aunt's, had a wire pull-bell with a glass knob, that could have been an item in a modern antique store. Doubt assailed him when he pulled the bell and listened to its nervous jangling in the hall, because it could have been that he was making a fool of himself and that things weren't what they seemed on Dock Street, but Rhoda had been waiting and he had been right about her.

"Oh, hello," she said, "won't you come in for a minute and meet my father and mother?" And then her voice dropped to a whisper, "And tell me your name again. I knew I was going to forget it, and now I have."

"Harrow," he said, "and see you remember it next time."

When she was most nervous, Rhoda appeared at her calmest, so that he had no way of knowing that she was afraid of what he might think of Mr. and Mrs. Browne. She had no way of knowing, either, that she was beautiful enough as she stood by the door to cancel out any other impression. At any rate, she had to invite him into the house because Mr. Browne had wanted to add him up. It was a very useful experience to him later when he realized that the meeting had a universal quality, and he had used it once nearly verbatim in *Flagpole for Two*. The crowded room, the imitation tapestry upholstery, the Brussels carpet, everything told mutely that the Brownes had moved and moved. Mr. and Mrs. Browne reminded him later of middle-aged actors and actresses making the best of things when a play was on the road. They were gazing at him with a sharp, pathetic interest that a parent is never able to conceal. It was a long way, he was thinking, from Betty Howland and the apartment that overlooked the Reservoir in Central Park. It was like stepping into another set before another audience and still being able to be himself. It was something to remember that through most of his life he had usually been himself.

"Well, this is a real pleasure, meeting you, Mr. Harrow," Mr. Browne said, "and it's kind of you to take our little girl out. Rhoda's always popular wherever she goes, but she hasn't had much time to meet any boy friends here yet. The name is Harrow, isn't it? I don't recall any Harrows in the local phone directory."

"What Mr. Browne means," Mrs. Browne said, "is that he is trying to get acquainted with all the names of persons in this locality. Mr. Browne, you see, has recently assumed the management of the Ford Motor Agency, but perhaps Rhoda told you, Mr. Harrow."

The whole story, with all its implied pathos, was told by Mr. Browne's overpressed, double-breasted suit and in Mrs. Browne's antiquated pompadour. It was only necessary to take one look at Mr. Browne to perceive that he would not be assuming the management of the Ford Motor agency for an indefinite period; but there was nothing sharp or unkind about these thoughts because Rhoda stood beside him, and they were Rhoda's parents. He did not mind their sudden eagerness and the avid way they looked at his gray suit and his straw hat. A parent had every right to make an estimate and he did not mind if they were thinking that there must be money somewhere, because Rhoda was beside him.

"No, I don't believe that Miss Browne had time to tell me," he said. "I hope you enjoy it here, Mr. Browne."

He did not blame Mrs. Browne for watching him. There was no reason why she should not have faced the possibility that he was up to no good, and at the time perhaps she was right.

"You don't live here, do you, Mr. Harrow?"

Of course she had to place him, poor bewildered Mrs. Browne, and it was doubly difficult for her then when he was having his own difficulties in trying to place himself.

"No, I don't live here exactly," he said. "I don't truthfully know where I'm living at the moment. New York as much as any place, I suppose, but right now I'm rather at loose ends."

"Oh," Mrs. Browne said, "I remember now. Rhoda told me you were here visiting a relative."

"Yes," he said, "my aunt. I'm very fond of my aunt."

"Mother," Rhoda said, "there isn't any reason to cross-question Mr. Harrow, or perhaps he'll be afraid to come again."

"Why, Rhoda," Mrs. Browne said, "what an idea. It's just the way I am, Mr. Harrow, interested in everyone."

"Well, Mrs. Browne," he said, and he laughed, "that's just the way I am, too."

"Besides, Mother," Rhoda said, "he hasn't asked for my hand in marriage," and she smiled, "and if he has any designs on me, I'll tell you later."

"Rhoda," Mr. Browne said, "I think that will be quite enough."

"And don't be ridiculous, Rhoda," Mrs. Browne said. "It's very kind of you to want to take such a bad-mannered girl to the pictures, Mr. Harrow. And you will have her back shortly after nine o'clock, won't you? There'll be lemonade and cupcakes waiting in the kitchen, dear."

Rhoda referred to the incident when they were outside, walking up Harrison Street.

"You were nice to them," she said. "I guess parents are all that way." It was nearly the only explanation that she ever gave of them, except to tell him once later that she knew he understood them.

"Why shouldn't I have been nice to them?" he had said. "They let me take you out, and it's true that they don't know much about me."

"Well," she said, "I guess you know all about us now. What did you say your first name was?"

"It's Tom," he said, "and your first name's Rhoda. I haven't forgotten that."

"You can call me by it," she said, "and I'll call you Tom if it isn't on too short acquaintance. Have you got designs on me?"

"I daresay," he said. "Don't blame me. Anyone would, you know."

She laughed, and her laugh fitted with the mellow light of six o'clock.

"Well," she said, "I'm glad you've come right out with it. I don't care, up to a point, and you like me, don't you?"

"Yes," he said, "considerably."

She laughed again more softly.

"Well, of course I like you or none of this would have happened," she said. "I used to be frightened, and then nothing was fun, and then I told myself I would have to get over it if I was going to get anywhere. Talking to you is like reading a brand-new book, and I've never seen anyone just like you, and I don't understand you at all."

The first lines were always drawn at a first meeting. He must have been like a book to her and she had tried and tried for years, but she had never understood much of the book. Then she added another thought. One of the reasons that he had loved her was that she was almost always partially but never brutally frank.

"Tom," she said, "since you've been so truthful, I think that I should be, and I want to tell you, unless I change my mind, that I have designs on you, and I also want to tell you my mother and father have." Then she giggled.

"What's so funny?" he asked.

"Nothing. It's only exciting," she said. "No young man wearing sort of tailor-made city clothes has ever taken me to the pictures. That was why Mother was so frightened. You can understand, can't you?"

"Yes," he said, "but don't you be frightened."

She laughed, and as they were walking to the Bijou Theatre, which was an unpleasant name but true even in those days, the sun had reminded him of Milton — "the gilded car of day, his glowing axle doth allay."

"I'm not," she said, "and besides, I want to know more about what you're like."

"I'd rather know more about you," he said.

"You will," she said, "I hope, and you mustn't worry about Father and Mother. You knew Pa was a failure, didn't you, the moment you looked at him? I love him, but he's a failure."

"Why, Rhoda," he said, "I don't mind. I like it if you love a failure."

"I love lots of the things you say," she said, "and I think you're very nice, but I don't understand you at all."

"You don't have to," he said, "as long as I understand you, Rhoda."

"Well," she said, "then let's not get complexes and things, because we're only going to the pictures."

The word "complex" then was almost as new as the new model Ford that Mr. Browne was selling, and where had she picked up the word? He could guess that not the girls at the typing school or Mr. and Mrs. Browne had used it, but Rhoda had always been in tune with the latest note of time.

"I don't know what you're about at all," she said, "but I do think you're more apt to get me out of everything than anyone I've ever known before."

"How do you define 'out of everything'?" he asked her.

"That's silly of you to ask me," she said, "because of course you know that every girl my age, even a rich one, always wants to get out of everything."

There was no one else who had quite the same answers to things as Rhoda.

By the time America had reached the year 1928, sexual morals, according to certain experts, had broken down, and this disintegration had been assisted by Mr. Scott Fitzgerald, whom Walter Price for no good reason had always called "Fitzy," and by the dim lights of those motion-picture halls where the almost silent films of those days — at least in the country — were accompanied by the piano. It could not have helped morals for young people in ill-lighted, badly ventilated halls to perceive the liberated actions of handsome actors and actresses moving in a more desirable world. Somehow, in the film world, the poor but honest girl always lived poor but honestly in a ten-thousand-dollar-a-year apartment which must have been confusing to other poor but honest girls. Somehow she always fell into the arms, to appropriate music, of the poor but honest boy, who drove a moving van and who never quite seemed to belong in the poor but honest girl's apartment, which she paid for out of her meager stenographic salary. A generation before, young people sat side by side on love seats, looking through stereopticons at photographs of Niagara Falls and of the Spanish-American War, but in 1928 you could see dreams of wish-fulfillment move. You could sit with the girl of your choice in the darkened theatre in 1928, and observe conventional varieties of love play as far as was permitted by a confused National Board of Censorship, and at the same time project your imagination into the doings on the screen. There was no wonder that sex standards were disappearing under this erosion, and no wonder that he and Rhoda Browne trustingly and conventionally held hands the moment that the lights were dimmed, like babes in the wood — not that this was quite the right way to put it from either of their points of view — until the lights went on again. There was no wonder that he and Rhoda Browne felt closer emotionally then they had before, after the picture was ended.

He had tried and tried, while casting his mind back to those years, to recall what under the sun the picture had been about that they had witnessed that evening, and he never could remember. What was more, he never cared, because he had been sitting beside Rhoda, holding her delicate, firm hand, and even at odd moments allowing his hand to rest upon her knee, not more than that, even though he may have had designs. It was by sheer accident that he had met her there at Dock Street, and only kind coincidence had permitted them simultaneously to speak. The gods were very good to him that night, because he knew after his few words with her, reinforced by slight physical contact, that he would never in the world again meet anyone with her validity or appeal.

The 6:30 show was over by about half past eight, but instead of darkness, there was still the glow of sunset.

"It just goes to show," Rhoda said, "that nothing much can happen at the 6:30 pictures on daylight saving time, and I think you'd better get me home by 9:15 this once."

"Would you like an ice-cream soda first?" he asked.

"I'm tired of ice-cream sodas," she said. "I wish it were dark enough so we could see the stars. I'd like to go some place and see the sky, but you can't ever see much of it here with all the trees and houses."

"There's the burying ground by the common," he said. "You can see a lot of the sky from there, if you're not afraid of dead people."

"I'm not afraid," she said, "I'm only scared I'll get briers in my silk stockings."

"I'll buy you another pair if you do," he said.

"My mother always tells me," she said, "not to accept gifts from men. Well, all right, but only if there are briers. You must be anxious for me to see the sky."

"Not especially," he said. "I'm only curious to know why you want to see it."

She glanced at him sideways in the waning light.

"Because it makes me wish all sorts of things I want," she said, "and I want a lot of things."

"You mean the sky's the limit," he said.

She did not laugh or even smile.

"That's what I do mean," she said. "I never thought of it in just that way."

"What sort of things does the sky make you want?" he asked, and she smiled her bright, quick smile.

"I'm afraid I want everything," she said, "and I keep being afraid it will all keep on being the way it is."

The burying ground by the common was a symbol of the past, perfunctorily maintained by the town and no longer employed for its original purpose. Instead, its slate stones and tombs were objects of curiosity and occasionally of vandalism; it had become part of the local custom, and it was considered correct for the local youth to walk there after the 6:30 show. He remembered that they sat side by side on a tomb belonging to a Captain Ezra Blood, a startling name, and the tomb was still there intact, as of the present.

"It's awful to be afraid," she said. "I wish I weren't afraid of being poor, and wandering around and ending marrying someone who's always going to be poor." She glanced at him and their eyes met, and even in the half light, he could see that their gray-greenish tinge suited the color of her hair. "You don't know what I'm talking about, because you don't know what it's like to want things and know you'll never get them. Clothes, diamonds, and limousines and things like that. I don't know if I'd care about having them — but it's knowing I'll never get them —"

"I know what you mean," he said. "I guess I want a lot of things I'll never get, but the trouble with me is I never know just what I want."

"That means you've never been poor," she said, "or had to want things."

"Maybe, but I've never been rich," he said.

"It's queer talking to you," she said. "I don't seem to know where I am with you, because I don't know what you are, I guess."

"I don't know what I am myself," he said, "but then, maybe no one knows exactly. Would you like it if I could get you clothes and jewels and limousines?"

"Yes," she said, "of course; only, if you started doing that, you'd have to keep me in them. I wouldn't want to start slipping back again."

"Maybe I could try," he said.

"I'd like it if you would," she said, "but besides, I'd like it if I were an honest woman."

"I don't know whether you can make people honest women, but I might try," he said.

The color was still in the sky and the clouds by the western horizon were still partly gold and partly purple. Whenever he saw clouds of that color afterwards, he always thought of fantasy. They were both dealing with a sort of make-believe that might possibly turn into reality, but even if the reality were possible, you did not have to face it unless you wished. There were few times in life as entirely agreeable.

"Suppose I were the Count of Monte Cristo," he said. "You've read *The Count of Monte Cristo*, haven't you?"

"Yes," she said. "I've been trained carefully by my mother."

"I didn't know mothers made daughters read *The Count of Monte Cristo*," he said.

"I didn't say that," she answered. "I read it when she wasn't looking."

"All right," he said, "suppose I were the Count of Monte Cristo and I could give you everything you wanted."

She shook her head.

"It's just as well you're not," she said. "I'd be terrible if I had everything I wanted, but the main thing would be to be sure you'd always be the Count of Monte Cristo. Do you think you always would?"

It was colder now the sun was down, and she stood up, but he knew what he would have said if she had given him the time to answer. He would have said of course he would always be Mr. Dantes, and he would have believed it, too.

"I suppose I'll have to go," she said. "There are cupcakes and lemonade in the kitchen. You're not going to go away, are you?"

"No," he said, "not if there are cupcakes."

"I mean," she said, "I know you're only visiting your aunt or someone, but — after all of this — I hope you're going to be here for a while."

He had never thought until then that he might just as well write his second play in the Judge's house.

"Oh, I'll be here for quite a while," he said.

"I don't see how you can be, if you have anything to do," she said.

Every thought and speech projected its pattern afterwards, and this one in particular.

"I haven't got anything to do at the moment because I'm out of a job, but at the same time I'm doing a little work," he told her.

Right there they reached the roadblock, the roadblock of the years.

"You mean you're working, and you're out of a job, and you don't have to work?" she asked him.

"That's right," he said. "Roughly that's what I mean. I mean, I don't exactly know what I'm doing myself."

"You don't know what you're doing yourself?" she said.

"That doesn't sound right. That isn't accurate," he answered. "I know roughly what I'm doing, but I don't know how it's going to come out."

Rhoda laughed uncertainly, but her laughter sounded like the temple bells of Mandalay, disturbed by an unexpected breeze.

"That sounds queer," she said. "I like you, but I don't understand anything you're saying."

There was always a gap between them, but they were walking side by side down Dock Street then, and everything seemed possible.

"You see, I'm writing a play," he said.

"You mean like Ibsen?" she said.

"I wouldn't call it straight Ibsen," he said, "not *The Wild Duck* or anything like that, but at the same time, it's a play."

"You mean you're so rich that you really don't have to work at anything?" she asked him.

"Oh, no," he said. "You see, I've written another play and they

245

hope to produce it on Broadway, and they've paid me a thousand dollars."

That was before inflation, but still, the sum had a different meaning for each of them.

"You're not just telling stories," she said, "that you write plays, and they pay you a thousand dollars?"

"No," he said, "that's accurate. I've written one and now I'm writing another."

"How long does it take?" she asked.

"You can't make any rigid estimate," he said, "but I'd say, if you have a clear idea, you ought to get something in shape in about three months."

"Four thousand dollars a year," she said. "That isn't much, is it?"

They were walking down Harrison Street, and the stars were out, but the elm trees obscured the stars.

"That's only the advance," he said. "If the plays are good enough, they'll run into a great deal more."

"How do you mean?" she asked. "If they give you a thousand dollars, isn't that all?"

"Oh, no," he said. "If a play's a hit on Broadway, it can be worth a good deal more than a hundred thousand dollars."

She did not answer for a minute.

"I don't understand what you're saying," she said, "but you did tell me, didn't you, that you have a play that may go on to Broadway? Could that one be worth more than a hundred thousand dollars?"

"Yes," he said, "perhaps."

"And they've given you a thousand dollars for it anyway?" she said.

"Yes," he said, "that's what they call an advance."

They were silent for almost a minute.

"I still don't understand what you're talking about," she said, "and I suppose you're exaggerating, but I've had a wonderful time."

"I've had a wonderful time, too," he said. "What are you doing tomorrow?"

"I don't know," she said, "but you can have a cupcake now."

They had reached the door of the Browne house, and now the dark was falling, but the sky was clear and it was possible to see the stars.

"I'd like a cupcake very much," he told her.

"And when you're eating it," she said, "after I've told my mother I've come home, I wish you'd tell me what you are. What does your father do?"

"He didn't do anything but lose money," he said. "He died of flu after the war, but he did take me to Jack's."

"What's Jack's?" she asked.

"In New York," he said. "It used to be a restaurant on Sixth Avenue before Prohibition. He took me there when he was drunk one night, and he sang me a little song."

"What song?" she asked.

Another thing about Rhoda, she was always avid for small detail.

"Oh," he said, "it was a silly song:

> "Stay in there punching, sonny,
>   Don't let your heart fall plop,
> Someday the nation will honor you, too,
>   As it's honored your dear old pop."

They were in the Brownes' kitchen, with its coal-burning stove and soapstone sink, and the lemonade and the cupcakes were on the table, just as Mrs. Browne had said they would be.

"I still don't understand you," Rhoda said, "but I do hope the nation will honor you, too — and you're not going to leave town, are you?"

"No," he said. "The idea would be ridiculous."

She had pulled off her cloche hat. The electric bulb from the kitchen wall bracket made her hair glow, and cast perfect shadows on her photogenic face. She was prettier than anyone he had ever known or ever would again. He moved to touch her, and she did not move away.

"Not here," she whispered. "Mother will be listening through the register upstairs."

But she did kiss him, once, in the shadows just outside the front door. There was nothing spectacular about the embrace, since at that time the gesture was conventional, but he never forgot the touch of her lips, nor her farewell whisper. No one ever again had whispered as merrily and beguilingly as Rhoda.

"Good night, Monte Cristo," she said. "I'll see you in the cemetery tomorrow afternoon."

XV

It Lingers Still, Thy Infinite Variety

THERE had once been a time when he had resented, though
he had always artistically admired, the inevitability of Greek
tragedy. From the opening scene onward, it never required an
interpretive chorus to make it clear that the hero, gifted though
he might be by the gods, would never extricate himself from
the difficulties into which the Fates had cast him. Aeschylus had
often seemed to him to insult the dignity of human will, and yet
he had to admit that there were times in any life when Aeschylus
and Euripides were doubtless right. There were times when, like
a swimmer in the surf off a Long Island beach, one would inadvertently be caught in an ebbing current and before one knew
what was happening, be carried out to sea. An experienced
swimmer had told him once that it was better to let the current
take you until its force died down, because man could never
beat the sea in an outright test of strength, and Aeschylus would
have added that man could never beat the Fates.

His experience with Rhoda Browne thirty years ago was something the Greeks might have understood better than the
moderns. There was coincidence in his having met her on Dock
Street just when he had left New York and Betty Howland forever; but coincidence, a Greek would say, was furnished by the
gods, and after he had met her, the ending was inevitable. He
was conscious of the efforts that Rhoda's parents and Rhoda herself were making. He could be amused by them, but he never resented them and never would have wanted them different.
There had been many sides to Rhoda that delighted him without his ever wanting them to change, and in spite of those sides

and those eager calculations, no one could erase the truth that he and Rhoda were in love.

You could debate with yourself exactly what the phrase "in love" might mean, and undoubtedly it never had meant the same thing to any two individuals. From his point of view it was not infatuation, because he had always seen her in clear perspective. He loved her humor and her honesty and he must have also loved her for the things that he could give her that she wanted, but why had she loved him?

"I don't know why," she said once that summer. "I don't understand you half the time. Maybe because you're so different. You're always new and strange — but I can tell you when I started loving you — in the kitchen eating cupcakes, when you said it would be ridiculous to go away; and it would have been ridiculous."

It would have been ridiculous, although common sense must have told him at some point that going away was the wiser thing to do. It would have been ridiculous after she had whispered that she would see him in the cemetery next afternoon, and his Aunt Edith had been pathetically delighted when he had suggested that he might stay on for a month or two and finish up his writing. As of now, if he could have done it over again, he would not have changed a minute of that time, for all of it was refreshing and most of it was comedy, and one of the most delightful things about that summer was that Rhoda and the Brownes had been impressed by his financial capabilities.

It was obvious, that next day, that Rhoda had given her parents some sort of balance sheet.

"Mother wonders whether you wouldn't care to come to supper tomorrow night," Rhoda said, "and Pa's going to buy some lobsters, in case you want to know."

There was another thing that he could not forget. He had been among the first to appreciate Rhoda's potential charm.

"Would you like to have me?" he asked her.

When he asked the question, he could remember that he had been trying to analyze her charm.

"Don't ask silly questions to get compliments," she said. "Or maybe you don't like lobsters?"

"I always like them," he said, "in the company of a pretty girl."

"That's a silly thing to say, too, because lobsters always taste the same. You remember what you said yesterday about silk stockings?"

"Yes," he said, "I remember."

"Well, look," she said, and she pointed at her ankle, "you can get me a pair and bring them around tomorrow night."

"I'll get you a dozen so you won't have to remind me any more," he said.

"A dozen?" she said. "Well, all right, if you'll help so I can get them upstairs without Mother seeing them, because Mother might think . . ."

He laughed; she could always make him laugh.

"Oh, no," he said, "not for a dozen pairs, and I'll tell you another thing I'll do. I'll buy a new Ford from your father."

There was still some money in the account.

"You mean you'll buy it on account of me?" she said.

She could always make him laugh, even when he knew that the current was taking him far away from the beach.

"That's right," he said, "and you won't get your stockings torn in the brambles any more."

He had learned one useful thing about the town long before he had met Rhoda, and this was that everyone's life there was an open book, whether one wanted it to be or not. Sin and sorrow, sex and continence were always written more clearly than the words on a wayside pulpit or the words on a poster advertising the latest Hollywood production. Thus he was not astonished to find when he had arrived at Harrison Street that evening that Mr. and Mrs. Browne had been able to learn a good deal about him. Mrs. Browne was alone in the overstuffed parlor with a faded framed photograph on her lap.

"Rhoda is working in the kitchen," she said. "She's much more of a homebody than I ever used to be. Mr. Browne will be here in a few minutes; it's wonderful that things are so busy at the agency."

"It does seem as though everybody's buying a Ford these days," he said. "Would Rhoda like me to help her in the kitchen?"

"Oh, no," Mrs. Browne said. "Rhoda always calls the kitchen a woman's world. I hope you like lobsters, Mr. Harrow."

"I've always been devoted to them," he said, "and I only hope they won't frighten Rhoda."

"That's very thoughtful of you to think of them in that way," Mrs. Browne said, "but Rhoda isn't easily frightened. I hadn't realized that your aunt was the Miss Fowler who lives in that delightful old gingerbread house near Johnson Street, Mr. Harrow."

Her intentions were obvious, but from the very first they had never alarmed or irritated him. On the contrary, his interest was stimulated, as it always was when he encountered something new. He had never been considered a desirable match before, and the feeling was agreeable. He could understand at last the reactions of a hero in a Jane Austen novel or of the Rockefeller or the Whitney boys, even though he and Mrs. Browne were a long way from the Whitneys. Still, as Tolstoy had said, if one had once seen a street fight, one could write about a battle; and besides, someone had to marry Rhoda someday; someday her knight would come riding. He had never minded in the least being cast as the Little Colonel's knight. He had always sympathized from the very beginning with the eagerness of Mr. and Mrs. Browne. It resembled the anxiety of shipwrecked passengers on a foundering raft, and yet the fact remained that the Brownes had hit the jackpot in the end, and had landed safely in a bungalow at Daytona Beach.

"It's known around here as the old Judge Fowler house," he said. "I have never been enthusiastic about my grandfather's taste in architecture, but perhaps you're right, that it is delightful in a way."

His motto had always been to try everything once. It was easier than he had thought, being a Count of Monte Cristo.

Mrs. Browne sighed, lightly and not lugubriously.

"The home where one has spent happy hours of childhood and youth must always be delightful in its way," she said. "Now, when you came in, Mr. Harrow, you surprised me poring over a photograph of my old home." She held the framed picture out to him, and he found himself examining the awkward outlines of a huge house with a bulbous front and a columned portico. "It's my dear mother's photograph of the old Rhyelle mansion in Baltimore, now unfortunately torn down to make room for a real estate development."

When Mrs. Browne became one of the Baltimore Rhyelles, she assumed a south of Mason and Dixon accent, a soft, almost imperceptible slurring of intonation which was never a part of her ordinary speech.

"The ballroom was in the large wing in the back, just yonder," she said. "I was presented there to Baltimore society, and I met Mr. Browne at that year's cotillion, not that he'd been invited. He had come with some other young men from the University of Maryland, not that he could not have been invited. The Brownes of Maryland are well known in the state." It put Mr. Browne in his place. Although she never admitted it outright, it had always been clear that the Rhyelle-Browne marriage had been a misalliance, and there was an intimation, also never put into words, that due to it, the doors of the Rhyelle mansion had closed on Estelle Rhyelle forever. Mrs. Browne sighed when she had finished her speech, and he could not blame her. Everyone had his own Rhyelle mansion somewhere.

"It's an interesting house," he said. "No wonder you like to look at it."

"I only like to at odd moments," Mrs. Browne said. "I don't believe in stepping backwards into the past, but I do wish you might have seen it. It would have made such a background for a play, and Rhoda says you're a playwright, Mr. Harrow. It must be fascinating being a playwright."

"Maybe she has it a little wrong," he said. "I wouldn't say I am a playwright exactly, but only trying to get to be one."

"But Rhoda says you've written and sold a play?"

A note of dismay in Mrs. Browne's voice made him answer

253

her reassuringly; he had never understood why he had always been anxious never to let down Mrs. Browne.

"That's true," he said, "I have written one and the producer has paid me an advance on it, and he's planning to put it in rehearsal sometime this autumn, and I am writing another while I'm waiting to see what's going to happen."

Mrs. Browne sighed, but it was a sigh of relief.

"It must be wonderful to be so successful so young," she said.

"You're right about my being young," he said, "but I wouldn't say that I'm successful yet — only hoping to be."

"I know you're going to be," Mrs. Browne said. "I can tell from looking at you. They used to say in Baltimore I was gifted in that way. Oh, here comes Mr. Browne."

Mr. Browne, that evening, was dressed in a blue double-breasted suit, and you could see that he was too anxious ever to be a good salesman. That was one thing to remember — never fall on your face with eagerness.

"Hudson," Mrs. Browne said, "perhaps it's enough of an occasion so that Mr. Harrow would like to take a little something."

"I guess you've got to come up with that again," Mr. Browne said. "What little something?"

Mrs. Browne was sweet and patient.

"Some of the something, Hudson, that you brought home from the sales convention," she said.

"Oh," Mr. Browne said, "why, you bet. You could do with a snort of rye, couldn't you, Mr. Harrow, seeing, as Rhoda says, you've been on the stage? It isn't bad hooch. Our main distributor gave it to me, so it's got to be good."

"I wish you wouldn't call it a snort, Hudson," Mrs. Browne said. "And Rhoda never said that Mr. Harrow was on the stage. He's not an actor, he's a playwright, Hudson."

"Well, it's still stage," Mr. Browne said, "and I guess this young fellow will excuse me if I call it a snort. He looks like he might be kind to a poor old man."

Then they were interrupted by a scream from the kitchen.

"Mother," Rhoda screamed.

254

"What is it, dear?" Mrs. Browne called.

"The lobsters, Mother," Rhoda screamed, "one of them's got away, and he's lost the plug out of his claw and the others whistle when you put them in the pot!"

"Please let me help her, Mrs. Browne," Tom said. "I'm wonderful with lobsters."

It was a prediction, not an established fact. He had never before thought of trying to be wonderful with lobsters. Rhoda was wearing an apron over her green dress with the red spots. Her sleeves were rolled up, and her hair was rumpled.

"That's what comes of trying to show you what a good cook I am," she said. "I told Mother it wouldn't work. I've always hated housework. I hate everything except riding in a limousine."

"I don't blame you," he said. "Where's the lobster who lost his plug?"

"He's under the sink," she said. "Let's leave him there."

"It might be a good idea," he said, "but I told your mother I was wonderful with lobsters."

"All right," Rhoda answered, "go ahead and be honored just like your dear old pop."

"You look beautiful, now that you're all aglow," he said.

"Never mind," Rhoda said, "here's the broom. Get the broom in front of him, and when he bites it, grab him."

It worked, like many of Rhoda's suggestions.

"If you know so much about it, why did you scream?" he asked.

"Don't be a dumbbell," Rhoda said. "To get you out here, naturally. I don't like the going-over they're giving you in the parlor."

"It's no going-over. Your father was going to give me a snort of hooch," he said.

"Well," she answered, "I can handle you without their help, and besides, I'd rather."

"So would I rather have you," he said.

"I bet you didn't bring the stockings," she said.

"You're wrong," he answered. "I brought them."

"Oh," she said, "where are they?"

"On a chair in the hall," he said. "I don't think anybody noticed the package."

"I'd better get it upstairs quick," she said. "You can watch the lobsters and I'll run up and wash my face and brush my hair. Do you approve of lipstick?"

The picture of Betty Howland returned to him, but the vision disappeared almost immediately, and after all, lipstick was not mandatory in 1928.

"On occasions," he said.

"Well, I'll try you out with it after supper," she said. "Pa's taking Mother out riding after supper in the demonstrator Ford. Mother arranged it." She giggled. "The young people alone — I wish I could be allowed to handle you without help. Don't you think I'm able to?"

"I think so up to date," he said.

"So do I," she answered. "You haven't changed your mind, have you, about buying a Ford?"

"No," he said, "I'll take it up with your father at supper."

"I don't mean to be grasping or pushing, or anything like that," she said. "You understand that, don't you?"

"Yes," he said, "but you do like people who live up to their promises, don't you?"

"You know," she said, "I wonder whether you aren't laughing at me half the time."

"Not half the time," he said.

"Well," she said, "promise you'll never make me cook."

"All right," he said.

The moment was more solemn than it should have been. They stood in the kitchen shyly, as though each had said something more than was intended. He had an impulse to draw her toward him, but she shook her head quickly.

"No," she said, "after supper. Watch the lobsters, Monte Cristo."

It was curious that since that night he had never learned much more about Rhoda's family, but at the same time he had discovered almost all that was necessary for a son-in-law to

256

know; and there were points beyond which curiosity should not go about a girl's parents if one were in love with her, and Rhoda was vague about them herself. She did not know what had happened to her mother's family, the Rhyelles, and frankly she did not care. Mr. Browne sometimes spoke of his boyhood days on the Eastern Shore of Maryland, but Rhoda had never cared about this either, or his business ventures — the chicken farm, the orange ranch in California, the hardware store in New Jersey, the insurance agency in Rhode Island. She knew only that none of them had worked. He might have pried further into the difficulties of the Brownes, but he had always had the grace not to do it. All that was necessary was to take Rhoda's family as they were, and they were not so hard to take. Mrs. Browne had been sweet and thoughtful, and Mr. Browne basically was a good old guy, and both of them had gratitude, which was something one did not always get from in-laws. He had never been able to blame Rhoda for her desire to escape from them because every child in the world always wanted something that childhood had not given, and Rhoda's had never given her security.

"You were kind to them," she told him that evening, "and they were awfully silly, weren't they?"

"I don't know that you'd call them silly exactly," he said.

"Of course you would," she answered, "throwing you and me together, and it's only a wonder they didn't make you run away."

"I don't want to run away," he said. "I wanted you and me to be thrown together. That's what I came here hoping."

"It would have scared off a lot of boys," she said. "Maybe you're dumb in some ways."

"I don't feel dumb right now," he said.

"Nobody ever does," she said, "when they're being dumb. All that Baltimore business — whenever a boy comes to call, Mother gets to Baltimore."

"You can't blame her," he said, "that was quite a house in Baltimore."

"Oh," she said, "the mansion. Do you believe it?"

"That's not a good question," he said. "You ought not to ask me that."

"Well, anyway, you were sweet," she said, "and of course I love them, I suppose. Oh, dear! I wish I could keep on believing."

"Believing what?" he asked.

"In their amounting to anything," she said. "Oh, dear, it's awful to wake up and start seeing things. I wish I didn't see so much."

"I don't see why you wish that," he said. "I like to see as much as I can. Maybe that's what we're here for."

"If I see too much, I get frightened," she said.

"Why, what's there to be frightened of?" he asked.

He remembered Rhoda's mother saying that Rhoda was not easily frightened, and now she looked worried rather than afraid, or perhaps exasperation would have been a better word. She scowled and her lips grew thin with impatience, but at the same time, there was a smile at the corner of them, and her eyes were bright. She still looked attractive, but then she always had at any time and in any place, and the dingy parlor only made a romantically contrasting background for what he saw in Rhoda.

"It's the same old record," she said. "Maybe every girl in the world gets frightened who isn't rich and who has a little sense."

"Frightened of what?" he asked.

"Why, frightened at what's going to happen to her," she said. "A girl's life is always a horrid, unfair dancing party. That's true, you know. It is a sort of dancing party."

She disengaged her hand from his, did a quick dance turn in the middle of the Brussels carpet and sat down opposite him in a straight-backed chair with her ankles carefully crossed, and her hands neatly folded on her lap.

"A girl's got to sit and wait for some man to ask her to do anything at all," she said, "and you don't know who he's going to be or what, and if he's awful you don't know whether you ought to say 'No' to him or not because then there may not be anyone else, ever, to ask you anything, but there's one thing you always know. You can't keep sitting here, pretending that you like the music. Somebody's got to take you away, but the frightening thing is, no one may ever ask you, or worse than that, no one you want."

She stopped and smiled, her sudden swift smile.

"Don't pretend that you're a wallflower," he said, "and it isn't hospitable of you to be away off across the room."

"Well, if you're asking me to join you," she said, "come over here and make the proposition and lead me back. Someone's got to ask me sometime."

He could never tell when they had reached an understanding. There were no perceptible stages, except for the beginning at Dock Street. Everything between them had been inevitable, but gradual. That night he had not asked her anything, and yet he must have known as sure as fate that he was going to, and just as surely that she would agree.

"I know," she said, "it isn't polite for me to talk about myself. People always say in advice to the lovelorn that you should draw your gentleman caller out. Ask him tactful questions. Get him to talk about himself. Do you want to talk about yourself?"

"Why, not especially," he said.

"And I don't know whether I want you to, either," she said, "because you make me feel how dumb I am. But, anyway, what's the name of this play you're writing now?"

"It's called *Little Liar*," he said.

"That's a queer name," she said. "Where did you get it from?"

"I got it from Hilaire Belloc's *Cautionary Tales*," he said, "from a poem about a girl named Matilda who screamed for the firemen when the house wasn't burning down, and finally when it was, and she shouted fire, they only answered, 'Little liar!'"

"Do you think I'm a little liar?" she asked.

"Not any more than most girls," he said. "Girls at some point have to be little liars."

"I'm glad you see it that way," she said. "What's your play about?"

259

"It's about a man who falls in love with his conscience," he said.

"Are you trying to be funny?" she asked. "How can anyone fall in love with his conscience?"

"Well," he said, "in this play, the man's conscience is a beautiful girl, and the man is in bed in his bedroom in the first act, after having done something that disturbs his conscience; and his conscience, the beautiful girl, keeps knocking and knocking, and finally she comes in because she is so tired of knocking. She's always been knocking on doors for years trying to get to him, she says, and he's never listened."

She was listening to him carefully, but she still looked puzzled.

"She comes right into his bedroom?" she said. "I wouldn't dare do that, but it isn't a bad idea. But how does he know that she's his conscience?"

"Because she tells him so," he said, "and he apologizes for never having listened to her before. He didn't know she was so beautiful, and he falls in love with her."

"He falls in love with her right in the bedroom?" she said.

"He has to in the bedroom," he said, "because it's too expensive changing scenes nowadays."

"What is she wearing," she asked, "when she comes into the bedroom?"

"Negligee," he said, "she's thinly clad. After all, consciences don't need many clothes."

"Gosh," she said, "I don't see how you thought any of this up. What happens then?"

"The curtain goes down," he said. "It's the end of the first act."

"You mean the curtain goes down right then," she said, "and you don't see anything happen? I don't think that's fair."

"It's better to imagine some things," he said, "and I don't think it's a bad first act."

"Well, I don't think it's fair," she said. "What happens then?"

"Why, in the second act," he said, "she falls in love with him and she loves him so much she lets him do almost anything he wants."

"I wish I had a conscience like that," she said, "only mine would have to be a boy. But what happens after that?"

"Well, that's the third act," he said, "and I'm working on it now. He quarrels with his conscience, and they get divorced, and he's back in his bedroom again, entirely devoid of conscience, and that's as far as I've gone, except that he's going to ask her to come back."

"Why?" she asked.

"Because he finds it very lonely to have no conscience at all," he said, "but just when he's made up his mind to get along without one, there she is, knocking at his door. He is just getting out of his trousers — conscience is always knocking at the door at the wrong moment — and she tells him to behave himself. Divorced or not, you can't get rid of conscience."

"It sounds sort of peculiar," she said. "But then, I've only seen a few stock companies act plays."

"There's nothing peculiar about having a conscience," he said. "Everybody has one."

"Have you got a conscience about me?" she asked.

"Yes," he said, "I think I have."

"That's nice if it's true," she said, "because most men don't seem to have much of any about girls. That's why you have to be on the lookout, always. It gets awfully tiresome being on the lookout."

"That's what he tells his conscience in the play," he said. "No one has much conscience about his conscience."

The house was very still, and he put his arm around her.

"Remember your conscience," she said. "She may not like it." But she did not move away.

"My conscience is getting on fine," he said. "How's yours?"

She laughed, one of those quick laughs whose echo always lingered in his memory.

"A girl doesn't need one, usually, as long as she deals with facts," she said, "and maybe you're beginning to be a fact. I sort of hope you are."

"I hope so, too," he said, "but maybe we'd both know better if you'd let me kiss you."

"That's a silly thing to say," she said. "You know very well I will. So stop talking and go ahead and do it."

One thing about Rhoda had always been that her frankness never spoiled anything. It did not spoil anything to know that he had done what she had been expecting, and that she had wanted him to do it.

"I've got on violet talcum powder," she said. "I'm glad it didn't make you sneeze."

"It didn't," he said.

"Well, dust if off your shoulder," she said, "it gets all over everything, doesn't it? I wish I had some French perfume."

"I'll get you some," he said.

"That would be nice," she said, "if I could think of some way of using it so Mother wouldn't notice, because I'm afraid she'd guess where it came from. Mother's quick about things, sometimes, when she gets her mind off Baltimore."

"Maybe I can find you some scentless perfume," he said. "It'll be in a clear, crystal bottle labeled 'Hide and Seek' or else 'Camouflage.' 'Camouflage' would be a better name, considering it's French."

"It's hard for me to tell whether you're ever serious," she said, "because you're always joking."

"It's a coincidence," he said. "I'm pretty serious most of the time."

"I wish I knew," she said. "Is it true this new play is about all these things, or are you just making it up?"

"No, I'm not making it up," he said.

"Do you think," she said, and looked at him almost shyly, "anyone will give you another thousand dollars for a play like that?"

"I shouldn't be surprised," he said. "They may pay a lot more, if the first one goes all right."

"I know you wouldn't be surprised," she said, "but still do you honestly think anybody will understand it?"

"Maybe," he said. "I've shown the first part of it to Mort Sullivan, and he says it ought to act, and they're looking around right now for fantasy."

"Who's Mort Sullivan?" she asked.

"My dramatic agent," he said. "I used to work for him before I started writing plays."

"Gosh," she said, "I didn't know you had a dramatic agent. When you get that Ford, we can go to the beach, and there's a roller-skating pavilion there."

"I can't wait to roller-skate," he said.

"Oh, don't," she said, and suddenly her voice broke. "Don't keep on being funny, because —" her voice broke again — "it isn't, for me. It isn't funny at all."

"Why, Rhoda," he said, "I didn't mean —"

But she spoke again before he had finished.

"Then kiss me and be serious," she said. "I've got to get out of this. I want to be where I can use French perfume, and I don't want it called 'Camouflage.' I don't want anything to be camouflage. Oh, Tom, I'm so afraid I won't."

"Don't be afraid," he said. "I'm not joking, Rhoda."

"I won't be, if you don't go away," she said. "You're the only person I've ever seen who — who —"

He waited, but she did not go on.

"Who what?" he asked.

"I don't have to tell you what," she said. "You know very well. Now kiss me good night again. I want to be asleep before Mother comes back, and I'll see you again at the cemetery tomorrow at the same tombstone. Good night, Monte Cristo."

"Why not be informal," he said, "and simply call me 'Monte.' I honestly wouldn't mind."

"Don't," she said, "please. This honestly isn't funny. But if you'd rather, I could call you 'Count.' Good night, Count — but I want to brush that talcum powder off you. That aunt of yours might not like it. Stand still where the light strikes you. You're dreadfully handsome, Count."

Without anything having been said specifically, nothing more was necessary. As an older generation would have put it, the young people were interested in each other, but he never

263

could agree with his Aunt Edith that Rhoda had thrown herself at him. The action had been simultaneous, and from the moment they had first seen each other, it was for better or for worse, and Rhoda had been right about the violet talcum powder.

His Aunt Edith was reading by the gas lamp in the front parlor when he returned to the Judge's house.

"Tom," she said, "I am not mistaken, am I, that you are covered with violet perfume?"

"I'm sorry," he said. "I thought I had dusted it off."

"It does not matter," she said, "the odor is not disagreeable. Did it come from that young girl on whom you were calling, Rhoda Browne?"

"Well, yes," he said, "now you mention it, Aunt Edith."

"I recognize that conventions have changed since I was young," his aunt said. "It must mean, then, that she has been embracing you on the first night you called on her formally. I'm sorry if I disapprove."

"I wouldn't say that she was embracing me, Aunt Edith," he said. "It would be more correct to say that I was embracing her."

She sniffed and he, also, was aware of the scent of violets.

"It is what a gentleman would say," she said. "But your admission cannot conceal the fact that the young girl was willing to be embraced."

She had put down her book and sat with folded hands, her ankles carefully crossed, though only partially visible beneath the hem of her long dress, in an attitude exactly like Rhoda's when Rhoda had said that a girl always had to wait for someone to ask her.

"How do you know she consented?" he said. "Perhaps she resisted my advances."

"No," she said, "no. It would have been more correct if she had done so, but if she had, there would have been less perfume."

"Well," he said, "the Judge's grandson doesn't kiss and tell,

Aunt Edith. Let's say that a friendly embrace is almost conventional now among unmarried members of opposite sexes of a certain age. It doesn't mean what it used to. In fact, it's only a form of politeness."

"I understand," his aunt said. "I am glad that you have been polite, and I realize that things have changed greatly. Your father, for example, was a very impetuous man in what I might term an amorous way regarding my sister, your mother, after his automobile collided with the tree. But it was at least ten days before my sister and Mr. Harrow reached anything approaching what you seem to have arrived at much sooner. Yes, I know that times have changed."

"It might have happened sooner, too, if my father hadn't been hurt in the accident," Tom said.

"That is true," his aunt said. "He sustained a broken arm and a fractured collarbone. I had forgotten. This Browne girl, I suppose, must be pretty."

"Yes," he said, "I think she is, Aunt Edith."

"I can understand that you might think so," his aunt said. "What I should have said is that I hope she is pretty from the standpoint of my generation."

"Yes," he said. "I see what you mean. That's just the way she is pretty. In fact, you might say she looks distinguished."

His aunt sniffed again. "I am glad, although it hardly seems possible," she said.

"Well, that's the way it is," he told her. "Her mother comes from Baltimore. She was a Miss Rhyelle."

"It is strange," his aunt said, "even when I was young, people of a certain sort always seemed to come from Baltimore. She's not a Catholic, I hope. So many people are Catholics who come from Baltimore."

"I didn't see any sacred pictures on the wall," Tom said, "but the Brownes may have sold their Fra Lippo Lippi's."

"The Judge, your grandfather," his aunt said, "prided himself on his religious tolerance. He associated on the bench with many Irish Catholics, some of whom were judges also. But the

Judge was never in favor of a Protestant-Catholic marriage, although he always added, as I add, too, that this opinion was intended as no reflection upon the Church of Rome."

"But, Aunt Edith," he said, "I don't think they're Catholics, and because I have violet talcum on my coat doesn't mean I'm going to marry Rhoda. I don't have to make an honest woman of her on account of it, do I?"

"There can be no reason for going to any such lengths immediately," his aunt said, "since the acquaintance has been so brief, but you must understand that everyone is talking."

All that surprised him was that everyone should have been talking already.

"How do you know?" he asked.

"Mr. Gorman has said so, and so has Marie," his aunt said. "You were seen together in the cemetery after the 6:30 motion pictures and again the next day, and this afternoon on the way back from the post office from the last mail, which contained a letter for you from New York in a young lady's handwriting, you were seen waiting for several minutes outside the typing school."

There were some places where you never could get away with anything, and he was glad that never in all their association had he attempted to conceal anything from his aunt.

"It looks as though you have me dead to rights," he said. "Yes, we have been meeting in the cemetery."

"I'm glad to know," his aunt said, "that cemeteries can serve a dual purpose, but I think perhaps I should go and call on Mrs. Browne myself if things have gone so far."

"But Aunt Edith," he said, "things haven't gone anywhere." And the strange thing was that, when he told her, he believed it. He should have realized that what was nowhere in New York was far in some places.

"Don't let us labor the point," his aunt said. "The Judge, your grandfather, taught me as a young girl about weighing circumstantial evidence."

"Listen, Aunt Edith," he said, "I only kissed her. That's all the circumstantial evidence. That and the cemetery."

266

His aunt shook her head.

"I still think I shall call on Mrs. Browne," she said. "It will look better in the eyes of everyone and will be fairer to Miss Browne since things have gone so far."

It was only fair to admit that his Aunt Edith had been correct. Things had already gone so far that they would never be the same again, so far that the lines of success and failure were drawn in his career already. It was not too late for escape, but even if he could have looked into the future, seen himself as he was, alone and taking another drink to escape from the present, he still would not have changed a line. There had never been, and there would never be again, anyone in the world like Rhoda Browne.

XVI

Life and Love Moved Faster Then

THOUGH trite, the remark was still significant, that the happiest time in a man's or a nation's life occurs usually during those periods in which no historian can think of much on which to comment. He had not intended, before he met Rhoda Browne, to spend his summer out of New York while writing his play, *Little Liar*. But the happiest things in life often occurred by accident. Nothing that came to him later in professional and other ways could compare with the days he spent that summer; but he could recall very little about that time that was definite. He could remember only a few of the things he had said to Rhoda Browne and not much about the hours they had spent together, for these had finally fallen into a sequence. But at the same time, he had never worked so hard. If the fantasy *Little Liar* were finally to give him a place, as many reviewers agreed, in future histories of drama, he could thank Rhoda. The best in art was born only of incentive, which might be fear, hunger, jealousy or cupidity, but the incentive that made him spend hours on *Little Liar* that summer was solely the drive to show Rhoda that he could earn another cash advance. He had often wished that he could turn the clock back and experience again the drives that had urged him, but drives, he now knew, intensify and diminish, but could never repeat. There was nothing again like the period when he had worked on *Little Liar*, never the same anguish or ecstasy, or sense of living, or the same total competence. A woman seldom understood that a man's work always existed in a world beyond her own, but there was no doubt that Rhoda showed interest in those days.

"Do you think they are going to give you another thousand dollars?" she asked. "I love it, when you read it to me, but maybe that's only because I love you."

"Rhoda," he told her, "let's leave ourselves out. Essentially it's a good play."

"I don't see how we can leave ourselves out," Rhoda said, "when we need more money if Mother and Pa are going to let us get married."

Although he had faced the fact of marriage many times when he had been working on *Little Liar*, the word still sent a shiver of finality up his spine.

"All right," he said, "if your father's making so much in his Ford agency, you can go and marry a millionnaire."

"I didn't mean that," she said. "I want you. I think you're going to do better than Father, honestly I do."

Aside from Rhoda and *Little Liar*, he had other things on his mind, including a constant correspondence with the Higgins office. It had finally been decided that *Hero's Return* was to be put into rehearsal toward the middle of September.

This meant that he, being the author, should return to New York the first of September for the casting, and thus the time for finishing *Little Liar* was briefer than he had thought.

When he received this communication from the Higgins office, it was the end of July and he was not satisfied with *Little Liar* yet. A difficulty with any play was that no one connected with it was ever finally satisfied. In any drama there was always a well-constructed turning point, but in life you were always too involved in living to make a successful analysis. Now he could see that he had still had command of the situation when the news reached him that his play would go into rehearsal. The sensible thing to do was to pack up and go to New York to finish *Little Liar* without any further interruptions. If he had wanted to, he could have left that morning, simply sending a note to Rhoda. Would he have missed her in New York, enmeshed in the novelty that faced him there? He might

269

have temporarily, although the chances were that he would never have married Rhoda Browne; but when he was actually living through that period of decision, the possibility never occurred to him. No one in love could be a cynic, and he was in love with Rhoda, and consequently without the capability of judgment. He was beguiled, and he never blamed himself.

He had developed a habit that summer of parking his Ford roadster on Dock Street opposite the typing school, knowing very well that concealment was impossible. He sat waiting for her that afternoon after the news came, mentally revising some of the final speeches of *Little Liar*, oblivious of the people and the sounds on Dock Street. He was happy without knowing that he had been happy until years later. In his preoccupation with his last lines, he was not conscious of contentment until he saw Rhoda walk out of the old brick building whose second floor housed the typing school. They each expected the other and each took it for granted that the other would be there. She was wearing a plain cotton print dress and she was carrying her shorthand notebook. As she had often told him, she never did care how she looked at typing school, and now that her father was making enough money to give her a dress allowance, she was not going to spend it on looking nice when she was learning things like shorthand and double entry bookkeeping. But her intentions made no difference. She could not change the radiance of her hair or the grace of her walk, nor could she conceal her pleasure that he should have been waiting patiently for her there.

"I'm glad you've put the top down," she said. "Let's go for quite a long ride, shall we?"

"All right," he said.

"I'm tired," she said. "It was an awful bore up there today doing speed tests. Every girl should learn to support herself if necessary, but I don't want anybody to tell me so again."

"I won't," he said. "I don't want you to support yourself."

"Well, just keep thinking along those lines," she said. "How are you doing with the play?"

"It's all there," he said, "but it needs some going over."

270

"You keep fussing with it," she said. "Maybe you're doing it too much."

"There are one or two things that I want to make better," he said, "but the main part of the fussing is over."

"It makes me nervous the way you keep going over it," she said. "I don't believe anything you're doing will affect it now. Why don't you send it the way it is, and start on something new?"

"So I'll get another advance, you mean?" he asked.

"Yes," she said, "that's what I mean. You ought to keep doing it without wasting so much time. You said you could do four of them a year. I'll bet if you put your mind on it, you could do six."

"I don't seem to be able to explain," he said, "that I'm not selling these plays for a thousand dollars. That is the advance they are giving me against royalties."

"Well, it's something, anyway," Rhoda said.

"But the point is," he said, "as I've told you, if the play's a success, I may get a good deal more."

"But you can't tell," Rhoda said. "I still think what you have now is the point."

"You're a funny girl," he said. "An awfully funny girl."

"I don't feel so funny," she said. "How much money have you got in your pocket right now? Is it quite a lot?"

"Quite," he said, "comparatively speaking. I think a little over fifty dollars."

"You think? Don't you know?" she asked.

"Not down to the last nickel," he said. "Would you like me to stop and count it?"

"No," she said, "but as long as you have fifty dollars, why don't you take me to a roadhouse somewhere and get me some dinner and a bootleg cocktail? I've never been to a roadhouse."

"I don't know whether there are any around here," he said.

"There must be some," she said. "We saw one in the movie last night, that part of the double feature called *She Stoops to Folly* — I mean that place where there was a dance floor, and there were drinks and waiters and sizzling steaks. You remember that roadhouse, don't you?"

"Yes," he said, "vaguely."

"Vaguely," she repeated. "Why is it you always keep remembering things vaguely?"

"I must have been thinking how to get another advance," he said. "The picture didn't hold me."

"Maybe because you were holding me," Rhoda said, and she giggled, "but there must be some sort of roadhouse."

"You mustn't believe everything you see at the pictures," he said.

"That's what you keep saying," she answered, "but it seems to me a lot of the things I see are coming true. You look better than Douglas Fairbanks, in a different way."

"And you look better than Pickford," he said. "Besides you're my sweetheart, not America's sweetheart."

"Maybe it would be better to be America's sweetheart," she said. "Why not ask somebody at a filling station where a roadhouse is?"

"All right," he said, "I'll ask."

The place they went to was called the Kozy Kottage Diner. He could remember the uncomfortable booth, the man in the spotted tuxedo playing the piano and the violent taste of the gin and ginger ale at one dollar a drink.

"Gosh," Rhoda said, "so this is really it? This must be like New York."

"Don't drink that too fast," he said, "or you may go blind. This isn't a roadhouse; this is called a 'speak-easy.' They have bigger, better and busier ones in New York. Why, there's one where writers go in the afternoon, where if the police make a raid, they can press a button and they can have the bar go right back into the wall. And anyway, there are always people in the front room just waiting to get arrested. They're paid to get arrested."

"You remember queer things," she said. "I can't imagine being interested in a lot of poor people sitting around waiting to get arrested."

"I suppose it's how you look at it," he said. "I like to imagine what they're thinking while they're waiting. It could almost be an opening scene for something. They have broken noses and wear dinner clothes so the police can pick them from the regular patrons. And that reminds me, I've been meaning to tell you, I got a letter this morning saying that the play's going into rehearsal in September, and they'll be casting it before that. I've got to think about getting back to New York."

Her lips trembled and her hands shook as she endeavored to pick up her gin and ginger ale in a sophisticated manner.

"Well, you're not going to go to New York and associate with a lot of actors and actresses and chorus girls unless I go with you," she said. "How soon are you going?"

"I don't see how it can be arranged very well for you to go with me," he said. "I'll come right back as soon as the play starts going."

She shook her head.

"They never come back in the movies," she said, "when they go to the city and leave the small-town girl. Anyway, I won't take a chance. I'll go with you. You don't think I'm going to let you go, do you?"

She always made him laugh at unexpected moments.

"You needn't laugh," she said, "I'll never have a chance at anyone like you again. All right, you've got to marry me."

"But I can't, Rhoda," he told her, "until I know whether I have enough money to support a wife."

He could still remember the exact tune being beaten out on the piano. It was "Smiles," not quite so dated then as it was at present.

"I know," she said. "It's awfully dangerous, but I've got to take a chance, that's all. I can't let you go without me. What are you laughing at?"

"Only smiling," he said. "There are smiles that make me happy. I never thought you'd propose to me in quite this way. All right, I'll take a chance if you will."

"All right," she said. "You'd better tell Mother and Pa to-

273

night, even if we have to wake them up, and we'll go to Niagara Falls."

"Niagara Falls?" he repeated. "Why Niagara Falls?"

"Because it's where people go to get used to each other."

"Not necessarily," he said.

"Well, anyway," she told him, "I've always dreamed of going to Niagara Falls. Is it expensive at Niagara Falls?"

He never had occasion to go to Niagara Falls again, nor had he afterwards any desire because he knew that he would suffer disappointment if anything had changed, and doubtless everything had, including the Falls themselves. He did not care to be introduced to the new Niagara Falls. He wanted the old Niagara of September 1928, where he and Rhoda spent those fleeting days, after their single night at the Wellington Manor House — before it became necessary to go back to New York in order to sit in the Higgins office listening to people reading parts for *Hero's Return*. The Falls of that vintage had been packed long ago among the flatcars of the great caravan of change, and now were locked forever in time's warehouse.

Was the Romanesque red brick depot still standing, he wondered, with its colored porters grown kindly from consistent encounters with happy young couples who had all of life ahead of them and who seldom cared about the cost of things? Were the souvenir shops still carrying on, that had once made Rhoda gasp with wonder at their machine-made moccasins and tomahawks? He still could not understand why Rhoda had immediately wanted him to purchase a pair of moccasins with a picture of the Falls upon them, American side. And what about the Canadian side, that swift transition from American to foreign soil, with customs and immigration inspectors?

"Do you know what I think?" Rhoda had said. "I don't believe that customs man thought we are married."

"He was only looking for liquor," he told her, "not making a moral research."

"Well, it's lucky he wasn't making an immoral research," Rhoda said, "or he might have found the pint."

"No, he wouldn't have," he said. "American officials seldom molest American women."

"There might have been a matron," she said. "They have them in the movies."

"Not for a pint of Scotch," he said. "Only to break up rings of diamond smugglers."

"Will you get me some diamonds that I can smuggle sometime?" she asked.

"Yes," he said, "of course. It wouldn't look right if I didn't."

"That's one nice thing about being married," she said. "All sorts of things all at once look right," and she laughed. "All the things I've always been told a nice girl shouldn't do suddenly look right — I mean, as long as people know we're married — as long as I have a wedding ring. It's a whole new sort of life."

"Maybe anyone's life is," he said, "when he's suffering from euphoria."

"I wish you wouldn't use long words," she said, "and you mustn't use up all your father's money, and maybe we ought not to keep walking across that bridge so you can have a drink."

"It's like marriage," he said. "It's all right to drink in Canada."

Was Goat Island still there, with the swirling eddies of water and the conclusive roar of the Falls behind it? He had heard of second honeymoons, but he would never have dreamed of returning there for such a purpose. He never thought, as he stood by Rhoda, watching in a stupefied way that constant swirl of water, that they were both about to go over the falls of change.

"I wish you wouldn't keep tipping the headwaiter a dollar," Rhoda said, "every time we have dinner in the main dining room. There's no use our acting richer than we are."

Could you still hear the Falls at night from the third-floor suite of the Iroquois — which he had insisted on taking because he had never previously occupied a hotel suite — always provided the Iroquois House still existed? Doubtless the sound of the Falls was there, but it would be drumming a different tune from the one he and Rhoda had heard in the middle of the night.

"It makes me feel as though I had never paid attention to anything before," she told him once, "and the noise is trying to tell us something, isn't it?"

"Yes," he said, "it's trying."

"But we don't know what." She shivered when she said it. "I hate not knowing. I always hate to guess."

"Everything's trying to tell you something, and no one ever quite understands what," he said. "That's why no one can ever be sure of anything."

"Well, I'm sure of one thing," she said. "I'm happy right now. I never dreamed I could be so happy."

"Well," he said, "that's something, and the same goes with me, in case you want to know."

"You're happy in a different way," she said. "You can't be as happy as I am because everything isn't so new."

"You're new," he said. "You always will be."

He had never made a truer remark. Every time he had ever seen her, there had never been the repetitions that threw most human relationships into lines of boredom. There was always something different with her in the same way that the month of May was different every year, in spite of how well you thought you knew it.

"There's another thing I'm sure of," he said. "I love you. Do you love me? You're like a water nymph," he said. "I keep thinking if I chase you, you may turn into a tree."

"You do think of the dumbest things," she said, "and don't you worry, I'm not going to turn into a tree or anything and I don't think water nymphs ever do. I'm going to be right around where you can take care of me. Of course I love you. Why shouldn't I?"

"All right," he said, "why should you?"

"Don't be dumb," she said. "Look at yourself in the mirror. Cinderella was grateful to the Prince when he chased after her with a slipper, and you're a prince — in a nice way, I mean. There's only one thing I worry about. I don't want to go back to mice and pumpkins. Please don't do something so that I have to go back. Please don't let the clock strike twelve."

"All right, I won't," he said.

"Maybe you can't stop it," she said. "Maybe you won't be able to think up ideas all the time. Please keep trying to think up good ideas."

"How do you know they're good when you say you can't understand them?" he asked her.

"When I don't know what you're talking about," she said, "I know you're being a genius. Whenever I get to understand what you're saying without thinking it over twice, it shows you're losing your grip."

"Well," he said, "I love you. There's nothing subtle about that, is there?"

"Of course there is," she said. "I don't see how I was lucky enough to find you. Gosh, I'm a lucky girl."

"At the moment," he said.

"Don't start saying things like that," she said. "It's got to be a permanent moment."

"It sounded permanent when I said those things in church, and I meant them, Rhoda."

"Oh, yes," she said, "you've got me and I've got you, and now what? You never seem to want to keep your mind on the now what."

"But I've told you I don't know what," he said, "so I can't put my mind on it."

"I don't mean the big what," she said, "I mean the little whats. What are we going to do when we get to New York? That's what I mean. Where are we going to live?"

"In a hotel, I guess," he said, "some low-priced one."

"Just a cheap hotel," she said, "and not go apartment hunting, the way they do in books? I want an apartment with a very soft, gray carpet in the bedroom and a chaise longue, and a dressing table with flounces."

"But we don't know what kind of apartment," he said, "or what I can afford. I won't know until we see what happens to the play."

She was silent and their thoughts were lost in the roar of Niagara.

"All right," she said, "maybe I was crazy to marry you, but I still think I was right."

"That's nice to know," he said.

"Oh, darling, I didn't mean it in that way at all," she said. "Being right has nothing to do with loving someone, and I fell in love with you right away, and being in love and common sense don't mix; but a girl has to make them go together. It's difficult being a girl, darling. I've told you and I've told you, she has to take a chance on something, and she doesn't have too many chances."

"All right, you put your bet down," he said.

"I know the way it must sound to you," she said, "but please don't forget I'm in love with you."

"All right," he said, "I'll hold that thought."

"Darling, I do really love you, but I'll tell you one thing, I won't have a baby in a hotel."

"People don't as a rule," he said, "they usually have them in hospitals."

"Don't laugh," she said, "please, because I'd like to have a baby, and it could happen, couldn't it?"

"It might very well," he said. "I shouldn't want to bet on its not."

"Well, then, I know what I'll do," she said. "When we get to New York, I'll start looking at all the very best apartments, duplexes with swimming pools and things like that, just in case we might be able to afford one."

"All right," he said, "it wouldn't hurt to look."

The time had not yet arrived when Arthur Higgins was customarily called old-fashioned by a younger Broadway generation, and he doubtless did end by being overcareful and conventional; but up to his last days, when he had attempted to the utmost of his ability to turn Emily into an actress, Tom had still looked on Arthur Higgins as the best producer he had ever known. Customarily, authors quarreled with producers, accusing them of rapaciousness and of cutting corners, and at the best of times there were misunderstandings over contracts, but Tom had seldom been through such difficulties with Arthur Higgins. After all, producers had to come from somewhere; they had to have capital or to know where to find it. Some producers had risen from the ranks of vaudeville managers; others had started as stock promoters. Others had been actors who had saved their earnings; others had started as stage-struck playboys. They had only one thing in common — what they liked to call "love of the theatre." You could take your pick of managers; some of them were stupid with a gambler's flair for hits; some were ruthless; a lot were maladjusted; and most, like actors, were obliged to be egocentric.

Arthur Higgins, as far as Tom Harrow could remember, fell into none of these categories. It was true that he liked to hear the sound of his own voice and in later years he was garrulous, but he always had discerning taste, intelligence, a good education, and impeccable manners. He was a graduate of the Harvard Law School, and had been a junior partner in a large downtown firm, and had been commissioned a major in World War I. He had become interested in the theatre when he had married an English actress named Helen Adair, who had come to New York with a Shakespeare company; but he had not fallen in love with Miss Adair in a theatrical way. He had met her at a house party on Long Island, and had not discovered for several weeks that she was on the stage, and when he did, as he himself had said, he had never held it against her. Helen was one of the few actresses he had ever known who did not try to act, and, he would sometimes add over the champagne at dinner, all Helen needed was to be herself. She made a convincing Ophelia without making the slightest effort to go crazy, and no one had a better speaking voice or a better judgment for a play script.

After marrying Helen Adair, his interest in the theatre had grown, but he was comfortably established in the law. He would doubtless have ended as a senior law partner if he had not acquired a client who was a playwright, Burton Millis, who had just finished *The Last Long Walk*, and had been unable to interest anyone in it. As Arthur had said once, himself, he had not cared much for the Millis play, which began with a meeting of a millionnaire's son with a taxi driver on the curb outside a nightclub. Helen had seen the lure of its improbabilities, and Arthur's aunt, who had died at just that time, had left him a considerable legacy. It was Helen who got him interested in *The Last Long Walk*, and there must have always been another side to Arthur Higgins which he had never known existed until his wife brought it out.

"It was," as Helen Adair used to say at the Higgins Sunday-night suppers, "right there in Arthur all the time, and he never knew it — his love of the theatre."

When Tom called at the Higgins office one afternoon around the first of September, Arthur Higgins was easily one of the leading producers in New York, although there was a rumor that Mrs. Higgins made the decisions — but there were always such rumors. He had visited the outer office often in the past as an employee of the Sullivan agency, but this was different. The people seated in the waiting room, all trying to look happy and all assuming a nervous watchfulness only apparent in people applying for a theatre job, were waiting to try out for the play he had written; and the knowledge gave him a feeling of responsibility more than elation. He saw them wondering who he was, examining his clothes and his walk, and before he was halfway across the waiting room he knew they had already recognized that he was not a competitor. You were an actor or you weren't, but neither did they know he was the author. This was the only time he had ever been able to wear the cloak of anonymity. The curious thing about the recollection was that he was piqued by the waiting room's lack of recognition when he should have been grateful.

When the girl at the reception desk looked up, he saw that her eyes were coldly gray and her face and figure were coolly beautiful. She had been cast exactly for the part a girl must play at that reception desk, and she did not know who he was, either, because she was a new reception girl.

"I have an appointment with Mr. Higgins at three o'clock," he said.

She looked at him studiously, as she had to when anyone tried to see Mr. Higgins.

"Oh," she said, "then you must be Mr. Harrow. Do you know your way to Mr. Higgins's office?"

"I'm afraid not," he answered.

"I'll show you," she said. "I'm rather new here myself."

She was trimly, freshly beautiful, but his interest was entirely impersonal. There had seldom been so much on his mind. It was only a great many years later that he could occasionally wonder what might have happened if he had not been married to Rhoda and in love with Rhoda — probably nothing, and any such afterthought was immature.

"I read a copy of *Hero's Return* yesterday," she said. Her voice had changed now that she had left the waiting room. "I thought it was swell, Mr. Harrow, not that everybody hasn't told you that."

"Why, thanks," he said, "too many people can't tell me that."

"I never thought you'd be so young," she said. "You look as young as photographs of Scott Fitzgerald."

"Now you mention it," he said, "I've seldom felt as juvenile as I do this afternoon. Is this the maestro's office?"

"Yes," she said, "it's Mr. Higgins's office."

Her voice was formal again; she was turning the bronze knob of a dark oak door. That was the first time he had seen Nancy Mulford, which only went to show that it was futile to make an intelligent guess about futures. He never guessed that he would end by being more dependent on Nancy Mulford than on any woman he had ever known. He knew only years later that another preview of his life had been shown him, if he had had the sense or the interest to perceive its outlines.

"I'll keep your hat if you'd like," she said.

It was thoughtful of her and it reminded him that he was entering a great man's presence.

"Thanks," he said, "and my gloves."

The gray gloves he was holding even in September had been partly a Broadway affectation and partly an imitation of his Uncle George.

"Mr. Higgins," Nancy Mulford said, "this is Mr. Harrow."

The office was Jacobean. Its heavy tables, tapestry-backed chairs, dark oak woodwork and some tapestries — generally bad ones depicting the rape of Europa or some less dramatic scene in ancient mythology — were considered appropriate then for an office in which the dramatic arts were discussed. If the setting ceased to impress him in later years, even to the point of appearing to him like a contrived arrogance, he was impressed that afternoon; and in memory he could never evade the feeling that he had been face to face with greatness. Arthur Higgins behind his dark oak table was always impressive, with his thin, patrician head, lighted by a diamond-leaded window to his left; and Miss Helen Adair — she had an actress's reluctance to adopt her husband's name — seated at one end of the table, gracious, beautiful in a Shakespearean satin gown, added to the impressiveness. As he crossed the length of the long room to clasp Arthur Higgins's genially extended hand, he could imagine he was a squire in a castle about to pay his devoir to the lord and the chatelaine.

"Well, my boy," Arthur Higgins said, "well met, if I may use part of a great quotation. Tom, I don't believe you've met my wife, who is especially here for this happy occasion."

"How do you do, sir," he said. "It's a great pleasure to meet you, Mrs. Higgins."

"Indeed yes," she said. "Dear boy, call me Miss Adair and later Helen, when we come to know and love each other as I'm sure we shall."

"Indeed yes, Miss Adair," he said. He had not meant to say "indeed yes" but it was always a temptation to deal in resounding phrases in the Higgins office.

"The play, . . ." Miss Adair said. "I adored every word of it, and all its crisp perfection; and so did my lord and master, didn't you, Arthur?"

Arthur Higgins gazed blandly through the Jacobean twilight, and then there was a faint flicker on his face, but not a smile.

"Indeed yes," he said.

Tom understood after that that anyone was a fool who underrated Arthur Higgins, and you could never be sure exactly when he was laughing inside himself.

"I wonder how you hit on the theme," Miss Adair said. "I suppose it came to you in a burst of inspiration, and the title captures it perfectly — *Hero's Return*."

"It sounds beautiful as you speak it, Miss Adair," he said, and then he tried his best not to look at Mr. Higgins, but his curiosity was too great. "I got the title idea from Stevenson's poem, of course."

"Oh, yes," Miss Adair said, "dear R.L.S. He did lay him down with a will."

"We must find an actor," Arthur Higgins said, "who can look like a soldier and talk like one, but I don't want him *What Price Glory?* — this isn't Stallings. I am thinking especially of the new boy, Albert Briggs. We'd better get him in to read, don't you think so, darling?"

"Yes," Miss Adair said, "although I love to talk to Mr. Harrow, dear. He's so much more literate than I thought he would be."

"It's a literate play," Arthur Higgins said, "and I think it's an acting play, and you don't so often get those two together, but there's one thing I think you ought to cut, an incongruity in my opinion, but we need not mention it now."

That was what they always did. They led up to it gradually, putting you off your guard by intelligent praise before they delivered the punch, but he was not aware of the technique then.

"What incongruity?" he asked.

"Where he sings that song," Arthur Higgins said. "In a mood of deep seriousness that verges upon tragedy, he suddenly sings a musical comedy lyric. It seems to me an inartistic clash of contrast. Don't you agree with me, dear?"

"Yes," Miss Adair said, "I am afraid perhaps I do."

He was to learn that the Higginses always stuck together and that Arthur Higgins was constantly looking for incongruities, but it was not an incongruity. It was dramatic contrast and in its place more tragic than any serious line.

"You mean," he said, "someday the nation will honor you, too, as it's honored your dear old pop?"

"That's it," Mr. Higgins said, "incongruous."

"Not if it's done right," he said. If he had not stood up for his lines then, he would have been like all the others who ended by letting Mr. and Mrs. Higgins write their plays for them. As it was, he was one of the very few who could argue with Arthur Higgins.

"I can see no right way of doing it," Arthur Higgins said.

There was a pause, and Tom Harrow realized that a new tension had crept into the room.

"You see, it's this way," he said, "he's been drinking. He comes on after the automobile smashup and they tell him the girl is dead, and he knows he's a hell of a hero. Well, he sings it and does a dance step — that's the way he reacts, that's all."

"Does a dance step?" Arthur Higgins said. "Oh, no, not a dance step."

"Yes," Tom Harrow said, "like a song and dance man. He says, 'Oh, she's dead, is she?' And then he goes right into it. I could show you what I meant if I had a hat and cane."

Arthur Higgins picked up the telephone beside him, an antiquated, upright instrument whose receiver hung on a hook, but there was no way of knowing then that it would grow antiquated.

"Ask Miss Mulford to bring in a walking stick and a hat right away," he said. "I didn't know you were an actor."

Tom had never been an actor except for being able to illustrate a line. He still remembered the business with the hat and cane, and he had often done it afterwards — people would ask him sometimes at Palm Beach and Antibes if he would mind doing that song routine in *Hero's Return*. Miss Mulford handed him his hat and Arthur Higgins's malacca cane.

"Well, it goes like this," he said. " 'Oh, she's dead, is she?' — and he gives a double shuffle, and then he repeats it: 'Oh, she's dead, is she? All right, strike up the band!

"Stay in there punching, sonny,
Don't let your heart fall plop,

284

Someday the nation will honor you, too,
As it's honored your dear old pop."

How am I doing, pals?' . . . That's all, and it fits if you do it
right."

Tom saw his father's face, and he could hear his father's voice
again in Jack's. It was inexplicable, what details stuck in memory.
He was not an actor, but he had given them the idea, and he
knew they were with him.

"I'm sorry you haven't had experience," Arthur Higgins said.
"I'd like to have you direct the play; but at any rate, I want
you at rehearsals regularly. Miss Mulford, find that place in
the script and give a copy to Mr. Briggs. Let him study it for
ten minutes. Send in the first girl out there who's been reading
those speeches in the living room scene. We'll do the juveniles
first because we'll need Miss Adair's reaction."

There was never any trouble for him in the Higgins office. He
knew his way around there instinctively after that.

"Let's see," Mr. Higgins said. "Helen, my dear, haven't we
dinner for Wednesday night open? If we have, how would it
be if Tom Harrow and his beautiful wife — she must be beautiful — dined with us, informally, *en famille?*"

"Indeed yes," Miss Adair said. "Will you tell us where you
are living so that I can call her myself and extend the invitation? And I also am sure she must be beautiful."

"She is," Tom Harrow said, "and I know she would love to
come to dinner, Miss Adair."

"If I call you Tom," Miss Adair said, "you may call me
Helen, and what, pray, is your wife's first name?"

"It's Rhoda," he said.

"Rhoda," she said. "I might wish that my mother had called
me Rhoda. And where is it I may reach her, Tom?"

"At the Hotel Bulwer, on West Thirty-fourth Street."

"Oh," she said, "I've never heard of the Hotel Bulwer, but it
is a resounding name."

She stopped. A girl was coming in, young and frightened,
holding a typed copy of the play, and Tom knew how she felt.

The mantle of majesty had descended on him by then. He was the author, and it was his first experience.

"My dear," Miss Adair said, "try doing that again."

"Doing what?" the young girl asked.

"Walking in again," Miss Adair said, "and this time, my dear, please walk, don't amble. Why is it no American girls learn to walk? Don't look startled, try it again, my dear."

"You are reading the part of Alice in the script, I believe," Mr. Higgins said. "I'll give you Stanley's lines. I start in the middle of page twenty, Act I, beginning, 'Well, well, look who we've got here, not that I give a damn,' and you take it on. No, not now. Get yourself ready and I'll repeat, 'Well, well, look who we've got here, not that I give a damn.' . . ."

The girl must have come straight from the Drama League. Who had sent her around, he wondered? Had she been obliged to sleep with anyone to get the chance, or had she been calling at the office day after day? The byplay and the speculation interested him more than the lines, and years later the incident came back to him when he was writing *All Ashore*. Her face and voice for no good reason stood out from all the others. Her hopelessness was touching. Her wish to be on the stage was fading into nothing. Where had she come from, and who was she? It was his persistent curiosity that had given his work vitality and his interest in people and motives was still as keen as ever.

"Thank you, my dear," Arthur Higgins said. "You'll hear from us. Thank you very much."

They were all silent until the dark oak door had closed.

"My God!" Helen Adair said. "Do you agree with me?"

"Indeed yes," Arthur Higgins said, "especially since she impresses you, darling, in such a fashion. I hope you agree too, Tom."

"Indeed yes," Tom Harrow said.

"Look here," Miss Adair said, "I begin to think you boys are making fun of me."

"Indeed yes," Arthur Higgins said, "I think perhaps Mr. Harrow is pulling your leg, my dear."

286

"Only figuratively," Tom Harrow said.

"Sometime when Arthur's out," Miss Adair said, "perhaps you'll venture to try it another way. I knew as soon as I saw that script we'd all get on. Call for the next poor thing, Arthur. Arthur always insists on cleaning up the bit parts first. What was the name of that hotel?"

"The Bulwer," he said, "on West Thirty-fourth Street."

"Oh, yes," she said, "the Bulwer, and the name is Rhoda. Do you frequently pull Rhoda's leg?"

"Well," he said, "I try."

"I think we'd better get the next girl," Mr. Higgins said. "I don't want you falling in love with another playwright this year. Next year, but not this year, darling."

XVII

There Was Enough to Take Her Shopping

THERE were occasions in his later life when he had actually
missed the Bulwer. He doubted whether this had ever been so
with Rhoda, who ever afterwards refused to stop at anything
she termed a second-class hotel. They frightened her, she said.
There was a nightmare quality in their dingy lobbies and in
their efforts to make the dark dining rooms look attractive.
Then there were the people, aging, about to lose their bridge-
work, and always the shaking old lady who had just forgotten
who she was. She did not mean to be unkind, Rhoda used to
say, and she could never understand why people like that always fascinated him, even after the hotel scene in *Flagpole
for Two*. He could see those people if he wanted, and get into
conversations with them if he wanted, but Rhoda could not
help being frightened.

Whenever she thought of the Hotel Bulwer, she always
thought simultaneously how dreadful it would have been if
they had always had to stay there, if he had been obliged to
get a position at fifty dollars a week or something in a publish-
ing company or a magazine or somewhere. What was even
worse was to think that someday, if things did not work out
right (and of course he could not always be successful), they
might have to return to the Hotel Bulwer, after they had been
used to other things for years. This could happen (he might
not be successful always) and they were accustomed now
to spending such a fearful lot of money. It was her fault, admittedly, because she was an expensive girl who grew more
and more expensive all the time, but being so did make her

frightfully insecure. She occasionally had nightmares in which she was a little girl again and her father was losing all his money and sometimes she would get Tom confused with her father. That was why she was afraid, even when she so much as saw a second-rate hotel.

He could appreciate her point of view, but there had been advantages about the Bulwer. For one thing, there were no possessions, except his typewriter and their suitcases. They had only each other at the Bulwer, no automobiles whose fenders you might dent, no Chippendale tables you might stain, no Aubusson carpets upon which someone might drop a cigarette, no jewelry to lose, no mink, no Waterford, no Lowestoft, no Renoir or Matisse or Picasso. For that brief interval, he had been free from the fetters that held him ever after, and he still could believe that they had been closer together then than they ever were again because of those beautifully limiting factors.

He could grant that their apartment at the Bulwer was not much of a place in which to have each other, but it had not been a double bedroom. It had been a suite, so-called, because he had not wanted to think of Rhoda all alone all day in a double bedroom while the show was in rehearsal; and besides, there had to be a place where he could do rewriting at night without keeping Rhoda awake. In spite of the prosperity of the era, the Bulwer was not one of those New York hotels that had pulled itself together to face new competition. It was not redecorated and it did not announce that it was under new management, and there was no appeal in the wheezy elevator to try the New Cuisine in the New Dining Room. Their suite looked out on an airshaft which gave the place an eerie silence, except for phonographs and domestic quarrels that echoed in the shaft in the middle of the night. The purple upholstery of the sitting room sofa and the two armchairs had fallen to greasy ruin. The reproduction of a Maxfield Parrish fairy palace was terrible; the double bed sagged in the middle in such a way, as Rhoda said, that neither could have kicked the other out of bed, no matter how much either one might have wished to. There was nothing that you gave a damn about, nothing that you coveted; there was nothing to do but love each other and be delighted with each other and hope that very shortly they would find some better dwelling place.

"Well," he said that autumn afternoon when he returned from those tryouts at the Higgins office, "have you been looking for apartments, Rhoda, the way you said you were going to?"

"Oh, yes," she said, "and kiss me again, please. When I'm here alone, I keep thinking I'm a little girl."

"Did you see any good apartments?" he asked. "Just to take your mind off our poverty?"

"No," she said, "I wasn't dressed for the good ones. I never made Park Avenue. The man only showed me cute places where you walk upstairs in old houses, and he tried to kiss me in one of those cute places."

"I don't blame him," he said, "and it does show you were dressed for something."

"It shows I'm not Park Avenue," she said. "I don't think he was the Park Avenue man. By the way, the man who runs our elevator is named Bill."

"Oh," he said, "just my Bill."

"He said he had a brother in a drugstore who could get us a pint of something anytime. I got him to get it. I haven't tasted it because I know it's wrong to drink alone."

"That's fine," he said. "That proves you have a reason to be glad to see me."

"Oh," she said, "I've got a lot of others. When you came in just now you looked like someone in one of those true-confession magazines that Mother never let me read, like someone from another world."

"Well," he said, "I am just back from one."

He did not know it; it took him years to see that he was always coming back from make-believe into her world of fact, and she had never been able to follow him into the world of make-believe. She had never been at home in its unrealities because she was nervous with unreality, more particularly the unreality of the theatre and of the people in it. You could make a parody of Ecclesiastes out of her thoughts: insecurity of insecurities, the Preacher said, all the theatre is insecurity. But Rhoda had always been a good trouper in those days. She had to be; and for his money, she was always better than the bunch of them. Goodness knew, he knew them all, the writers and producers of his time, the actors and the actresses, Hollywood, Broadway and London, and there was friendship, and love and admiration, devoid of inevitable pretense. Yet he could understand that this was something that Rhoda had never wanted, or something Rhoda had never seen. He could pass in review the great figures of the theatre, alive and dead, down to the level of the younger ones beginning to be. He was still a part of the world of make-believe that in the end had made all worlds unreal, but he could not blame Rhoda for never having understood.

"The Higginses are asking us to dinner," he said, "on Wednesday, informally, just *en famille,* and Miss Adair will telephone you."

"Don't be so snooty," Rhoda said. "I know my high-school French, but — oh, my God, darling, I haven't anything to wear, even *en famille.* Look what happened when I was looking at apartments."

"I know," he said, "but according to what happened there, people are still able to get together and we'll have to buy you something to wear *en famille.*"

"We haven't got the money," she said.

"Never mind the money," he said.

She put her arms around his neck and her head on his shoulder and began to laugh.

"That's where I want us to be," she said, "in the never-mind-the-money land. I'm tired about minding about money."

"Just hold me tight," he said. "Just hold onto my coattails and maybe I can get you there."

"In a big way?" she asked.

Then he began to laugh, too. From the very beginning her preoccupation about money and security had never greatly disturbed him, and besides, they were in love.

"By God," he said, "you're the queen of the gold diggers, aren't you?"

"Don't," she said, "don't say it like that. You see, I really love you, Tom."

Love, to use a new expression, was, no matter what one said about it, in the end a highly personalized affair. Their love had been personalized, and he was very glad it had been, because the memory of it was still fresh and strange and different by far from other memories. He knew she loved him because she always gave in her way as much as he gave her. They were crazy about each other in those days and they both must have shared a feeling that they were on the verge of something rich and strange. You never could separate the components of love and you were a fool to try when they were blended into the most potent potion in the world.

"I'll take you shopping first thing tomorrow," he said, "because I want to see you looking swell, baby."

Songs then were different and they danced to different tunes, but there was no change in meaning, and she must have known darned well, baby, that he had given her quite a lot of other things besides love.

It was a pity he knew so little about women's clothes before the theatre had made him a specialist on the subject, and perhaps Rhoda had helped in that interest. Ever since that morning, he had always looked at beautiful women with an appraising eye, wondering whether their dresses would be becoming to Rhoda. He remembered that Betty Howland had spoken of a fashionable place — one that depression had driven out of existence long ago — and its name now eluded his memory, but he still could remember the perfume, the discretion of the carpets and the comfort of the chairs and a Parisian sophistication. The lady in charge of the floor had been gracious, and he had handled the situation in the best way he could. He was a beneficent, rich young man, well-dressed, married to a simple country girl, and Rhoda had looked simple in her tweed suit.

"I want a very simple but becoming dinner frock for my wife to wear tomorrow night," he said. He could not remember whom he had heard use the word "frock" but it sounded well. "And I should also appreciate your advice regarding the accessories. We're dining with Mr. and Mrs. Arthur Higgins, the producer, tomorrow night."

"Oh," the floor lady said, and her face cleared, "Mr. Arthur Higgins. Did he send you?"

"He might have, but he didn't," he said. "I'm Thomas Harrow, the playwright."

He could not have thought of a better thing to say. The word cast a glow of the arts and made Rhoda sweet and simple like his high-school sweetheart.

"Oh," the floor lady said. "Oh yes, Mr. Harrow."

They were snobs at heart in those places when dealing with the arts.

"Something simple," he said, "but at the same time becoming."

"Yes," the floor lady said. "I think I know what you mean, but I wish the young lady had a slightly different hair style."

"She can get a different one," he said, "this afternoon, can't you, dear?"

"Yes, dear," Rhoda said.

"The best way to make up our minds," the saleslady said, "is to have a few simple things modeled, and the hair style of our first girl is something of the style I mean, if you'd care to watch her, Mr. Harrow."

She walked down the length of the room and disappeared behind a velvet curtain while he and Rhoda sat in painful silence.

"The bitch," Rhoda whispered. "I don't think she thinks we're married."

"It doesn't matter," he answered.

"It matters to me what she thinks," she whispered. "My mother brought me up to be a good girl. I'm going to take my glove off so she can see my ring."

"By God," he said, "I think perhaps you'd better, darling."

He thought of that place again long afterward when he saw *My Fair Lady*. The scene at Ascot brought it back, and the music fitted with that distant mood. He could remember his sense of creative triumph, more poignant and perfect than anything later, and rightly so, since never in his life again would he deal so closely with that species of human value. It was he who had brought Rhoda there; it was he who had selected the evening gown.

"While we're here," he said, "we'd better make arrangements for a day and afternoon dress, but only the evening one must be ready tomorrow, and I'll be glad to leave you a check on the Fifth Avenue Bank."

It sounded well. He was glad that his uncle had opened an account for him there while he was at school.

"It really isn't necessary, Mr. Harrow," the floor lady said. "Mrs. Harrow does look fetching, doesn't she?"

Of course it was necessary. Dresses or frocks were cheaper then, but what with accessories, Tom must have been committed for nearly eight hundred dollars before they were on the street.

"I don't know how you can act like a millionnaire," Rhoda said. "You shouldn't have done it, darling."

"Of course I should," he said. "I said I wanted to see you looking swell, didn't I, baby?"

"But Tom," she said, and he knew she was torn both ways, "we're beginning to spend all the money in your account, and we don't know what's going to happen."

"Don't you see it doesn't matter?" he said. "You've got the dresses, haven't you?"

There you were again. It was something she could never see — the value of a moment. She could never tell the things that existed on which only a sense of being alive could place a value. She could accept the theory, but never the fact that there was sometimes safety in the throwing-away of safety.

When Cliff Wisehall, who had provisionally promised to do the directing of *Hero's Return*, found himself unable, because of pressure, to attend the first four casting sessions, Arthur Higgins became annoyed, although no one knew better than he that annoyance was valueless in dealing with theatrical impresarios. It was apparent that as Cliff Wisehall's reputation grew greater his flamboyancy increased in a direct ratio. When Arthur Higgins remonstrated, Cliff explained that he was trying to get the feel of the play, and until he could get the feel, it was futile for him to pick actors. He was trying and trying to get the feel, sitting up all night, pacing the streets all day, to get the feel, and frankly, it eluded him. He wondered whether Tommy — he had begun calling Tom "Tommy-my-lad" after their first meeting — actually had grasped the inner meaning of the play himself. He also wondered whether Arthur Higgins understood the inner meaning of the play. If either the maestro or Tommy-my-lad did understand, just let them tell him.

It began to dawn on Tom Harrow — after a conference that ended, like others he sat in later, in a barrage of finely balanced rhetoric — that Cliff Wisehall had not got around to reading the play; and finally the same truth dawned on Arthur Higgins, who said late one afternoon that he would direct the play himself.

Arthur Higgins both presented and directed *Hero's Return*, and Tom Harrow learned more of the feel of the theatre in those days with Arthur than he ever needed to learn again. Arthur had learned, by patient experiment, to reconcile the unreality of a stage set with the actualities of living as understood by an audience. He always insisted that his actors must know where they should be every second they were on stage and know what they were doing, and why. There were plenty of actors and actresses who dreaded the Higgins direction, but those who adjusted admired him. Later Tom knew others who were able to achieve more memorable effects, but no one with the Higgins thoroughness or logic. It was his first experience of seeing a play, a figment of his own imagination, start from the beginning and move into tangible shape, and ever afterwards he had never tired of this intricate process.

The cast first met in a private dining room in the Hotel Astor. They had already assembled when he arrived, sitting on banquet chairs like a class about to attend a college lecture. A new cast, he often thought, resembled a crew signed up for a long voyage in the age of sail, all listening with anxiety for the good word from the captain. Of course many were friends who had signed up together on other voyages, but others were new, silently eying each other with a competitive jealousy peculiar to their profession.

"Well, here's the author," Arthur Higgins said. "He's late, but we can start now."

"I'm sorry, Mr. Higgins," Tom said.

"No one has a right to take time away from other people," Arthur said. "Remember, after this, everyone on time. And, now the author's here, we'll spend the morning reading through the play. I want the people in the opening scene to move to the far end of the room. All right, my dear — you're the young sister, aren't you? I'm sorry, I forget your name." It was one of the ingenues, a girl who was new on the stage.

"Delia Duneen," she said.

"Thank you," Arthur Higgins said, "I won't forget again."

As a matter of fact no one did, after *Hero's Return* opened. She was not billed as a leading lady until later, and she was established after that.

He had met all the cast before, but he had never seen them together and he had never previously been through the experience of listening to any long work of his own read by a group of strangers. No one could ever tell, playwright, director or actors, what might eventually happen to a play while it was in rehearsal. Everyone was groping in his own sort of darkness, particularly in the first reading. While he listened to these strangers stumble over his lines, he was beginning to perceive the theatre's utter lack of self-concealment. Everyone was involuntarily subjected to the criticism of everybody else, and it was a sort of criticism that demanded self-reliance or inordinate vanity or the help of others. He always understood afterwards why people in the theatre were always drawn together, apart from the rest of the world, and why so many of them were generous and considerately kind. You knew people better in the theatre than in other environments because you had to. There was not much to know about some, but you always had to know what there was and you had to remember through the years tastes and capacities.

Well, in the end, he had known them, nearly all the great ones and the lesser ones, and their faces and voices now formed a procession through his memory. He could see the ending generations of his early days, the Drews, the Marlowes, the Keanes, the Sheldons and the Thomases. He could recall the first time he had met John Barrymore and the last. He had seen youth grow to middle age and disappear, and he had seen the authors come and go. It startled him to realize that so many of them only a few years his senior were gone already — O'Neill, Howard, Barry, and Sherwood. He had seen new ones take their places, the Millers and Williamses. The truth was, if he lived much longer, he would get to be a grand old man of the theatre himself. He had known them all and he could believe he had been backstage ten thousand times, kissing the leading lady and the supporting girls and telling each that she had been glorious, and saying it was the best performance he had ever seen and predicting that the play would run for a thousand years. You had to keep your head to discount the flattery, but there was genuineness beneath the convention. There was the strong wine of friendship, the common bond and community experience. You were a part of the brotherhood and, once you were, you were never wholly like anyone outside the boundaries.

He could see why Rhoda had never really been at home with those people, although she had always looked at home. She had always been uncertain in the presence of make-believe and she could never sort out as he could the values of illusion and reality.

"The trouble is," she said, "I don't like insecurity."

She had never said a truer thing. The theatre was as insecure and fickle as public taste.

"And you're insecure yourself," she had said. "That's what makes me so nervous, Tom. You're getting more that way all the time."

Frankly he was already beginning to suspect the word, and it happened, when Rhoda had made that particular remark, he was less secure than he had ever been afterwards. She made it the day they were going to try out *Hero's Return* in the theatre in the Hotel du Pont in Wilmington, Delaware. He had not been sleeping well; he had been rewriting several scenes that were more on his mind than Rhoda was. In the theatre, insecurity constantly moved into some new sort of insecurity. If you were once successful, you always had a fear that you would never be so good again, and so, whatever happened, there was always insecurity.

XVIII

He Heard about Hal in Wilmington

IT WAS always possible to argue over the virtues or defects of tryout towns — New Haven, Philadelphia, Wilmington or Washington, or Boston — and the audience reaction to opening plays differed in each of these cities, but no tryout town could be perfect, and Wilmington was convenient because there was the theatre, right inside the hotel. Thus the ordeal of an opening night, the clash of personalities, the trauma of watching a play run through for its first time before a paying audience, and the final post-mortems and rewrite hours, all those things that made a first night hideous, could take place under one roof.

"I don't see why, if you're so nervous," Rhoda said, "you and I can't have supper alone, instead of being even more nervous with Arthur and Helen Higgins."

"Please stop calling her Higgins," he said. "She's Helen Adair — she doesn't like to be called Mrs. Higgins."

"I don't see why she can't take it," Rhoda said, "I have to be called Mrs. Harrow, don't I?"

"You didn't have to be, once," he said. "Remember the idea was that you decided to take the chance."

"I know," she said, "I had to. You'd never have come back. You'd have forgotten all about me. In fact, you keep forgetting me the way it is."

"I've got a lot of things on my mind, Rhoda," he said. "This business is sort of like having a baby. Everyone says so."

"Oh, my God," she said. "Suppose we should start having a baby?"

"You don't think you are, do you?" he said.

"I don't know," she said. "That makes you frightened, doesn't it?"

"Not frightened, only startled," he answered.

"Well," she said, "I'm glad you didn't say that it makes you startled 'on top of everything else.' Everything that happens lately is on top of everything else, isn't it?"

"That's right," he said, "everything is on top of everything."

"I never knew there could be so much to get on top of," Rhoda said. "Aren't you going to wear a dinner coat?"

"No," he answered.

"I don't see why," she answered. "Arthur Higgins always does, and you needn't be cross about it."

"I'm not going to wear a dinner coat on top of everything else," he said.

"There," she said, "don't say it that way. If you wore a dinner coat, you wouldn't look so much like a genius. You're getting to look more and more like one all the time."

"I wish to God I were one," he said.

"Well, hook up my dress," she said. "You still like it, don't you?"

"Yes," he said, "except for the hooks."

"I don't believe anybody could be worse with hooks than you," she said. "I wish I had a maid."

"I wish you had, too," he said.

"Don't be so cross," she said. "I know you're worried. Do I look all right?"

He had never seen her look better. The dress went with her hair and eyes. The only thing that disturbed him was that she had never looked so expensive.

"What'll we do if it doesn't work?" she said.

"If what doesn't work?" he asked.

"You know," she answered. "The play — and you're afraid it isn't going to work, aren't you?"

"That's right, I'm afraid," he said.

She moved her bare shoulders impatiently.

"I wish I understood any of this," she said. "I don't see why

300

you and Arthur Higgins don't know whether the play is going to be good or not, after all the weeks you've been going over it and over it — and instead of that you all get more and more uncertain."

"That's right," he said. "I thought it was good when I wrote it, but I don't know anything about it now. I guess that's how it is with plays."

"But lots of people have seen it," she said. "Haven't they told you what they think?"

"It doesn't matter what they think," he said, "because they didn't pay to see it."

Bridge was entirely different when you played for even a small stake, and the same was true with a play. Once an audience had a stake in a play, there was a psychological release that built a new relationship between audience and players. If you wanted to be philosophical, perhaps this condition was like all phases of life; if you wanted to live you had to pay, and if the management gave you a complimentary ticket, you did not live. It was interesting that Rhoda had echoed that thought that night.

"Yes," she said, "I guess everyone's got to pay."

Her remark still annoyed him. He never had been able to discover just what Rhoda had paid for. She had always got in with what was still called at the box office an "Annie Oakley." She had always had a free ride, ever since he had met her on Dock Street, but then perhaps no ride was ever wholly free.

"Tom," she asked him, "did you ever happen to know any of the du Ponts?"

"You ask the damnedest questions," he said. "No, I don't know any of them."

"There must be lots of them living around here, mustn't there to have this big hotel and everything?"

"Yes," he said, "there should be lots and lots."

"Do you think any of them will be at the play tonight?"
"Why do you care?" he asked her. "I don't know."
"I'd just like to see what one of them looks like," she said.
"God almighty," he said. "They must look like other people."

301

"But Tom," she said, "they aren't like other people. They aren't like you and me."

"I don't know whether they are or not," he said, "and I don't care. I don't want to be a du Pont."

"I know you don't," she said. "That's what I don't understand about you, because I'd like to be one."

"All right," he said, "all right — and exactly why should you like to be a du Pont?"

"Don't get cross, Tom," she said. "I'd like to be a du Pont because they don't have to worry in the way we do. No matter what happens, there they are."

Rhoda, more than political arguments, had made him into an approximation of a liberal. Instead of being amused, he was angry, which showed that the strain of the play was telling on him.

"All right," he said, "I'd rather worry than be a du Pont."

"I don't see why you say that," she said. "I hate to worry, and no du Pont has to."

"Listen," he said, "there might be a revolution."

"A revolution?" she said. "Don't be silly. Look at this hotel."

"Listen, baby —" he said.

"Don't you call me baby," she told him. "You've been picking up all sorts of words since this play has been in rehearsal."

It was consoling to believe that he had been justly angry.

"Listen, baby," he said, "to have this on top of everything else is more than I can take tonight."

"There you go again," she said, "on top of what?"

"Listen, baby," he said, "I have to worry about the play and about you and me, and what are you being but a selfish little bitch?"

"Would you kindly say that again?" she asked.

"Yes," he said. "Who were you when I saw you in front of that typing school? Who brought you to the Hotel du Pont, anyway? Who paid for that goddam frock you're wearing? I repeat the phrase with pleasure, you're a selfish little bitch."

It hit her between wind and water, because once you showed Rhoda the picture, she was able to see it, almost always.

302

"That's right," she said. "I guess you're right."

"Well, as long as you admit it," he said, "stop crying, Rhoda."

She did not stop, but there had never been anything painful about Rhoda's weeping because she was always attractive when she cried.

"I know you're right, dear," she said. "I know I'm selfish. Mother's always told me so, and I love you, and I know all the things you've done for me. Tom, you're wonderful and there isn't much I can do back for you."

"You don't have to do anything," he said, "you only have to love me."

"Oh, Tom," she said, "of course I love you, and I always will — only I wish we didn't have to worry."

"Listen, baby," he said, and for once she did not mind if he called her baby, because she was crying in a nice way and her head was on his shoulder, "everybody has to worry."

"Yes," she said, "except the du Ponts, the Fords, the Rockefellers and people like that."

"Listen, baby," he said, "maybe they have to worry, too, in different ways."

"Oh, Tom," she said, and she sobbed, "I don't think I'd mind so much worrying in a different way."

He held her closer. After all, she had taken his mind off the opening, and furthermore, he was master of the situation.

"Listen, baby," he said again, "if you would only stop it, everything would be wonderful. Just you let me do the worrying."

"But, Tom," she said, "I have to worry, too."

"Oh, no," he said. "Can't you stop it, Rhoda?"

Her sobs increased but she still was beautiful. He could almost think, much as he hated Victorian similes, that Rhoda was like a lily of the valley in the spring.

"But I've got something more to worry about," she said.

"Well, put it off," he said. "We've got to have supper with Arthur Higgins. Rhoda, I don't mean to be cross, but I've a lot on my mind tonight."

"I've a lot on mine, too," she said.

"I can only repeat," he told her, "you're being selfish."

"Maybe I am," she said. "But Tom, I really am going to have a baby."

He had never brought himself to tell Harold of that moment. There were some things one never could discuss freely, and this was one of them. In a few episodes in life, at least, there came a first time which you knew could not be the same again. Rhoda's news had seemed incredible that night and at the same time like a gift from the gods. He had tried later to recapture the portents of that moment by the aid of the written word and the skill of actors, and once or twice the result was not bad, but it had never been the same. You could not live through a first time twice, and no one could ever do it for you, and there it was that night, on top of everything.

"Darling," he said, "don't cry. That's the best thing I've ever heard."

"How's that again?" she asked.

"It's the best thing I've ever heard," he said. "It makes me feel like a du Pont. It's all right, I'll take care of everything."

He wished there had been more times when she had needed to believe him as much as she had then. Everything might have been much better if he had not taken care of her too quickly, too easily and too well. A time of stress and struggle would have brought them together, and Rhoda could have taken it if he had not hit the jackpot quite so soon. Neither of them knew, he was glad to recall, that the scales were already weighted down. All that they could know of that present was the joy that they took in each other and a sense of confidence and fulfillment that was gone before you could recognize its worth.

"Darling," she said, "I never knew you were so wonderful."

It was still something to remember that they had stood alone and self-sufficient and that there had been a union of their thoughts and wishes.

"And I don't want you to be anything else," she said. "I love you just the way you are, and if he's a boy, I want to call him Harold."

"Harold?" he repeated after her. "Why Harold?"

"Because he lost the Battle of Hastings, the way his mother did," she said. "I never expected there to be a Harold, but I'm awfully glad because I love you, darling."

Then the room telephone rang, reminding him that they were late.

"Hurry and wash your face," he said. "It's a good thing you don't puff up when you cry."

No matter what might happen to a marriage, the play moved on, and in the end everyone on the program owed his first allegiance to the play.

"Have you two been quarreling?" Helen Adair asked.

"Why no," he answered, "not at all."

"Well, if you haven't been," she said, "you've been making love and it's almost the same thing."

"Helen," Arthur said, "let's not think any more quaint thoughts. Helen only means you're looking charming, Rhoda dear — Venus rising from the sea."

"Arthur," Tom said, "how is it you think of things like that?"

"Because I've had a drink," Arthur Higgins said. "The shaker's on the table, and there are orchids for the girls beside the cocktail shaker, Tom."

"Orchids," Tom said, "I should have thought of orchids."

"You will eventually," Arthur said. Arthur was in a dinner coat and pearl studs, impeccable in spite of the endless days and sleepless nights. "I've sent flowers to the girls backstage in both your name and mine. Sandwiches and salad are coming up and black coffee. I've never believed in prisoners eating a hearty breakfast."

"Arthur," he said, "do you think it's going to be as bad as all that?"

"We don't know," Arthur said, "but we may three hours from now."

"Don't look so worried, dear," Helen said to Rhoda, "Arthur's always like this before openings, bitter and nasty nice."

"We should go backstage before curtaintime and say kind words," Arthur Higgins said. "Then you and I will watch from the back of the house."

The worst of it all, and this never changed with years of experience, was standing at the back of the house watching the waiting audience. There was a hostile impersonality in the voices and in the rustling of the programs. He could never get rid of a tenseness that verged on stage fright, and the uncertainty never changed. He had first faced that night one of the theatre's most hideous dangers, that once you had lost the attention of an audience, nothing could bring it back again. The first sight of the set, the first motion of the players, their first speeches, grew vitally important. Standing together in back of the darkened theatre while the curtain rose, revealing the sitting room of a small-town home, he was aware of tension in Arthur Higgins.

"Yes, son," Arthur said later in New York, "in the first two minutes most of your chips are down. A play's like a newborn baby. If it breathes in the first two minutes, maybe it will live to grow up."

He was aware even then of the first stirrings of life in *Hero's Return*. The first moves of Albert Briggs made the play move: the door opening to the left, the tired man returning to the scene he had left two years ago — and the pause, the incredulity. Albert Briggs had understood the elements as Arthur Higgins had been sure he would. Arthur Higgins had wanted someone who would give a suitable character interpretation of the part, not necessarily an actor with a public, and Albert Briggs had not been well known before that night. In fact, *Hero's Return* made two stars, Albert Briggs and Delia Duneen. Tom Harrow must have known, that night, that nothing mattered so much as the craft to which he was dedicated, and even Rhoda and her secret vanished while he watched his people live.

The show as it had played in Wilmington was closer to being set and ready to move to New York than they had thought it would be; but there was some cutting and a new series of lines for the final curtain, and the revisions had to reach the actors early enough so that they could be tried in the afternoon run-through. They got back to their rooms at one o'clock and Rhoda had been tired, but he still had the impression that she always looked prettier as the night wore on.

"I wish you could come to bed," she said, "instead of sitting up writing, and if you keep having to do this as a regular thing, I wish you had a wine-colored silk dressing gown, that writers and artists wear in the movies when they are on one of those Italian terraces having breakfast with their mistresses."

"How do you know their dressing gowns are wine-colored?" he asked.

"They'd have to be," she said, "if you had one. I'll buy you one as soon as we get some money. The funny little man who comes around with the railroad tickets and pays the hotel bill and things said we ought to get a piece of change from the box office tonight. That's true, isn't it?"

"Yes," he said, "I guess so."

"There's one nice thing about being on the road," Rhoda said, "Arthur Higgins pays all the expenses."

"Don't forget it's very generous of Arthur," Tom said. "There's nothing in the contract that makes him pay for us both."

"Well, anyway, the first thing, I'm going to buy you a wine-colored dressing gown. There must be some in Wilmington. The du Ponts must wear them, don't you think?"

"Maybe none of the du Ponts are writers," he said.

"They don't need to be," she said, "but maybe some of them have mistresses."

"Maybe. I wouldn't know," he said. "You don't need it, but you'd better get your beauty sleep."

"I'm glad if you think I'm beautiful," she said.

"You know I think so, and I've told you that before," he said.

"I still don't believe it," she said, "unless you tell me. Tom, everything's awfully strange tonight. All those people talking and kissing each other and calling each other 'darling.' Are theatre people always like that?"

"Yes," he said, "I guess they're volatile. But what's so strange?"

"We seem to be moving around so fast," she said, "into Niagara Falls and sex and that Hotel Bulwer and new dresses, and then down here and all this, and then going to have a baby."

"All right," he said, "blame it on the Bulwer."

"I'm not blaming either you or the Bulwer," she said. "But everything's moving so fast I can't remember what I used to be like."

"I thought the idea was that you didn't want to be what you were like," he said.

"I know," she said, "but it's unsettling when you begin not to be able to remember. Now kiss me, and not the way the hero did when he met his high-school sweetheart. Good night, and don't sit up too long."

He could never estimate the lapse of time, but he must have been at his typewriter an hour or so when he heard her speak to him again. He had not heard her enter the room and her voice startled him.

"Tom," she said, "you're not angry about our going to have a baby, are you?"

"No," he said, "on the contrary, I'm getting more enthusiastic every minute."

"All right," she said. "I only wanted to know, and I won't interrupt you any more. I love you, and I'd rather have you than the du Ponts, in case that worried you."

"Why, thanks, dear," he said, "it's been worrying me all night."

"And now you'd better come to bed," she said. "You must be finished with that by now."

It had always been a problem when to stop writing plays and dealing with characters, and get back again to being married.

There could never be an adequate preview of the world of tomorrow, no way of realizing until much later how close he had been to Rhoda, or how near he had been to grasping the elusive. A word or two would have done it, and those words might not have been associated with the act of love. Had she been willing to give that night while he had been unwilling? It was too late now fully to reconstruct the scene, and no way of realizing then that opportunity was moving and that each advancing minute would add to the static, unbreakable side of a relationship. There was a time for everything under the sun, but you seldom knew the time.

"Do you have a feeling," she said that night, "that everything is beginning to move so fast that we'll have to run to keep up with it?"

"Yes," he said. "If it keeps on going this way, there won't ever be any time for you and me — but of course it's going to stop."

"I wish we could stop, just you and me," she said, "and watch the rest of it move. Just you and me on solid ground."

"I know what you mean," he said. "There'll be lots of time for you and me, but it's got to be our kind of time."

He never should have taken it for granted that he and she could be much alike, and perhaps it was something to be thankful for that neither one of them had ever tried too ploddingly to understand the other.

XIX

Don't Look at All of It Just Yet

HE MUST have dozed off, but the Scotch-and-soda that Harold had poured for him was still firmly clasped in his hand, and his arm was resting on the arm of the incongruous leather chair that had come from the Judge's library. The silence of the room, which was what he noticed first, was like the silence of the Judge's library. The town was always still after a certain hour, but for a moment after he realized he had been dozing, it was hard to separate the past from the present. For just a second, but one could not measure the time, he thought that he was at school again and that he was in the Judge's house and that he had fallen asleep reading a book from one of the hidden shelves. There was always that bewildering interval between sleeping and waking, and the troubles of the day and the dinner that the Bramhalls had attended had caused him to drink more than usual, so that it was an effort to sort things out; and while he did so, he had the disturbing impression that he might be lapsing into senility.

Was he in the Judge's library or not? There was a split second of panic while he struggled with the thought that he might never again know where he was. Then the libido, or whatever you chose to call it, had pulled his consciousness together. He was not in the Hotel du Pont, and Rhoda was not asking him to come to bed. The present was breaking through the shadows of the past. It was after dinner, and the Bramhalls had gone. Rhoda had been a ghost, and she was gone; and Emily was upstairs, probably snoring softly, although Emily had always been sure that he was the one who snored. Harold had gone to bed, and Harold had turned into a very nice boy who could mix the drinks efficiently. Harold must have learned how in some officers' club, or on Makalapa Row where the admirals had their houses at Pearl Harbor. Walter Price, too, was gone. He remembered that Walter had fallen asleep and that Harold had aroused Walter with the cheerful efficiency of someone who understood people who were gone with liquor. Harold must have learned this know-how in Guam or in the Philippines or in Makalapa Row. He remembered distinctly, after the Bramhalls had gone, that he had asked Harold to give him another Scotch — and there it was, still in his hand. He was sitting facing shelves of the Judge's books, but he was now in the Saebury house that he had remodeled, no longer in the Hotel du Pont in Wilmington, Delaware, working on the second act of *Hero's Return*. He was in the Saebury house and he was a damn fool to have bought it, and the bank had called his loan — but he had not spilled his drink, which he now perceived had grown lukewarm. Now was the time to finish it so that sleep could knit up the ravelled sleave of care, to quote Shakespeare, not that sleep ever knitted the sleeves of his care any longer. It was always just as ravelled when he awoke in the morning as it had been in the evening, and he was growing tired of apt quotations.

There were times when stirrings in a house were highly disquieting — the ghostly creaking of some beam or board due to some pressure of construction or heat or cold, the abrupt tapping of a twig against a windowpane due to an eccentric veering of night air. Heard in the middle of the night, such sounds, all subject to rational explanation, occasionally would move into the realm of superstition that common sense could never quite invade. His thoughts that day and night had set up in him a perfect receptivity such as the late William James had discussed in his *Varieties of Religious Experience*. If he had been listening intently, he would have been better prepared, but he had heard nothing until he was aroused by the sound of steps descending the front stairs, and the steps had a ponderous slowness with which he was unfamiliar. Their steady progress had brought his mind back to the three measured taps on the stage before the curtain rose at the Comédie. In spite of wit and reason, he sat transfixed by a childish sort of dread that the footsteps were coming to carry him away to a bar of judgment; and for no good reason except that there were eccentricities in everybody's mind, he had the childish memory of the routine of the Punch and Judy show. Punch had done away with Judy and the policeman, but the Devil got him in the end. There had been a rap-rap before it had happened. It was the Devil, coming to take Punch away. Doubtless free guilt contributed to his illusion that destiny in the shape of inevitable ending was moving down the stairs. The steps were not the steps of Emily with the clatter of her mules, nor the easy steps of Hal. The steps, growing nearer, were not stealthy but excruciatingly slow. His concept of destiny and free guilt could have lasted only a second or so before he realized that each careful footfall carried its burden of years and waste. He was no longer facing dread, but there was no relief when he realized it was Walter Price, because Walter, in his shabby woolen dressing gown, in the doorway with the light reflected on his partially bald head, was a harbinger of the inevitable tomorrow.

It was all well enough to remind himself that Walter Price was some ten or twelve years his senior and had led an irregular and dissipated life, and that he had not yet reached by a long shot Walter's phase of physical shakiness. Still, there was a grim thrust of time in Walter, a sharp nudge, a warning of what was coming. The glimpse of Walter, unguarded and disheveled, revealed the unalterable truth that, given a year or two, time would be pushing Walter, like Punch, off the stage. Walter was nearing the van of the big parade, following the stream of human frailty, of all ambitions, on his way to where Mort Sullivan had gone and Arthur Higgins and Helen Adair. He was on his way toward that bourne they wrote about and that one fact, after birth, that was completely unescapable. These were obvious facts, but now there was an urgent reminder that not only Walter but he, too, was a part of the big parade. The

312

younger generation, the younger writers, and Hal and Emily were waiting for him to pass the stand in review. Time was gently nudging so that he would make room for someone else. The show was never over, but pregnancy was continuing, drums were beating, and you had to march along.

"Why, hello, Walter," he said. "What happy chance has brought you back?"

"Several combined chances," Walter said. He still looked like a sergeant major in the big parade to oblivion, but there was warmth and friendliness in his reappearance, reminiscent of an earlier day before one was conscious that the big parade was starting. "The thought that you might still be here alone and in the need of company, for one thing, and then a habit of mine that I cultivated from my experiences as a brigade adjutant in World War I, a habit practiced by Napoleon."

"I never knew you were the adjutant of any brigade in World War I," Tom Harrow said.

"Dear boy," Walter said, "in a life as full as mine, it is difficult to tell even one's best friends everything. Now that I'm here, how about a little drinkie? That was another reason for descending the staircase," he laughed softly, "not that I'm a nude. I never was a believer, nor was Mr. Ziegfeld, in full exposure."

The band was striking up; the parade was marching on. Few young people in the unappreciated vigor of their youth would now understand that the allusion of Walter's, so archly put, referred to a picture in a show of cubist art in New York in 1913 — the *Nude Descending a Staircase*. The parade was moving on.

"I'm very glad you're down here, Walter," Tom Harrow said, "in many different ways. The drinks are over there and your presence zips everything together like a zipper."

Walter Price succumbed to a falsetto burst of laughter.

"Tom," he said, "you've always had a delightfully macabre sense of imagery. There never has been anything exactly like your dialogue — the sudden moment, the sudden, unexpected turn. And we truly do need a zipper to pull together past and present."

The atmosphere was like the cold bathtub and gin days on Lexington Avenue. There was still a meeting of minds, the curious and useless rapport between them that Rhoda had often criticized.

"Yes," Tom Harrow said. "Are you all right? Have you found your little drinkie, Walter?"

"Yes," Walter Price said, "the bourbon, like the sands of time, is running low, but I'm unzipping it right now."

"Let's not overlabor a good thing," Tom said. "That's the trouble with these comedians, Benny and the whole damn lot of them, but what was it you were saying you did that Napoleon did?"

"Napoleon?" Walter Price said. "Napoleon? Don't tell me, I'll get the connection in a moment."

It was summer again on Lexington Avenue and Rhoda had gone to the Cape or Watch Hill or wherever it was she went when he had to be in town.

"When you were a brigade adjutant in World War I," Tom Harrow said, "you cultivated some habit from Napoleon."

Walter Price laughed again.

"Dear Tom," he said. "Now I'm here beside the bourbon and the Scotch, how about a drinkie for yourself?"

"Not at the moment," Tom said. "What about Napoleon?"

"Oh, that," Walter said. "Why, merely, Tom, that when I was in my salad days preparing for entrance examinations to West Point, I dabbled somewhat in Napoleonana."

"Now wait," Tom Harrow said, "don't tell me you went to the Point. It doesn't fit in with Harrow, Walter."

"That is the trouble with the modern craft of playwriting," Walter Price said, "everything has to fit in, or as dear old Arthur used to say, everything has to hold water."

"All right, as long as you hold your own," Tom Harrow said.

"Now just a minute," Walter said, "when have I never not? Name me a single instance."

314

"It doesn't matter," Tom said, "as long as you carry it on both shoulders."

"Dear boy," Walter said, and he wiped away a tear, "you always think of something new, but we were talking about Napoleon. Napoleon had a faculty for taking cat naps, in case you don't remember."

"There weren't any cats," Tom Harrow said. "Josephine had a dog that bit Napoleon. He couldn't take cat naps."

"Not on the nuptial couch," Walter said. "Are you sure you don't want a little drinkie? Like all great generals, Napoleon was able to doze off at odd moments and then to wake in a split second with the whole battle plan back in his head. I practiced this when I was adjutant of the old Third, and very useful it was when the Boches counterattacked in the Bois des Rappes — asleep one moment, leading my men the next. Did I ever tell you about that counterattack in the Bois?"

"It must have been a great war," Tom Harrow said, "World War I, I mean, simpler, more like the Civil War."

Walter sighed.

"Tom," he said, "your intuitive sense is a signature to everything you do. Yes, there was a Civil War quality with the caissons rolling along, a quality so apparent in the play *Secret Service*. Did you ever see Gillette in *Secret Service?*"

"No," Tom said, "but I saw him in my extreme youth in *Sherlock Holmes.*"

"A pity," Walter said. "He was better in *Secret Service*. By the way, I wonder whether you have met a young client of mine, a playwright named Vincent O'Keefe."

The aimlessness of Walter usually deserved attention. When you least expected it, after long locutions with footnotes and appendices, something would lead to something, and now the name of Vincent O'Keefe moved forward suddenly, solid and challenging.

The name, intuition indicated, had appeared as the end result of a carefully woven fabric, and the real reason for Walter Price's reappearance was now approaching. For as long as Tom had known Walter Price, Walter had been pulling promising

315

young playwrights out of hats, and they had always possessed the insubstantial qualities of conjurers' rabbits, and always disappeared in an ectoplasmic fashion.

"Vincent O'Keefe?" Tom Harrow said. "Why no, I've never heard of Vincent O'Keefe."

Walter sighed in a patient manner.

"You will hear of him in a very resounding way," he said. "In all my searches for talent I have never encountered talent of the same impact. The moment I read a line of his, I knew I was in the presence of greatness. I knew there was no time to be lost and I didn't lose a minute."

"So that's what you've been leading up to, is it?" Tom Harrow asked. "You don't mean you're taking on another play?"

Walter raised his glass.

"Only in a promotional way," he said. "There will be no trouble getting any number of people to participate in the production costs. It's a comedy, Tom, reminiscent of *Once in a Lifetime*, but with a gusto and a genius far exceeding Kaufman and Hart; a comedy about Hollywood."

It had always been hard to understand the enthusiasms of people like Walter Price, that flourished on disillusion and failure or, when they withered, were re-created immediately into something new.

"Walter," he said, "don't you know that Hollywood's been funny so long that it's stopped being?"

"Not under the magic of this new boy of mine," Walter said. "Every line of this play is hilarious, and most of it is sidesplitting. All I ask you is wait till you read it."

"I'm going to die someday," Tom Harrow said, "but I'm not going to die laughing at a total stranger named Vincent O'Keefe. Who is he? What did he ever do?"

"That's the beauty of it," Walter said. "He's never done anything."

"Where did he come from?" Tom asked.

"He came from Harvard," Walter said. "He wrote the play in his senior year in a creative writing course, produced very successfully by Harvard and Radcliffe students."

"That makes it a valuable piece of property," Tom Harrow said. "Where did you find him, Walter?"

Walter poured himself another drink.

"I didn't. He found me," he said.

"How did he do that?" Tom Harrow asked.

"He was thumbing over the yellow pages of the telephone directory," Walter said. "Don't laugh, Tom. I put my name in the yellow pages last year as a happy sort of afterthought, with a small squib about myself, in a neat oblong box."

"And he came upon the squib?"

"Yes," Walter said. "He was discouraged, and he had been drinking."

"Look here," Tom Harrow said, "you haven't paid him an advance, have you?"

He had not yet lost the faculty, and he hoped he never would, of growing interested in problems that were not his own. His curiosity was now attempting to construct this unknown Vincent O'Keefe. He could see him dressed in chino trousers, soiled buckskin shoes and a sweatshirt.

"I shall pay him an advance," Walter said, "the day after tomorrow, in accordance with the terms of our contract, and it will be the wisest of many wise investments I have made. Did I ever tell you of that flutter of mine on Wall Street back in '28?"

It was delicate of Walter not to approach the point too bluntly, but the ending was inevitable and Tom Harrow felt a keen compassion.

"How much are you going to pay him, Walter?" he asked.

"It may seem high to you," Walter said, "but considering I'm introducing a new figure in the theatre, very little. Five thousand dollars, Tom."

"Good God," Tom Harrow said, "five thousand dollars?"

Walter raised his hand in a gesture that demanded patience.

"Not all as an advance, of course," he said. "I'm sorry I've not been clearer. Promotional costs, plus the advance will amount to five thousand dollars."

Walter had made himself very clear. He was short of money

317

again. It was not necessary for him to go on, but circumstances forced him.

"You wouldn't mind, would you," he said, "letting me have five thousand, Tom, until the promotional work is over?"

Now that Walter Price had asked the question, it was like moving from one element to another. He was facing reality again, at least as he understood reality, and his own experience that night was similar. He had been in the library, half asleep. The drinks he had taken had changed his point of view and the direction of his thoughts, but they had made nothing vague. His mind had been dallying with the past and the experience was much like swimming underwater. Nothing Walter had said had brought back the present until Walter had asked for five thousand dollars. Now he was on the surface again, no longer young or married to Rhoda Browne, no longer standing on the threshold of success in a brave and safe world. He was in his fifties, a very different age, and closer to being dead broke than he had been since he had lived in the Hotel Bulwer.

"Why, Walter," he said, "it's natural for you to ask me. I want you to know I'm glad you have." It hurt to see the relief on Walter's face.

"Dear Tom," Walter Price began, and his voice choked, "no one ever had a better friend."

One of his troubles had always been that it hurt him to say "No," and he had a moment's clear vision of all the money he had loaned. This had been expected of him because openhandedness had been one of the attributes of the theatre, but still he had always been an easy mark. It was disconcerting to find himself automatically thinking where he could find five thousand dollars for Walter Price.

"Walter," he said, "it's painful to recall right now that I had quite a lot of dough once, but I gave half of what I had to Rhoda and then there's the Hopedale alimony."

"Dear Tom," Walter Price said, "you don't have to remind me what you did for Rhoda or the quixotic manner in which you have been providing for Hopedale. It makes me all the more vividly aware of your generosity. Of course, as I must have told you, if things had ever been straightened out regarding the Alabama claims, the shoe would be on the other foot and I would be begging you to ask some assistance from me."

He knew that he should tell Walter directly and get it over, but he eagerly grasped the opportunity to delay.

"What Alabama claims?" he asked.

Walter laughed comfortably. It was sad to hear him since the expansiveness of his mood reflected his deep relief.

"Surely it's the lateness of the hour," Walter said, "that makes you forget the Confederate ship of war *Alabama*, built in England, that preyed so successfully on Yankee merchantmen. The British government, after the peace, agreed to reimburse Yankee shipowners for their sunken ships, and the Price shipping was badly hit by the *Alabama*."

"The Price shipping?" Tom said. "What Price shipping?"

"Dear me," Walter said, "I've surely mentioned the old Price packets that once plied so successfully between this continent and Liverpool until the *Alabama* swooped upon them."

"Now wait a minute," Tom Harrow said, "I don't see how the *Alabama* could swoop upon Price packets if your family fought for Dixie in the Civil War, and if they were almost burned out by General Sherman."

Walter sighed.

"Oh dear," he said, "I never realized that I had never told you. The packets belonged to my Great-uncle Walt, who stood for the Union and who quarreled bitterly with the Colonel, my grandfather. But in time, due to death and attrition, I found myself heir to Uncle Walt's Alabama claims."

"What happened?" Tom asked.

Walter Price sighed again.

"What invariably happens," he said. "The papers got lost somewhere in Washington, and now there are no Alabama claims."

It was like most of living; you started with something and suddenly it was gone. He was very young when the song was popular, "I'm forever blowing bubbles." There was a silence in

319

the room, now that the bubble of the Alabama claims was dissipated.

"Walter," he said, "I hate to say it, but I'm another Alabama claim."

The confidence of Walter Price and his serene belief in friendship remained unshaken.

"Sometimes, Tom," he said, "the obliquity of your wit leaves me a trifle in your wake. In exactly what respect are you an Alabama claim?"

Tom no longer desired delay; he was the matador at the end of the bullfight. He was tired of facing reality and it might be that he could escape from it again if he could insert the sword at the proper point between the shoulder blades.

"In every respect," he said. "I haven't got five thousand dollars, but I might let you have a hundred or two if you hurry and cash the check."

Walter's expression gave him a sharp twinge of guilt, the widened eyes, the sudden sagging of the facial muscles.

"Tom," he said, "it's hard for me to believe you're serious."

It was easier now that the worst was over. He found himself speaking with less effort, like a runner who has gained his second wind. He was saying that it had been hard for him to realize the facts himself and that he was hardly adjusted to them yet. As Rhoda had often said, he had always been incredibly vague about money.

"You remember *Porthos of Paris*," he said — "that musical that was fixed up as a capital gains setup? The bank put up the cash and I put up my securities as collateral, all I hadn't given Rhoda, and then my personal note for another seventy thousand. I let my enthusiasm run away with me, Walter, but you do remember *Porthos of Paris*, don't you?"

Walter Price nodded. It was impressive how quickly he had adjusted himself to a friend's disaster, until one recollected that Walter had been living on intimate terms with crisis for many, many years.

"Granted it did not have a run," Walter said, "it was *succès d'estime*."

It was one way of putting it. The compassion of the theatre was around them both and the room was quiet with a midnight silence. Then Walter spoke again alertly, with an agent's professional sharpness.

"No sale of the picture rights?" he asked. "After all, it was a Broadway production and a deal could have been made for the costumes."

The costumes were the trouble. The public was tired of costumes.

"You see," Tom said, "the note falls due next month. I'm putting this place on the market and the furniture will be sent to Parke-Bernet. I've a new play, but still I've got to raise the money."

"My God," Walter said, "are you sure you don't want another drinkie?"

"No," he answered, "not at the moment, thanks."

He was up from the bottom of the sea, right there with the actual — so much with it that he could see the unreality of Walter Price.

"Does Emily know?" Walter said. "It will be very hard on Emily."

Walter, when he once got away from himself, could estimate a situation and Walter had always possessed a knowledge of character. Also, having been in the agency business, Walter had learned the value of warm, human interest. Tom Harrow had a brief vision of all the situations in which Walter must have participated, warped and distorted by the lenses and prisms of the Price imagination. Emily's voice was back again as he had heard it in the hall that morning.

"She knows," he said. "She had what you might call a 'race-track reaction.' She's been stamping on her pari-mutuel tickets, and now maybe it's too late for her to bet again. I can't help feeling sorry for her. She's very cross and she has no place to go."

"May I ask," Walter asked, "if you wish she had some place to go?"

It occurred to him that it had been a number of years since

he had given any serious thought to his relationship with Emily. She was there and she was a part of the eternal problem, and he did not want to give his attention to Emily now.

"All women become tiresome on occasions," he said, "and occasions seem to increase the longer you know them. Even Rhoda was tiresome. I think perhaps I will have a drink, merely due to the power of your suggestion."

He walked over to the drink stand and poured himself some Scotch. He had never approved of using liquor as emotional insulation, but he had to admit that it had helped this evening to absorb those shocks that wore one out.

"You never were the secure type, Tommy," Walter said. "Really, if I may say so, Rhoda should have accepted that."

"Let's not be hard on Rhoda," he heard himself say. "Give her credit for buying her tickets before the first race."

Tom Harrow put a cube of ice in his glass and walked across the room to the Judge's chair. He was glad to observe that he could walk easily and steadily, that his syllables were not slurred, that his mind was clear, that he was not sleepy.

"I looked a lot better to her than some of the local entries," he said, "even if I weren't stable. But now we're on the subject of racing, I don't like colts that are too stable."

"And you went right out in front," Walter said. "By Jove, there was nothing like you in the old Price barn."

"The old Price what?" Tom Harrow asked.

"The Price racing stable," Walter said. "The colors were cerise and white. Surely I've told you of my Uncle Joe's Kentucky breeding farm? Our Derby winner, Thunderbolt, was at stud there for fifteen years."

"Thunderbolt?" Tom said, but he was thinking about himself. "I wonder what in hell it was that I ever saw in Emily."

He took a swallow of whiskey, and he was shocked to realize that he was tiring of the taste. Brands of Scotch, he was thinking, were like brands of human relationships. You could put your money on the twelve-year brands or the eight-year-olds, or you could move to lower prices, but in the end Scotch was Scotch, and human relationships, too, had their unbreakable patterns. He looked sharply at Walter Price, afraid that Walter might have fallen asleep.

"I suppose," he said, "after a mood is over, no one can understand just what it was that got him into an emotional involvement. But some people seem to hold a mood for years and years, while I always seem to be moving on."

"Tommy," Walter said, "it's the artist in you that changes."

That was the old excuse: it was all right to fall flat on your face, all right to love them and leave them, all right not to send a check to the wife and kiddies, as long as you were a creative artist. The license of the creative artist was a slogan of the theatre, a part of the Decalogue of Hollywood, but had it any meaning?

"I thought she was a cheerful girl," he said. "But as soon as I married her, she began having temper fits and lachrymose hours. I didn't know that she was spoiled as well as dumb — I wasn't in the mood."

"Tommy," Walter said, "I would not say that Rhoda was dumb."

"No," he said, "not Rhoda. Emily. But I don't blame you for getting confused, Walter. They all get the same — impatient with me in the end. Look at Hopedale. No, I'll take that back, I don't want to look at Hopedale."

"No," Walter said, "it would be easier to look at Rhoda."

"Goddammit," Tom Harrow said, "I don't want to look at her, either, and I don't want to look at Margaret Cadova — do you remember the Cadova girl?"

"Oh, yes," Walter Price said, "at Antibes. I don't blame Rhoda's having been annoyed."

He was walking down an unpleasant glade which he had not traveled for some time, but in any case, he preferred at the moment the past to the present.

"Rhoda wasn't seriously annoyed," he said. "She knew it didn't amount to anything. Nothing ever did, you know, when Rhoda was around. By God, she almost made me practical; at least she made me save the money and take advice from practical friends."

For a moment he had a memory of Rhoda at Palm Beach, years ago.

"Walter," he said, "I really am terribly sorry I can't help out."

"Dear boy," Walter said, "I'm able to take these things better than you, I fear. It's you I'm worried about. It doesn't seem possible — no, not possible."

"I have to pinch myself occasionally to realize it," Tom Harrow said. "In fact, I've been pinching myself at odd moments since I got the news this morning."

"If you want a word of advice from one who knows," Walter said, "it is well to allow hard realities to creep up upon one slowly. This softens the absoluteness of the shock. *Don't look now* has always been my motto for the first day, and for the second day: *Don't look at all of it just yet.*"

"I've been looking," Tom Harrow said, "but still I can't see all of it."

"Dear boy," Walter said, "I think we had both better toddle upstairs to bed, and I'll give you a sleeping pill."

Some puritanical reflex he may have inherited from the Judge made the idea repellent, and sleep at the moment seemed like a weak apology as well as an escape.

"No thanks," he said. "You go on up, Walter; I think I'll stay down here awhile."

He had no desire whatsoever to go to bed, or anywhere. He was sinking again to the bottom of the sea where wreckage lay, festooned with Shakespearean coral.

"Dear Tom," Walter said, "do you remember when *Hero's Return* opened in New York?"

"Yes," he said, "you're damn well right I do."

It was a silly question, and Walter should have known it even at that time of night.

"It's incredible," Walter said, and his voice was on a higher note. "After that night I thought you'd never have to worry about anything again. Well, Tom, good night."

XX

To Put It Very Frankly, He Was Feeling Fine

HIS FIRST play opened at the Empire, a large house for a play
by an unknown. It was the name of Arthur Higgins that had
filled it in the beginning, but when the Empire was finally
closed, most newspapers mentioned *Hero's Return* in their lists
of outstanding plays that had been produced there, and his own
name alone had always carried him after that. He was glad to
remember that he had asked his Aunt Edith to the opening,
and he was quite sure that he had not felt relieved when she
had refused, saying that the journey would be too much for
her. He had never regretted, either, that he had insisted that
Rhoda ask her parents, although they were a further complication in the midst of the final hysteria.

"Darling," Rhoda said, "I don't want to hear about Baltimore
right now. And whether it's a boy or a girl, Mother will want it
named Rhyelle."

"It does fit either sex, doesn't it?" he said.

"Don't," Rhoda said. "You always joke about things that are
serious, and it always makes me feel unstable."

"All right," he said, "things may be tottering, but I don't see
what we can do to help it."

"Well, it doesn't help to get Mother and Pa right here in the
Bulwer with us," she said, "and you know Pa will expect you
to pay for everything."

"All right, Rhoda," he said, "if the play's a hit the bill won't
hurt me, and if it's a flop it won't make any difference."

"Oh, Tom," Rhoda said, "what are we going to do? Just answer me that — what can we possibly do?"

"Listen, Rhoda," he said, "I've got a lot of more immediate things on my mind. Just remember that no matter what happens, everybody ends up by doing something."

"Oh, my God," Rhoda said. "We'll even have to move out of the Bulwer."

He never could grasp the exact meaning of Rhoda's worries. He could not comprehend why Rhoda, who had never liked the Hotel Bulwer, began to clutch at it as a life preserver in the last days before the opening.

"That's right," he said, "no matter what happens, we're going to get out of here."

"Don't laugh," she said. "We may end up in a rooming house in Brooklyn or the Bronx or somewhere."

"Not necessarily," he said, "but if we do, we can hang the diapers on a fire escape, and I haven't the remotest idea where we could hang them in the Plaza."

"Don't laugh about the baby, either," she said. "As if everything wasn't bad enough without it. I never dreamed, even for a single minute, that we'd begin having a baby in almost no time flat."

"Well, anyway," he said, "we're not having it in minus no time flat."

It was a relief to see that the set expression around her lips relaxed.

"I suppose I should have thought," she said, "but then, it wasn't all my fault."

"Why don't you admit you enjoyed it when you didn't think?" he said. "I did, personally."

She laughed. It had not been so difficult in those days to make her laugh.

"I've always liked the things I shouldn't do," she said.

"You should," he said, "and anyway, you don't look as though you'd done anything."

"Don't I at all?" she asked.

"Not the slightest," he said.

"Well then, we won't have to think about it yet," she said, "and maybe we won't have to tell Mother yet. I wish you hadn't bought those clothes for me. Tom, have we any money in the bank?"

"Almost none," he said. "But don't worry, we'll get some, Rhoda."

"Besides," she said, "these clothes won't be any use for months and months."

"They're all right now," he said. "You'll look wonderful when the show opens."

"Oh, God," she said. "I wish I felt wonderful."

He frequently wished the same thing for himself in those last few days, but he doubted if anyone ever had felt good before an opening in New York. In spite of the telegrams, the flowers, the reassuring speeches of confidence, the last hours had a quality that nothing could relieve. Having a baby was not wholly one's own fault, but having a play was. He had never been as worried about Rhoda as he had been about the play. He must have begun to realize that Rhoda was less vulnerable than the play, and then there were the actors and the Higgins money. Everything was on his shoulders as everything always was before a Broadway opening.

"Well, well," Mr. Browne said, "I never thought I'd have a real live playwright for a son-in-law."

"You can't tell how things are going to turn out, can you?" Tom answered. "I feel alive at the moment but I can't say I feel real."

"You look real, Tom dear," Mrs. Browne said, "and very handsome in your tuxedo, and isn't Rhoda lovely? I wish her grandfather could have seen her."

"Yes," he said, "she's looking lovely."

"And happy, too," Mrs. Browne said.

"I'm not happy," Rhoda said. "I'm absolutely sick with worry."

"Well, anyway, you look happy, dear," Mrs. Browne said, "and lovely, with the gardenia that Tom gave you — and thank you again for my gardenia, Tom. That's the way a wife ought always to look — happy — and that's why Tom looks so happy and cheerful, because you do, dear."

"He isn't," Rhoda said. "He's only pretending. People are always pretending around a theatre."

"That's right," Tom said. "I've got to be going now. Here are the tickets. I'll meet you at the theatre, Rhoda."

"You mean you're not going to have dinner with us, or anything?" Rhoda asked.

"I'll eat afterwards," he answered. "I've got to go to the Empire."

"But you've just come back from there."

An uneasiness that he never lost on future occasions had returned to him. He had never been able to eat on an opening night and there was always a conviction, stronger than any call of conscience, that he must be back at the theatre. His reason might tell him there was nothing further he could do, but his responsibility toward the players was closer than any family tie. It was hardly fair to call the theatre a dedicated life, when you knew how undedicated many of its greatest figures were — but when it called, you answered. You left wife and children and the real world, when it called.

"But Tom," Rhoda said, "aren't you going to be with me when the play begins? I can't stand it by myself."

Here was an example of the divided loyalty that had ruined nearly all his life. He never had been able to be two things at once or to develop the requisite split of personality, and neither had most of his contemporaries, but at least he had seldom been ruthless. He had been glad to give Rhoda anything unless the theatre intervened, and Rhoda had never understood that the theatre, not he, gave her everything.

"I'll be with you," he said. "I've got to see the show out front."

He had to see the show out front. He had to get the feel of the audience, and nothing mattered but the show. Rhoda, on such nights afterwards, was pure abstraction, and he could not help it if she was jealous of the theatre. Sultans could make adjustments in a harem, but it was always hard to have two mistresses, even if one was only figurative, in New York.

"I'll be with you before the curtain goes up," he said, and he took his wallet from his pocket. He remembered that the wallet had looked juvenile, dating from his days in college and that it did not go well with his dinner coat which was almost new. He drew out two ten-dollar bills, his last large bills, but he handled them carelessly. He still could not regret that he had always handled money carelessly.

"Go somewhere and have a good dinner," he said. "You tell her where, Mr. Browne, some very nice hotel. I'll be with you at curtaintime."

Then he kissed her. He remembered the scent of her hair and the scent of the gardenia. Her dress was beautiful and she did look very happy, although her hands were cold as ice.

If there was one thing he had learned in the course of his career, it was how to estimate an audience. As of the present, he could walk into a theatre before the house lights dimmed, and tell from the murmur of voices whether the audience would be intellectual or stupid in its mass reaction. One must never forget that an audience was as essential to any play as its lines. An audience, that variable cross-section of individuals of diverse attainments and backgrounds, must be collectively as well as individually intrigued, amused and educated, but education could be achieved only by subtle indirection. An audience could be shocked, but not too much; or frightened, but not too much; it could be charmed by whimsy, but not too much; it could be made to laugh, but it was worth remembering that people could not move indefinitely from one laugh to another. A good audience might have appreciation, but it was never constantly intellectual. Its attention in the mass was childish in its vacillation and it disliked holding a thought too long. If you lectured to it unduly, it would squirm and cough, and an audience never had to be polite since it had paid to be present and had a right to be critical of its investment. There was no wonder that everyone, down to the ushers in the aisle and the soft drink venders in the lobby, feared and respected any audience; but in the main, an everyday audience was predictable. It was only a first-night audience that was not. Attention constantly wandered. Distinguished individuals in the front rows could become more important than the actors or the lines, and a critic's facial expression more intriguing than a love scene. Applause, though violent, was so lacking in validity that one could seldom honestly be sure what the score was until the papers with the reviews were on the street.

He was more conscious, when he found his seat beside Rhoda in the orchestra, than he had ever been before of the beat of voices and of a cruel undercurrent of curiosity. He remembered that Rhoda's vivid interest had disturbed him, but, after all, she could not share his sentiments, and now that he had written a play he would never be amused by a first night again.

"Where's Arthur Higgins?" Rhoda asked. "I don't see him anywhere."

"He's at the back of the house somewhere," he said. "He's restless; he likes to move around."

Curtaintime was deliberately late, but still near enough so that there was nothing more that anyone could do. Now and then the voices around him would move into definition, like voices in a stream of consciousness.

"The name of the man who wrote this play," he heard someone behind him saying, "is Harrow, Thomas Harrow. I've never heard of him, have you?"

"No," he heard someone else answer, "but Arthur always has a penchant for young men."

"In what way do you mean?" the first voice asked.

There was an interval of quiet laughter, a bit of dialogue which was typically first-night.

"Do you want to move around with Arthur Higgins?" Rhoda asked.

"No," he said, "I'd rather take it here beside you, darling."

"I think it's fun seeing everybody," Rhoda said. "It's much more exciting than Wilmington. There are so many more people with jewelry and everything, and lots of them must be really rich. I don't see what you mean about taking it. You ought not to be acting as though you were going to the dentist."

A dental chair and a first night were not so far apart except that on a first night there was never any novocaine. There was nothing to relieve the reality of complete exposure.

330

"Where are the critics?" Rhoda asked.

"Don't shout," he said. "They're ahead of us in the aisle seats so they can rush out quickly to write the good news."

"Is that one over there a critic?" Rhoda asked. "If he is, he can't be very good, because his shirt is dirty and his coat isn't pressed."

"Linen is no criterion," he said.

"Darling," Rhoda said, "you ought to be excited. It's all your party, isn't it?"

"Christ, yes," he said.

"Don't say that," she said, "you'll shock Mother."

"All right," he said, "I wish it weren't my party."

"Don't say that, either," she said. "It's the first time I've really liked anything since I saw Niagara Falls."

"Baby," he said, "we're going over it now in a barrel."

"Don't mention baby, either," she said. "You ought to be dreadfully proud."

"Jesus," he said.

"Don't say that, darling," she told him. "Mother's right beside you. Aren't you excited at all?"

"Yes," he said, "hold tight to the inside of the barrel."

"What are you talking about?" she asked. "What barrel?"

"Any barrel," he said, "and we're inside it, not outside it."

"Darling," she said, "think of all these people coming to see your play. I wish I'd written it."

"All right," he said, "you can do the next one. I'd rather have a baby."

"Don't keep saying 'baby,'" she said, "just when I start feeling happy. Oh, my God, Tom, what are we going to do if all these people don't like it?"

"It's companionate of you to get around to that point," he said.

"Anyway," she said, "of course they're going to like it. Please don't get me frightened, Tom."

He held her hand and it was still cold as ice.

"Look," he said, "there could be a lot worse things than this, Rhoda."

He did not believe what he was saying. There could be death, destruction and ruin — but nothing could be worse than the first night of one's first play on Broadway.

There were some writers he knew with such a resilient enthusiasm and with such a poignant narcissism that they never seemingly tired of any line they had written. Unfortunately he had always found that once he was finished with anything, he was finished. He could polish and revise, but there eventually came a point when perspective would depart, and when finally every word would be stale and distasteful. When he heard the opening speeches of his play that night, his anxiety grew because of his deathly weariness at their repetition. He knew by heart each lilt of voice, each gesture, but his uneasiness was worse between the acts.

"Wouldn't you like to walk outside and listen to what people are saying?" Rhoda asked, when the first act ended.

"No," he said. "It doesn't make any difference what they're saying."

That was correct. A play was done when it opened and curiosity regarding its reception was fruitless.

"Tom," she asked him, "do you think it's terrible?"

"I don't know," he said. "It doesn't do any good to be frightened."

But he could feel a cold paralysis of a theatrical fear that was different from any other in its physical and mental elements. It was more than fear of failure or disgrace. There were minglings of self-pity and dread of the future, and he had never subsequently been able to analyze the mixture.

"They seem to be listening, don't they?" she said. "And I haven't heard anybody cough."

He did not answer and she tugged at his sleeve.

"Tom," she whispered, "what's the matter?"

"Maybe you shouldn't have taken a chance on me," he said.

"Tom," she said, and her voice broke, "don't say that. When are we going to *know?*"

"When the reviews come out," he said. "When we see the *New York Times*. We'll have to go to Arthur Higgins's party and just wait."

"Oh," she said. "All we do is wait and wait."

His nerves were on edge.

"Stop being a goddam little bellyacher," he whispered. "I'm the one who's taking the beating, not you."

"No," she said, "me too."

He never had any adequate recollection of the performance as a whole, except that it had seemed ragged. The actors were uncertain of their timing, and seemed out of touch with the audience from start to finish, and in the third act Delia Duneen dropped two lines, and, even though Briggs improvised, the sequence was meaningless. The parts that he thought had depth and poetry only grated on his nerves. When the applause grew louder and the laughter sounded more natural, he listened in disbelief. He already knew that the stage had its own rules of behavior, one of which was to applaud excessively when a first-night curtain fell. He left Rhoda and Mrs. Browne as soon as the applause started, and reached the indescribable plainness and disorder of backstage which was to be part of his life. He stood for a minute in the wings watching the cast change order each time the curtain fell. There was a gloomy dusk in the wings created by the glare of the footlights, and an ugly businesslike reality that counteracted the unrealities of the stage set. He did not realize that Arthur Higgins was standing beside him until he heard his voice.

"It may be genuine applause," Arthur Higgins said. "This has gone on two minutes longer than is conventionally necessary, and it still keeps up. Did you like the performance, Tom?"

"I couldn't follow it," he answered.

"Listen to the hand Briggs and Duneen are getting," Arthur said. "It is more than is absolutely necessary. George —"

Then he saw that George Rosen, the assistant stage manager, was with them.

"George, tell Duneen to go out alone."

It was instructive to watch Arthur Higgins gauge the reaction without excitement or emotion.

"They are sometimes kind to a new face," Arthur said, "but this may mean more. It isn't dying down. George, keep the curtain

333

down ten seconds longer, and if it keeps up, send out Briggs."

When the curtain was down the sound from the house was deadened, but the applause was still insistent.

"All right," Arthur Higgins said, "send it up again. This really is longer than is conventional. It's always very tricky; you never can be sure."

His voice was drowned out as the curtain rose.

"It's a smash hit, Mr. Higgins," George Rosen said. "Listen to the lovely hand they're giving Mr. Briggs."

George Rosen was a young man then, with a great future ahead of him, and he was now out on the Coast — where, if he had wanted, he could have bought the rights of *Porthos of Paris* — but he had been assistant stage manager, then.

"You can't trust them," Arthur said. "When those people get in the right mood of mass hysteria, they will applaud their grandmother's funeral. They may think better of it in the morning."

"But still, sir," George Rosen said, "they are going for Mr. Briggs in a very big way."

"Yes," Arthur said, "but the reviews will tell better. Send the curtain down, George, and tell Briggs and Duneen to go out and kiss each other lightly and then we'll send it down for good. Nothing resembling a clinch, George. Sex must not enter into it, you understand, now the show is over."

"It might be a lovely touch," George said, "if you and Mr. Harrow, Mr. Higgins, went out to take a bow."

"Never make such a suggestion again," Arthur Higgins said. "If they saw Mr. Harrow and me, they wouldn't believe the play. Excuse me, Tom, nothing personal intended."

They were still applauding when the curtain rose on the chaste embrace.

"I think I can honestly detect an undertone of enthusiasm," Arthur Higgins said. "Tom, would you like to go out alone? The new playwright — it won't hurt, if the reviews are good."

"No," he said, "it's bad enough right here."

"You're being debonair," Arthur said. It was still difficult to hear him in the wings.

"The hardest trick is to be debonair when you take it on the

334

chin," Arthur Higgins said. "Keep the curtain down, George, and dim the footlights. Put on all lights on stage. Bring on the cast, and go and kiss Duneen, Tom, and tell her she was wonderful. Shake hands with Briggs, in a very manly way, and then kiss the other girls. Don't kiss them too hard because you'll have to do it all over again at the apartment. Yes, on the whole it might be wise to hoard the osculation, Tom."

Tom wished that at the *In Memoriam* meeting held for Arthur Higgins he had remembered to quote that bit. He had said only that Arthur was the greatest trouper he had ever known, and who wasn't the greatest known trouper when he died?

"You are all over queer perfume," Rhoda said. She made the remark in the taxi when they were on the way with his family-in-law to Arthur Higgins's apartment.

"Yes," he said, "it's mostly Duneen, I think. Arthur made me kiss them all. It's etiquette."

"I'd just as soon you didn't kiss Duneen too often," Rhoda said. "She's too pretty for her own good."

Now that the play was over, he was able to think of Rhoda and of how she would adjust herself to everything.

"I do think Miss Duneen is lovely," Mrs. Browne said, "with fine features, but she is not *distinguée*. She has not the patrician look."

"Yes," he said, "you're very right" — and he noticed that his voice had assumed the inflections of Arthur Higgins — "she isn't and Rhoda is. The thought crossed my mind the first moment I saw her."

He was glad to hear Rhoda laugh.

"Don't you believe him, Mother," she said. "It didn't cross his mind at first that you came from Baltimore."

"I'm sure it crossed his mind that you were a lady, dear," Mrs. Browne said.

"There used to be a race-track man down in Maryland I used to know," Mr. Browne said, "who once said he could always guess the blood lines from looking at a filly."

"Hudson," Mrs. Browne said. "What are you giggling at, dear? I don't think your father's very funny."

335

"I'm nervous, Mother," Rhoda said. "I can't help it until I know what's happened to the play."

"What's happened, dear?" Mrs. Browne said. "Why, it was marvelous from start to finish, and everyone clapped and clapped except some men in the row in front of us who left in a very rude way right in the middle of everything."

"Mother," Rhoda said, and the weary patience of her voice showed how quickly she could move to another way of life, "those were the critics. They had to leave to meet their deadline."

"I still think they might have done it more politely," Mrs. Browne said. "Everything was perfectly lovely. I'll never forget how everyone else clapped."

"I know, Mother," Rhoda said, "but applause doesn't mean anything on a first night, and I'm not sure the play or the audience became alive."

Rhoda never forgot words or phrases; she was quoting Arthur Higgins.

"Why Rhoda, it was magnificent," Mrs. Browne said. "Wasn't it wonderful, Hudson?"

"Yes, Estelle," Mr. Browne said, "it was a hundred per cent, and I don't think we've thanked Tom enough for asking us down to see it. It's the finest time I've had in years."

He was glad that he had asked the Brownes and that at least someone had derived some happiness from the ordeal.

"There's only one thing . . ." Mr. Browne said.

"You're the one who always picks holes, Hudson," Mrs. Browne said. "What thing?"

"I didn't know Rhoda would marry a famous man," Mr. Browne said. "It's going to be tough for me to get on with a famous man."

It was easy enough to laugh, and to suggest that they wait to see the papers, but at the same time the house at Daytona Beach might have been much farther inland if it had not been for that remark of Mr. Browne's.

That ride in the dark uptown on Park Avenue, past the glittering windows of the apartment buildings, was a last link between a past and a future that he was hardly beginning to discern. He was approaching a set of values unknown to him except in an academic way, and no one in the world could explain any human value academically. It was not Rhoda's fault that she had failed to grasp that future in the same way that he had. He was leading and she was following. Besides, no two people ever reacted in the same manner to any given situation, and the complexities of that future were with him still. The complexity of the creative urge and the riddle of artistic integrity were all intermingled with tenets of love and marriage. He could see, now, that he was inevitably more involved in that future than Rhoda ever had been.

For example, that party at the Higgins apartment was bound to have more overtones for him than for her. Beautiful as she had looked, light and easy as she had seemed, she was bound to be less aware than he of the significance of that party. In spite of the strangers gathered in the Higgins living room, the party had a tribal quality. They all were waiting for the word; the livelihood of many guests depended on it. Like hundreds of similar gatherings he had attended later, theatrical democracy was behind it. The Higgins office force was waiting to express a word of hope and cheer; there was champagne and there were cold things to eat. The sight of the table in the Higgins dining room made Tom suddenly hungry. Arthur Higgins, even in his last days, had always insisted on champagne.

In the Higgins apartment, defiant loyalty temporarily overcame petty jealousies. There was a murmur that seemed rehearsed when the Brownes, Tom, and Rhoda entered. He had never been as much the center of anything before, walking in with Rhoda. Perhaps he already had a premonition that he would be the center of similar gatherings for years to come, that voices ever afterwards when he entered a New York drawing room or restaurant would drop for an appreciable moment, that ever afterwards he would be the center of critical likes and dislikes, enthusiasms and enmities.

"Here he is," Arthur Higgins said, crossing the room to meet him. "Here's the hero."

It was solid corn, but the speech also had a sort of authentic old-school quality in the Higgins apartment. The room, with its

337

tapestries, its dark woodwork and its upstairs gallery, was a larger, more gracious projection of the office. There was nothing that exactly resembled its spirit any more unless some odd corner of the Cloisters up the river, but the late Charles Dana Gibson would have been entirely conversant with the background. A moment's pause after Arthur Higgins's courtly speech made Tom aware that everyone was waiting for a bon mot in return, and that he had to be right out there with Arthur Higgins.

"Good evening, Arthur," he said, and he waved his hand to the office and theatre personnel and other guests with whom he was only half familiar. "Let's not cheer yet. The poor devil may be dying."

It was nearly his first experience in delivering an apt, informal line. Arthur understood such grace and waited until a ripple of mirth subsided.

"But you could still do with some champagne, couldn't you?" Arthur said.

"Yes," he said, "I really could."

A waiter arrived who looked like a Gibson waiter, with a tray of glasses.

"One moment," Arthur Higgins said, "before we lapse into easy conversation." He was made to be a master of ceremonies, and he had always loved that sort of thing. "The last few years have been a bright period for the American stage. I predict that everyone will know this news tomorrow, but in the meanwhile, I am proud to propose the health of one of our newest and finest playwrights."

It was a time to be quiet and to touch glasses with Arthur Higgins, and to face the fact that Arthur might be right.

"Darling," Helen Adair said, "the interesting thing is that Arthur means it."

He was able to tell himself that everyone meant things when caught in a theatrical emotion, and that such an outgiving was like the bubbles of champagne. Then he was shaking hands with everyone and their faces still returned to him with his memories of the Higgins apartment. He saw Mort Sullivan and the girls from the Sullivan office; and Walter Price, thin and handsome in

338

those days; and Waldo Francis, who handled the publicity; and Dick Brogan, his assistant; and Curt Winternitz from the box office; and Nancy Mulford; and Bess Moriarty, who ran the switchboard; and Celestine Guin, who was wardrobe mistress; and Marie, whose last name he never did remember, who was Duneen's maid; and Gus, the call boy; and Lou Achir, the stage manager; and George Rosen, his assistant; and Bob Solomon, the assistant business manager.

Then he was meeting the Higginses' special guests and friends, and the financial backers, and shaking hands with Mr. and Mrs. Paul J. Merriman, Mr. Higgins's lawyer; and Mr. Benjamin F. Chew, Mr. Higgins's financial adviser; and Mrs. Chew, who lived in a charming estate in Bronxville. He was meeting Spike J. Maxwell, who had roomed with Arthur Higgins at Harvard; and General G. Wesley Jones and Mrs. Jones, now at Governors Island, who were deeply interested in the play because General Jones, then Colonel Jones, had distinguished himself in the Bois des Rappes, mentioned in the play. The general lost interest on learning that Tom had not served in World War I.

"I wanted to go, sir," Tom had told him, "but I was not in the age group."

He could remember the lines in the general's face and he was sure the general had understood and applauded the psychology of heroes. Then Arthur Higgins introduced him to Mr. and Mrs. Arthur Twining Hertime.

"Tom," he said, "these are special friends and they are especially anxious to meet you because they are sharing some of our financial burdens."

Mr. Hertime laughed in a very jocular way.

"Don't tell tales out of school, Art," he said. "We are very pedestrian people, Mr. Harrow, but may I call you Tom, and may I call your gorgeous wife Rhoda? We are so pedestrian that Mrs. Hertime and I enjoy a change sometimes, don't we, my sweet? And we have certainly enjoyed this evening."

"And I am certainly sure after this evening," Arthur Higgins said, "that you are going to make some change out of it, Art."

Mr. Hertime laughed again.

"Whether I do or not," he said, "it's been more fun than a barrel of monkeys, meaning nothing personal. Hasn't it been more fun than a barrel of monkeys, Angela?"

"Yes," Mrs. Hertime said, "but you mustn't mind him, Mr. Harrow, and neither must your ravishing wife. What did you say your first name was, dear?"

"Rhoda," Tom Harrow said.

"Rhoda. It's one of my favorite names," Mrs. Hertime said. "Haven't I met you somewhere, dear, at Palm Beach or somewhere?"

"Palm Beach?" Rhoda said. "No, but I wish you had."

"Did you hear that one?" Arthur Hertime said. "She wishes she had! Tom, if I may take the liberty of saying so, your wife is as witty as she is beautiful. Waiter, bring me some more happy water. Here's looking at you, Mrs. Harrow — but may I call you Rhoda?"

"Why, yes, if you'd like to, Mr. Hertime," Rhoda said.

"It's a deal if you call me Art," Mr. Hertime said. "Angela, I've got an idea. These kids must be very, very tired. Do you get the idea? Why not take them down to the beach with us next week, after the show is set?"

"That would be a lovely idea, Art," Mrs. Hertime said.

"Well, it's a deal," Mr. Hertime said. "We'll get you a drawing room for Thursday night. How about it, Tom?"

As it happened, he had no real chance to answer because Arthur Higgins spoke immediately.

"Of course they'll come, Art," he said. "The play will be entirely set by then."

Thinking of it in retrospect, there was always such a thing as a quid pro quo, and Arthur Higgins could not be blamed for using them as currency.

"But I haven't any summer clothes," Rhoda said.

The wine was working, wine and the excitement.

"It's all right, Rhoda," Tom said, "I'll get you some tomorrow."

"But Tom —" she began.

"It's all right, Rhoda," he said, "they'll keep — you can use them later."

340

"Besides, it's off season," Mrs. Hertime said. "We all of us just camp out off season."

He did not know that a door to yet another world was opening, a fateful world for him and Rhoda, the unexplored land of the very rich. He could never see the glamour of that world as Rhoda had, and it was possible to ask what would have happened to him and Rhoda if the Hertimes had not asked them there. What if they had only stood at the gate looking in instead of stepping across the threshold? Yet they would have stepped across the threshold eventually. Rhoda might have hesitated, but his insatiable desire for new experience would have moved him.

"Thank you very much, sir," he said to Mr. Hertime. "Rhoda and I would appreciate a rest, and we've never been to Florida."

"Don't call me 'sir,'" Mr. Hertime said. "Call me Art. It will be an enormous pleasure to have you with us, Tom."

Later, when from experience he could draw finer distinctions than he could then, he knew that the Hertimes, if they were not top-drawer in the way the Bramhalls were, were not in a lower echelon. Wealth, like good Burgundy, needed maturing, and a consciousness of inherited wealth could not be acquired in a single generation, and Mr. Hertime's grandfather had founded the Hertime Smelting Company.

"They always know what they're doing," Rhoda had said, "and somehow you and I never know. I mean, we're never sure."

"That's right," he said, "we can't afford to know."

Rhoda had actually described the boundaries of that world. It cost a lot to afford to be sure, in money and in character, more indeed of either than he had ever possessed.

He might let his thoughts wander, but in memory he was still in the Higgins apartment recalling the sharp uncertainty that had possessed him. When young, you were always uncertain, and there were different uncertainties later, like those of a physical checkup in a hospital. There you could wait in an antiseptic room, reading an antiseptic book, knowing that in a little while you might be told in a nice way that your life span was drawing to an early close, but there was no vanity in life and death, no fear of artistic failure. It was only your fault in an academic way if your liver or gall bladder had gone wrong. On the contrary, you were entirely to blame if your play became a flop.

He had eaten one slice of Virginia ham and one slice of Tennessee smoked turkey and a little mixed green salad, and had drunk four cups of coffee, and a considerable amount of champagne, but he was thinking all the while of the tumbrels moving to the guillotine. They could all blame him, Higgins and the players, and the champagne did not help. He was the French aristocrat waiting for the knife to fall, but the end came somewhere around one in the morning. It was Simeon, from the accounting department, who brought the news. Simeon, who was pale, redheaded and aggressive, arrived unnoticed until he approached Arthur Higgins. Then there was a collective sigh because Simeon was carrying proofs from the *New York Times* and *Herald-Tribune*. Although Simeon must have read them earlier, it was not his place to register delight or disappointment. This was the function of Arthur Higgins, one which he had performed many times before.

It was possible still to re-create Arthur, who had put on his horn-rimmed spectacles, holding the limp strips of paper while Mort Sullivan read over his shoulder. Silence had spread over the apartment, like the voice of conscience. It was possible still to see the faces, but perhaps anyone else could recall as vividly as he the details of a first dramatic triumph. He could remember the choking dryness in his throat and his frantic effort to look composed. Arthur Higgins had raised his voice to draw everyone's attention, but speaking skill was unnecessary at the time since everybody was waiting.

"I have never read reviews out loud," he said. "I can only say these do not surprise me in the least, and I will read a headline. 'New Genius on Broadway' — and it is not ironical. You had better look at these yourself, Tom, and then let everybody see them."

Actually, he never fully read those first reviews and afterwards he developed a mental block which prevented his carefully reading any reviews of his work, but the words and phrases still leaped at him. "Youthful yet mature." "A finely faceted, dramatic

342

diamond." "Heartrending in its sheer simplicity." "Luminous and deep." "A companion piece to *They Knew What They Wanted*, though told in its own brave style." "Will take its place with the best of contemporary theatre." The words in his memory sounded hackneyed now, like the quotes of all reviews, but in that moment a new assurance and a new power came over him that he never entirely lost.

"Here," he said, "read them, Rhoda."

Then Mort Sullivan spoke to him.

"Boy," Mort said, "how does it feel?"

Tom was glad that he had told the simple truth.

"Frankly, it feels fine," he said.

He never could believe in Mr. Kipling's thought that triumph and disaster were two impostors that should be treated just the same. He preferred triumph to the other, and he still believed that anyone who was not a fool, including General Washington, had doubtless given triumph special treatment within limits. He had never been ashamed of feeling fine.

"Tom," Rhoda said, and her voice was insistent above all the other voices, "Tom, they don't say this about everybody, do they?"

"No," he said, "not as far as I know, Rhoda."

"Then it means," she said, "that everything's all right, doesn't it?"

"Yes," he said, "it looks that way."

"Can't you be sure?" Her voice had risen. "Is there any catch or anything to it? Does it really mean we won't have to worry any more about this?"

"Yes," he said. "I rather think it does."

"Well," Rhoda said. "Well!" He saw that the color had drained from her face and that her knees were sagging.

"Rhoda," he said, "are you all right?"

"I will be in a minute," she said. "Just put your arm around me. I don't need smelling salts or anything, but I feel a little faint."

"You mean —" he began.

"I don't mean *that* at all," Rhoda said. "Don't be so silly. A baby doesn't worry you to death. It *really* is all right, isn't it?"

343

"Yes," he said.

She looked better, and he doubted whether anybody had noticed.

"Here," he said, "take a drink of this."

"Darling," she said, "it doesn't seem possible, does it? I mean Palm Beach and everything."

Then her voice was lost among other voices, since everyone was speaking. In the turn of a second hand he had become a Figure in the Theatre. Only the other day he had read on the dramatic page of the *New York Sunday Times* that he was a Figure in the Theatre, and he still did not know exactly what it meant, because he had never been able to cultivate an interest in the critical arts even when he had been a subject. He could see, intellectually, the value of criticism, but he never had felt at home with the men who wrote it, because their compulsions ran on different tangents from his own. Their ideas were to his mind inaccurate, even when they offered praise. Praise was old to him now, but it was new that night. In fact, so new that he allowed himself to take pleasure in it when he and Rhoda were riding alone in a taxi back to the Bulwer.

"Frankly," he said, "I'm feeling fine. Are you feeling fine, Rhoda?"

"Yes," she said, "but it's awfully hard to stop worrying just in a single minute."

"Anyway," he said, "we're going to have champagne for breakfast. We'll give it to the room clerk to keep on ice."

"Is that why you asked Arthur for those two bottles?" she asked. "Gosh, I never thought of having champagne for breakfast."

"Then think about it now," he said. "Rhoda, do you love me?"

He had nearly dropped a bottle getting out of the taxi, and he had twisted his ankle as he recovered himself. He was limping when he gave the bottles to the night clerk at the Bulwer.

"Well, Mr. Harrow," the night clerk said, "how does it feel to have a real hit on your hands?"

That was what they always asked — how it felt.

"Boy," he said, "it feels fine. Doesn't it feel fine, Rhoda?"

344

"Yes," she said, "it does, but I wish you could think of another way to say it."

Later on he had tried to think of other graceful ways, but there was no other sensible way to say it. He had wished many times later that he could feel that way again, relaxed, which is why he had twisted his ankle getting out of the taxicab, free, so much in love with Rhoda, so elated and so sleepy, or so full of wit and humor, so shot through with good ideas — but then, that sort of thing could happen only once.

XXI

King Midas Would Have Understood Palm Beach

THE ANCIENT Greeks, he often thought, were people he would have liked and understood better than the Romans of the Augustan age. The Greeks produced better dramatists, and their mythology had been a source of delight to him ever since he had encountered Bulfinch in the Judge's library. No wonder the Freudians had turned to the Grecian myths in their endeavors to explain the subconscious mind. Although it was a pity, perhaps, that Greek mythology should have gained popularity due to the efforts of Dr. Freud, it proved its appeal had touched the heart of the Great Interpreter from Vienna. It was startling to hear words like Oedipus and Narcissus tossed drunkenly about at Westport week ends and used by Emily, who had never read *Oedipus Rex;* but King Midas, as far as he knew, had not as yet been turned into a medical symbol, perhaps because a king had been seemingly interested more in money than in sex, although, according to Nathaniel Hawthorne, he had loved his daughter, but not in a way to interest.

He had thought of King Midas upon awakening in the Hotel Bulwer next morning. It was half past ten in the morning; it was amazing how soundly he and Rhoda had slept then without the aid of any sedation except champagne. The telephone in the other room was ringing. His ankle gave him a twinge when he got up to answer it, and his pajamas looked unaesthetic. It was a time for silk pajamas now and silk lingerie for Rhoda if they were going to Palm Beach. The call was from the Higgins office.

There was a queue in front of the box office about ten blocks long, an exaggeration, but it conveyed the idea that advance orders were coming in so fast they were sending three more men over. The show was in, and how did it feel, Mr. Harrow, to have a hit on your hands?

"Boy," he said, "in spite of everything, it still feels fine."

Then he called the dining room. There was no room service at the Bulwer, but he told the captain there that he would give anyone five dollars who brought up his champagne in a bucket of ice, with two pots of black coffee. Rhoda must have awakened while he was talking.

"What's that," she asked, "about champagne and coffee?"

"Just something to pick us up," he said, "before we go out and start spending money. How are you feeling, Rhoda?"

"It doesn't seem right after everything," she said, "but I'm feeling fine."

"You'll feel better after the champagne," he told her. "They just called up to say there's a line buying tickets at the Empire ten blocks long."

"Ten blocks?" she said.

"It's only a figure of speech," he said, "but it's long enough so we'll get some cash from the Higgins office after the champagne. And then I'm going to see you get dressed from the skin right out, and no maternity dresses, either. Remember, we're going to Palm Beach, and then maybe we'll go to Cartier's."

"Cartier's?" she said.

Midas would have understood, or Pandora. Rhoda's hair was unbrushed, but it looked beautiful.

"Tom," she said, "you sound as if you were making something up."

In spite of the pain in his ankle, and even before the champagne arrived, he thought she looked like Venus on the Ludovisi throne. She had the same true simplicity as that bas-relief, the same scorn for illusory adornment. The truth was she did not need illusion, or make-up, or anything that morning.

"I know what you mean," he said, "but I think we'll get used to it by degrees."

347

He should have said he was afraid they would get used to it, and he would have been right to fear. The times that were best in living were always the times in which one did not believe.

He could grant that he might have experienced too many things with time, but still he believed he was right in being shocked by the appearance of Palm Beach the last time he saw it as compared with the autumn of 1928 when he had been there with Rhoda. Lake Worth had become a septic tank, and the great American odor of potatoes, popcorn, and fish frying in vegetable oils penetrated almost to the shops on Worth Avenue. And what of the Ocean Boulevard? The Joe Davieses might still be there, and maybe the Kennedys, but why did all the houses look like frosted cakes, and the palm trees and the pigeon plums and the Spanish bayonets and the hibiscus bushes appear grotesque? They had not looked so when he and Rhoda had seen them. And surely the people had been different. Surely the people had not been so dull when he and Rhoda had been there, or was it that experience simply blunts every novelty? What was it that made his blood pulse fast at Palm Beach once?

"It doesn't seem real, does it?" Rhoda said.

"That's right," he said, "and let's hope it never does." But then, eventually it did. To hell with palm trees now. To hell with the softly sweet tropic scent of Southern waters, and mimosa. But things were different once — the first bougainvillaea, the first scent of Southern seas, the first glimpse of all those interesting people whom one had read about but never seen.

The Hertimes' limousine, a replica of that mythological Packard, was at the station to take them to the Hertimes' house on Ocean Boulevard, and he had never felt so wide awake, so susceptible to new impressions. Mrs. Hertime had been full of information. They were all good friends after the journey, although Mrs. Hertime was still timid with him. As she had said herself over drinks the previous evening, when they had all dined together in the Hertimes' drawing room, she had never seen anyone before who talked just like a witty story in the *Saturday Evening Post,* and she hoped he wouldn't be bored with them and that it was selfishness to take him down before the season had started, but there were people who loved to be there before the season, when it was quiet.

"Now, everybody who first comes here," Mrs. Hertime said, "always wants to know the names of trees. Now, that over there that's all over the place is a banyan tree. I think it comes from India."

"It must have," he told her. "Mowgli would have liked it."

"Who is Mowgli?" Mrs. Hertime asked.

"Oh, come," Mr. Hertime said. "He's in that *Jungle Book* you used to read the kids."

"Oh, yes," Mrs. Hertime said.

"And I know what those trees are," Tom said, "they're palms. I know it from Palm Sunday."

"Oh," Mrs. Hertime said, "nobody told me you were a Catholic, but Ralph can drive you over to early Mass."

"He needn't bother," he said. "I've only seen the palms outside of church."

"He hasn't been inside one since we were married," Rhoda said. "That was the First Congregational, and it scared him half to death."

Rhoda had never been in a Packard limousine before, but she looked as though she had ridden in one always. In fact, in the traveling suit he had bought for her, she seemed as if she had always been at Palm Beach. She might, in fact, have been "Miss Palm Beach" in a much more emphatic way than any one-piece bathing girl. She was born to exist in places like Palm Beach, and the reason must have been that Palm Beach spelled then and still spelled the securest sort of solidity that he had ever known.

"It's dreadful that so much is closed," Mrs. Hertime said. "You see, the hurricane season is hardly over."

He could admit the phenomenon of the hurricane, of which he had read in juvenile fiction and in Joseph Conrad, but he could never believe — news to the contrary, and in spite of Sodom and Gomorrah — that God could let loose a hurricane on Palm Beach without giving most serious thought to the possible repercussions; and the Hertimes, in their maroon limousine with its bicycle-spoked wheels, also seemed hurricane-proof. As things

349

turned out, Mr. Hertime had been so firmly rooted to the rocks of financial reality that he died, in the mid-Roosevelt Thirties, as Mrs. Hertime had assured Tom once, just a little richer than he had been at the end of 1928, which only went to show that this sort of thing was a gift.

Tom had never had that gift, and perhaps Rhoda had already begun to realize it. In spite of her new trousseau, in their new pigskin suitcases, the suspicion may have been dawning that he was not quite the man she had believed he would be. She must have learned in the Hertimes' Packard, even before the butler and the second man came down the front steps to get out the luggage, that a thousand dollars wisely spent at Bergdorf's and a clip from Cartier's could not buy the pedestrian wizardry of the Hertimes. They had some other magic gift. Presley Brake, to whom Rhoda was now married, had it, and Rhoda must have learned part of the secret herself, in order to have found Presley. But no one had told him what the secret was, and now the truth was dawning upon him, that old dogs could only seldom learn new tricks.

"Anyway," Mrs. Hertime said, "the caretakers are starting to tidy up the shrubbery and the swimming pools and take the shutters off some of the houses."

He was surprised that Mrs. Hertime, who was Midwest, and as she liked to say, just folks, in spite of the chauffeur and the yacht and all the other things that Art had wanted, had not referred to the houses as homes — but she must have known that this could not be appropriate. You could never, somehow, think of the representative Palm Beach dwellings as homes. They were closer to being castles in Spain, or monuments to cumulative achievement, or to immature dream desires, but you could never call such specialized buildings homes. The architects who were so feverishly building in '28 must have examined photographs of the Alhambra every night before they went to sleep, after caviar entrées and indigestible dinners — and then they must have dreamed. These dwellings had the frothy quality of designs squeezed out from different tubes by chefs to adorn the surface of an important piece of pastry, but this impression was neither disturbing nor inappropriate as he faced that new wonderland on that distant Sunday morning. In the eyes of their owners, they were meant to be escapist confections, that should not, even if they did, sit heavily on mind or conscience.

"Oh, look, Art," Mrs. Hertime said, "those nice young Bramhalls are here. Their house is all opened, and a colored girl is shaking a mop out of the upstairs window. Tom and Rhoda would just love them, and I'm sure that they'll be cocktailing at the Everglades if it's open."

The indiscriminate changing of nouns into verbs was a novelty to him then that fitted all those sights.

"Yes, honey," Mr. Hertime said, "it looks as though they were. I thought they were going to their place at Antibes this year."

"Perhaps Marion is sandwiching-in Palm Beach," Mrs. Hertime said, "or maybe Dick is too busy."

"That's so," Mr. Hertime said. "Bankers are busier than bird dogs. Did you ever meet Dick Bramhall, Tom?"

"No," Tom said, "I don't believe I have, Art."

"You're such a congenial cuss," Mr. Hertime said, "I keep forgetting you're in show business. Dick Bramhall is Bramhall Box."

"Bramhall Box?" Tom asked.

"That is, his father's Bramhall Box," Mr. Hertime said. "Dick is in the Guaranty, and if you want my opinion, he has one of the shrewdest investment brains in America. He handles my portfolio when I'm busy with new ideas. You two young fellows have got to get together."

"You wouldn't know he had an investment brain or anything when he's down here vacationing," Mrs. Hertime said. "Dick and Marion are the nicest young people. And what do you think the name of their yacht is, Rhoda? It's named *Bramma*. That shows you what fun they are — Bram for Bramhall and Ma for Marion. She says she's a good little old-fashioned wife, and old-fashioned wives come second."

"Tom," Rhoda said, "am I old-fashioned?"

The thought came to him that she was as full-panoplied as though she had been Minerva stepping from the cloven head of Zeus, but it was not a formidable thought. He had never been as

351

physically in love with her as at that moment, and ever afterwards he could understand why people were forever getting mixed up with other people in Florida.

"You're not old-fashioned, but you like things right," he said.

"Not right," she answered, "only level. I like things so I know where they'll be tomorrow."

"Then you ought to get out of this market, honey," Mr. Hertime said. "No one knows where it's going to be tomorrow."

The Hertime house was still standing when he had last been down there visiting the Bramhalls with Emily, and he had walked alone to look at it and had even ventured a few steps up the pebbled driveway. They were the same round pebbles that the Hertimes had used, and as they slipped and rattled beneath his feet, he could remember how the maroon Packard had sounded. The harsh winds that scoured the Florida East Coast had weathered the massive pseudo-Moorish hacienda with its Byzantine influence. The house had been intended for the heavy gaiety of another era, a happy moment in history, little concerned about the future. The lives of Art Hertime and others like him at old Palm Beach had represented a truly noble effort. Those people had wanted avidly to be happy, more perhaps than any other group that he had ever known.

Happiness, or its approximation, enveloped him mistily the moment the Packard drew up beneath the porte-cochere. Lytton, the butler, was smiling and so was the footman, who wore a striped waistcoat; and so was Jim, the head gardener, smiling, and Suzanne, Mrs. Hertime's personal maid.

"We'll share Suzanne between us, dear," Mrs. Hertime said to Rhoda, "and they'll have the ocean-view suite, Lytton."

"Is everything all right, Lytton?" Mr. Hertime asked.

"Oh yes, sir," Lytton said.

"Let's see," Mr. Hertime said. "It's a quarter of twelve. Drinks in the patio at 12:15. Luncheon at one, and, if it's possible, we might have some pompano with nuts over it. Has any more Bollinger come in?"

"Yes, sir," Lytton said. "Mr. Farraday brought over five cases yesterday. He was sorry the labels were discolored by the salt water, but everything is legible."

"Good old Max," Mr. Hertime said. "Somebody down the street must be going short if we've got five cases. All right, Bollinger and pompano, and the yacht at two. I want Mr. and Mrs. Harrow to see what there is to see. Is the Everglades Club open yet?"

"I believe not yet, sir," Lytton said.

"Well, Angela honey," Mr. Hertime said, "then I guess the Bramhalls won't be cocktailing there. Say, Tom, is 'cocktailing' grammatical?"

"I'm not exactly sure, Art," he said, "but it's a very attractive word, particularly when Mrs. Hertime uses it."

"Now listen, son," Mr. Hertime said, "break the ice and call her Angela. Let's get the Bramhalls to do a little cocktailing here at six and then dinner. How about it, Angela? And how about some good red roast beef? Dick and Tom will get along like two separate burning houses. And now Tom and Rhoda might like to get upstairs and take off their corsets and scratch until it's drink time in the patio."

Their rooms were more beautiful than the downstairs rooms of the house, done in pecky cypress. The beds, the bureaus, and the tables had also been made of cypress. The curtains were of gray-blue light silk that went beautifully with the walls. Rhoda had never felt the uneasiness that was often with him at Palm Beach. She hurried from their sitting room to the bedroom to the boudoir-dressing-room to the bathroom, while he stood by admiring the bluish-green water of the sea across Ocean Boulevard, still trying to analyze his discomfort. Then Rhoda threw herself into his arms in a most unexpected way.

"Oh, darling," she said, "I can't bear it. It's all so wonderful."

"If you mean it's different from the Bulwer, you've got something," he said.

"That's why it's wonderful," she said. "It's so different from anything I've ever known. It's like magic."

"It's different all right," he said, "but I hope there isn't magic."

"Why, Tom," she said, "what's the matter? You've been so

happy ever since we had champagne for breakfast, and now you look so solemn."

"Maybe if we rang the bell we could get a half a bottle of Pommery," he said. "Lytton could bring it up. Do you think he's Bulwer-Lytton's grandson?"

"Tom," she said, "you don't sound like yourself at all."

"Maybe I'm not. Maybe, now I come to think of it, I'm afraid."

"Afraid?" she said. "What are you afraid of, unless it's of being happy?"

"I'm afraid I might begin to like this sort of thing too much," he said. "Lytton and the limousine."

He put his arm around her waist and held her close, and he was happy for a second.

"You certainly cuddled into that car," he said, "like a cat on a cushion."

She pushed herself away from him.

"Don't muss my hair," she said, "and besides, we ought to get ready for drinks on the patio. Why shouldn't we like all this too much?"

He could not make a specific answer, and he still could not delve into the vagaries of artistic conscience.

"We don't belong here," he said.

"Maybe not," she said, "but at least I want to."

"I mean," he said, "I can't be like these people, Rhoda."

"Of course you can," she said, "and so can I." And she kissed him.

The kiss took away the ominous note.

"To hell with the patio," he said. "Let's be late."

"But, Tom," she said, "Suzanne or Bulwer-Lytton might come in."

"I doubt it," he said, "with those hand-wrought Spanish locks."

"I wish you'd keep things in some sort of sequence," she said.

Well, that was the way it had been once. You did not need sequence when the drums had beat that tune. You could move from one mood to another then and forget the shadows, and yet at the same time the cleavage between them had already started with his moments of uneasiness.

"You see," Mr. Hertime had said, "we have to play sometime."

Perhaps that was not such a bad way of describing just what went on down there on parts of the Florida East Coast, but nobody as far as he knew had ever fully explained what "play" meant as the term was used.

"Now, before starting afternoon activities," Mr. Hertime said after lunch, "I suggest that Tom and I slip into my Worry Room."

Why did he have a worry room when he came down there to get away from worry? It was possible to ask him, but hard to evaluate the answer.

"It's my little joke," Mr. Hertime said, "isn't it, Angela honey. Because I've given up worrying long ago. Let's go in there and call up New York and ask about the market and the show."

If the Worry Room was a witticism, its appearance was not jocular. It contained a flat desk, two telephones, scratch pads, and sharp pencils.

"Yes," Mr. Hertime said, "sometimes you've got to charge your batteries. In summer it's Watch Hill. You've got to see Watch Hill. . . . Long Distance, please."

Mr. Hertime held a telephone contemptuously, in a firm, ritualistic manner.

"Hello," Mr. Hertime said. "Is that you, Charlie? I'm here with Tom Harrow who wrote that show. How's our little market project going?"

There was the rattle of a voice on the receiver, but Mr. Hertime was not worried.

"All right," he said. "Let it ride. And now about the show at the Empire . . . Well, well, well."

Mr. Hertime smiled.

"Well, well, well. It's sold out solid and Metro and Warner are bidding for the picture. You get the point now, don't you, Tom, why I call this the Worry Room?"

He believed that his powers of comedy automatically increased when he came to places like Palm Beach and Antibes, but anyone could panic the Hertimes and the Bramhalls, and the same was true with the Ordway Gibsons and the Ogelthorps and the

Stewart Enderbees — not the ones who were mixed up with Coca-Cola and not the Enderbee Ointment Enderbees, but the other ones — and the Maurice Jakeworths, who owned the Rainbow Farm Stables. No matter what you said, they always laughed at Palm Beach, and that was doubtless why the Bramhalls had always said that the moment they had laid eyes on Tom and Rhoda, in the Hertimes' patio that evening, there had been an instinctive, congenial bond between them.

He had been more impressed by their clothes than their faces, and Marion Bramhall did have a beautiful figure, though not as good as Rhoda's, and her Burgundy Shantung dinner dress, he was afraid, was better than Rhoda's. When it came to Dick Bramhall, Dick already had his look of executive integrity and Dick was one of the first people he had ever known with a crew cut. He had never thought they would always be dear friends, but Marion Bramhall had reminded him again and again of what he had first said to her.

"You must go out on Dick's and my boat sometime," she had said.

"I'd love to," he had said, "if you don't pull up the anchor."

Marion had never forgotten that bon mot or the sly twinkle that had come into his eye just before he made it.

"Oh dear," she said, "we won't pull up the anchor. It's called the *Bramma*, you know."

"I don't see why you didn't call it the *Maddick*," he said, "not that we're on a first-name basis, Mrs. Bramhall."

"Dick," she called, "did you hear what he said? Why didn't we call the *Bramma* the *Maddick*, and we're not on a first-name basis, but we're going to be. We're all going to love each other, aren't we, Dick?"

But the important thing that evening had occurred after dinner when they were out on the patio again admiring the colored electric lights in the patio palms that made them look, as Mrs. Hertime said, like tropical Christmas trees.

"Oh no," Marion Bramhall had said, "they look like those trees with jewels out of the *Arabian Nights*."

In the red, green, and white glare from those whispering

palms, he found himself talking after dinner with Marion Bramhall, while across the patio Rhoda and Dick Bramhall were engaged in a low-voiced, earnest conversation.

"How does it feel, Tom, to have a real live Broadway hit on your hands?" Marion Bramhall had asked.

"I'm glad you asked me that," he had said. "Just between you and me, it feels fine."

"It must be wonderful to write so divinely," Marion Bramhall then said. "My father used to try to write. He used to lock himself into his den every morning after Grandpa died. He was interested in eighteenth-century English writing, I think."

"Tom," Rhoda said, and her voice had that wind-bell ring that it always had when she had encountered something delightful, "Dick has a wonderful suggestion for you now the play is going so well. Tom, I want Dick to tell you himself."

"I know," Tom said, "take out life insurance. Someone told me that before we came here, Rhoda."

"Tom," she said, "be serious. It isn't entirely about life insurance."

Dick Bramhall cleared his throat, not in a harsh way.

"I don't mean to be rushing in where angels fear to tread," Dick said.

"Don't worry," Tom answered. "Angels never care how much they step on me."

"Oh, Dick," Marion Bramhall said, "just listen to him. He says things like that all the time."

"Well, it just occurred to me," Dick said, "that we might talk sometime about setting up a custodian account and having your royalties and other earnings paid into it, and then we could sit down and work out a portfolio of insurance and securities. I'd gladly give you some advice sometime."

"Well, that would be fine," he answered. "Someone was talking the other day about a good stock called Electric Bond and Share."

"There," Rhoda said, "that's exactly what I mean, Dick."

Dick Bramhall coughed again.

"I don't mean to rush in where angels fear to tread," he said again, "but maybe Rhoda has a point. I wouldn't buy anything but Liberties just now. The time to buy stocks is when the market gets too low. Now if we had a custodian account . . ."

He added that such an account would be new business for the bank, and he was there to get new business, but anyone could tell that Dick Bramhall had made that tentative offer on the first evening of their acquaintance because he was basically kind, and Dick Bramhall was one of the few basically kind investment men he had ever known.

"I did it," Dick Bramhall told him later, "because you and Rhoda were babes in the wood under those lights in the palm trees. I did it because I knew what would happen to you if I didn't. I've got so at the bank I'm able to read faces a little."

"Do you mean I have a weak face?" Tom asked.

Dick Bramhall shook his head.

"No," he said, "not weak. Financially incapable. Now Rhoda, on the other hand, has a financial face."

The beauty of Rhoda, her clarity, and her gaiety had concealed from him what Dick Bramhall had seen.

XXII

Happiness Was Just around the Corner

HE SHOULD have learned, as Rhoda had. He should have listened, while he had the chance, to the sayings and the maxims of great men like the Hertimes and the Bramhalls. If he had paid heed, the grinding in the street would not have been so low tonight; but, truthfully, he could not have listened then any more than he could now, because he was not made to hear their Ben Franklin type of wisdom. He had not been born with the patience and perception to discover the grains of wisdom that existed in the sayings of Henry Ford, Sr., and Andrew W. Mellon. He had other fish to fry, and his own activities in the winter of '29 were time-consuming. Success sparkled like the breakfast champagne at the Hotel Bulwer before it went flat and he was bored with it, but he had to face the aftermath: new friends, new problems, new vistas, and the never-to-be-wholly-grasped essences of his craft. The truth was he preferred the words of Sophocles, Molière, Shakespeare, Ibsen, Shaw and O'Neill to the pontifications of Rhoda's big parade — and he still preferred living to security. He did not mean that there was not pleasure in the easy inflow and outflow of large sums; but he had always been bored with advice on how to keep them. It was true that he had always been financially impotent, and, frankly, he did not care.

"But you can't know," Dick Bramhall said, "whether you can ever do anything like *Hero's Return* again."

Right as rain. Of course you never knew. It was the fear that moved creation, but Bramhall did not understand the drives of uncertainty. He measured them in money, which was not the honest measure.

"You don't have to explain," he could hear his voice from the past answering the Bramhall voice. "I know what you mean. Maybe I'm afraid you're making me too damn safe. If I save too much money, why should I try to do it again?"

"I don't quite follow you on that one," Dick said. "There's some connection in the sequence I must have missed."

It was a difference in conditioning. Arthur Higgins would have understood, but not Dick Bramhall, and after all, why should he?

If it had not been for Dick, the best friend he had ever had, as Rhoda had reminded him on several occasions, the royalties from *Hero's Return* and the motion-picture money, too, flowing to his bank in a constant stream, would have gone, as Rhoda put it, "down the drain" — a phrase which she had picked up in the big parade. But there was always some return for money or effort, no matter how it might be squandered, in experience and memory. And these might have paid some sort of dividend, and accrued some sort of interest, that would have surprised the Bramhalls and the Hertimes.

When they got back from that Palm Beach visit, Arthur had given him a room in the office where he could work on *Little Liar* and they moved from the Bulwer to a small suite in the Plaza while they were looking for an apartment; and the secret was out now about Rhoda and the baby. *Little Liar* was what had taken most of his time, and there were problems newer and different from any at Palm Beach: problems of flatterers, of importuning parasites, of friends and enemies. The rewards of literary success were vastly greater, then. Ever afterwards he had always felt deep sympathy for new figures in the American drama. He could wince at adulation, for there was nothing easier and nothing worse than believing you were better than you were. There was nothing more enervatingly consuming than the poison of conceit, and he could still thank his Providence that he had got *Little Liar* to the condition of an acting script before he had ever become a literary figure. No wonder he was busy; no wonder he had no time to worry about money or about where they were going to live.

It was Rhoda and Dick Bramhall who fixed the budget and piped the tune. He might have been a fool not to notice. He had never worried greatly why it was that, no matter how busy he and Rhoda were, there was always time to see the Bramhalls. They had always been great friends and, as far as he knew, there had never been any talk; and there had been no reason for any, because Bramhall was not that kind of man. Actors, playwrights, and promoters, and sometimes lawyers, could afford to be — but no good investment banker. But why else had Dick Bramhall been so kind and patient, if he had not been in love with Rhoda? He could see the picture now, and his respect for Dick Bramhall grew as he saw it. If Dick had loved, he had loved from a distance, or he would not now be Chairman of the Board. Then there was Rhoda. Rhoda would not have had it any other way because Rhoda had loved him then, not Bramhall.

He was already growing used to the mutations of Rhoda's voice, so that he could quite accurately fit those alterations from the norm with her moods.

"Darling," she said, "I know you're busy, but do you miss me?"

"Yes," he said, "I always do."

"Oh," she said, "half the time you're more in love with that play of yours than you are with me."

It was what any wife might say, and he was already experienced enough to feel a twinge of guilt.

"That isn't so," he said. "I forget about it as soon as I see you."

"Oh no you don't," she said. "You're in love with that man's conscience. It makes me nervous when I think that you can think of things like that."

"You shouldn't be," he said. "That whole idea came to me before I ever saw you."

Obviously she was leading up to something or she would not have called him at the Higgins office.

"Darling," she said, "I've been house hunting, and finally I've found a most wonderful apartment."

"You mean," he asked, "you're settling for one on Beekman Place?"

"Oh no, dear," she said, "not with elevators and men with

361

gloves. This is informal and perfectly beautiful, and something that all our friends will feel at home in, even your queer new friends. It has a back yard and we can plant a garden."

"Where is it?" he asked.

"It's on Lexington Avenue in the Thirties," she said. "Now please don't ask questions until I see you. It's two stories in the dearest old brownstone-and-brick house, and it looks just like something built out of a box of blocks."

"Oh no," he said, "not out of blocks."

"Wait until you see it, dear," she said. "It's just the way New York ought to look. Dick says so."

"Who?" he asked.

"Dick Bramhall," she said. "What other Dick is there?"

"I don't know," he said. "I'm on a first-name basis with a lot of Dicks these days."

"He's been awfully sweet," she said. "When I called him at the bank about this place, he came right around to see it. Marion's at her Parliamentary Law Club."

"What sort of club?" he asked.

She laughed, not because it was amusing, but because she was impatient. He could already identify the laugh.

"I know it's a queer name," she said. "But anyway, that's what it is, and they talk about things. You know how Marion likes to talk."

"You're damn well right I do," he said. "She must be wonderful at that club. Do you think she's filibustering?"

She laughed again.

"Well anyway," she said, "Dick knows you're going to be crazy about it, and we're here at the Plaza now. Dick thinks it would be nice if you came up if you could. He has some figures and things to show you. He says we ought to be on a budget."

Then he began to laugh, himself.

"Yes, I'll come right over," he said, "and if it makes you happy, we'll go right on a budget."

The banks, the custodians, the contracts, the lawyers, the agreements, the investment portfolios with their neat blue covers and their rustling pages — and God only knew how the covers had started being blue — he was accustomed to those things now. He had learned to sign docilely where he was told — "not here, Mr. Harrow, but there on the other line that has the red seal on it." If he could not face figures, he had learned to make a good attempt at facing facts, but it was different then. The lease that Rhoda and Dick presented to him at the Plaza was the first one he had ever signed and the account of his income from the Custody Department was the first of its sort that he had ever seen.

"Just sit down and look it over, Tom," Dick said up there in the Plaza. "I'm afraid Rhoda's tired after all that house hunting. Sit down and read it and then see if you can tell me that you don't believe that figures talk."

When it came to figures, Tom had always implicitly believed everything Dick told him and he had never regretted it. He was new at numbers, but the sound of Dick's voice gave him a feeling of being able to put a bundle he was so clumsily carrying upon shoulders trained to bear burdens — and after all, that was what trust departments of banks were for. Why blister your thumbs cutting coupons when people like Dick Bramhall could get people to do it for you?

"A lot of money does seem to be coming in," he said.

It was approximately the right thing to have said for Dick would have paid a clever remark no heed.

"The account is coming on nicely," Dick said, "and a few acquaintances who know about theatrical properties tell me that the earnings will be the same for a very appreciable length of time. It isn't so very much money, but it's new money — and new money is always interesting."

"I suppose you mean there are all sorts of things you can do with new money," Tom said.

"Tom, I wish you wouldn't interrupt," Rhoda said. "Dick's given this a lot of thought."

He felt no resentment. He only felt, as he felt afterward, poignant and humble gratitude for the skill and patience Dick displayed.

"We are in a position now," Dick said, "where we can begin to make a tentative budget, and I've made a vague sort of break-down — not on that sheet, the other sheet."

"Tom," Rhoda said, "you're holding it upside-down. Dick, I told you he was hopeless about numbers."

He was not annoyed. Rhoda and Dick together never had annoyed him.

"I'll be awfully glad to take your combined word for it," he said. "It will be all right with me if I earn it and you two budget."

"You're missing a good deal," Dick said. "It's fun budgeting with Rhoda."

It was not intended as a joke. He could not remember that Dick Bramwell had ever cracked a single joke about money.

"Well, just so long as you don't carry the budgeting to bundling, it will be all right with me," he said.

A blush suffused Dick's Palm Beach tan.

"Now, Tom," he said, "you know I didn't mean it that way."

It was time to laugh loud enough to permit Dick to join in the general merriment.

Somehow those budgets had always followed the same uninspiring pattern.

"There seems to be a whale of a lot for Miscellaneous, Dick," he said.

"I know," Dick said, "but I think we can afford to be generous, Tom. The insurance comes first and then I'm assuming you're going to write lots more darn good plays."

"Well," he said, "the goose can keep on trying if you don't squeeze him."

"That's exactly the point and picture I'm presenting," he said. "In a few years the hope is that your savings backlog will have reached a point where there won't be too much squeeze."

"But there ought to be some squeeze," Rhoda said. "Remember what I told you about his being lazy, Dick."

"All right," he said, "just a little squeeze."

"Please listen, Tom," Rhoda said. "Now tell him about the apartment, Dick. It's a darling place, Tom, and I told the man we'd take it."

"You told him we'd take it without my seeing it?" he asked.

364

Rhoda had already moved a long way from Niagara Falls.

"Dick wanted you to see it," she said, "but I decided we ought to take it before someone else could snap it up. Tom, it's going to be wonderful — an enormous living room, big enough to dance in — and it's going to look like you."

"I thought you said it looked like a house built out of blocks," he said. "Do I look like something built out of blocks?"

"Darling," she said, "the rent's ridiculous for two floors in that big house, and our own stairs. Dick, isn't the rent ridiculous?"

"The bank only wants to break even," Dick Bramhall said. "It's being held for the land — and I was surprised, personally, at the plumbing."

"In a nice way, I hope," Tom said.

"It's — er — noisy," Dick Bramhall said, "but in wonderful condition for one of those old brick-and-brownstones. It was the Rossiter house, and old Mr. Rossiter must have gone all the way on the plumbing."

"Who were they," Tom asked, "the railroad or the steamship Rossiters?"

He said it as a joke, but Dick weighed the question.

"The old gentleman, from what I've heard, was in railroads mostly," he said, "but partly in copper."

"That explains it," Tom said, "copper piping."

"As a matter of fact, the hot water is all piped in copper," Dick said.

"Darling," Rhoda said, "you're just going to go crazy over it when you see it."

"All right," he said, "maybe I'd better sign the lease while I'm still sane."

"Right there," Dick Bramhall said, "on the line with the red seal at the end of it."

Everyone who had lived in New York for an appreciable period of time had developed the impression that the place had been steadily going to the dogs since the first time he saw it, and, in Tom Harrow's estimation, everyone sharing this conviction was correct. New York was not what it had been when he first remembered it in the days before World War I. It had been almost the New York of O. Henry in those days, but later it had lost its geniality and graciousness. Its taste for spaciousness and food and comfortable living had been dissipated. It had digested too many disparate and desperate people. It had contorted itself too often while struggling with its perpetual growing pains. Its manners, never good, had steadily deteriorated, along with its traffic and rapid transit. The newer, brighter civic efforts, like Rockefeller Center, were more brash than beautiful. The marks of the old graciousness, the occasional residential street of brownstone houses with their stoops and basement entrances, now filled him only with malaise. Those places were mere faint memories of yesterday; and, when he thought of it, the old house on Lexington Avenue, whose first two floors and back yard he and Rhoda had occupied, had been exactly this. Yes there had been a difference, and he feared he knew what the difference was. It 'was the gap between youth and age. New York had always been a town of youth, no place for valetudinarians.

During the Roosevelt era, a rash of histories of America had been published coping with the economic and social wrongs practiced by capitalists (notably Mr. Jay Gould, who never, in these volumes, seemed to have done right) upon the exploited masses. Not so long ago, while turning over one of these newer interpretations, he had come upon an illustration of a parlor of a well-to-do family in the 1880's. It had immediately reminded him of that strange house on Lexington Avenue. The house had been bought by the bank, along with the other houses on the block, to become in the next few years the site of an apartment building. But the house itself had never given hints of its eventual dissolution. Although its gutters leaked and water made stains on its brownstone façade, it had the complacency of the picture in the history book.

Its hot-water heating system, doubtless the latest word in comfort when Mr. Rossiter had installed it, was almost a parallel to the heating systems of the Palace of Knossos at Crete, or to the ruined Roman villas on the Palatine. The plumbing, too, was truly surprising; the toilet bowls had floral designs. The parquet floors could not be imitated today, because no carpenter pro-

366

tected by a zealous union would take the pains to lay such floors in New York, where the lifetime of a building seldom exceeds twenty years. Its sliding doors, its walnut finish, were reminiscent of an early Gothic novel.

"Darling," Rhoda said, "it's going to cost us almost nothing, and, do you see what I mean?"

"Yes," he said, "I can see exactly what you mean."

"And there's a little man and his family who lives in the basement," Rhoda said, "who will look out for the furnace and the fireplaces for almost nothing. His name is Balsamo. Dick spoke to him and made the arrangements."

"Balsamo?" he said.

"I think that's what it was," she said. "He's very friendly."

"That will help," he said, "if he's friendly."

"You see," she said, "this is something that your friends and my friends both will understand."

It was the first time that she had mentioned that difference between her friends and his friends. The break had been more intuitive than actual, but she had understood the Hertimes and the Bramhalls better than he.

"You see," she said, "it's both theatrical and practical — and wait till you see upstairs. There's a huge bedroom for us and a room for two maids and one for Harold."

"Who's Harold?" he asked.

"Don't be silly," she said. "If it's a boy, I told you I want to call him Harold."

"All right, if he's a boy," he said, and she kissed him.

"Dick says there are auction rooms," she said, "where you can buy things very cheaply if you wait."

"All right," he said, "I want a four-post bed and a clock to go over there, and I suppose we ought to have a crib or a cradle."

"Not a cradle," she said. "Harold wouldn't like it. We're not coming over in the *Mayflower*." And she kissed him again.

"There'll be lots of things," she said, "rugs, curtains, all sorts of things. I'll do most of it, but I want you to like it all."

"Why, Rhoda," he said, "I'm going to love it all."

She looked again at the large, high-ceilinged rooms.

"To think that you and I should end up in a place like this," she said.

"Don't put it that way," he told her, "this is only a beginning."

It was queer to think that they both could be right, with such conflicting statements, because, now he looked back on it, it was a beginning and also the beginning of the end. The same thing doubtless happened in other marriages and would happen in more to come; the worst of it was, that most of mankind (excepting always those who were helped by psychoanalysts, either of the Freudian or the Jungian school) never knew where they were going until they had got there; and when you were there, you could never find a backward turn.

He was amazed now at the obtuseness that had been around him like a fog in those first years in New York, for it was the one time in his life when he did have everything; but he could remember thinking then that there would be more, lots more, that he and Rhoda were only barely moving toward a broader firm foundation of marital contentment. There would be the child and more plays, better plays. There would be more friends, trips abroad, more times when he and Rhoda could get away together, more ways that he could make her happy. Now he could wonder if he did not have some faint premonition then. Happiness seemed always to have been in the retrospect or in the future, and this might have been true with Rhoda, too.

"Wait," she was always saying, "until we get the heavy curtains up."

"Wait," she was always saying, "until we get Harold's nursery fixed."

"Wait," she was always saying, "until we have our first big party and use the Sheffield candelabra, and wait until we get the right sort of worktable for your room upstairs. Everything is going to be marvelous when everything is done."

It was going to be, and of course they had been happiest while they were waiting.

If the living room in the apartment did not look like the picture in that American history book, it always had the dignity that belonged to its generation. There was a colored maid named

368

Myra, a very good cook-waitress who came by the day from Harlem, and also there was a cleaning woman for two days a week; and then, of course, when Hal arrived, there was a baby's nurse and someone else. He could not recall their names and faces any longer, but Rhoda had learned to run a household as readily as she had learned everything else, and they always were able to save money. He wished now that he had been more interested in these details, but he could only remember, now, his contentment whenever he reached Lexington Avenue and his delight at having Rhoda there to meet him, while all the little things he should have treasured had slipped through the meshes of his memory.

Hal was to arrive in late June, which explained why they had stayed in town all summer and why afterwards he could agree with New Yorkers who said that New York was at its best then. At least it was so in those days, and the two floors were cool. Rhoda, who had never cared for flowers until then, had got a little man — she had now reached the stage where she could call a great many people little men — to plant some things in the back yard, and another little man installed an inexpensive garden fountain. He remembered the musty odor of the yard of an evening, pervading, but not unpleasant, like other New York backyards that had been turned into gardens in those enlightened days. It did not matter whether or not the plants did well; you could always get the little man to put in new ones, and you could always listen to the dripping of the fountain.

"Darling, the stock market keeps going up all the time, doesn't it?" Rhoda said.

"Does it?" he asked.

"Don't you even look?" she said. "You read and read the paper."

"I look sometimes," he said, "and I'm going down to one of those offices sometime next week. I want to see the tickers. They say boys run around and chalk numbers up on blackboards in a place called a customers' room."

"Remember not to buy anything. Remember what Dick said," she told him. "It's all too high."

"I don't want to buy anything," he said. "I want to watch the faces. I want to hear the talk."

"With all those friends of yours," she said, "who come around for drinks, I'd think you hear enough conversation without going to a stockbroker's."

"There are different kinds of talk," he said. "I want to get it classified."

"You mean dialect and things like that?" she asked.

"No, not that," he said. "Some people say one thing; others with the same thoughts express them differently. Stockbrokers talk alike and bankers in a slightly different way. I like to listen for the difference."

"Does Dick Bramhall talk like a banker?" she asked.

"Yes," he said, "he's the norm for a banker."

"It isn't very nice of you to be horrid about him," she said, "after what Dick's been doing about everything."

"It isn't horrid to say that someone talks like a banker," he said. "Don't you wish I'd talk like one?"

"Sometimes, not always," she said. "Tom . . . ?"

"Yes?" he said.

"Tom, after the baby's born and we have a good nurse and everything, couldn't you and I go away somewhere and have a trip — not Niagara Falls, but somewhere farther?"

"That sounds swell," he said. "Somewhere without the Bramhalls and the Hertimes."

"And let's make it without the Higginses," she said, "and without the people from the *Hero* who keep coming around, and especially without Delia Duneen."

"Why without Duneen?" he asked.

"Because I'm tired of seeing her sitting around loving you," she said, "and thinking how much happier she could make you than I can."

"Duneen?" he said. "Why, Duneen can't think as long as that consecutively about anything but herself."

"Never mind," she said, "she keeps getting you mixed up in her thought sequence."

"Darling," he said, "I'm not mixed up in any Duneen sequence.

She's a sweet but stupid little girl. Don't worry about Duneen."

"All right," she said, "and don't you worry about Dick Bramhall."

"I don't," he said, "why should I?"

"And you needn't take that tone about him," she said. "I don't think he's very happy with Marion."

"Did he ever tell you so?" he asked.

"Oh, no," she said, "he wouldn't dream of telling a thing like that."

"You bet he wouldn't," he said.

"That isn't kind," she said. "Don't keep saying things like that about Dick. Anyway, let's go away somewhere. Abroad."

"That's fine," he said. "Whereabouts abroad?"

"Oh, anywhere," she said. "Let's go to France. They say it's beautiful in Antibes."

"Who told you?" he said.

"Why, Dick," she said. "And he says the exchange is very favorable. The poor French keep having trouble with the franc."

It was strange to recall the echo of her words, now that the poor Americans, despite enlightened struggles, were having trouble with their dollar. He could hear the dripping of the backyard fountain still. Of course each drip was counted and had to be paid for, but this did not amount to much. Superficially none of it amounted to much — not Dick Bramhall, not Duneen. If two people really had each other, they had everything and needed nothing more. There were no Bramhalls or Duneens those summer nights while he and she were waiting for the baby, only the fountain, which was connected with the city meter, but everything in life was metered in some way or other, and someone was always ringing the bell and saying, "Gas man, here to read the meter."

Perhaps obstetricians, and midwives before them, had always gone to great pains to make childbirth appear like a simple, merry affair. He had been lulled into a sense of security by having Dr. Jellison, who had been recommended by friends of the Bram-

371

halls as the best man in New York, say that Rhoda would have an easy time of it.

"You see," he said, in one of his early talks — it had always been his practice to see each couple together — "your wife has a beautiful pelvis."

It had seemed to Tom stuffy of Rhoda to be annoyed.

"I don't know why he should have made that remark in front of you," she said.

"Well, he was only dealing with facts," he told her. "I don't think anything personal was intended."

"It sounded personal to me," Rhoda said, "and I'm going to speak to him about it."

Rhoda was already learning how to put people in their places and until after Harold was born Dr. Jellison made no more than a veiled anatomical remark again.

But the knowledge that she was going to have an easy time of it had made them both confident. He remembered that in spite of the pains that had started, as they had about six in the early evening, she was in high spirits driving to the hospital.

"I don't mind it as long as it's your baby," she said, "and I'll look better when it's over. Now don't look worried, Tom."

"I'm not," he said, "as long as he said it's going to be all right."

"Of course it's going to be all right," she said, "and it's going to be a boy, and I don't want you around until it's over."

The longer he lived, the more convinced he became that you had to pay for everything, whether it was for failure or success or routine living. He had never, like governments or citizens he could mention, attempted avoidance, but the practice was unfair because, more often than not, other people were involved when the chips were down. Rhoda had been talking so much about security that he was already beginning to revolt against it. There was no safety in living, and in the end, about all you got out of life was learning how to face truth without side-stepping to avoid it.

Rhoda had been in the delivery room for about an hour and Tom had been waiting alone in a small reception room when he saw Dr. Jellison in his clean, white duster walking down the corridor. He saw the doctor for several seconds before the doctor knew he was being watched, and there was no way of forgetting those seconds because it was very seldom that one saw behind the academically compassionless medical front. For that second or two Jellison was more human than he had ever appeared. His step was slow and he looked deathly tired — until he saw that he was being watched. Tom Harrow had always distrusted doctors after that, even the best or ablest of them. He had never liked the arrogance of their assurance or their priestlike assumption that they were different from other people. Granted that all this was necessary in their profession and a part of their professional conditioning, he still did not admire it. You could have them as friends until you were a patient, and then inescapably the veil dropped down.

"Oh, there you are, Tom," the doctor said. "Well, it's a boy — seven-and-a-half pounds."

Tom felt no relief because he had seen the doctor's face and had observed the hesitation in his step out there in the corridor.

"Rhoda thought it was going to be a boy," he said. "How's Rhoda?"

There was no longer a trace of uncertainty. If he no longer trusted doctors, he admired them; when he had a doctor in a play produced in 1938, he knew the scene was good, because his mind, when he wrote it, was back there in the hospital with the aura of ether that had emanated from Dr. Jellison.

"She's having a transfusion," he said. "She hemorrhaged just when I thought the party was over."

Again that frightful American barbarism of turning nouns into verbs struck him as one of the worst parts of medical semantics; the lighthearted business of calling such a thing a "party" showed that the doctor was modern, and Dr. Jellison was still trying to maintain the pose when he went on with the rest of it.

"I'm afraid once will be enough," he said. "But we'll talk about that later. I'd better go back now."

There was no use analyzing the sort of fear Tom had felt. Times might change, but moments of sickly terror never did. Circumstances might alter significance, but not the moment itself. The terror that he felt was that Rhoda might be leaving him. All their times together, which were more vivid than the separate times themselves — all the small things that made up a personality — were mingled with the memories: the wiry, unbrushed look of her hair when she awakened in the morning; the softness of her face when she was aroused from sleep; the swiftness of her smile.

She was deathly pale when he saw her and there was a sickly smell of ether in her hair.

"Darling," he said to her, "I am awfully glad you're here."

"I'm glad I am, too," she said. "I didn't want to lose you. There's so much we can do. We'll have a wonderful time."

They had been closer together then than they had ever been before or since, and you could not take away the essence of that memory.

"Have you seen him?" she asked.

"Who?" he said.

"Why, Harold, of course," she said.

"No, not yet," he said. "All right, we'll call him Harold."

Watching through plate glass while the baby was held up by a nurse who would still have been ugly without a gauze mask, Tom had not been impressed, at the time, by Harold.

It was appalling to him, occasionally, when he found himself in the company of learned men, to realize his own lack of deep specific knowledge. He could skim the surface of many subjects, but he had no grasp of any except on the single one from which he gained his livelihood. He knew a few of the basic principles underlying writing better than the average professor of literature or drama. This was only natural, since these people were theorists, not obliged to live by writing. The best of them seldom realized that craftsmanship or the ability to use words was the basis of all artistic effort. These individuals, preparing their lectures and writing their doctorate theses, spoke eloquently of art and life; but few of them appreciated how far life itself diverged from the printed page or the spoken line of the theatre. Writing was a heady brew, but it was never life itself. Actors or characters on a printed page did not behave like normal human

374

beings. The problems of people in drama were not like those in real life. They were tenser, crisper, more sudden, more contrived, and limited by human patience, because those situations were the work of men, not gods. Situations had to be shaped and made comprehensible. They never could be vague, as they often were when molded by the gods. There were a great many clever people who did not know what life was about, but the audience had to know the meaning when you wrote the show. In those days, when they had everything, that was often the trouble with broken marriages — and he had seen a lot in his time — you seldom knew they were broken until they were smashed. All those people on the side streets of the city, those dextrous men who riveted broken porcelain — even their skill never made the object the same again, and they were better at it than the psychiatrists and the lawyers. But his mind was still back there at the time when they had everything and all the while everything had been slipping through his fingers.

XXIII

It Was Foreshadowed on Lexington Avenue

HE COULD think of a passable simile, now that his mind was on the subject. Once he had gone on a fishing trip in the Laurentians. He had never been so far away from anything as he had been on the string of lakes out in the woods in that canoe. Seth Maxwell had one guide in one canoe and he had one guide in another. His guide's name was Gus, and Gus was at home in a canoe. On their way to the fishing area, they paddled for two days from lake to lake, and when the lakes ended, generally in a swamp, it was necessary to carry the canoes, the tents and the food to the shore of another lake. Gus, who had a bad cough and a birthmark on his neck, could handle the canoe and most of the gear himself, but there was always plenty left. The experience had been so unusual and so uncomfortable, and he had known so little about getting in and out of canoes or handling rods, that the thing ended by being amusing.

He appreciated afterwards the solitude of the country through which they traveled. He must have seen the spruce trees and poplars and the lakes and the beaches with their rocky promontories through a subconscious eye because he had felt no immediate reaction to their beauty. He remembered the trails of the portages with stones on the downslopes that rolled beneath his feet. He had fallen several times, unbalanced by the pack on his back, but there had been one beautiful moment that stood out in that discomfort. Close to noon on the second day, when he was in the middle of a portage called Half Mile Carry, he had come upon a spring beside the trail, rising in a sandy bowl beside a granite boulder. Ferns and mosses grew around the spring's edge and a clump of alders shaded its small basin, but erratic spots of sunlight moved in patterns when a light breeze moved the leaves of the alders. The whole sight was unexpected and the unexpectedness added to its beauty. There was a glint in that spring like the sun on Rhoda's hair. He had never forgotten the scents by the spring's margin, not the same as Rupert Brooke's stream, but they were as unforgettable, unforgotten. There was the acrid smell of the emerald-green moss and the pungent odor of the broken fern fronds that he crushed as he had knelt beside the spring. He tossed aside the pack he was carrying and he plunged his cupped hands into the clear water. It was icy, numbingly cold and his bodily reaction was delightful as he lifted his cupped hands above the surface. He was thirsty, but he knelt staring at the water in his palms and watching it slip in tiny streams between his fingers; like sand in an hourglass, he thought, except that this was ice-cold water and the drops hit the spring's surface in a golden, jewel-like way, making patterns more irregular than patterns of raindrops. He was holding the sands of time, except that this was water, and then his hands were empty and his thirst was back. He had allowed the water to vanish without drinking. Rhoda used to say that he forgot her half the time. She could never understand that his mind could be in two places at once and that part of her was still always with him.

You should drink while you had it, and not let water slip through your fingers. The drops had returned to the spring like life to a greater life and he could see them now as a bittersweet symbol of what he and Rhoda had held once together.

There would be a drop for the afternoons when Hal would come to the parlor from the nursery. Hal had been a modern anachronism: a nursery child, unduly excited by occasional social contacts with his parents. "Don't pull the cigarette box off the table, dear." "Watch it, Hal, watch out for the fire tongs." In his memory there were always other people in for drinks or for tea. Rhoda had become fascinated by the ritual of tea and she had picked up a silver service from one of the estate silver people off Fifth Avenue. Tea was not a favorite beverage, but she loved to pour it, and it was a pleasure to watch her at the table in the afternoon. He wondered whether she remembered that he had rehearsed her in the act. There was always some actor or writer and usually some friend of Rhoda's whom she had met at lunch or at her discussion club, now that Marion Bramhall had got her to be a member. Her friends were always eager and excited when they embarked on this antiseptic adventure that they doubtless called Bohemia — not that it was, because the Harrows were delightful and literally in the *Social Register*, since he was not an actor and Rhoda was not an actress; but still, he wrote for the stage and she was perfectly charming. There was a restrained excitement among Rhoda's friends when they came in for tea or something stronger. He had always enjoyed watching them in this dangerous milieu, but it never paid to jest about them afterwards with Rhoda — not when his own friends burned holes in the carpets and kept drinking more and more bathtub gin, not when friends like Walter Price insisted on telling off-color stories.

There would be the break when Harold appeared.

"Here's Harold," he could hear Rhoda say. "This is Harold's hour before his bedtime. 'Harold's Hour,' by Longfellow."

This had been his line originally, but she had taken it over and he could still remember the soft, infectious note of her laugh that always followed.

"Come and kiss Mummy, dear," she used to say, "before Daddy gets you drunk on his Martini."

Harold always did well in that interlude while his nurse stood in the doorway. He ran into the parlor and rolled over on the rug, limbering himself like a member of a college football team. He could shake hands very nicely with Rhoda's friends and answer questions nicely and then he could change right over and adapt himself to the people from a less settled but possibly merrier world.

Hal understood Duneen, for instance, who always loved to come around, not out of gratitude, but because she loved the family, until she and Rhoda had some sort of quarrel. Harold did not mind when Duneen knelt on the floor and held out her

378

arms and said in her very best voice, "Come here and kissums auntie, sweetums."

He could remember the disturbed wrinkle on Rhoda's forehead when Duneen got off that one; he should have written her a better speech and rehearsed her in it, just as he had rehearsed Rhoda at the tea table. Harold, on the other hand, had needed no rehearsing whatsoever. Harold had enjoyed being kissed by Duneen, and after all, why not? He had even enjoyed playing bear with Walter Price and listening to Mort Sullivan recite A. A. Milne. Harold was more of a trouper than Rhoda had ever been, and he was an extrovert right from the beginning.

"Do you think he loves me too much?" Rhoda asked once. "I don't want to get too emotionally involved with him to the exclusion of you, darling."

Rhoda should never have read so many books on child psychology; they had not been necessary when it came to Hal, but she never had been a fool about Hal, because she had lots of other things to worry about.

Rhoda had also begun to read books on love and marriage when they had everything, almost before the everything was imperceptibly growing less. The frank discussion of the marital state, of sexual difficulties and of day-to-day adjustments to male and female philosophies was fashionable when they were on Lexington Avenue and he could only hope that the fad had now become so tiresome that it was running itself into the ground. However, perhaps this increasing bibliography did fill a long-felt need, since obviously the institution of marriage was not working as well as it had in a previous generation, or in times when women understood less about their manifest destiny than they did at present. At any rate, it now seemed to Tom that all through his life women — that is, good women — took themselves more seriously each year and studied more and more carefully how to integrate themselves and their husbands and children into the Home. Naturally those books were a great help, being all clearly if dully written largely by disciples of what would now be called the do-it-yourself school. Out of curiosity, and also to please Rhoda, he, too, had dipped into enough sections of this literature to realize that there were authorities in the medical and university worlds who could tell you exactly what to do in bed and out of bed, how to be patient, how to overcome frigidity, how to combat impotence, and, in fact, how to understand that sex could be fun as well as beautiful. After his first encounter with this five-foot between-the-sheets library, he had not enjoyed it, and he could remember that once he had taken the matter up with Rhoda.

"Rhoda," he said, "if it's all the same to you, couldn't you keep that book on married love off the bedside table, or put it in plain paper wrappers so whoever makes the bed doesn't have to see it?"

"That's an awfully self-conscious remark," Rhoda said. "You take such a liberal view about most things, but you're puritanical about sex."

"That isn't fair," he said. "My position is only that I don't need a psychologist from the University of Mexico Medical School to tell me. Maybe I know as much about sex as he does."

"That's awfully conceited of you," she said. "You haven't made a study of it like the man who wrote this book."

"All right," he said, "do you want me to make a study of it?"

"No," she said, "don't be ridiculous, but it wouldn't do you any harm to read it so we can talk about it together."

"Rhoda," he said, "there are a lot of other things I'd rather talk to you about when we go to bed besides that book."

"I don't know why you should be so sensitive," she said. "Men are so ridiculous in some ways, especially American men, as it says in the book. Don't you want to be a good lover?"

"Now wait a minute," he said. "Now that we're getting personal, books on how to do it aside, do you have a good time in bed with me, or don't you?"

"I think that's a vulgar way to put it," she said.

"Well, what about Chapter Three in the professor's book?" he said. "That's personal enough, isn't it, and who's being a puritan now?"

"Darling," she said, "he's personal, but I wouldn't say he's vulgar."

"And I'm not vulgar, either," he said. "I'm asking a straight question. Now give me a straight answer, do you or don't you?"

"Of course I do," she said. "But there may be more to it than we know about. Haven't you any curiosity? Don't you want to know?"

"How can there be any more to it?" he said. "And it's only between you and me, and we don't need the professor."

"Darling," she said, "it's queer when you're so sophisticated in some ways, that you're so narrow-minded and almost prudish in others."

"I wouldn't say I was prudish," he said. "I just don't need the professor. And you don't, either; or, if you do, read D. H. Lawrence, or Burton's *Arabian Nights*."

"Darling," she said, "they aren't scientific and besides, they don't relate it to other parts of marriage."

"How about just letting it go," he said, "and letting it relate itself?"

"Darling," she said, "you may not know it, but that's the basic trouble with most American marriages. Listen, let me read you this one sentence in Chapter Two."

"Don't," he said. "For God's sake, don't."

"Just this one sentence," Rhoda said. " 'The indifference of the married couple or their ignorance of the integration of the marital sex relationship with the daily round of nonsexual marital activities lies at the root of the misunderstandings that eventually cause two thirds of marriage shipwrecks.' What do you think of that?"

The probity of the printed word always influenced women more than men. He could quote that awkward sentence word for word, but its meaning was clouded and its facts were still disputable.

"I think it's terrible," he said. "Now don't read any more. I don't want the professor with us in bed."

"Just one more sentence," Rhoda said. "Another one out of Chapter Two. 'The husband, more particularly the American husband, is more reticent regarding the sex relationship than the awakened American wife. It should be the duty of the wife to encourage and, in fact, insist on frank and fearless discussions regarding sexual compatability.' "

"God damn," he said, "it sounds like a bridge hand. North led out his ace when he should have led the two of clubs."

"There's no reason to swear or be vulgar," Rhoda said. "Now, here's a sentence out of Chapter Four. 'It may seem to some that the subject of sexual afterplay may not merit a full chapter by itself.' "

"Here," he said, "give me that book for just a minute, will you, Rhoda?"

"Darling," she said, and she laughed, "I knew you couldn't help being fascinated once I started reading. Oh, Tom, what are you doing? Stop it."

He had tossed the book out of the window before she had finished, and he had never regretted the act. He had been wrong in his idea that there were no sharply dramatic moments in the humdrum hours of living. It was one of the few times he had ever seen her lividly angry.

"Get right into your clothes," she said, "and go out and get that book!"

"The hell I will," he said. "It didn't hit anybody."

"Don't be mid-Victorian," she said. "Go out and get that book! What will people say if they find it on the sidewalk? And what are you laughing at now?"

As another of those manuals on marriage had said — this one by a more whimsical, genial professor — little husband-and-wife jokes lubricated marriage wheels, and this turned out to be one of them. Even Rhoda eventually began to laugh at her reaction about the book on the sidewalk and its presence on the bedroom table. There were lots of things to laugh about when Rhoda was around.

In fact, as he could see their story now, it fitted into no compendium of marriage. It may have had the dreary outlines of case histories, since there was nothing new under the sun and strains in all relationships could be classified, but it had its own values, since nothing with Rhoda in it could be like anything

382

else. That was the difficulty with generalizations; there could be no set rules for any two people, and when blame was dished out, everyone had to take some of it. If he had worried more about Rhoda's worries, if he had not been in such revolt against the crowd at Antibes, if he had taken Rhoda more seriously, if he had lived more in reality and less in imagination . . . But then, it was always possible to go on indefinitely with such conditions, and what was the end result? Invariably one began to have the suspicion that the end was in one's stars and that human will and wish were not what they were cracked up to be.

There was nothing ominous about the individual digits of the column that made everything add to nothing. He had sometimes wondered whether, if Rhoda and he had ever talked things over carefully, anything could have been achieved, but he doubted it. No one off the stage or out of the pages of a book could ever tell the exact circumstances that caused personal decision. One thing was sure: it was not argument or logic, it was something more basic and threatening because it was usually unknown. It she could never explain, a balance and a conflict of desire. He must have been that way with Rhoda — a summation of things could understand it and he could never blame her. He could only watch again the drops of circumstance escape him between his fingers as he had watched them long ago, and the process was inevitable since it was all a part of life and living.

Drop . . . and there was the crash in October, '29. They had not suffered from it measurably. The *Hero,* in spite of a year on Broadway, ran through the winter to good houses, and he had previously sold the picture rights for a very large sum. Then *Little Liar* was a hit, and, even with business doing badly, the royalties had been substantial and the picture rights were large again. There was enough money in the account to buy a long list of common stocks at bottom prices in the summer of '32. Rhoda was the one who was always going to the bank and discussing investments, just as Rhoda was the one who got him to go into temporary partnership with Arthur Higgins and later induced him to produce and direct a play, himself, in '34 before he had finished *Flagpole for Two.* They had not suffered from the depression; on the contrary, they were growing rich when the New Deal pump priming started. Drop . . . and Hal was starting to go to school. Drop . . . and there was Antibes and the season when the *Hero* played in London. Drop . . . and there was a summer in France, but he would much rather go back to Lexington Avenue and to the September party they had given there not long after Hal was born.

"I know there's no one much around," Rhoda had said, "but Dick and Marion are in town, and the Hertimes are staying at the Ritz. And there are all your theatre people rehearsing. Don't you think we ought to have a party? If we don't have too many people, we could have the drinks out in the garden."

Anyone involved with the theatre as he and Rhoda were, was always giving a party of one sort or another to celebrate something. Those things were part of a convention, a social tax demanded of anyone successful, a gesture of kindliness or simple generosity. He and Rhoda gave many other parties, usually on Sunday nights, the freest time in show business, and Rhoda learned quickly that no one was any better than she at giving an evening party, at arranging the table, the salad and the Virginia ham or at telling the maids for the evening, or the man who came in from the club, exactly what to do. Entertainment had become a routine, as graceful and as beautiful as one of Rhoda's evening gowns, by the time they reached Park Avenue, but Tom was the one who had first set the scene. He was the one who had first directed her, back in September of '29 when Rhoda was still recovering from Hal and still had to pretend that she knew more than she did. Impossible as it might have seemed subsequently, Rhoda was still shy and apprehensive then.

"Tom," she had said, "don't laugh. I know you're going to be derisive, but I think we might feel more sure about things if we bought a book of etiquette and read it out loud."

"Where?" he asked. "In bed?"

"I knew you'd make a joke of it," she said. "You always laugh, but everything's so new."

"That's right," he said, "and everything is better when it's new."

He could think now of all the new things: the emerald, the

384

dresses, the gold slippers, the runabout, and presents for Hal. They all of them wore out in time, or were turned in for something else, but the first sight was what he still remembered and the last sight seldom mattered.

"I'll show you how to run the party," he told her.

"But I don't see how you know," she said.

She never understood that different people had different capacities for observation. Without ever doing so consciously, he stored details in his mind and he had been to enough parties already to know the accepted routine. All that was necessary was to get the caterer that Arthur Higgins used and then to add a few touches — the Chinese lanterns in the garden, the extra candelabra, and champagne, plenty of good champagne. There was no reason to bother about the works of Emily Post if you had a suitable dry vintage and some light, good food. There was no need to worry about throwing the right people together, for everyone was always congenial if there was champagne and if the flow was judiciously controlled by someone like Marcel, who ran the Higgins parties. Marcel and his two waiters could estimate the saturation point of everyone. There was never too much or too little when Marcel was on the job. . . .

It was time to light the candles and the lanterns in the garden. Marcel and two assistants were there and, even without candlelight, the table was an achievement.

"I wonder whether anybody's coming," Rhoda said. "Do you think we told them the wrong day or anything?" She had not yet lost her uncertainties, so that every party was still like an opening night. He never worried whether anyone would come or not. The show was the thing: the table, the glasses, the lanterns.

"You won't care if we have some champagne," he said.

"But we ought to care," Rhoda said, "and not use champagne like a crutch."

"Why," he said, "that's what champagne's for. That's why they spoil good wine by charging it with gas. Marcel, will you open us a bottle, please?"

"Yes, Mr. Harrow," Marcel said. "Certainly, Mr. Harrow."

Marcel was a snob, like other people who worked in the radius of the theatre. Tom was conscious of the exact balance of Marcel's respectful tone, but he was already accustomed to respect and its intoxication had evaporated.

"It is good champagne, isn't it?" she said. "Tom, you're awfully clever about these things. You're so much more at home than I am. How many people do you think are coming?"

"It's hard to tell," he said, "because a lot of them will bring friends at the last moment, but we have enough of everything, haven't we, Marcel?"

"Oh yes," Marcel said; "indeed yes, Mr. Harrow."

It showed that Marcel had learned a great deal from the Higginses.

"You'll stay with me, won't you, Tom?" she asked. "Because I can't remember names and faces the way you can. Don't go off in a corner and talk with anyone."

"I'll be right with you," he said. "There won't be any corners."

"Maybe I ought to go up and see if Hal's all right," she said.

"He's all right," he told her. "I looked at him before I came down. He's sound asleep, but his Nanny's wide awake. Marcel, could you remember to sneak her up a glass of champagne?"

"Oh yes," Marcel said. "Indeed yes, Mr. Harrow — but none as yet for Master Harold."

The room was growing dusky but still the gleam of Marcel's teeth was bright and Marcel did not joke with everybody, or remember the name of everybody's son — not that this sort of thing mattered any longer.

"I hope everyone's going to get on together, Tom," she said. "There are so many different people. Maybe we should have had two parties and not mixed them up."

"They'll get on," he said. "Your people are always crazy to meet my people. It's the great adventure."

"But they never understand each other," she said.

"That's right," he said. "Your people think my people are basically amoral and my people think your people are basically stupid, but they both know that money helps. They are like you. They sense solidity."

386

"Oh, Tom," she said, "please don't start making fun of me."

"I didn't mean to, dear," he said, "and anyway, a backlog is no joke — according to insurance companies."

"I wish you wouldn't keep calling them *my* people," she said. "But you like them, don't you?"

"Yes," he said, "but I wish they wouldn't keep treating me as though I were a foreigner."

"It's because you're getting to be famous, Tom," she said. "It makes them nervous. It makes the Hertimes nervous. But you like the Bramhalls, don't you?"

"Yes," he said, "I like everybody now I've had a drink. And you like my people, don't you?"

"Oh, yes," she said. "I like them better all the time. I love Mort Sullivan, and I don't mind Walter Price, and I love the Higginses. And I'm even getting so I think I like Duneen."

"Well, well," he said, "that's wonderful."

"But I don't like that new one who's going to be the man's conscience, that Laura Hopedale," she said.

"She has a good speaking voice, and she's a pretty girl," he said.

"Yes," she answered, "but she's selfish. You can see it in her face."

Rhoda should have understood that most girls had to be, to get on.

"Tom," she said, "you don't think I'm selfish, do you?"

"No," he said, "but you don't have to be."

Then the doorbell rang. Myra was there to open it.

"Well," he said, "it's started," and he kissed Rhoda. "Don't worry, I'm right with you."

Everything around him had been changing ever since, assuming new shapes with the rapidity of waves on a stormy sea, including literary tastes. Out of gale-tossed thought had come philosophies, new modes of artistic expression, sometimes fascinating only because of their confusion. *Lady Chatterley's Lover* had appeared. Tom and the late D. H. Lawrence would have blushed at the antics of characters subsequently dreamed up by the young hopes of modern American literature. Then there was Mr.

Joyce and his *Ulysses* — and be sure to read the chapter in which the heroine gave free rein to her subconscious. These thoughts, the last time he had perused them, seemed like pallid stuff now that our boys and girls could use all the bad words freely and now that sexual aberrations were old hat. And yet he believed that Joyce might survive the rest of them. But what about all those people in the Judge's library? There was a light run on Trollope lately, but what about William Makepeace Thackeray? He was now only someone to be passed off with a nervous shrug in a small Ivy League lecture room. He was aware of a lack, in the Victorians, of what modern publishers called "lustiness" — or did this mean that his own taste was becoming dulled by a newer, braver, lustier world?

Old-hat though it might be, when he thought of their party that September night, his mind moved to the Belgian ball in *Vanity Fair* with its news of Napoleon's advancing armies. It was a quiet, old-fashioned and stilted passage, but it remained sound. His had been another festivity before another Waterloo, on Lexington Avenue that night, and it was strange that the parallel should never have occurred to him until more than a quarter of a century later. Everything had been there, if he had only had the wit to see it: all the moods, emotions, and main characters had appeared in that vanished Victorian room. The mood was implicit in the lilt of the voices, and in the banality of the champagne humor, in all the wit that was not wit, though some of it was amusing in retrospect.

Sitting quietly now in the library late in the night — and it was doubtless later than he thought — holding an empty whiskey tumbler and aware of the small-town nocturnal silence, different from any other silence, he could recall the guests of that other night, and their names and faces, far more clearly than he could any he had encountered in New York six months back. Players, playwrights, critics and managers had been moving in from the country then, for Labor Day was over. He could hear himself saying, standing beside Rhoda, "Rhoda, you remember Gilbert

Smythe" — and that would have been Gilbert Smythe from the old *New York World.* And now he had no knowledge as to whether Gilbert was alive or dead.

"Rhoda, this is Norman Wyatt from Hollywood. You remember, he's come to New York to talk to me about a script."

Norman was the one who died of an overdose of sleeping pills just before the war, but he had an old pro's mind for plot.

"Hello, Honoria, darling. Rhoda, of course you remember Honoria."

If Rhoda did not, she should have. Honoria had been in the front row of one of the *Scandals* and had just married Boris Klutch, who was being spoken of as a new David Griffith of the movies. . . . Klutch was the one who had run off to Tahiti a year later, at a time when Tahiti was a fashionable running-off place. Then Honoria had married Guy H. Nestling, the oil man, who, incidentally, had once been a close friend of the Hertimes; and when that had broken up, she had married Clarence Hugee, ten years her junior, the fashionable film juvenile; if he remembered rightly, Honoria had pulled a gun on Clarence in the Brown Derby or somewhere. He could not remember when he had last heard about her. The drifting dunes of time had covered a lot of people who had been conspicuously active before the Twenties had become a dust bowl of the past. . . .

"Duneen, darling," he heard himself saying, "you're looking marvelous. How is everything at the Vineyard? Is it still safe to swim on your beach in the altogether?"

It was only a casual question and there was no reason at all for Rhoda to have been annoyed. He had only been to the Vineyard for a short week end to see the Higginses on business.

"Tom," Arthur Higgins was saying, "I've brought along Burt Sturgess. I thought you boys ought to get to know each other."

That was the Burt Sturgess who had written the play about the evangelist, the name of which had now escaped him; the Sturgess who was once going to be a new adornment of the American drama until Hollywood had got him. Hollywood nearly always got them. Why was it that Tom had managed to escape, and where in heaven's name was Burt Sturgess now?

"Laura, dear," Tom said, "thanks ever so much for coming. Rhoda, here's Laura Hopedale."

At least Rhoda had recognized Laura Hopedale, and back in those days Laura had been something to remember. Laura, who was then still an ingenue, had what was called around the theatre a "spiritual quality." Her dark eyes had a startled look, and when she smiled she had a pleadingly wistful expression. With such attraction, it was already being said that she had a future in the pictures as well as on the stage. Her close-up was disastrously compelling. Her expression had not changed much when she was in North Africa with a USO troupe considerably later, and even then her complexion had been vastly better than most movie actresses'. Her words came back to him; her voice, with its soft and alluring huskiness and its almost perfect modulation, was as fine a speaking voice as he had ever heard on any stage or any picture set.

"Oh, Tom," she said, "it's enchanting to have a glimpse of you in your own milieu. This, all of it, is so entirely you."

"Rhoda had quite a lot to do with it," he said. "I'd call it seventy-five per cent Rhoda."

"Oh, now," Rhoda said, "I just shopped around for the things. He's the one who arranged everything. He's good at setting scenes, isn't he, Miss Hopedale?"

"Call me Laura," Miss Hopedale said. "It seems as though I've known you always, dear."

"I'm good at setting scenes," he said, "but I hope I never make them."

"That's true," Rhoda said, "he never does make them, Miss Hopedale — excuse me, dear, I meant to say Laura."

All the characters were there that night, or almost all, who had a part to play in the scenario of his middle years, and yet there was no warning of a distant drum. He was willing to bet that a soothsayer had never said, "Beware the Ides of March" — or if he had, that Julius Caesar had never heard him.

"Here come the Hertimes, Tom," Rhoda said. "How sweet of you both to come. Tom was just saying that he hoped that you weren't going to forget."

390

"Oh, sweetness," Mrs. Hertime said, "we wouldn't have missed this for anything. They may grow corn but not interesting people like this in the Mississippi valley. That's just what Art was saying in the taxi, weren't you, Art?"

"I sure was, honey," Art Hertime said, "and I might also add, not even at Grosse Pointe, Michigan. Say, Tom, I've got a tip for you. Buy yourself a few shares of Packard tomorrow and put them away and forget it."

"Art, honey," Mrs. Hertime said, "aren't you forgetting something else?"

"Forgetting what, sugar?" Mr. Hertime asked.

"To introduce our overnight guest, Art."

"Oh," Mr. Hertime said, "excuse me, sweetness. . . . We brought along with us one of our closest friends and one who I hope you'll agree with us is one of the finest guys in the world, Presley Brake — you know, the one who started the new investment trust, Monolith Security Mutual. Pres, I want you to meet one of the cutest and most brilliant couples in New York, Rhoda and Tom Harrow, and I know you'll all get along like a house afire."

"I know Rhoda's going to love him," he could still hear himself saying, "if the middle name of that investment trust is Security."

"That's its middle name" — and he could still recall the dry and lisping precision of Presley Brake. Presley already was growing bald, but the thinning hair gave his features and his thin nose reliability and balance. "Security is something you have to watch carefully just now."

"It's awfully nice that you could come, Mr. Brake," Rhoda said.

"Come on, Pres," Art Hertime said, "let's get a glass of happy water before these actors and geniuses drink it all up on us."

Presley Brake was slightly corpulent already, but perhaps this impression was based only on prejudice. There was no indication that he was another Marquis of Steyne. He had always been a colorless man, devoid of imagination, but again, this possibly was prejudice. There was no reason to think charitably of him any longer. In fact, there was no reason to think of him at all any more. . . .

"Well," he had said to Rhoda, "that balances the party. Get a few figures from the financial district in, and everything has sanctity."

"Sanctity?" Rhoda said.

"Maybe that isn't the word," he answered. "I guess the word's validity."

"Anyway," Rhoda said, "it's a good thing we know some people who know about finance, because you know that you don't."

"That's right," he said, "and I don't want to know."

"That's a pose," she said, "and you know it. Who's that coming in now, the very pretty young girl in the gray silk dress? What play is she rehearsing for?"

"Oh," he said. "She's in the Higgins office. She's been working on the acting script for *Little Liar*."

"I thought you said Miss Hopedale was the conscience," Rhoda said. "I'd rather have this one for my conscience."

"She doesn't act," he said. "She works in the Higgins office. But she is pretty, isn't she? Her name is Nancy Mulford. . . .

"Hello, Miss Mulford," he said. "I don't believe you've seen my wife since the party after *Hero* opened."

"You don't remember me, of course," Nancy Mulford said.

"I ought to," Rhoda said, "and we ought to be friends, if you're typing Tom's new play. You know, Tom met me — in fact, he picked me up — outside a typing school. Perhaps he has a weakness for girls who type."

"Only if they type beautifully," he said.

Then they were alone again, he and Rhoda, and the voices were louder in the room.

"Why were you so formal with her?" Rhoda asked. "Why didn't you kiss her and call her darling, the way you do Duneen?"

"Because I'm old-fashioned at heart," he said, "and it wouldn't do in the Higgins office, and she wouldn't like it."

"That's true," Rhoda said, "she isn't on the stage."

Everything was there that night, all the people and all the elements that were to make up success or failure in his life, except Emily, who was still in Indiana with blond pigtails, no doubt, and freckles on her nose.

392

At that moment, on Lexington Avenue, they were moving out of what one might still call the Age of Confidence into the Age of Christ-I'm-Confused, in which he had spent most of his active life and in which he was dwelling still. They were moving through regimentation to social significance, to a region where theory was indistinguishable from practice. They were moving into electronics, to war, and thence to atomic fission. Wishing was immature; he could only wish that he were back on Lexington Avenue with a foreseeable future ahead and with Rhoda beside him in her new party dress.

"Tom," she said that night, "I'm awfully glad we had the party."

It was easier to be glad about things in the Age of Confidence. They were still not surfeited with too much to be glad or sorry over. It was a simpler age, full of error, no doubt, but he wished again that he were there.

XXIV

Too Dark Downstairs for Sleeping

It was very late at night and nothing had been gained by sitting alone with semiconnected reminiscences except spasms of regret and the feeling of surprise one always had at how fast time had moved and how little was left to show for it. There had been a girl one summer in New York, and never mind who she was or what had happened to her. At any rate, there was no free guilt about her as there might have been about some others he could bring up. She was a college girl and interested in the theatre in a more intelligent and less emotional way than was true with most.

It had been summer in New York, quite a while after the Lexington Avenue days. He was alone in the Park Avenue duplex, getting his meals out, except his breakfast. He was in town as usual getting a play ready for casting and Rhoda and Harold had gone to Watch Hill. For the life of him he had never been able to do any work at Watch Hill, in spite of its coolness, comfort, and swimming and everything else. At the end of an August afternoon, he had gone to have a cocktail at the Patricks'. It had been Bill Patrick, the writer, who was married to a nice brunette named Molly at the time, and who had a house in the Turtle Bay development — the one with all the back yards in the block put together, forming a communal garden. Bill Patrick was finishing a novel and Molly had said that Turtle Bay was better than the country what with the garden and everything. He wished he could get the exact date of that summer correctly, but it must have been after Repeal, judging from his memory of bottles on the table out there in the garden.

There were a number of people whom one might properly call interesting, in that they made their living from writing, painting, or acting. It was strange that the average American housewife felt that people who wrote were interesting. He had already become acutely conscious of the fallacy, and those guests of Bill and Molly Patrick were unusually tired of being interesting that afternoon. He was finishing his cocktail and getting ready to leave when the girl arrived, and it would have been impossible not to be impressed by her in that environment. It was not her beauty that attracted his attention. Her figure was good but her face was plain. What was unforgettable and appealing to him, at that moment, was her expression of wide-eyed innocence that matched the cotton print dress she was wearing. You could tell that she never before in her life had seen so many interesting people. The wonder would wear off, given time and opportunity, but it had not when she stood there in the garden uncertainly, because Molly had gone into the house for something, and at best Molly was always careless about introducing people.

"May I get you something to drink?" he asked. "I don't believe we've ever met before. My name is Harrow."

"I'm Augusta Drew," she said, "and if I could, I'd like some gin and ginger ale, with very little gin."

"That's a college girl's drink," he said. "You must still be in college."

"Why, I am, as a matter of fact," she said. "Next year will be my second year at Vassar."

"A cradle for heroines," he said. "Don't go away, I'll be right back with your gin and ginger ale."

"Excuse me," she said, "did you say your name was Harrow?"

"Why, yes," he said, "Harrow's the name, and Harrow's my nature, if you don't mind Dickens."

"Not the Mr. Harrow who writes the plays?" she asked. "But you don't have to answer that one. I can tell you are. You couldn't be anyone else."

Her look was something he could not forget. He had never seen it on Rhoda. That was the thought in the back of his mind when he poured her a very little gin and a great deal of ginger

395

ale, and he remembered that he had asked himself an obvious question: Why had Rhoda never looked at him like that? Was it because she had always known too much about him, or was she basically too wise?

"I was thinking of going somewhere for supper," he said, "and it would be much pleasanter if you cared to come along."

"I'd love to," she said, "but are you sure you want me?"

Truthfully, he had not been sure; he had wanted the moment to stay preserved without its being spoiled. But it had not been spoiled. He had taken her to 21; she had never seen the place.

"It must be wonderful to have everyone know who you are," she said.

"Not any more," he said. "The catch in it is that nothing keeps on being wonderful."

"This keeps on being, for me," she said.

He had never forgotten, not that there had been much to forget. He talked to her about what he was writing, something he would seldom have done with Rhoda. He talked to her about Harold and about Watch Hill.

"I'd ask you up to the apartment," he said, "but there's nothing worse than an apartment in midsummer."

He was conscious that he did not want anything to spoil it, and nothing had. He had not even touched her hand until he had said good night to her in front of the building where she was staying.

"Good night. You're the nicest man I'll ever know," she said.

It was nothing much, but still something to remember. If he had ever seen her again, something would have been spoiled; and he never had seen her. Rhoda had known him too well, but not from their first meeting had her face ever worn that look, and maybe it was for the better. Undoubtedly he would have grown tired of it in time.

He must have dozed off for a moment, and he was glad he had, because the short space of oblivion, which was not unlike the dimming of the theatre lights that marked a lapse of time, finally broke the chain of his recollections. That dimming, which

396

could not have been much more than a minute's lapse, brought him back to the present again, and he discovered Hal was in the library. Hal was in a Liberty silk dressing-gown, something that someone must have given him for Christmas. He looked as though he had been asleep, but he also looked alert, with a nautical alertness he had not lost as yet.

"Hi, Pop," he said. "You know it's getting late?"

"Is it?" Tom asked. "Thanks for telling me, Hal, and, now you're here, how about sweetening up my drink with a little Scotch and water? If the ice has melted, never mind, the English never do."

Hal took the glass with a lieutenant, j.g., alacrity — but he also looked concerned, although the concern was not annoying since it meant that Hal was fond of him.

"You're kind of living it up tonight, aren't you?" Hal said.

The remark was devoid of reproof, but Hal still looked concerned, and an answer was temporarily difficult. It occurred to him that he would have to have a frank talk with Hal in the rather near future regarding the financial situation. Hal did not know the news unless Emily had told him, but Tom was in no mood for serious talk at the moment.

"Thanks," he said, when Hal handed him the glass. "I wouldn't say I'm living it up, as you put it. It would be more accurate to say that I'm living it down, not that anyone ever can. I've just been sitting here thinking."

"Well," Hal said, "they must have been long, long thoughts."

"Not long as much as disconnected," Tom said. "You're not old enough to let your mind run on at such length about anything, except sex, while as for me, I've done quite a lot of living up and down. I was thinking about the apartment in New York, the one we had when you were a baby. It was a nice place, and maybe we shouldn't have moved."

"Say," Hal said, "you've had a fight with Emily, haven't you?" It was not a time for serious talk.

"Has Emily been telling you?" he asked.

Hal shook his head.

"No," he said, "but she woke up and asked me to come down

397

and see what you were doing. She said she was worried about you."

"I suppose she is," he said. "It's funny, when I first met her I never thought that Emily was the worrying kind."

"She's upset about something, all right," Hal said.

"Yes," he answered, "but let's not talk about it now. In the morning, maybe, but not now."

"That won't be so long," Hal said. "It's pretty close to daylight."

"All right," he said again, "in the morning, perhaps, but not now."

"Anyway," Hal said, "I can always tell when you've had a fight with Emily, because you begin thinking about that apartment on Lexington Avenue."

Tom found himself experiencing one of those rare moments of surprise. It was impossible for any parent fully to realize that a son could be grown-up and reasonably mature.

"That's observant of you," he said.

"Well," Hal said, "I've spent quite a lot of time observing you, off and on."

In the very near future it would be necessary to have a serious talk with Hal.

"I'm afraid it's been more off than on," Tom said. "I'm sorry about it from your point of view — I mean about everything smashing up. It must have been tough for you, being pulled two ways at once, but you've come out of it pretty well, and . . ."

He was glad that he had made this speech because he could see that Hal was pleased.

"There weren't two ways to it particularly," Hal said. "I always thought you didn't have a square shake. I was pretty young at the time, but I told her that at the time, with you away at the war and everything, she shouldn't have done it that way, and you didn't get a square shake."

He felt an emotion after Hal had spoken that was connected with the eternal tragedy always surrounding what is euphemistically called a broken home, and combined with the sadness was gratitude for Hal's loyalty.

398

"Listen, boy," he said, "things are never so simple. Just remember things like that are all mixed up. I gave your mother quite a lot of trouble, boy, in various devious ways. I couldn't be a sound domestic type."

"Anyway," Hal said, "you were always a hell of a lot of fun at home. Maybe she thinks so now. And anyway, she shouldn't have pulled the switch when you were away at the war."

He found himself wishing for a moment that he were as young as Hal, an age when everything seemed clear-cut.

"Listen," he said, "really, it's not as easy as that. I was restless, you know. Goddammit, Hal, I didn't like soundness. Does she still talk about security?"

Hal shook his head.

"Not any more," he said. "She doesn't have to, any more."

Tom laughed, but he stopped almost at once.

"You see," he said, "she was always afraid things wouldn't last. Everybody has his own type of fear, and I never was afraid in just that way. She didn't want me to go to the war, you know, and she was right. I was too old for that show, anyway, and then along came Presley. Nothing's ever simple."

"You wanted to go, didn't you?" Hal said. "Personally I thought it was a pretty swell thing of you to do. Maybe I think so still."

There are a few unchanging qualities in a father-son relationship. There may always be a vestige of hero-worship that cannot be completely erased by disillusion or common sense. His mind went back to his own father and to that vanished night at Jack's. The memory made no sense, but a son's regard for a father cannot be assessed wholly in terms of sense.

"It's not as easy as that, Hal," he said again. "I wanted to see the show. That's the trouble with show business; it makes you selfish. You don't want to be left out of anything. You always want to see the show."

"She should have waited until you got back," Hal said.

"It wasn't a waiting time," he said. "It was an upset time. It would be fairer to say that I shouldn't have gone. It was being irresponsible, as she said, and I really was too old."

399

"You weren't so old," Hal said. "Anyway, you didn't look it. I've got your picture still."

"Hal," he said, "when you're around forty, it's too late to play soldier. I'll say one thing for it, I knew it right away. I was as miscast as hell, but still I wanted to see the show."

"Well, you got into the fighting," Hal said.

"Yes," he said, "by accident, and I was still as miscast as hell."

It was a transient episode. His memories of Rhoda were much clearer and more valid than his memories of the war.

"Of course," he said, "it was a surprise, the 'dear-John' letter, I mean, but maybe I had it coming to me. A lot of dear-Johns did."

"Say," Hal said, "you'd better go up to bed before you hang one on, Pops. Remember, you're going up there tomorrow."

"Yes," he said, "that's so. It hasn't skipped my mind."

They were both silent for a moment.

"Come on," Hal said, "go up and get some sleep, Pops."

Tom was too wide awake for sleep and he did not want to lie still, staring at the dark.

"Did she say why she wanted to see me?" he asked.

"No," Hal said, "she just said it was important and that she had to see you."

The whole weight of the day pressed down upon him, and it had been an endless day, what with all the traveling backward and forward in the past.

"I don't see what can be important now," he said.

It sounded like an epitaph, which was what it was, and when anything was finished, you could never put life back into it again.

He thought of the last time he had said good-by to her. There had been one of those pointless quarrels that had grown frequent enough to be commonplace, though they had both learned that nothing resolved itself in quarrels.

"But where are you going?" she said. "You can't just go away and leave us here."

"I've told you," he said, "that I can't tell you where I'm going."

"But what's going to happen?" she said.

"I don't exactly know," he said, "so don't ask. You've got plenty

400

of money if I don't come back, and the will, and powers of attorney."

"Oh, God," she said, "I never thought you'd do it."

It could have been that her never thinking so and never believing was what had finally made him do it.

"Rhoda," he said, "let's not go over it again."

"You and your damned uniform . . ." she said. "But you'll be doing something. What am I going to do?"

"Behave yourself, I hope, and look after Hal," he said.

"Just for one more time," she said, "are you really going to leave us?"

They had been over it, and she knew.

"You won't even miss us," she said.

"Of course I will," he told her.

Her voice broke.

"Everything we had is gone," she said. "Don't you feel it? Everything."

"Look," he said, "I've told you nothing's gone. I love you more than I ever have. I've told you that."

"Yes," she said, "you love me because you're going." And perhaps this had been true, but still he loved her.

"Well, anyway, good-by," he said.

She threw her arms around him and she sobbed.

"Good-by, Tom," she said. "I'll do the best I can."

He had spent so much of his time listening critically to voices that he was an authority on the subject. The pitch of a voice or its emotional content could build a scene or mar it beyond recognition. Sometimes a voice could arouse him from his dreams, the voice of someone long ago dead coming urgently from the darkness. As he considered those words of Rhoda's, he was amazed at how perfectly preserved they were, without blur or blemish.

"Good-by, Tom," he heard her say, just as though she were in the room, and he thought again of all the things he might have said.

"I am sorry," he might have said, "that I haven't been able to give you everything you want."

401

"Rhoda," he might have said, "everyone alive has different things to give and can only give so much."

"Rhoda," he might have said, "you've got to give back something in return. You've got to give enough to make it even."

Some speech like that was needed for a suitable ending, but he was glad that he had never made the speech. In retrospect, he saw that Rhoda had given him all he should have wanted. He had asked her to write him and not to forget the A.P.O. number, and then he was out in the hall ringing for the elevator, holding nothing but his overnight bag, since the rest of his equipment was in Washington. There were courteous attendants in the building and there were a few famous last words. The younger men had left the apartment staff already and thus the elevator operator was nearly old enough to be his father.

"Good luck to you, Mr. Harrow," he said.

"Thank you," Tom had answered. "Thank you, James."

Their voices, too, were preserved against the elevator's reassuring descending note and with them the strain of the parting was almost over. He was experiencing what must have been a typically selfish male reaction: relief at having escaped a disturbing scene, in the knowledge that there could be no repetition.

Then the scene shifted and Hal was speaking to him.

"Come on, Pops," he said, "you've got to get some sleep. You'll want to look corn fed and happy when you go up there."

Hal might be lacking in imagination, but he had balance. There was obviously no use sitting up any longer, conjuring voices and shadows.

He got to his feet with almost no difficulty. In fact, he was surprised to observe that he was steady on his feet and the knowledge made him identify himself with one of those debauched heroes, so popular in turn-of-the-century drama, who were usually saved from themselves by the honest sweetness of an innocent girl. But where was the pure, sweet girl? Not around the house, nor anywhere else any longer.

"What's that you're saying, Pops?" Hal asked.

"I was saying," he said, "where is the pure, sweet girl?"

"I don't quite follow you," Hal said.

402

"No reason you should," he said. "I wasn't asking you to, and if I had, you'd be a demnition fool to want to do it."

There was style in that remark. He was like the late John Drew and completely steady on his feet.

"There's just one thing," he said. "That guy isn't going to be there, is he? That's all squared away, to use your language, isn't it?"

"I guess I'm not with you yet," Hal said. "What guy?"

There was no slurring in Tom's speech, but he was aware, now that he was standing, that his self-control was not what it should have been. It was high time he got some sleep.

"Your goddam stepfather," he said. "He won't be there, will he?"

"Oh, him," Hal said. "No, of course he won't. I told you, didn't I? She wanted you to know particularly that this was going to be a private talk. Besides, he's a self-effacing guy."

His emotional response was erratic and he was unable to control it.

"He's a self-effacing, goddam son-of-a-bitch," he said.

He was immediately ashamed and he had not realized that bitterness could be stored so long. Bitterness was the worst of human failings.

"Well, well," he said, "I seem to be a shade uncomposed tonight. I shouldn't have used hard words. Your mother wanted him, that's all. The guy was only a symbol, a symbolic son-of-a-bitch. Don't hold my elbow. I can get the hell out of here and upstairs alone."

"Sure you can," Hal said, "I never said you couldn't. I'll put the lights out, Pop."

"Leave them on," he said, "lights don't make any difference. Leave them on tonight."

"What's the idea?" Hal asked. "Why keep them on?"

The half-senile flash of anger he had felt had evaporated and he was in control of everything.

"It's not an idea, it's a whim," he said. "I just don't want to go to sleep when it's dark downstairs."

There was a trace of sense in the whim. In a few minutes he

would be in the dark, but, if the lights were on, there would still be part of him downstairs, and he did not want to be in one piece at just that moment. Instead, he wanted to be like a good investment list with a suitable balance between stocks and mature bonds.

"The stocks will be upstairs, but the bonds can stay down," he said.

"How's that again?" Hal asked.

"Never mind," he said. "I'm whimsical, but don't turn out the lights."

"Right," Hal said, "if you want it that way."

He was conscious of a resentment against Hal, not due to Hal's personality or kindness. It was more tragic, the unexpressed resentment that age always felt towards youth, the knowledge of moving to the edge of the picture. Tom was in a vulnerable position because of overindulgence, where anything he said could be used against him, but he was still, if he might say so, in considerable command of his faculties.

"Say," Hal said, "what happened to you today?"

"It's nothing that can't keep," he said. "I'm tired now. It's nothing tragic, just remember that."

It occurred to him that there were only two dominant tragedies in life. One tragedy lay in the mistakes one made, and the other in growing old, but everyone made mistakes and everyone grew old. He could not recall just then, and he was proud he could not, who had written "Grow old along with me, the best is yet to be." It was one of those literary falsehoods that had done much to turn him against poetry. The actuality was that the older one got the less one was lulled and mellowed by the past, the less wise one became in spite of experience. The less you had, and the less you became, and the hell with it.

"To hell with it," he said. "I'll see you in the morning, Hal."

Upstairs the reading light was on and his pajamas were folded at the bottom of his turned-down bed, and the door that communicated with Emily's room was ajar.

"Tom," she called, "are you all right?"

This was irritating. In the first place, why shouldn't he have

404

been all right, and in the second, if he weren't, why should she have cared? He forced himself to remember that the worst of her problem was that she was obliged to care.

"Poor Emily," he said. "Grow old along with me, the best is yet to be, and just you wait and see. Good night, Emily, I don't want to talk about it now." And he closed the door.

Emily did not speak again. She had made the wrong selection back there in Arthur Higgins's apartment and now she was fearing that even this selection might move on. He was tempted to speak to her again, but it took a longer time than you ever envisaged if you started to converse with Emily, even in the small hours of the morning. Rhoda, on the contrary, had always been frank enough to say that she was sleepy.

"I don't see why you wait until I am sound asleep," she always said, "before you have any interesting ideas."

He had felt so tired that he had thought that he would sleep immediately, but he should have remembered that was a fatal fallacy that sleep invariably followed fatigue. As soon as his bedside light was out, he was much wider awake than he had been during that lonely interval in the library. He was acutely conscious of the night sounds, and he was sure his mind was moving so alertly that he could see beyond the night. His thoughts were deflected on a new, pre-last-war line. He was seeing through the dark, with extraordinary accuracy, places he had taken Rhoda, never against her will: an inn on the road to Oxford, and rooms at New College where they had been asked to tea. He could remember a house party at Sussex, where the people were partly Mayfair and partly intelligentsia. He could remember Claridge's and the horses' hoofs on Brook Street, and Berkeley Square and Grosvenor Square, and the Bond Street tailors and the theatres whose curtains rose at reasonable hours. Rhoda had caught the feel of London, just as she had of Paris, but Rhoda was at home anywhere. He could see the Place de la Concorde from the gallery of their sitting room in the Hotel Crillon. They had both been very fond of the Crillon in those days, and the chestnut trees along the Champs Elysées were in full bloom.

He had done a lot for Rhoda in a way very different from the Hertimes' or the Bramhalls' and very different from that of anyone like Presley Brake. He had shown her a side of life that they had never seen, or, if they had, one which they could not appreciate. Only a year or two ago someone had told him, intending it as a compliment, that he was very much like the late Scott Fitzgerald in that he had a similar veneration for wealth and power — a complete untruth. Rhoda was the one who had cared for these. But he could see now clearly, in the dark, that he had been dealing in another sort of currency and he was not justifying himself when he admitted that he did not care for money in itself, but only for what could be exchanged for it.

"You never think," Rhoda said. "You let it run through your fingers."

Very well, he had let it run through his fingers. There were other types who could hold it and never let it go, but there was one thing that even they were not able to hold, and that was the sand of life, and if you couldn't hold onto that, why hold money? He had a distinct realization that he had wasted something, but it was impossible to tell what was waste when all creative effort was a distillation of experience.

He could see Algiers again as it had been the first time he had seen it, standing with Rhoda on the deck of someone's yacht. There was always a good chance to get on a yacht in those days if you were sufficiently entertaining at Antibes, and they were more entertaining than most people. It was morning when they anchored in the harbor of Algiers. The houses that rose up on steep slopes, forming terraces of walls and roofs, looked more French than he had believed they would, though, according to Frenchmen, Algeria was an integral part of the Republic. He had walked through the narrow streets with Rhoda and he was positive that they had stopped for tea at the beige-colored Hotel Aletti. He could remember its terrace overlooking the harbor. Even the Kasbah, to which they had gone with a guide under careful supervision, was more French than *Arabian Nights*. He had not dreamed, naturally, of the auspices under which he would see the place again. There had been rumors of war, but if one came, he could not see it in Algeria. He had cared more about motoring in the back country and visiting the remains of a lost Roman city than about visiting contemporary Algiers, but he had never thought of France as a projection of older Rome.

He could even remember that he and Rhoda in Algeria had gone through at least one argument about money.

"Let's talk about something else," he said.

"I know," she said, "I know you think it's stupid."

"I don't think money's stupid," he said, "I only think it's dull."

"That's a tiresome attitude," Rhoda said. "It may be dull, but what would we have done if dull people hadn't told us how to invest your savings? I don't think it's kind of you to say they're dull."

"I didn't say they were," he said. "I said that money was."

"You think Dick and Marion Bramhall are dull," she said.

"Not always," he said, "I just think they're different from you and me."

"And I suppose you think Presley Brake is dull," she said.

It was three in the afternoon. They were among semiarid hills, driving back from somewhere, and they had just passed the well of an Arab village.

"He isn't entirely," he said, "but I don't like him."

"Why don't you?" she asked.

"I don't like the shape of his head," he said, "and I don't like the sound of his voice, and all he cares about are motor cars and money."

In retrospect, this was not a bad thumbnail sketch, even if it might have fitted several other people.

"Tom, you're an awful snob," she said. "You say that because he hasn't got an Eastern accent."

"Look," he said, "we're having a nice time in a very peculiar country. I want to see what's going on and not talk about Presley Brake."

"All right," she said, "I never said I wanted to talk about him, either."

She was the one who had brought him up. She was the one, not he, who had him on her mind. He had never given a damn, and he didn't now, for Presley Brake.

They had never quarreled vociferously because they both were easygoing people. They had never been through those marital scenes so hilarious in drama and so tragic in private life — no shrieks, no shouts, no throwing of small articles. Could it have been that there had been too much repression between them both? He could not honestly believe so. On the contrary, they were both naturally considerate, but it might have been that they had been too civilized. Years had passed before he could have a glimpse of himself as she must have seen him, erratic, careless, with a juvenile desire to be a playboy. But at least they had both lived. Furthermore, he wished that he felt like a playboy now, that he were as alive as he had been then, or as aware, instead of trading both for cynical, weary wisdom. The swap was inevitable, perhaps, but it was still a bad exchange.

XXV

The Army Had a Name for Them

THE THING that happened had to happen somewhere, but it was incongruous that the Hotel Aletti should have been the place — not the Aletti as he had seen it first, but the Aletti in the war, down at the heel and deathly threadbare like the whole city of Algiers. Though war had touched Algiers almost as lightly as Paris, the blight of war, not its physical aspects, had made the city drab and devoid of the character he had previously remembered. It exhibited a waning of spirit more than physical hurt, and the echoes of a defeated nation constantly caught one's ear. The shelves of the shops were bare and so was the Hotel Aletti, an empty shell, its furnishings ruined. The main dining room was stripped of its silver and napery. The plates passed by tired waiters, had come from defunct hotels in the States or from vanished ocean liners; the napkins were wrapping paper; but the rooms could have been much worse. He was lucky to have obtained one, with his rank of lieutenant colonel, the most meaningless and most fluid rank in the army. He was on the Army staff after a motion-picture assignment that he had started with evaporated during the sporadic street fighting outside of Oran. It had ended when he had called across the street in French to a French officer. He was doing staffwork in Algiers, and not only his French but his ability to get on with the British had been a help. Now it was summer in Algiers, shortly before the invasion of Sicily, and he had been there long enough to realize that Rhoda had been right. It had been a piece of selfishness for him to go. He was not of much use, even though he was popular around G–1 and was able to handle confidential information without its going to his head; but, selfishness or not, he was in the orchestra out front watching the most terrible yet the greatest show on earth and one that had always made men leave home.

Mail from the States had arrived that afternoon, but he had been too busy to read his letters until he was back at the hotel; and even if he had not been occupied, he would not have read Rhoda's letter sooner because he had never cared to read her letters at headquarters. His room at the Aletti overlooked the harbor, and he could remember the lengthening shadows and the afternoon light reflected on the water. His familiarity with stage sets enabled him to replace each article of furniture in his memory. There was a worn-out carpet, there were dingy blackout curtains, soiled walls, a bureau, a three-quarters bed with a sagging spring and olive-drab army blanket, a wardrobe with a cracked mirror, two chairs, one straight with a broken seat, the other with plum-colored, frayed upholstery, and a hat rack with his helmet and his gas mask hanging on its hooks. He had poured himself a small drink of bourbon into the cup of his canteen because he was tired and pleased to be hearing from home. He balanced her letter in his hand a few minutes before he opened it, observing that the postmark was Watch Hill, and he reconstructed the details of the house they had rented there for several summers. It would be approximately five hours earlier there than in Algiers, and he could think of Rhoda on the beach with Hal; he wondered how much Hal had grown. She would be tanned, and the sun always made her hair lighter. The memory was both near and distant. Lately he had been able to understand the contradiction, since like many others he had learned to place home and its attributes into a realm of a very remote possibility; and this was a practical point of view, the quicker attained the better. In the loneliness that necessarily accompanied an army overseas, it helped one's general attitude to be concerned exclusively with the present and not to bother with the past.

He could afford to relive those hours now that he had not seen Algiers for fifteen years. He lay in the dark, and with the

410

clarity that darkness brings to thought the letter might as well have been before his eyes again. He could see the bold, rebellious, slanting handwriting that had always reminded him of a schoolgirl rebelling against her teachers. There was always anticipation whenever he opened one of Rhoda's letters, because she wrote the way she spoke, impulsively but never stupidly, and he could always read a dozen of her thoughts between the lines. What impressed him, now, was his utter lack of suspicion. He never knew until he had read the first two sentences that his letter from Rhoda was one of those letters that the Army had a name for, and there was an appreciable lapse of time before he could read it intelligently.

He could recollect it word for word, but he still refused to give himself the pain of drawing upon the accuracy of memory. His instinct for preservation had helped, because even then he had tried to see himself as another person and not himself. He had rehearsed himself, as he would an actor who had received the news; he had tried to cultivate an actor's professional virtuosity. It was the theatre that saved him back there in Algiers. He had seen the simulation of so much emotion that it governed his behavior.

From the moment he finished the letter, a part of himself must have observed the scene curiously, with a knowledge that it was a valuable experience professionally. He could not say that he welcomed it, but part of him admitted that this was an opportunity to observe behavior under the influence of grief, a species of behavior which he had studied often academically. He was sure back there in Algiers that, given the faculties he now possessed, he would have observed with interest the processes of dying — and as it was, a part of him was as dead as the corpses on the road near Oran.

He sat recovering from the blow, knowing that he was as much in shock as a battle casualty. In shock body and mind acted defensively, so that it was impossible to tell at first the extent of damage, which became apparent only after the first impetus of the thing was over; and by then you could only hope that processes of healing might begin. It must have been his own desire for preservation that helped him put Rhoda from his mind.

There was nothing, he was sure, less predictable than the human mind or the caprice of will. It was no wonder that the *Book of Common Prayer* made reference to omissions and commissions and implied that devout congregations were miserable sinners. All one could do was to live under the leadership of the Chief Justice of the mind, and the mind was always more interested in the preservation of the ego than in abstract truth. He could see that defense mechanism had been in control of him already, and that after the shock there had come a wave of indignation which sounded to him now like an oration on Armistice Day. It was dastardly of Rhoda, his mind was saying, to have played this trick upon him while he was far from home fighting for his country, or at least a member of the armed services trying to be useful. He perceived the flaccidity of the argument, but Rhoda had been ungenerous and ungrateful. Then, with this meretricious indignation was combined an element of pride, and no one could tell how much of this one possessed until faced by disaster. Some of his pride must have been drawn from the stage, where appearances often counted more than fact. There was pride in keeping the production in correct proportion, pride in a traditional façade, and never mind what lay behind it.

He remembered that he had poured himself another drink and that he had been careful not to take too much because he was to dine up on the hill with his boss, General Whelk, who was a West Pointer disapproving of civilian officers, and they were going to work on logistics. The thing to do was to live in the present and to remember that Rhoda and Hal were in a country so hard to reconstruct that they were already in the past. When he had finished his second drink, he opened the foot locker beside his bed and took out a writing tablet and an air-mail envelope.

Dear Rhoda, he wrote, *I have received your letter. I am sorry you have not felt that you could wait until this show got finished here, but then, that is your privilege. I am writing to my lawyers*

to get in touch with you at once. Please give my love to Hal.
Sincerely . . .

Of all the letters he had written her, this was the last, and he
could still believe it was admirable in that it expressed his
feelings better than pages could have done. He was aware of
the glacial quality but he could believe she deserved it. There
was always that doubt, that question of what might have happened if he had written differently, but there were lots of things
that one could do only once. He could address that letter only
once; he could put it only once in the pocket of his blouse. He
could put his cap on in that same way only once and look at
himself in the cracked wardrobe mirror. He had lost weight
since New York; summer had given him a coat of tan in spite
of his work indoors. In his uniform he looked nearly like a pro,
because he had studied the mannerisms. He had even been able
to fool some people on the hill until they had seen he did not
have the ring, but no one could be like General Whelk without
intensive training. He was new wine in an old bottle, or was he
doing right in quoting from the Scriptures?

The general had sent a jeep down from the pool.

"Evening, Sergeant," Tom said to the driver. "I hope I haven't
kept you waiting."

The sergeant looked like a pro himself, and at least he had
been through basic training.

"No reason not to wait, sir," the sergeant said, "I've had my
chow. It's a lovely evening, isn't it — the kind that makes you
wish you were back home, doesn't it?"

They were civilians together in spite of the uniform. It was a
civilian army until one reached the higher echelons or encountered an occasional survivor from the peacetime regulars.

"If you think of home," he said, "it means you have a nice
home, Sergeant. You're married, I suppose."

"And two kids," the sergeant said. "Yes, sir, I have a lovely
home."

"Well," he said, "there's a saying — I wish I had my book of
Familiar Quotations here — that anyone who has a wife and
children gives hostages to fortune."

413

"That's a fact, isn't it, sir?" the sergeant said. "It kind of slows you up. If I may be frank, colonel, I get a lot more of a charge driving you than most officers. You've always got something to say that's on the ball."

"As long as it isn't a lovely charge," he said, "and this isn't an order, but if it's all the same with you, Sergeant, would you please not use the word 'lovely' again until we get there?"

"Say," the sergeant said, "what's wrong with the word 'lovely'?"

"Nothing, Sergeant," he said, "except it makes me gag tonight. The younger writers are using it and it is frequently employed in fiction in the *New Yorker* magazine."

"Jesus, sir," the sergeant said, "you really know your way around."

Tom was adaptable, and besides, headquarters was like a stage. He remembered a profile that had been written about him by one of those bright young men with a gift for words and a penchant for collecting comical details. Maybe the author had given a key to his character in one phrase he remembered, "the affable Mr. Harrow." He was glad he had not been called "tweedy and affable" since *affable* in itself was enough. Did affable mean a placating manner, smacking of cowardice? Did it mean a commercial desire to please, a Dale-Carnegie-calculated drive to make friends and influence people, or merely proper manners? You never could tell how contemporary taste might succeed in warping the meaning of a word.

He had been a figure that appealed to a naïve quality in the army. There were generals who, in their peacetime lives, had never come in contact with Figures, and now the net of war had brought them great Figures wholesale. They collected them indiscriminately — pugilists, ball players, movie stars, professors, writers, artists, singers. He was glad he had got in G–1 originally because he could speak French, but he might have stayed because he was a Figure that could answer affably when asked how he had so many ideas for plays. He may have kept the sergeant waiting, but he was just on time when he knocked on the door of the general's quarters.

"Good evening, sir," he said.

The general's room on the second floor of the converted resort hotel, looking over the orange trees and the bougainvillaea of the garden, was as spacious as his rank demanded but as plain and neat as Sparta. The general was writing a letter. As the waning light fell on his thinning hair and graying temples, it occurred to Tom Harrow that he would be a dead ringer for Julius Caesar if he had only possessed a better voice. He had been put into G–1 because of ability. It had been no kick upstairs and he was not yet on his way to Washington.

"Hello, Tom," he said, "pardon me, I'm writing a line to Mrs. Whelk. There's a courier going out tonight who will take it in the pouch. The old lady gets nervous if she doesn't hear from me twice a week. I hope you write Mrs. Harrow regularly."

"Yes, sir," Tom said. "In fact, I just wrote her a line at the Aletti and also a kind of a business letter, too. Would it be asking too much, sir, if you could get them off with yours?"

"No, no," the general said, "as long as one is for the Lucky Little Woman. My motto is, always write the Lucky Little Woman."

The general would have been beautiful as Shaw's Caesar. He could even wonder what the general would do if he should come in contact with Cleopatra in Cairo.

"Tom," the general said, "open that closet over there and get the bourbon off the right-hand shelf, and two glasses by the washstand, will you? And there's clean water in the bottle. Pour out two stiff snorts before we go over to the mess."

"Why, that sounds fine, sir," Tom said, "but not altogether like you."

"Don't kid me," the general said, "you knew it was coming. Listen to what I've written: '*And now I must close, Myrtle. Tom Harrow — I told you I had him with me, didn't I? The one who wrote the play you and I saw in New York back in '39 — is with me, and we're going to have a little snort. Pinky Greenway tried to take Harrow from me last week but he didn't. Tom sends you his regards and wishes you were here.* Right?"

"Right, sir," Tom Harrow said.

415

"You know," the general said, "for a civilian you're a good Joe. Here's looking at you, Tom."

The pain left him for a moment.

"Why, thanks a lot, sir," he said.

"Don't kid me," the general said. "Say, before we go to the mess, I might tell you I was Up There half an hour ago, and got what I wanted."

There was a good reason to be startled because what the general said indicated an ending of an episode.

"Congratulations, sir," Tom said.

"Thanks," the general said. "It will be nice to be dragging out of here. I'll be going up Casablanca way the day after tomorrow. I'm taking Pugsy White with me. If you weren't married to such a lovely girl, I'd put in for you, too. Pour me out a little more."

It was a time to pour the drinks carefully.

"Sir," he said, "I'd like to be in the show."

"You did all right, son," the general said, "at Oran, but this may be the business this time."

Tom found himself clearing his throat.

"If you want me, sir," he said, "I know a little Italian, and I'd like to see the show."

The thing had been on a professional basis and he hoped that he had paid his way. His mind had been on the Dumas Musketeers back there in the general's quarters. When he looked out of the window and saw the orange trees and the bougainvillaea, the curtain of unreality dropped down. He was Raoul setting forth with the Duc de Beaufort now that the king had taken away de la Vallière. The difficulty was that neither God nor Dumas had made Tom as capable as Raoul, but his mind was off his troubles.

XXVI

You Always Fell Down Somewhere When Running Through the Script

WHEN he had gone out to Hollywood to do a treatment of *Little Liar*, Antoine Lasalle, who had been proud to admit that he had been born on New York's East Side, at that particular time was one of the greatest producers on any lot. Tom Harrow had made a great hit with Mr. Lasalle and still called him 'Tony'. In fact, they had got on so well together that Mr. Lasalle had insisted that he and Rhoda come out from New York at his expense and stay as his guest personally at his Beverly Hills home, Château Lasalle, and, as Tony had said, the swimming pool was so long that if you swam the length of it, you had to have the personal gym instructor, who was always on duty, take you back in a wheelchair to the bar. The occasion for the invitation was the World Première of the film *Little Liar;* and Antoine was an artist in those days, having done that movie, *Women Without Men*, which had grossed five million — and if that wasn't art, what was? In fact, Tony was in a position to wear an opera cloak to the World Première of *Little Liar*, and Fifi Lasalle's string of pearls had snapped just when they were all putting their feet on moist concrete to commemorate the event, but who gave a damn, as Tony said? There were lots of other oysters, and new shoes and slippers had been supplied for everyone. Somehow Rhoda had never got into the spirit of the occasion, and she had worried all that night about how to get concrete off pearls, not that they were hers, but Tom had enjoyed himself that night.

417

The studio crowd had wanted to do something nice in honor of Mr. Antoine. The plan was to give him a surprise at the party he was going to throw at the château after the opening, and the thought was to get a little skit together and there was a lot of acting talent around happy to be in it. The main problem was to get someone to write the skit and he had been asked to do it and had whipped the whole thing out in two hours. The idea was amusing at the time. In some respects he had been a new Milton, writing *Comus* for the benefit of royalty. It was a long way from the great Puritan to the bathing cabañas at the far end of the château swimming pool, and Milton himself would never have dreamed of the lighting and equipment that had come up from the studio. Naturally a different, non-*Comus* tempo was required at Beverly Hills, but the *Comus* plot had not gone badly when translated into the Brown Derby vernacular and the saving of the virtue of Melesande Miller, who had played the conscience in the *Little Liar* film, had been something that brought down the house for any one of a number of reasons and most of the reasons were right there in the audience.

There was no reason to have thought of this ancient and somewhat bawdy occasion, which marked the height of Hollywood greatness, if it had not been for a lyric he had written, sung by Percival Rodney who had played the part of Comus. Percival had been the fashionable funny man in those days, although he was now a sad hermit, living somewhere near Palm Springs, who ate only Indio dates and yoghurt. Percy had never been funnier than when he had sung a lyric called "Running through the Script." It was a pity that most of it had long ago evaded Tom Harrow's memory, but he could remember the chorus as he lay staring into the dark. The music had a happy lilt; it had been written by Joe Bushkin in the studio, who could think up ten tunes an hour back in those days.

If a body meet a body [some of the patter went] running
    through the script,
Should a body blame a body, if a body slipped?

Running through the script [was the way the chorus went],
Running through the script —
Be careful; don't fall on your ass, while running through the
   script.

Rhoda had said that night that the whole thing was vulgar,
and she was shocked that anyone in his position should pander
to such a boor as this Lasalle, which certainly was a made-up
name, and when were they going to get out of the château? No
doubt he had always been too pliable, too affable, and no doubt
he possessed a vulgar streak. Yet if she had wanted financial
comparisons, as he had told her back there in the château, Tony
could stack up with Hertime any day, and why were they always playing around the Hertimes? It had not helped that
Rhoda had begun to cry when he made this remark, but this
was beside the point at present. A snatch of the chorus persist-
ently kept moving through his mind: *Running through the script
— Be careful; don't fall on your ass, while running through the
script.*

His life had been, in its final version, the running through of a
series of scripts written by Providence instead of by himself,
and of the two, he believed he was the better writer. His life
was one long script that already contained hints of the ending
and also a painful series of pratfalls. The studio in which it had
been directed and the stages had been his world with limitations not unlike those in Culver City. There were the same sort
of scenes made overnight with nothing but two-by-fours supporting the fronts of imposing buildings. The art departments
and technicians were remarkable. Give them a few hours' notice
and they could whip up a street in London, Paris or Peking,
and a crowd of extras could bring the scenes to life, and time
could be moved back and forward. Most of one's actual life was
consumed in walking past similar stage sets. You were always on
some lot or other, and you were forever acting out a script,
listening to directions hurled at you by conscience or the subconscious. Actually, he had had surprisingly little to do with
preparing the life script that he had acted. His name was on it

as clear as the carving on a tombstone, but this did not alter the fact that the whole business had been ghostwritten so badly that most of it could not possibly hold attention.

That dingy, inexpert production was now moving into its final act. There had been an interminable quality surrounding every part of the progression, but when the action was over he had the impression that everything had moved with remarkable celerity. The time lag seemed incredibly short from childhood until the present, and the intermissions were confusing. His life with Rhoda seemed closer to yesterday than the true yesterdays that had intervened, and there were unrealities so inartistic that they left no permanent conviction, like Rhoda's letter and the war. These were interpolations which no one in his senses would have used, and yet they, too, were speeded up in recollection. One was always running, never walking through the script and only when you were getting through with it did you know that time had ticked like a clock without a pendulum.

It was hard to pick out Sicily in the script, since incidents there had no particular relationship to past or future and all that held them together was a struggle for survival that had often placed physical fatigue above actual danger.

That sequence had begun and ended so quickly that its sharper fears were dulled. The interlude now had a spurious sunset aspect, enabling him to return to some of its moments wistfully. He had never been so well physically or so intensely aware of everything around him. Part of this awareness must have been due to apprehension, but he had not broken under strain. In place of the weight he had lost, the rest of him was tougher. By the time he reached Palermo, it had seemed a lifetime since Algiers, and his face had reflected the life. Its bone structure was more pronounced and humor had left his lips, and it could have been that Hopedale had been right about him when he had met her there in Palermo.

"You never looked this way before," she said. "You're wonderful."

420

This was one of those inconsequential and badly balanced speeches characteristic of the script. He had met her at a USO show to which he had gone without knowing who would be in the troupe. It had been a hot night outside the city and he had stood in the dark among several thousand officers and enlisted men, all lonely, all drawn there to catch a glimpse of what might approximate the life they had left behind. The stage as usual was a boxing ring, cut from the surrounding blackness by powerful, inartistically arranged lights. The sound of the generators that made them operate added to the confusion, and as always happened, the microphones were not functioning.

He had to hand it to Hopedale when, in spite of the handicaps, the crowd had been right with her from the start, and she had always been and still was an excellent mimic, and she always possessed an arrogant nerve that could make her go through with anything. He respected her performance, but, during the first minutes he saw her on that dazzlingly lighted platform, his only thought was of incredulity that he should be seeing in Palermo any woman he had known in his other life.

The chance of having a few minutes alone with anyone like Laura Hopedale, when it was necessary to compete with all the high brass, was almost nil in Palermo. He had not forgotten the amazed looks of some outstanding military figures at the party afterwards. She was dressed in a practical uniform that was mandatory for war theatres, but Hopedale could always give style to anything. She was talking to a three-star general when she saw him, and, as she said later, the general was a dull and concupiscent old man.

"Tom," she called as soon as she saw him, "think of seeing you in a rat race like this."

As she had told him later, she had always liked men, but not so many men. She had never been able to get on with women, but she really felt a new desire to try, she said, after her stay in Palermo.

"My God," she whispered, "you look wonderful."

"So do you," he said, "but then, of course there's no standard of comparison."

"That's the beauty of it," she said. "Its the only place I've ever been where there are no standards whatsoever. How is dear Rhoda?"

"Oh," he said. "That's so, Rhoda."

"What do you mean by that?" she asked.

"Nothing much," he said. "Did you say you were without any standards?"

"No," she said, "I only said there weren't any standards, and it's not my fault."

"No," he said, "of course it isn't, as long as you don't blame it on me."

"Harrow," she said, "I'm not blaming anything on you. My God, you look wonderful. There's so much I want to tell you."

"Dear Laura," he said. "I don't suppose it would be possible, but I'd like to do some talking myself. I feel like Othello tonight. I could tell you a lot of stories if you were Desdemona."

"I've always wondered what it would be like to be alone with you," she said, "but we never had a half a chance, did we? Your face is awfully tanned, but you're not as dark as a Moor. Okay, I'll be Desdemona."

"Where?" he asked.

"That's a good, intelligent question," she said. "Do you really want an intelligent answer? Soldier, are you really lonely?"

"Yes," he said, "I'm really pretty lonely."

"Well," she said, "what would Rhoda say?"

He still was gratified that she had wanted him over all the competition.

"Rhoda's interest would only be academic, as things stand," he said.

"Poor dear," she said, "do you mean what I think you mean? You ought to tell me about it. You ought to tell someone everything."

"I agree," he said, "but where?"

"Oh, well," she said, "they keep knocking on my door. They always do all night, but you can take me home. I'll have to explain it to that dirty-minded old man I was talking to. God, it's tiresome when three thousand sex-starved officers try to make you simultaneously every time the plane hits the runway, and then in the air there's the pilot."

"I'm just another," he said. "I'm trying to make you, dear."

"Yes," she said, "but you don't try so intensely. You lack the West Point training."

"That's what I hear all day long," he said, "but I wish you wouldn't tell me, too, that I'm not West Point."

"Thank God you never went to that place," she said. "I've always loved you. I never knew how much until right now."

"Values get magnified in a place like this," he said. "Not that I care — I merely bring it up."

"Harrow," she said, "I'm going to make you care. I'll have to go now, but wait around and you can take me home — I mean to that hotel."

He was sometimes disturbed by dreams which, though formless afterwards, had been so eloquent that they would awaken him from deep sleep and leave him uncertain as to where he was. In Sicily, where regular sleep had been denied him for long periods and where what there was of it could only be snatched at intervals, as someone overcome with hunger might snatch at food, he had been adjusted to those uncertain moments. He had awakened in jeeps and in strange rooms in shell-torn hill towns. There was usually a moment on waking when the past was comfortably around him and when he thought he was in New York or at least in Washington. He could still remember with a sharp embarrassment that had never left him, waking that night in Palermo and knowing that he was not alone. There was, incidentally, one thing he could say for Laura Hopedale, not that he could not have added a number of others: she was what one might call a graceful sleeper, never wakeful, never restless. If her sleep was not the sleep of the just, it was more attractive than sheer justice. It had a serenity of its own, the reason for which, he had grown to understand, arose from Laura's belief in herself.

"Rhoda," he said, "is that you?"

He realized where he was directly after he had spoken, and

he hoped frantically that his voice had not awakened her, but it had. Laura had a way of always waking when she knew she ought, and she always knew exactly where she was.

"Try again," she said, and she began to laugh, and he could not blame her.

"I'm awfully sorry," he said. "It's just conditioned reflex, ingrained habit."

"Oh well," she said, "I hoped I'd broken you of the habit already. Never mind, I'll keep on trying."

"It won't be difficult," he said, "almost no trouble at all."

He had said it because it was high time he said something of a complimentary nature, and the memory of her answer still startled him.

"I know it won't," she said. "She's not the type that would be good in bed."

"Listen," he told her, "I know it's all over, and nobody has to remind me of it and I know I shouldn't have brought up her name, particularly under the circumstances, but simply out of justice, Laura, I really ought to say that Rhoda's the sort of person who's good at anything."

It was difficult to imagine a more indelicate conversation or one that could have made him more disturbed; yet he was always glad that he had made this speech about Rhoda, for he had made the record clear, and, curiously, Hopedale was not annoyed.

"Tom, dear," she said, "I love it when you're loyal."

He had not known her so well then, of course, as he had later. There was never anyone he had known, man or woman, who possessed the same sort of indestructibility. In a woman's college it might have been called "quality of leadership"; in the theatre, most markedly among the critics, it was usually called "presence"; it was something that had always made her noticed, no matter how terrible the play. It was an assurance that still made her one of the glamorous figures on the Coast, who could compete with the youngsters regardless of age. It was only after one got to know her that one realized her assurance had the hardness and sharpness of obsidian, but then, there was no use in going on about Hopedale. It had all been a mistake, for which he was to blame more than she.

He had seen his lawyer in New York shortly after V–E Day. The land was swarming now with internal revenue agents, social security agents, farm and veterans' agents, not to mention secret agents representing foreign powers, but in spite of proliferation, the great professions still existed that had formed the background of his life, the keystone of the arch, that trinity who, more than love, had made his world go around — the dentist, the doctor, and the lawyer.

Curiously, his reactions to these professions remained constant. In spite of the marked fallibility of individuals, he still believed that doctors, lawyers, and dentists were endowed with an infallibility greater than that of common men in that they were selfless individuals. Try as he might, whenever he entered a dentist's office timidity would seize him, not so much because of apprehension as because of respect for the white-jumpered man whose nimble fingers would never admit error and who could converse brightly and sometimes sing while performing feats more intricate than any accomplishment of a watchmaker. It was different in a doctor's office. There one put aside confections and trinkets like detachable gold bridges and faced antiseptically the facts of eventual dissolution — not that this fact would occur immediately. The doctor behind his desk and the pretty receptionist would keep you on your feet a while longer. "Well, well, Tom," the doctor would say, "excuse me for keeping you waiting, but I've been performing a tonsillectomy, an appendectomy and a couple of hysterectomies." He could still feel the graciousness of this confiding camaraderie and still feel himself, in spite of some disillusions, in the presence of something beyond his world.

He felt the same about lawyers. These fellows had often been ribbed by dramatists. Shakespeare had begun the fashion, and if he had not been mistaken, Molière had continued. Mr. Galsworthy, an admirable playwright in his way, had a milk-sipping lawyer in his drama concerning the gentleman card-cheat and the Jew. You could laugh at them, but like the doctor, they were there when you needed them, full of cool compassion, imbued with an intricate wisdom drawn from books in the law library which he had never seen them enter.

More than in the doctor's office, in the office of a good sound law firm (and thank God his law firm was a good sound one) you were in the shadow of tradition. You could feel it in the sure, academic quietness, the confidential secrecy of the partners' rooms, a little quaint, a trifle out of date, but with that aged-in-the-wood quality that denoted considered judgment. It had seemed to Tom from the beginning that he had required lawyers for one thing and another, and the firm, to which Dick Bramhall had sent him long ago, could handle anything. It was a firm, as Dick had said, that had deliberately not allowed itself to grow like many of the others, but it was as good as any in town, or better. For years he had gone there as trustingly as a little child with problems of plagiarism, contracts, drunken cooks, his income tax and his will, and they had never failed him. There was a friendship between a lawyer and client of a different depth and quality from the friendship existing between doctor and patient. It was a mellower and a wittier friendship, but when one came to grips with things, one always knew when the maestro was talking. The name of the firm had its own rocklike appeal to confidence: Cathcart, Brewis and Balch. It made no difference that the grasses had been growing on the graves of these three partners shortly after the turn of the century. The validity of the names was still there. Mingling with their office furniture and their moldering calfskin tomes, their ghosts walked with the pay envelopes into the back rooms where girls were typing out the briefs. Their ghosts appeared at the partners' annual dinner when Jack Scheaffer, now senior partner, arose, helped by two junior partners because of arthritis, and raised his glass of Burgundy to drink to the Loved and the Absent. There was probity in that old firm name, just as there was probity in the bills sent to its clients. For instance, when Harry Bleek, who was handling his affairs twenty years ago and was still handling them, sent him a bill for so many conferences, for so much study and for the preparation of this and that, he always also sent a covering letter of explanation.

There was a saying that one's lawyer ought to be a part of one's self. This may have been a sound idea, but in spite of their long association, Tom Harrow could not consider Harry Bleek as his alter ego, and on the June day when he came from Washington and climbed up the subway steps into the sunlight of Bowling Green, he still felt uneasy as he considered their approaching meeting.

He should have known there was no reason for concern, because the firm could handle anything and, as Harry had often said playfully, one learned more about human nature trying cases in the probate court than most analysts discovered by stretching patients out on couches. However, human nature as seen through the steel-rimmed spectacles of Harry Bleek, a homespun affectation, was different from life as Tom Harrow had observed it, more sharply defined, more governed by a compilation of rules, and also more naïve.

There were no new lines on the face of the middle-aged receptionist. The only thing new in the comfortable outer office was a freshly fashioned plaque entitled "Roll of Honor," placed beside the other two plaques, for the Spanish War and World War I — still entitled "The Great War" — plaques that bore the names of employees and a few of the more junior partners who had shouldered muskets.

"Good morning, Miss Prothero," he said to the receptionist. "Is Mr. Bleek ready to see me, do you think?"

Miss Prothero looked at him with a kindness that was almost maternal, although he was sure that she had never been a mother, on or off the record.

"Oh yes," she said, "I am almost sure that Mr. Bleek is waiting for you." That was the legal way — never stick your neck out until you had to lay it on the line. "I'll check to be certain. Are you back for good, Mr. Harrow?"

"No," he said, "I'm over from London carrying a few papers, a kind of office boy, Miss Prothero. I'll be going back as soon as they find some other papers for me to carry."

"I'll tell Mr. Bleek you are here," she said. "In the meanwhile, in case he's busy, wouldn't you like a cup of tea?"

"No," he said, "but thank you just as much. Even in London I never drink it until the sun is over the yardarm."

The remark echoed with tinny banality from the yellowing photographs of New York in the Great Blizzard that hung in the reception room.

"Mr. Bleek wants you to come in right away," Miss Prothero said. "He's not in his old office — in the next one up the hall to the left. Mr. Hotchkiss died last year, you know."

He sounded insincere when he said that he was sorry that Mr. Hotchkiss had died; he had never met Mr. Hotchkiss. The character of the Hotchkiss office, which smacked of early Americana and hooked rugs, showed that partners did not move everything with them as they moved up the hall, but Harry fitted into it.

Harry had said over the telephone that they had been understaffed during the war and thus he had been compelled to pull more weight in the boat than previously. Still, he did not look tired.

"Well, well," Harry Bleek said. "So the hero's returned again."

When you considered his uniform and the ribbons, of the sort that were passed about like popcorn, the comment was apt and perhaps ironical, but it was impossible to tell whether irony had been intended.

"The hero wishes to God he could stay returned," Tom said. "This hero is tired of being a hero. Confidentially, I never should have gone to this war. I'm afraid the journey wasn't worthwhile."

"Oh, don't say that, Tom," Harry said.

"All right," he said, "I won't if that's the advice of counsel. From over there in London, it seemed to me that things are moving pretty smoothly, Harry."

"Yes," Harry said, "we honestly felt quite happy about the small newspaper reaction. Probably we have the war to thank. I was a little unhappy about the bitter tone in the *Time* announcement. Of course one couldn't keep such VIP's as you

428

and Rhoda out of *Time* — but then, it did seem to me that *Time* was waspish about Rhoda — but then, you know how *Time* can be."

"I don't remember," he said. "How was *Time* waspish?"

"Here it is in the folder," Harry said, "from that section called 'Milestones': '*Divorced.* Soldier playwright, Thomas Harrow, by his wife Rhoda, the latter charging cruel and abusive treatment while he was with the Armed Forces overseas. In Reno, Nevada.' Of course, as I told them over at Smythe and Harrington, Rhoda should have braced herself for that sort of reaction."

"I'm sorry," Tom said, "if people are waspish. I'm not, you know."

"I know you're not, Tom," Harry said. "Have you seen Harold yet?"

It was an easy question that deserved an easy answer, and yet he found it difficult.

"No," he said. "I'm afraid I won't, this trip. The school's up in Massachusetts and I only have a day or two. Besides, from what you wrote, if I went up, I might disturb him."

"You don't know how much he wants to see you," Harry said. "You know he loves you, Tom."

"It's good to know," he said. "I wish he wouldn't blame it on Rhoda. Do you remember the old song about, 'Don't blame it all on Broadway, you've got yourself to blame'?"

"Tom," Harry said, "it's like old times seeing you, and of course I knew you'd take it like a soldier."

"Listen," he said, "not soldier, office boy."

"What makes us all happy in here," Harry said, "is that it hasn't got you down. Yes, maybe you'd do better not to see Harold until things have blown over. One thing at a time isn't such a bad motto when dealing with children in anomalous situations. Maybe it's wisdom to let new developments take their course."

Harry coughed involuntarily, which was the only sign of nervousness that he ever displayed, and it was time to ask the obvious question.

"What new developments?" Tom asked.

"Hasn't Rhoda written you?"

"Several times," he said, "but I've returned her letters unopened, at least with the censor's seals unopened. Wasn't that advice of counsel?"

Harry Bleek nodded and coughed again.

"I'm very glad you did, Tom," he said. "That's what I'm here for, as insulation, so you will not get yourself needlessly disturbed."

In spite of the difference between a doctor's and a lawyer's office, both had a somewhat similar atmosphere of suspense and dread. It was clear from the cough and the shuffling of papers that the insulation was coming off.

"Well," Tom said, "the disturbance is over, isn't it? I did what she wanted, didn't I?"

"Oh, yes," Harry said, "absolutely, everything that is basic is done. We have a letter here from Rhoda, a nice letter. She's a civilized girl, you know."

He wanted to say that he knew that she and the whole thing were civilized, but it was not civilized to lose one's self-control.

"All right," he said, "what's in the letter?"

He could still remember the impersonality of his lawyer's voice, demonstrating that a counselor could be at one moment personal and at another as aloof as the fates.

"Well, the first thing you've probably guessed already, because talk's been going around. I've warned you, haven't I, that you must expect to be talked about? First, she gives the news that she's marrying this man Brake, Presley Brake. It doesn't surprise you, does it?"

There was no way of hiding everything, and he felt indecently exposed.

"I hadn't heard," he said. "When you write her, give her my best wishes, will you? Now, is there anything else?"

"The else," Harry said, and blinded justice, the scales, and the sword were gone, "is something that surprised and pleased me and I do hope you're going to react in a similar way, Tom, because no matter how you construe it, it is a generous gesture."

"I can't wait," he said. "Go right ahead if it's pleasant."

"As you know," Harry said, "I've always thought you were

430

quixotic in the separation agreement. Although it was a splendid piece of generosity, I would have objected more strenuously if she had not given you the custody of Hal."

It was a time to keep his mind carefully on the words, but instead he thought of Hal.

"Considering the situation," Tom's mind was back on the words again, "none of us here felt there was any need of your giving her half your cash and securities, and now it seems that Rhoda agrees. The fact is, Tom, that this second husband of hers is very wealthy, and she wants to give the settlement back."

If there had been fewer things to think about at once, life always would have been happier, but usually it was impossible to get one thing separated from another.

"She wants to give it back?" he said. "I don't quite get it."

"That's right," Harry said. "She wants to return it."

"With those common stocks that were bought in the Thirties," Tom said, "the whole thing must amount to pretty nearly five hundred thousand dollars on paper."

Harry Bleek nodded. "If they were sold, there would be an enormous capital gains tax," he said.

"Goddammit," Tom said, "she always wanted security."

Lawyers always had their own professional way of dealing with human values.

"But don't you see," Harry said, "no doubt he's making a settlement on her. Believe me, he can afford it, even with the gift tax."

The impulses that made one act were never the logical ones. Given perspective, he could not tell whether he had been still in love with Rhoda at the time or whether his main feeling had been jealousy.

"All right," he said, "thank her and tell her I still don't want it. Don't forget we've been over all this before I ever consented to the divorce. She accepted that money because I told her I would not consent unless she did. The agreement's signed and sealed and she can't give it back now unless I agree. I don't agree. Let her keep the money. Money's been the main basis of our difficulties and I can get along with what I've got left."

431

There was a cold, disapproving silence.

"I wish you'd think that over," Harry said.

"All right," he said, "consider it thought over. Just tell her I refuse."

There was another silence.

"Tom," Harry said, "do you mind if I ask you a somewhat personal question? I wouldn't if it were not germane to your situation, and if we had not been friends so long."

"Why, no, of course not, Harry," he said. "Go ahead and ask it."

"Are you planning to marry Miss Hopedale? It's been in the Hollywood gossip columns, you know."

It was not a bad maxim to tell the truth and nothing but the truth. The only difficulty was that one never knew exactly what the truth might be, because truth very seldom precipitated out of thought in a true, crystal form, and all sorts of extraneous half-truths had a way of mingling with it.

"The thought has crossed my mind, but not seriously," he said. "I've not taken the matter up with Miss Hopedale even off the record. Does that answer your question?"

He had never seen Bleek in court, but he could believe that his persistence might be something in the nature of an achievement.

"Then there is a possibility?"

"Oh yes. I take it you disapprove?" he said.

In the last analysis, how much did he know about Harry Bleek, in spite of their years of relationship as lawyer and client? Harry was another of those façades behind which there was not much reason to look, except from intellectual curiosity, and Tom had never ventured to look very far.

"Both as a lawyer and as a friend," Harry said, "I cannot say that I either approve or disapprove. I have not had the pleasure of meeting Miss Hopedale, only of reading about her and seeing some most alluring photographs. Maida and I never go to the theatre much because the commute to West Redding is pretty hard at night. Besides, Tom, I have given up long ago advising friends or clients about their private lives, save as regards the possibilities of potential legal entanglements, which I am sure you, and Miss Hopedale also, will have the good taste to avoid. I can only venture one remark. I suppose you will — and I believe you should — marry someone. The position is more normal than single blessedness."

His mind had moved automatically to the Bleeks' faithfully treated salt-box house in West Redding.

"I don't know what I'm going to do," he said, "but I do feel goddamn lonely."

Sleep did not cut it off. As he lay there sleepless, everything moved on and there was too much of everything. Confessedly he had handled life as clumsily as alcoholics handled liquor. He had not built up a calmness or a tolerance to life. He had not possessed the patience to take the good with the bad, nor had he absorbed the knowledge that one had to take them both. There were all sorts of less gifted people than he who had made a success of living, and now that it was too late he believed he had the reason. He had been too concerned with other things to live. He had been too busy with illusion to worry over reality.

If he had been in another mood, less worried with introspection, he might have brought up that shopworn excuse that had served him many times before, the one which people in the theatre were forever using: loyalty to one's art, a form of dedication that condoned mundane irregularities. But living, as far as he knew it, was mainly made up of half loyalties, and often in his professional life he had only been half loyal. There were the trips to Hollywood which one could shrug off as useful technical experience, but they were there, and he had gone for money. He had to admit that it was his fault that others had driven him to produce a number of shallow plays for money that had diverted him from his own work. There was only one thing he could say. He had never trespassed against his own work and he could believe that it was one of the few trusts that he had kept, but was the trust worthwhile?

He turned on the bedside light and got to his feet, and the

light that pushed the darkness back from the room and from the blackness of the windows made things better.

The solution to the problem was, of course, the sleeping pills behind the mirrored door of the medicine chest in his bathroom. He had never started taking them until he had met Laura Hopedale, and they were not a habit with him even now. They were something to use in an emergency and not as a means of escape, but he knew the exact dosage. Given three of the yellow ones, and there were plenty in the bottle, he should be sound asleep in half an hour. Before he opened the medicine cabinet, he saw his face in the mirror. Time, of course, had marked his face; his hair was graying, but thank heaven he was not bald and thank heaven his face had not grown flabby. Standing there, seemingly looking at someone else, he could see that his face was handsome still and, thank heaven again, it was not immature. It even reflected traces of intelligence, and his eyes, in spite of the drinking, were bright and steady. It was the face he had known from day to day ever since he had watched it when he had started shaving at the Judge's house. But now there was something, that disturbed him: it was both his own and a stranger's face. It was another façade, and now he was frank to admit that he did not know what went on behind it. He could only make a guess, which may have been all that mortal man could ever do, in spite of that command that still was inscribed on what was left of the Temple of Apollo at Delphi.

He had been to Delphi once, with Rhoda, on a cruise they had taken to the Aegean during their last year at Antibes. He could remember his walk through the shattered ruins of the Periclean Age. He could remember the eagle circling over the distant mountaintop, and the bright glare of the sun, and the columns of the temple, gilded with age and sunlight. "Know thyself," was the command — not that he could read the Greek — and an excellent piece of advice it was. The only difficulty with it was that, like all advice, it was hard to follow. He had honestly tried to know himself, again and again and again. Indeed, there had even been occasions when he thought he had known himself, but self, at least insofar as he was acquainted with it, was forever chang-

434

ing; something new was always being added. Possibly all that anyone could do, in spite of the help of religion and of healers of the mind, was to have a polite, respectful bowing acquaintance with the ego, a sort of relationship that did not permit heart-to-heart discussions or true confessions.

It was disconcerting, while standing there looking at his image, which might not even be a true one due to the eccentricities of reflected light and to the fallibility of human vision, that he did not honestly know what sort of man he was. He only knew that he was there and that he could not escape. He thought; therefore he was. But even thinking was eccentric, depending on liquor or the liver or desire. Still, he thought, and therefore he was, and he had to do the best he could with being. At any rate, he had had enough of it. The title of it was like one of those last plays of O'Neill's, *A Long Day's Journey into Night,* and it was time to go to sleep.

XXVII

Emily Wasn't Feeling Very Well That Morning

BEFORE he was aware of a disturbance in his room, he knew that it was morning. Artificially induced drowsiness was still with him, combined, unfortunately, with the aftereffects of Scotch and water. Conscience told him even before he was awake that he was not in the nonsmoking, nonalcoholic, nonbarbiturate state of a model man. This did not mean that he suffered any specific physical malaise, but he was still coping with a lethal blankness that was not natural, and through this veil of discomfort, he heard Emily's voice. It was morning and it could only be Emily. Arthur should have known better than to have been infatuated so long by Emily. Arthur, too, had fallen while running through the script.

"Tom," Emily was saying, "Tom, dear, are you awake?"

He had learned from experience that it was never wise in an offhand way to underestimate the power of Emily. She had asked him that same question many times before in the period of their marriage, and once he had considered it indicative of Emily's scatterbrained quality until he eventually found that Emily's brains were seldom scattered. On its face the question was foolish, since she had asked it when he was asleep, but it had a purpose. It was a means of awaking him because she wanted to talk to him and it was more graceful than telling him in so many words to wake up. He gave his usual answer before opening his eyes.

"I was asleep," he said, "but now I'm awake."

Emily, too, gave her conventional answer with the same remorseful surprise she always used.

"Oh, darling," she said, "it was stupid of me and selfish not to have noticed. I thought you were cat-napping — I didn't know you were really asleep."

"Well," he said, "I imagine no irreparable harm has been done, Emily."

When he opened his eyes, he was aware that it was later than he thought, another sunny day with a hint of the beginning of summer in it. Then he saw that the door between their rooms was open and the half-opened door made him wonder idly how long she had stood waiting before she had ventured to speak to him. Without being able to explain how he knew, he was conscious of an atmosphere of studied preparation, an atmosphere that made him wish his mind were clearer, and Emily's appearance did not deceive him. She looked as though she had just jumped out of bed and thrown something over her, but that was the way Emily always appeared when she wished to have a serious morning's conversation. She undoubtedly remembered that he had once been charmed by this early-morning look, and occasionally Emily would forget that there could be too much of a good thing. Her beautiful ash-blond hair that amazingly was no darker than he first remembered it would not have been so *négligé* unless she had deliberately rumpled it; and her face would never have been so attractively unmade if she had not already passed a damp washcloth over it, and the tossed-over quality of her kimono was overdone. It was a lacquer-red kimono that Emily had purchased at the Royal Hawaiian on a trip they had taken to Honolulu. There was a white Fujiyama against the red background. But combined with this landscape, for no good reason except that the Japanese were an unpredictable people, were a number of white cranes, some in flight and some standing on one leg. He remembered, and something told him that Emily herself was quite sure he would remember, that he had once called it her "expectancy coverall." The kimono was draped about her in a careless way that would have shocked Madame Butterfly, but it had been made for Western consumption. And there was one more thing that was too deliberate to be real. Emily was in her bare feet, and, unlike some other women

437

he could mention, she had always been attractive when barefoot, with straight, almost Grecian toes that always sprang back promptly after being cramped in pointed slippers. If Emily had really popped half-thinking out of bed, the first thing she would have done would have been to pop into her mules, much as an aroused fireman would pop into his breeches before sliding down the brass pole. She had come in barefoot because she had wanted to have a good look at him before asking him her question and the tapping of the mules might have disturbed him.

"I wouldn't have dreamed of waking you," she said. "You came up so late after everyone had gone. You must have been down there worrying, and ordinarily I would have come down and worried with you, except you were so cross last night — only to me. You were so sweet to everybody except me. You were just as cross as a bear with a sore head to me, last night."

He wished that he might think idly of the origins of a bear with a sore head, but there was not time.

"Yes," he said, "I was annoyed with you last night, in particular when we were dressing for dinner. That's when family rows usually start in a good play, don't they? There's always a comedy value in a conjugal quarrel if the man is snapping his suspenders and the wife is snapping her garter."

But Emily was not listening. Her mind was on something else.

"You're not still cross, are you, dear?" she asked. "I didn't mean half what I said. I was awfully tired yesterday. Tom, you're not really cross, are you?"

"I don't know yet," he said. "I haven't pulled myself together yet."

"Tom," she said, "you're feeling all right, aren't you?"

"Oh, yes," he said, "I guess I'm feeling all right."

"What you need," she said, "is a good cup of coffee. How would it be if I asked Alfred to bring our breakfast upstairs and we had it in my room? And I won't complain about crumbs in bed. Do you remember when you used to call me 'the Princess and the Crumb'?"

"Yes," he said, "now you mention it. In fact, I'm rather sure my recollective faculties aren't failing yet."

"Oh, darling," she said, "who ever said anything about your faculties failing?"

"At the moment I can't recollect," he said. "Perhaps I'll be able to after I've had a shower, and don't correct me — don't say I should have said, 'after I've showered.'"

"Darling," she said, "you do feel better than you did last night, don't you?"

"I won't know," he said, "until I've showered."

"Darling," she said, "I'll ring and have breakfast brought up. Don't worry about anything until you've had your coffee."

"Thanks," he said, "I'll have breakfast downstairs. I've got a lot to do today."

The change that came over her ingenuous, early-morning face made him feel sharply sorry, even when he told himself that his weakness had always been feeling sorry for people, in particular the girls. He had felt sorry for Emily when she spoke to him when he went to bed, and now his sorrow increased. He saw that she was desperately afraid, afraid of his displeasure and of her sudden lack of security. He wondered if she had been doing mental arithmetic. If so, she would have known that she could not count on comfortable alimony. The cornucopia was growing empty. The goose was running out of golden eggs.

"Tom," she said, "couldn't we go away somewhere for the day and talk about plans and things, just you and me, and we could take a picnic?"

She had always hated picnics. The mere suggestion was a measure of her desperation. He felt sorry, but at the same time he did not care, and, with the sun outside and the morning moving on, that lack of caring was the worst of it. Nevertheless, it was still hard to explain specifically why Emily's suggestion should have filled him at the moment with such irrational repugnance. It may have had something to do with that awkward reminiscence of the Princess and the Crumb, which not only brought his mind back to a younger time but made him wonder how he could even then have enjoyed eating breakfast in bed with Emily; and the suggested picnic was still worse. Emily had reached the age where any exertion caused a run in the nylons. Then there was a picture of Emily eating a sandwich. The only time they had ever tried such an experiment, insects of all kinds had begun attacking Emily; black ants, beetles, and caterpillars deliberately left their ordinary environment to crawl over her in a different and more aggressive manner from any they had practiced when crawling over him.

"It's awfully kind of you to suggest such an outing," he said. "Some other time, but not today."

"But Tom," she said, "I'm only trying to be helpful. I'm only trying to share your troubles."

"That's very generous of you, Emily," he said, "but not today."

"Tom," she said, "that's what a wife is for, isn't it, to share her husband's troubles?"

The generality reminded him of Rhoda, but here the parallel ended.

"I suppose that's one of the things she's for," he said, "on paper."

"Tom, dear," she said, "it doesn't help to be cynical, and I don't think either of us should adopt a don't-look-now attitude if things are as bad as you say they are."

"That's right," he said, "we mustn't sweep it under the rug. Don't worry, I'm going to face facts fearlessly just as soon as I've showered."

"Tom," she said, and there was a catch in her voice that was not the Higgins catch. The truth was that she was afraid of what he might do, and the relationship was new to him. She had never been afraid of him before. "Tom, please don't be evasive. Can't we face this together?"

The worst of it, as he weighed those words, was the realization that they had never truly faced anything together. He had never wanted any such support from her, and now it was too late. The traveling clock on his bedside table showed that it was a quarter of ten, not an unusually advanced hour, since the theatre had made him an habitually late riser, but he had a sense of impending events. It was time to start moving.

"There's going to be plenty of time to talk about this, plenty of time," he said, and he pushed back the bedclothes and got up.

As he did so, Emily's glance told him that he was not as attractive in disarray as she was, and anyway he did not feel in the least alluring. Once when he had been in a hospital for some reason or other, and he had rung and rung for the floor nurse, he had got out of bed, although he had been told he should not move. The nurse had come in the moment he was looking for his slippers and her expression had been very much like Emily's.

"Tom," she said, "where did you get those pajamas? I never bought them for you."

"It's all right," he said, "nobody else did, either. I bought them in Baltimore last winter when Alfred forgot to pack pajamas."

"They look dreadfully," she said.

"Yes," he said, "both they and I, but we'll look better after we've showered."

"Tom," she said, "don't say 'showered' again. It drives me crazy the way you harp on a word, and it isn't very funny. I noticed it the first time I met you. I think it's a nervous habit."

"I guess it is," he said, "I guess it's a means of hiding inadequacy."

Emily sighed. It was her rehearsed sigh of exasperation, but there was also a wistful note of failure in it.

"Tom," she said, "please. We've got to mean something to each other. I simply can't worry the way I have all night — worrying and doing nothing."

It was no time to talk and, looking at Emily, he knew she was willing to talk interminably.

"Emily," he said, "there isn't anything to do right now. I'll have a long talk with you later, but I've got to do some telephoning now and write some letters. I've got to call up Harry Bleek. I'm going to ask him to come down here. Harry will get us straightened out."

"Well, at least tell me what you are going to do today," Emily said. "If I can't do anything else, I can plan the meals."

441

He had to admit that she had a right to make the request.

"After all, we are married," she said, "in case you've forgotten, and Arthur Higgins advised me not to, in case I never told you."

"That's all right," he said, "you've told me, but Arthur never did."

"At least," she said, "are you going to be in for lunch, or are you going to leave me again listening to Walter Price? He's your guest, not mine, and I can't take it indefinitely."

"Don't worry," he said. "I don't think Walter will be here indefinitely, but I won't be in for lunch. There'll be telephone calls and going over accounts. I'll have lunch sent out."

"Oh," she said, "lunch with Mulford again, is it?"

"Don't," he said. "Be big, be kind and generous, Emily."

"I am kind," she said. "I'm very sorry for Mulford and for all the other people around here who have to assuage your ego. You're getting to be more like Arthur Higgins every day, except dear Arthur was always sweet about it." Then there was a change in her voice. "Tom, I gather you're not going to be around this afternoon. Will you want the new car or the station wagon?"

"How did you know I was going out?" he asked.

"Oh, never mind," she said, "but I suppose you'll want the new car. Tom, we've got to have it out. We may as well face it."

She was standing up straighter and, with an adroit shift of her shoulders, she made the red kimono less like a peignoir and more like the draped gown of a Roman matron. He should have known that something unexpected was coming the moment she had asked him if he was awake.

"Aren't we facing enough right now," he asked, "without bringing in something new?"

"Tom," she said, "why can't you be frank? You're going to see that woman."

From long experience he knew exactly whom Emily meant. She had often referred to Rhoda as "that woman" and to Laura Hopedale as "that bitch." Emily always kept things straight. It spoke well for Rhoda that the terms had never been interchangeable.

"How did you find that out?" he asked. "Did Hal tell you?"

She looked resignedly noble as she stood there gazing at a spot some inches above his head, noble and very gentle.

"No, dear," she said. "In case you're apprehensive, Hal hardly ever tells me anything, but I heard you and Hal talking about it downstairs last night."

"Oh," he said, "you mean you came down and listened?"

"That's what you always say about me," Emily said. "You always think I'm listening, don't you?" She laughed gently, "I would call it a bad conscience if I didn't know you better, dear. Tom, I was worried about you, and I have a right to worry, haven't I? I knew you hadn't come upstairs and I knew that Hal was concerned too, and I know how devoted he is to you. When he went downstairs, I knew he was afraid that something might have happened to you, and so I followed him as any real wife should do. Of course I heard you talking, but it was an accident, not eavesdropping, and don't say it was." Her voice broke. "Because I have enough without that to make me unhappy."

He found himself looking at her bare feet. If she had worn her mules, he would have heard them tapping on the stairs; but, in fairness, she might have been in such a hurry to be sure that nothing had happened to him that she had forgotten her mules.

"You were asking Hal why that woman wanted to see you," she said. "I couldn't help but hear, dear, because the door was open and your voice was loud, the way peoples' voices get with alcohol."

If one began talking with Emily, she talked and talked, and the morning was moving on, and, as Emily had said, he needed a cup of coffee.

"I hadn't meant to tell you," he said. "I would have except it would only have been another complication." He was annoyed to find himself speaking volubly and guiltily when there was nothing whatsoever to be guilty about. "Rhoda called up Hal yesterday and said that she wanted to see me. They're staying up at the Wellington Manor House for a few days, and as long as she said it was very important, I told Hal I'd go."

443

"Tom," she said, "does that woman want to see you about me?"

It was a silly question, but he could not blame her for being curious.

"Now, Emily," he said, "I don't see why you should come into this. You've hardly ever met her, have you?"

Emily breathed in deeply, and this was always a bad sign.

"I know what she wants to see you for," she said, "just as sure as if she'd told you. She wants you to leave me. She wants to have you back."

He experienced a strange sensation that was like a note of freedom, a note of hope, a note of the impossible.

"Don't," he said. "Don't let's be sillier than necessary, Emily. I haven't seen Rhoda since she wrote me that letter to Africa. Let's keep things on an even basis."

Emily's voice grew louder, and it was not her acting voice. "You love her," she said, "you've always loved her. Don't tell me you don't still love her."

The worst of the moment was that what Emily had said was true, and the devastating simplicity of it shocked him.

"Emily," he said, "it doesn't do any good to go on like that. I'll be back in time for dinner and I'll promise to tell you everything that's happened — but don't let's be silly, Emily."

"You love her," Emily said, and her voice was still louder. "Why do you deny it? Why can't you face up to anything? You loved her so much that you married that bitch, and that's why you married me, because you still loved her. You wanted me to get you away from it. I've tried. I've tried, Tom, but I can't keep on trying."

It had been a long while since he had felt so uncomfortable. He had never dreamed that Emily could be capable of upsetting him in just that way.

"Emily," he said, "it doesn't do any good to go on like this. This sort of thing doesn't help."

Few palliatives were ever more futile at such a time than words of reason. It was an occasion when nothing was helped by anything.

"Why are you such a coward?" she said. "Why don't you stand up like a man and admit you love her?"

Like a lot of Emily's questions, it led to nothing useful. He did not want to hear any more. He wanted to get away. He did not like to admit that he was afraid of Emily, but he wanted to get away. The older one got, the more anxious one was to escape from truth and revelation because one learned that they were increasingly incontrovertible.

"Emily," he said, "please stop this nonsense. Go and get some clothes on. I've got to take a shower."

When he had slammed and locked his bathroom door, he was aware that he had hurried, in fact had scuttled past her furtively, and her voice rang through the closed door. Arthur Higgins had always maintained that players must be heard to the outermost limits of an acoustically bad theatre.

"It isn't nonsense, Tom," she called. "You love her. You've always loved her. You're going away and leave me — don't say you're not. You're going away and leave me, Tom!"

She was still talking when he turned on the shower, although her words were indistinguishable; she was still talking, and she had made him run away. His thoughts were as confused as her muffled voice until he realized that they were moving, in a familiar repetitious pattern, along the sad incline of severing human relations over which the thoughts of others must have run before the Neolithic period. He was wondering again what he had ever seen in Emily that had made her charming to him and acutely desirable. He was wondering what refraction of mental light, what secret conjuring of mirrors could have made her seem once mentally and physically compatible and the ultimate answer to life's great unsolved problem. It was shocking to realize that he had asked himself these identical questions about Laura Hopedale as well as about several other women whom, by the grace of God, he had not married. What was it that inevitably happened to him, given a certain mood and place? Was his judgment of women invariably fallacious, or had they all been different once, only to slump into a slough of change while he alone remained discriminatingly superb?

445

There had been something that had attracted him. He must have been, even in his worst moments, observant enough and intelligent enough to have separated sensible selection from the biological urge. On the other hand, it could possibly be that there was nothing whatsoever sensible in natural selection. Nature was always marking the cards and stacking the decks and Nature may have been amused by eventual upset and disillusion. At any rate, Nature did not care as long as desire continued or could be renewed by another face, or another type of charm. Nature did not care about monogamy or marriage counsels and Nature was wary of all forms of sublimation. Nature's business was to let the race go on until Nature capriciously wearied of the species. What about the dinosaurs, or again, what about Peking man?

The dining room, when he came down, gave him an illusion of repetition that be welcomed, since it removed part of his thoughts from the scene upstairs. Besides, his mind was adroit in moving from scene to scene and in show business hysteria was always just around the corner. The whole dining room might have been yesterday instead of today. The misty sunlight of late May again coming through the window had the same value as yesterday, creating the effect that he had tried in vain to approximate with artificial lighting. Outside, the sunlight on the budding lilacs and on the soft, timid green of the just-evolved elm trees gave a note of hope. In fact, there was nothing in the world as hopeful as a New England spring or as maturely melancholy as an ending New England autumn. O'Neill had felt the beat of both these seasons, and, once felt, they created a mental climate that could never be erased.

Walter Price was sitting at his place looking exactly as he had yesterday, except that he was wearing a fresh white shirt. Its freshness showed that he must have arranged for Alfred to get Ruth to wash and iron it for him. Say what one might about Walter, with colored people he always had a way due doubtless to his association with them on the old plantation. As he had often said, no one but a Southern gentleman really understood

Negroes; and colored people, even up at Harlem, he always said, recognized a Southern gentleman. Walter was eating exactly what he had eaten yesterday, grilled kidneys, and he himself must have arranged with Alfred to obtain these, because Emily had always winced at the idea.

"Good morning, Walter," Tom said, and his own voice sounded like yesterday. "Are they giving you everything you want?"

Doubtless because of the kidneys, Walter had adopted his British intonation, showing that his thoughts were with the Price branch that had crossed the channel with William of Normandy and were depicted on the Bayeux tapestry.

"Good morning, dear old boy," Walter said, "you're looking very fit this morning. Fit as a fiddle, to use an American anachronism."

"That's right, Walter," he said, "to quote from a recent American ballad, fit as a fiddle and ready for love."

"Oh dear," Walter said, "not at breakfast, Tommy. It's been my observation that love usually takes a holiday at breakfast."

Tom was glad to be back with Walter and to be dealing with facts of friendship, more durable than love. At least they could still each accept the other and understand the other and tolerate and be amused by the other — always within limitations.

"Perhaps you're right," he said. "I hope Alfred remembered your gin, Walter. Next time you come, I'm going to have a bathtub rack made especially for gin bottles."

Then he remembered that there could not be a next time in that house, but Walter, if he recollected it also, ignored the thought.

"Oh, no," Walter said, "Alfred did not forget the gin, the warmth against the cold, the spirit of fortitude against misfortune. That is a thought that comes over me whenever I plunge into my cold tub and swallow from a bottle of House of Lords, not that House of Lords is absolutely necessary. You should try it yourself sometime, Tommy."

It occurred to Tommy that he had tried too many things, so

447

many that his curiosity might be ebbing, so many that experience in the end was a continuous production line.

"I've always heard that some of the world's greatest thoughts have emanated from bathtubs," he said. "Personally, I wouldn't know. Personally, I shower."

There he was again. Emily was correct; he was repeating himself, but he had always been entertained by his own humor.

"Good morning, Alfred," he said. "I'll have the same breakfast, please."

"Good morning, sir," Alfred said, "will you be having lunch with Mrs. Harrow and Mr. Harold?"

"No," he said, "send some out to me when you send Miss Mulford's."

"The kidneys are delicious this morning, Alfred," Walter said. "But speaking of thoughts of bathtubs, I had a most entertaining thought sequence this morning. For the life of me I cannot understand how it happened to leap the way it did out of the stream of memory."

"No one ever knows," Tom Harrow said. "Personally I was struggling with a few thoughts myself last night." But Walter was thinking of his own experience. He was off to the land of myths.

"I was thinking of Jimmy Finnegan's gym," he said.

In spite of the years, Tom never could tell where Walter's inventiveness might move next.

"Jimmy Finnegan's gym?" Tom said. "Where was that, Walter?"

"Oh, a noisome place west of Sixth Avenue," Walter said, "where fighters used to train. You've heard of Jimmy Finnegan, 'Sunny Jim' Finnegan, the writers used to call him. Sunny Jim, the lightweight. He lasted ten rounds with Benny Leonard — But surely you remember Sunny Jim."

"No," Tom Harrow said, "no, I don't remember."

"I keep forgetting," Walter said, "that we are not quite contemporaries. It would be a few years before your time. Sunny Jim was always one of my admirers, before I hung up my gloves."

448

"Why, Walter," Tom Harrow said, "I didn't know you either hung up or put on gloves."

"Well, well," Walter said, "it was only detail. Ever since I began boxing in the Yale gym as an undergraduate with the boxing teacher, Tex Tellegan, I always had a weakness for the sport. There's nothing like it for keeping down the waistline."

Walter was watching him and did not continue with his vanished boxing career. You could never be sure how much fact Walter perceived when his mind was in the realm of myths. It was disconcerting sometimes to discover how much Walter knew in terms of plain, cold truth.

"Tom," Walter asked, "can we hope that dear Emily will join us looking like Brunhilde in one of her damask housecoats?"

"Emily wasn't feeling very well this morning," Tom said. "I don't think she's coming down for breakfast."

"Dear Emily," Walter said. "The news, I suppose, the news. Strange, men can take bad news and rock with the punches, as we used to say at Sunny Jim's, but women cannot take it like men, although they can stand physical suffering much better. Even Maxine Elliott would wince at misfortune. Dear Maxine, she used to understand me, but then, with the age differential, the understanding was more maternal than otherwise. Dear Maxine — but she could not take bad news."

When he looked at Walter Price, he felt free from a number of cares, because the bad news that Walter had taken in his lifetime was virtually continuous and enormous in its total, but Walter had absorbed it. Walter had escaped from it. In fact, it was even possible that Walter was happy, no longer defensive, merely contemptuous in the face of new advancing failure.

"Walter," he said, "I don't care so much about myself. What with one thing and another I've had to think about money, but I've never cared about it seriously. I'm only sorry about your five thousand, and I'm sorry about Emily. None of it is her fault, after all, and Emily's always done the best she could."

He immediately disapproved of his frankness, because it occurred to him that it was almost the unkindest thing a man

449

could say about a woman — that she had done the best she could. The appraisal was insufferably patronizing, even when sprinkled with the powdered milk of human kindness. Yet the truth remained that Emily had done the best she could and the truth remained that there had not been much more for her to do, and this was his fault because, he realized, he had never honestly wanted her to do any more. He had only wanted her beauty and her cheerfulness and occasionally her sympathy. Now, having been so frank, he felt himself impelled to move on further.

"Perhaps, Walter," he said, "I've never asked enough of any woman. Maybe I've never known how. I've always expected them to do the asking. Somehow I've never got around to asking back."

"Dear old boy," Walter said, "that is very nicely put, but then, in my experience, women always jump the gun when it comes to asking and it's all a man can do as a rule to get a mild request in edgewise. Which reminds me of my experience with the Contessa Maria in Florence — good form forbids my telling you her high and resounding title. Dear Maria — did I ever tell you about Maria?"

"No," he said, "I don't think you ever have, Walter."

"Well, remind me of it sometime, old boy," Walter said. "There's nostalgia in that memory as well as sadness, and Maria, though from an environment quite different from Emily's, shared many of Emily's drives. But never mind it now."

He could not understand why Walter had stopped about the Contessa; it was unlike Walter to stop. It made one confused and it put one off, but in the pause that followed that lack of reminiscence, he found himself discovering that there was something he wanted very much to learn from Walter Price.

"Walter," he said, "am I right in my idea that Emily has changed considerably since I met her at Arthur Higgins's? I'm trying to think what she was like, and it's damned funny, I can't exactly remember."

"Dear old boy," Walter said, "I see your point. It is much like myself and the Contessa, our first chance meeting on the

Ponte Vecchio. I can only remember the charm of it, and I do know she was very different later. For example, when she tried to stab me after tea at Doney's."

"Good God, Walter," he said, "why did she try to stab you after tea? What did you do at Doney's?"

"Dear old boy," Walter said, "you know as well as I that one never does anything at Doney's, but I'll tell you some other time. We were talking about Emily and not about dear, dead days in Florence. You may remember that I was there when you met. I was aware, if I may say so, of the mutual attraction, as was dear old Arthur. Dear Arthur, I can recall his happy relief and I can recall what he said after you had taken Emily out to the opening at the Lyceum. 'Walter,' he said, 'I do believe that Tommy might look out for Emily.' And do you know what I said to dear old Arthur?"

"No," he answered, "what did you say, Walter?"

"I said, 'Be careful, Arthur, not to throw them too obviously together.'"

"Oh," he said, "you did, did you?"

"Of course I did not use those words, old boy," Walter said, "but I was sympathetic with Arthur's anxiety and his answer was typically Arthur. 'Tommy needs some woman to look after,' Arthur said. 'He never will need any woman to look after him.'"

He was sure that Walter was finally dealing with accuracy. It sounded like Arthur Higgins. Tom could perceive his own inadequacy now that it was, as usual, too late, but Walter was continuing.

"Dear Emily, there were so many others who wanted to look after her."

He could remember all the others. There were Henry J. Alvin, in the wholesale jewelry business; and Bassett Tomkins, from Toledo; and Merton Hewes, another director from Hollywood; and Coburn Croll, the new curator of an American Wing being added to a museum in Des Moines or Wichita or somewhere. They had all wanted to look after Emily, and he had won the wanting contest. It was unfortunate for Emily. Those others may have lacked charm and glamour, but they

451

would have been far better. He knew what women wanted —
Rhoda had told him. And he had let Emily down.

"Walter," he said, "may I ask you a question? It's going to put
you on a spot, but I'd like to know. Do you think I'm slipping?"

He saw Walter's eyes widen. He was watching, fascinated,
because it did not matter whether Walter told the truth or not.
Walter could not hide the truth, no matter what he said.

"Slipping?" Walter asked. "Slipping in what way?"

It gave him a sickening sensation when Walter hesitated.
He could tell himself that Walter's opinion was nothing, but at
the same time he knew this was not true.

"Professionally," he said. "Go ahead and tell me — am I slipping, Walter?"

Walter would not tell him in so many words, but the answer
would be there.

"Tommy," Walter said, "I don't see what's worrying you."

"Go ahead," he answered, "and tell me, Walter."

"Why, Tommy," Walter said, "you're the best in the field. I
don't have to tell you that. It's the consensus of opinion. You
have maturity, Tommy. I wouldn't worry — you're better than
you were."

It was pathetic, the relief he felt, and Walter was still speaking.

"I see now," he said. "You heard Emily yesterday talking here
at breakfast. I remember the door was open."

He nodded and there was no reason to apologize.

"Tommy," Walter said, "it's only dear Emily. Dear Emily, she
was only seeking for security."

"Jesus," he said, "let's not use that word again. I've got to go
out. I've got to call up New York, Walter."

"Tommy," Walter said, "a stay with you has always been a
delightful interlude. I can't remember whether or not I mentioned last evening that I'm going north to Ogunquit this morning."

"Why, no," Tom said, "I can't remember your saying it. I'll
miss you, and I'm glad you've been here at just this time."

"Dear old Tommy," Walter said, "telephone New York. I'll

452

wait to say good-by to Hal. If I can get that play in summer production at Ogunquit, there will be no trouble finding capital. I'll wait and say good-by to Emily. I suppose she'll be down before long."

"Oh yes," he said, "Emily will be down. Forgive me for leaving, Walter."

Old friends were the best friends was the way the saying went, but none of those sayings was invariably correct. He felt regret and also pleasure that Walter Price was leaving. Old friends knew too much and one knew too much about old friends. One could read between the lines too often and too far. One could detect too easily pity and compassion. Walter had underlined nothing, but Walter's knowledge of that first meeting at Arthur Higgins's apartment was too accurate to require explanation. Walter had been an open book all the while he had been speaking. Walter had as good as said that Emily should have married someone else. Walter had as good as said that he had always disapproved and now it was too late. There was only one consolation; it had been too late from the beginning and now it was time to call New York.

XXVIII

Mr. Harrow Would Much Rather Not Wait for Half an Hour

THE LIGHT in the converted carriage house was too bright and too cheerful and it seemed to him that Nancy Mulford sitting at the table and sorting out the mail also looked too bright.

"Walter Price is going away this morning," he said, "up to Ogunquit to see about the summer theatre."

"He finally asked for a loan, then," she said.

He nodded. He was glad to be with someone who knew everything so well that there was no reason to explain.

"There's no reason for you to worry about the mail," she said, "and I've done the new draft of the third act. You've got it pulled together." She smiled faintly. "You always do better when you're worried."

"You really think it's better?" he asked.

"Yes," she said, "it's good. It doesn't need any more. You never help by working over things too much."

"So you don't think I'm slipping?" he asked.

"I always think you're going to be sure of yourself sometime," she said.

She never had been able to sympathize with his perpetual uncertainty.

"Well, anyway," he said, "Walter says I'm not slipping."

"You asked him, didn't you?" she said. "I don't see why you do things like that. You don't look as though you'd slept well."

"Not very well," he said. "There was a little trouble at the house last night. The news, you know."

"It must have been bad," she said, "but after all . . ."

"After all, what?" he asked.

"After all, you're not going to the poorhouse," she said.

"Yes," he said, "I know. I told you not to be upset, and I'm not upset any longer. I've worked my way through it; it took me most of the night, but I'm not upset."

"I'm glad," she said, "that makes me feel better." Then she shook her head sharply. "I'm sorry I said that."

"I don't see why," he said.

"Because it doesn't belong in the script," she said, "and speaking of the script, I hope you're not going to pull it to pieces any more. You'd better run through it just once this morning and I'll send it to New York. You'll feel better when it's over."

"Running through the script," he said, "running through the script."

"Yes," she said, "I know the rest of it. You do feel better this morning."

"Yes," he said, "and I'll tell you why if you want to know, because I have charm and no character."

"I know what you mean," she said, "but it isn't exactly so. You always have character when you're running through the script."

"You mean I don't fall down?" he said.

"No," she said, "not in the script you don't."

"That's the nicest thing you've said for quite a while," he told her.

"Don't make me feel like a secretary," she said. "And you can strike that out, too. It isn't in the script."

"Now that I look at you," he said, "you didn't sleep so well last night yourself, did you?"

"No," she said. "I didn't know exactly what you were going to do. But never mind."

"I'm all right," he said, "I really am. Now get me New York. I've got to speak to Mr. Bleek, and don't go away and close your office door."

"You're not afraid to talk to Mr. Bleek alone, are you?" she asked.

"No, embarrassed," he said. "He's got to come up here and bail

455

me out again. All charm, no character. God, I wish I had some character."

"If you had the kind you mean," she said, "it wouldn't go with the script."

"Running through the script," he said, "running through the script."

"It's there on the table," she said, "and it'll be better if you do something this morning."

"All right," he said, "I'll work on it until two. I'm having lunch sent out here. I don't want to go back to the house. It's got too much unresolved guilt. Honestly, it kept me up all night until I took three pills."

"All right," she said, "and I'll give you a drink before lunch. What are you doing the rest of the afternoon?"

"Oh," he said, "the rest of the afternoon. That's right, I didn't tell you. I wish you'd tell Alfred to have Michigan's latest art triumph ready and brushed and polished by two. I particularly want the big car. Mrs. Harrow called up Hal, that is, I mean, Mrs. Brake called up Hal. They're staying at the Wellington Manor House. It sounds like a college dorm, doesn't it? She wants to see me privately. I don't know what she wants, but I think I'd better go."

"If you'd like, I'll drive up with you," she said. "I mean, if you can't tell what it's going to be about, and I don't think Mrs. Brake would mind."

He was sure that Rhoda would not mind. If she saw Miss Mulford in the new car, she would only say it was characteristic, that he could never face anything alone.

"I think I'd better go by myself," he said. "This is do-it-yourself day. I'm going to speak to Mr. Bleek myself and drive the car myself and fix the script myself and eat my lunch myself — but you can mix me a drink before lunch. And now get Mr. Bleek, and please don't go away."

Her clear voice as she placed the call with the operator made him believe that everything was pulled together. It was suggestion more than fact when he heard her voice because she had always pulled things together and she had seen him in every mood.

It had been years since he had thought it was necessary to hide his thoughts or feelings from her. It was one of those situations that they loved in Hollywood and one which was understood in America at least, the business relationship between a man and a woman, a strange mixture of the impersonal with a deeply personal understanding. Sex did not have to enter into it, and perhaps that was what made the thing for him unique. Nothing ever had to be resolved, except in Hollywood. The great thing about the co-existence was that it was not conjugal. There simply was no competition and no need to put a face on things. She had seen him in every possible mood, drunk and sober, elated or discouraged, sad or angry. She could make a sound prediction of his reactions; she knew his weaknesses without using this knowledge as a weapon; she knew them much better than he knew hers, and the beauty of it was that he did not have to know about hers. The only effort necessary for him was to do his work, and there would be no disturbance, no extraneous detail. It was completely peaceful there as he heard her speaking.

"Yes," she was saying, "but Mr. Harrow wants to speak to him."

She put her hand over the transmitter, efficiently and carefully in a way she had done for years. He could not understand why the gesture should make him wonder why she had never married.

"He's in conference now," she said.

"Oh, hell," he said, and when she smiled he was certain she had known exactly what he would say.

"He wants to know whether it's important, or whether he can call you back in half an hour," she said. "He would rather not leave the conference."

Doctors and lawyers invariably shared this common attribute which consisted in an annoying superevaluation of their time and the implication that they were different from other people. It had always exasperated him, that he was one of these artistic ne'er-do-wells to whom time meant nothing.

"You don't have to tell me that," he said. "You know I wouldn't call him at all if it wasn't urgent. Go ahead, get him on the wire."

She smiled, but her voice had not lost its musical formality.

"Mr. Harrow is sorry to bother Mr. Bleek," she said, "but he does say it's urgent. He would much rather not wait for half an hour."

She nodded to him and smiled again.

"Mr. Harrow's right here," she said, "if you can put Mr. Bleek on. Good morning, Mr. Bleek, Mr. Harrow is right here."

It was a part of the game she had always played, the game of keeping him off the telephone until the other one was on. She had always welcomed his delaying slightly. He seated himself carefully before the writing table and put his own hand over the transmitter when she passed him the telephone.

"Don't go away," he said, "please don't go away."

He waited for a moment, counting a thousand and one, a thousand and two, a thousand and three because he knew it would make her happy.

"Hello, Harry," he said, "I'm sorry to have kept you waiting, but I didn't know I could get you so soon. I've just been at the doorway of my study here, watching the birds in my feeding station. There were two cedar waxwings this morning, and a grosbeak."

When a telephone connection was good, there was no need, given imagination, for a television.

"Were you literally looking at birds," Harry Bleek asked, "or were you saying that simply because Maida and I have a feeding station?"

"Frankly, I was only speaking poetically, Harry," he said.

"Listen, Tom," Harry said, "I'm just in the middle of an important meeting, and if you'll excuse my saying so, I don't care momentarily about birds, poetically or otherwise."

"All right," he said, "never mind the birds for the moment. I very seldom do, even when they're bathing."

"Tom," Harry Bleek said, "not being a genius or an eccentric, and being seldom able to amuse other people by my whimsies, is it all right if you and I get down to the point? I was told that this was urgent. Is it?"

He smiled at Nancy Mulford, hoping that she had heard the question.

"Yes," he said, "I'm afraid it is urgent, Harry, but I felt the very urgency demanded that I might set the scene."

"Very well," Harry said, "I understand you now. I must apologize and say that I've temporarily overlooked my experiences with genius. From my observation, when you behave like this you're usually in a jam. All right, what's the jam this time?"

Tom Harrow found himself shaking his head. In the end he was never able to compete with a legal mind.

"Do you think you could take the night train up here?" he asked. "Or a plane? You're right, I'm in a jam and I think maybe you'd better get up here, Harry."

"I'm calling for my schedule," Harry said. "If it's bad, I'll take the night train, and you can send that colored professor of yours to meet me. How bad is it this time?"

There was patience in the "this time," a patience that showed the client was incorrigible, a patience without the charity to admit that anyone after his formative years was, to a certain extent, incorrigible.

"Harry," he said, "I don't know how it is. I try and try in many very earnest and thoughtful ways, but I never do seem to be able to get back to normalcy. I have only one consolation, Harry, the United States of America, that great nation in which we live, has never got back to normalcy either, not since the late President Harding."

"Tom," Harry said, "will you kindly be cooperative. What is it this time? Is it money this time, or women?"

He found himself moving as uneasily as a Catholic in the confessional.

"If it's all the same to you," he said, "I wish you'd take my word that this is serious. I can't go into it over the telephone, but I will say this: in my experience and in the work we've done together hitherto, women and money are more or less synonymous."

"My God," Harry said, "is it Emily?"

He moved again uneasily. He had never believed in indulging in true confessions over the telephone.

"Not Emily in particular," he said. "It's a mixture of everything, and all my fault, Harry, entirely my fault. But this time it's mostly money."

"I think you'd better be more explicit," Harry said. "Hopedale's not bringing suit, is she? Not again?"

"Oh, no," he said, "it isn't that. I'm only reaping my just deserts."

"I think you'd better be more explicit," Harry said. "Is there any sort of threatened action? I ought to know before I take the train."

He was feeling tired.

"Listen, Harry," he said, "you'll find out when you get up here. There's quite a lot to do, but if you want to know any more, go down and see Myles Summerby at the bank. I'm afraid he's going to tell you some things I haven't told you about."

He had known that the conversation would take it out of him, and he had been correct. Such conversations always reminded him of the disorder of his life. They were always raising the question of what everything was about. As long as he could remember he had been moving from one thing to another so constantly that now he was afraid to be still.

"Well," he said to Miss Mulford, "here we go again. Mr. Bleek is taking the night train, so tell Alfred to get up early and go in to meet him in the new car. It won't hurt Mr. Bleek to see it. We'll have to sell it, I suppose. You know, this thing has taken it out of me. Maybe I'd better have that drink right now."

"No," she said, "not now, not if you're going to see . . ." There was a moment's hesitation, as though she were seeking for the right word, "Mrs. Brake this afternoon. You know she wouldn't be amused. Is Madame unhappy?"

"I wouldn't say she was cheerful," he said, "and I don't blame her. The truth, is, Madame is getting on my nerves."

"Not again," she said. "It doesn't ever help you. Did you tell her there's going to be plenty of money? You'll always be able to earn enough."

"But no property," he said. "I think she has a feeling that she might outlive me, and you know, she could be right. The moral is, don't marry them so young. Do you know, I wish to God it weren't just one thing after another? Peace in our time, that's what I want."

"You wouldn't like it," she said.

"I wish you wouldn't make pronouncements," he said. "How do you know I wouldn't like it? I've never had it."

"You could have had it if you'd wanted it," she said.

He was tired of talking about himself and thinking about himself, but there was no way of getting his mind off the track.

"You're wrong there," he said. "Anybody who has to use his head and pull things out of the air and go on the road with shows doesn't have any peace, ever."

"You'll feel better when that play is mailed to New York," she said.

"Do you really think it's all right to go?" he asked her.

It was a question which he would never have asked any woman to whom he was married because he would have suspected the answer, but it was different with her. She knew the theatre as well as he did, almost.

"It's set," she said. "It ought to go down now so that they can start with casting. It won't help to pull it around any more. You always pull things around too much. Sit down and read it through, without thinking how to make it different."

"Maybe you're right," he said. "I ought to get over thinking that things or people can be made different when they reach a certain point. But I can't read the play right now. As soon as I start, all sorts of things will start in my mind. I've been thinking too much lately."

"If you want, I'll read it to you," she said. "I'll stop you if your mind moves off."

"You haven't read this one aloud, have you?" he asked.

"No," she said, "I don't like to until they're set."

"All right," he said, "it might be a good idea. Did I ever tell you you read very well?"

"You have," she said, "but not for quite a while. *Act I. The Baker living room on Long Island.*"

"Just a minute before you start," he said. "You aren't thinking of walking out of this job and leaving me, are you?"

461

There was a pause, and she smiled. She looked almost as pretty as she had in the Higgins office.

"No," she said, "I may have had some ideas once, but it's all too late now. There's nowhere to go."

"If you don't mind my saying so," he said, "it's a great relief to me that you think it's too late now, and I hope you'll please hold that thought."

"I'm rather glad it is too late myself," she said. "But, as we were saying — *Act I. The Baker living room on Long Island.*"

"Oh dear," he said, "it always starts in a living room, doesn't it? But we might move it from Long Island to Connecticut, to show that civilization is moving north and time is marching on."

There were good and bad readers, and he had encountered all varieties. There were the overdramatic and overemotional readers, and those who attempted in a most painful way to interpret the whole cast of characters. Then there were the mechanical and perfunctory readers, whose very monotony made you forget the lines. Mulford was somewhere between all these categories. Her interpretation was honest. She never attempted to give a play qualities it did not possess. She never even overworked herself to put it in its best light. Always, when she read a play of his, she could give him a feeling of perspective and the illusion that he was listening to a stranger's work, and there could not have been a more valuable attribute. It was her voice that created the illusion, clear and cool as the voice of justice. Her voice had a transparent quality that never interfered with the lines. And yet it always held the attention.

Now it erased the morning and the day and the night before, until he was back where he belonged, to the only thing that mattered. He had been careless with human relationships and with money, but never about his work, at least when he was working, and they could put it on his tombstone if they wanted. The only trouble was that he had worked only sporadically when it was necessary for him to extricate himself from the complications of living. Now he was emancipated, living in an environment of new problems and proportions which not only approximated life

462

but were beyond life. There was only one thing about them
about which he was certain — all those elements were better
than the irrationalities and actions of the world of the flesh and
the devil.

XXIX

Once One, Always a Bread Thrower

HE WAS tired of the timeworn maxims that in the end, if one lived long enough, turned out to be only half-truths. One of the worst of them was that obvious observation that there was always a first time for everything. There had to be a first time, just as there had to be a last time, and once he had been young enough to wonder why anyone should care whether there was a first or a last. Once he had been young enough not to indulge in the morbid interest of looking back to first times. At any rate, now that he did look back, first times were not necessarily the best times. The first time he had slept with a woman, for instance, had no golden halo of retrospect. In fact, he could still be embarrassed by his shyness and inadequacies. Nothing in that experience made him long now for the return of youth. He could only feel gratitude that the first time was over. But there were other first times that never lost their shock and novelty. The first time that he had seen death was an experience that repeated itself with an equal vividness. The first time that he had heard his own lines spoken on a stage was the same as all subsequent times because his amazement and interest had never lessened. But also there were first times that could never be repeated — ones, indeed, that could never be adequately re-enacted in the imagination — the first time one fell in love, or the first time one became aware of the blessedness of silence, or the beauty of the written word. The first time that he had driven with Rhoda to the Wellington Manor House was another of those unforgettable times, never to be repeated, never to be relived in thought.

464

After all, one might marry again and again, but in the strictest sense one was only married once.

The long road to the Wellington Manor House, with its landmarks gone or vastly changed, was not the same as the earlier road. He and Rhoda had driven there in his Ford. There was no comparison between one of those high-priced new cars that endowed their owners, according to the advertisements, with cachet, distinction, and discrimination and that distant Ford of his — except that both vehicles ran on gasoline. The road along the coast and through the country had been already, back in those late twenties, a tourist road with gas stations and tourist homes, and antique shops and fried-clam stands. But compared with the road on which he was now traveling, the one of his memory was like a quaint chromo that one would buy just for a laugh for the rumpus room. There were no bird baths for sale then, no statues of the Virgin Mary, no china ducks or quaint dwarfs to carry home to put upon the lawn. There had been no aquariumlike restaurants with carhops to bring you out a frappe (that now rhymed with wrap). But why torture oneself with comparisons? One could only go over that road to the Wellington Manor House once as he had with Rhoda. You could only do that sort of thing once, and maybe it was just as well that time could break some molds. It would have been like a second honeymoon if they had ever tried to do it again, and there was always sadness in even the best of second honeymoons. He could not understand why Rhoda had ever wanted to go back and see the place, except that Rhoda never did give up when it came to certain things, and women always reacted in a different, more sentimental way to the past.

Their suitcases had been on the back seat, as tattletale as rice and ribbons. His, though worn, were of good quality, marked T.H. because even in those days before the money rolled in he had always liked good luggage. Rhoda's two suitcases, on the other hand, had been purchased by Mrs. Browne at a local store. They had been covered with a patent-leather fabric, and on each and on the glossy black hatbox were Rhoda's new initials

465

in lacquer-red: R.B.H. *Just Married* would have been a super-fluous subtitle. He had worn a plain gray suit. Rhoda was in what Mrs. Browne had called her "going-away dress," also bought off a local rack, with the short skirt of the period and the waistline that came almost to the knees. But then, Rhoda had always looked well in anything, and at any rate, they were going away.

"Isn't the Wellington Manor House sort of awfully big," Rhoda asked, "and full of all kinds of rich people, from everywhere?"

"I don't know," he said, "but I hope you're right."

He could remember the brightness of the day, and the clear, northern sunlight.

"Well, I've got my evening dress," she said, "but I wish you'd brought your tuxedo, in case there's dancing after dinner."

"It will be all right," he said, "if you want to dance. These things I have on will be all right. It's toward the end of the season, anyway, and people go there to rest. They don't go there to dress."

"You can't tell," Rhoda said. "You've never been there."

"No," he said, "but my father used to stop there when he went up to Bar Harbor."

"Isn't it funny?" she said. "We wouldn't be going here at all, if he hadn't wrecked his car. Are you sure it's all right about the room?"

She had asked the question several times before and he shared her anxiety.

"Oh yes," he said, "I telegraphed a deposit, you know."

"And you're sure it got there?"

"Yes," he said, "it got there."

"I suppose it's silly of us," she said, "if we're going to Niagara Falls, to be going for one night in just the opposite direction. We should have taken the train and gone into Boston."

"We can drive back tomorrow and leave the car and take the train. It was too late today," he said. "If we have to go to Niagara Falls, I'd rather start this way."

"It's going to be awfully expensive, isn't it?" she said.

"Never mind," he said. "You can only do this sort of thing once."

"Yes," she said, "and maybe it's just as well."

"Maybe," he said, "but I wouldn't know."

"I wouldn't know," she said. "I don't know whether it's going to be nice or not, or anything."

"There's one thing about it," he said. "It's been done a great many times before."

"I don't care how often it's been done," she said, "you and I have never done it."

"It isn't because I haven't wanted to," he said.

"All right," she said. "But anyway, we've never done it. Will there be bellboys and everything at the Wellington Manor House?"

"Yes," he said, "I guess so."

"And will everybody be looking at us?"

"I wouldn't be surprised," he said. "But just remember, lots of people have been doing this sort of thing for years and years."

"Yes," she said, "but not you and me. That's what I can't get over. It's you and me, and it isn't everybody else."

Time had given that remark a texture which had been lost on him back there.

"Don't make it sound as though we were going to the dentist, Rhoda," he said.

"I didn't say that," she said. "How can I tell, when I don't know anything about it? Gosh, I wish I weren't a virgin."

"Someone has to be a virgin at some point, sometime," he said.

"Even a man?" she asked.

"Yes, even a man," he said.

"Well," she said, "are you a virgin, too?"

It annoyed him to feel that he was blushing, but then, Rhoda was always saying something unexpected.

"You never asked me that before," he said.

"I know it," she said. "It never occurred to me until now. Are you, or are you not?"

"Not in the strictest sense of the word," he said.

She laughed and the music of it was still not lost.

"Well," she said. "At least one of us knows something. You don't mind my bringing this up, do you?"

"No," he said, "anything you bring up is always all right, Rhoda."

Then there was a catch in her voice. It was hard to remember that Rhoda occasionally was not a realist.

"It's all right, anyway, because I love you," she said. "Tom, do you love me?"

"I wouldn't be here if I didn't," he said.

"You don't feel I threw myself at you, or anything like that?" she asked. "Because I suppose I did."

"No, Rhoda," he said. "Things don't work that way. We threw ourselves at each other."

"Tom, it's going to be wonderful so long as it's you," she said. "But before we get there, stop a minute so that I can get my hair combed, and be sure I look all right, and you don't mind me with lipstick, do you?"

"No," he said, "you always look all right."

She always had, even in that going-away dress and cloche hat. Fashions had never made any change in Rhoda. She had always looked all right.

"And remind me to take off my left glove," she said. "The wedding ring, you know."

"Yes," he said. "Take off both gloves. It would look funny with one on and one off."

"Yes," she said, "and it's American plan, isn't it?"

"Yes," he said, "you can eat and eat."

"And there'll be music, won't there?" she said. "Are you sure there'll be dancing after dinner?"

The dialogue seemed strange in his memory. The Fords of that time were wonders of their species. They were moving among the spruce trees, and the country seemed more bright.

"There must be dancing," he said, "or my father wouldn't have stopped there on his way to Bar Harbor."

"That was quite a while ago," she said.

468

"I know," he told her, "but I'm sure there'll still be dancing."

"Tom," she said, "do you think your father was a virgin when he got married?"

"I can't answer that question, Rhoda," he said, "because he never told me."

He had first read the *Odyssey* in the Judge's library, but he had read it often since and had once thought of putting a portion of it into dramatic form — not the part about Calypso, but the homecoming, which had a Rip Van Winkle quality that was bound to make good drama. The rest of the *Odyssey* was as confused as life itself, though admittedly he did not know exactly how minds worked in the Bronze Age. He only knew that a return to old scenes or a wish to return had a universal appeal because it was a common, shared experience. He was Ulysses in his nearly self-thinking automobile, driving up the road through an Ithaca of his own contriving.

The landmarks were faintly familiar, but the present was part of another day which gave the past impossibility, and this sense of unfamiliarity was most unpleasant because it made him feel that he was not identifiable with the new age. The small towns were still there, with their churches, and their houses grouped to express an older tradition. But the motor road was broader, and the main streets of the towns were cluttered with a conglomeration of parked cars with which he had no sympathy. The elm trees which lined the streets were dying from a new disease, and their dead limbs were like the bones of the past. Yet there was a note of hope. There was always a note of hope. The brave days of an age to come already formed a variegated carpet along the highway. Personally, he could call this carpet mediocrity, but doubtless he was wrong. Some people must have liked the hideous braided rugs dangling from lines to attract the motorist. Some people must have felt at home in the tangle of traffic, and in the cars, as sportive to his eyes as the ending of a new geological species. Some people must have liked the clusters of small new homes sown along the road like dragons' teeth. Some people must have liked them, since the inhabitants of these new homes, judging from the play yards and the juvenile wash upon the lines, had been indulging very freely in procreation. Then there were the new flat schools to house the product; and kennels selling pups — everybody in that brave new world must have been a dog lover; and driving ranges where one could hit golf balls; and motels that looked like Washington's Mount Vernon, or like a collection of Swiss chalets; and cocktail lounges, giant steaks and grand-slam cocktails. They expressed a part of a wish that was not always material, an aspiration that had always been a part of his country — Life, Liberty and the Pursuit of Happiness. In the end he could sympathize with this appeal, since he and Rhoda had once pursued happiness there themselves.

There had been a glow over that road when he and Rhoda had driven on it, sunlight and the scent of spruce and a feeling of country stretching on either side of them, in which anything might happen. At any rate, he and Rhoda had been happy enough so that there was no need to sort out impressions.

"Tom," she said, "we must come back sometime, a long time from now, so we can remember it all again."

It had not been a good idea. It was a game in which you threw the dice just once. Memory was better than fact. Memory had endowed the Wellington Manor House with the sentimentality and color that one encountered in a romantic pastel illustration in a book of legends. It had never looked that way, he was positive, when he and Rhoda had driven up to it. The velvet lawns, the rolling hills in back, with forests resembling Fontainebleau, the alluring gingerbread trimmings like those on the old United States Hotel in Saratoga he knew had never been there at all. They had sprouted from his imagination like exotic flowers in a seed catalogue. In spite of their reality, they had never existed. It had not been a rather forlorn survival then, when he and Rhoda had turned up the drive. It was a sanctuary — a place of tea and soft music, of rockers on the wide veranda, but the idea of sanctuary had somehow gone out of fashion. It may have been that the disturbances of his generation had proved the futility of ever trying to get away from anything. No one except the very old, who knew no better, wanted rest any longer. Only the very old maintained the error that they could get away from it all by staying in one place. The Wellington Manor House had its clientèle and its waiting list in older days, but it was different now. It hurt him to see signs saying that the Wellington Manor House was only ten miles away, completely renovated, under new management, tennis, boating, bathing, fishing, a cocktail lounge, free parking, championship golf course. The Wellington Manor House was just around the corner, but why the fanfare? A glance at the parking lot was enough to show that there was room in the Wellington Manor House, room for everyone, discriminating or not, and room on the championship golf course.

He wished that the Wellington Manor House, with its new paint and its effort at sprightliness, did not make him feel his age. The place was like an old actor trying to be a part of the present. It taught a rather ugly visual lesson that one should not try new tricks after a certain space of time. The air had a new chill in it when he stopped the car at the broad steps that led to the deserted veranda, with a row of empty rocking chairs; and now and then one of them moved in the faint afternoon breeze as though invisible guests were there watching him drive up. A bell captain in a fresh new uniform was on the drive even before the car had stopped.

"Good afternoon," the bellboy said. "If you'll give me the key to the luggage compartment, sir, I'll help you with your bags."

He had always enjoyed trying to guess what bell captains were like when out of uniform. The boy at the door of the car was young, and his posture indicated military service. One could guess that he had entered the army at eighteen, had finished his hitch and was now working his way through college.

"I'm not stopping," he said. "I'm here to call on one of your guests — Mrs. Presley Brake."

"Yes, sir," the boy said. "Mrs. Brake is in the lobby waiting. May I park the car for you further along the drive?"

"Why, yes," he said, "thank you very much."

It occurred to him that the brisk bellboy, with his crew cut, was a fair norm of youth. He represented what everyone invariably lost after a certain age, and the gentle motion of the de-

471

serted rocking chairs accentuated the bereavement. When he had last seen the Wellington Manor House with Rhoda, and a boy had come to take the bags, he had thought the boy was not so much younger than he, and now that unattainable time was back for a moment. He took a dollar from his pocket. He had been remiss in many things, but he had always been generous with gratuities.

"Keep the keys in case you have to move it," he said. "I won't be here very long."

The season now was spring and the hotel had just opened, which, on second thought, might have accounted for its emptiness. Returning to any place one had known years ago inevitably conveyed some species of disillusion, but old impressions were always intermingled. He could understand that most of what he remembered had not been true memory, but imagination. Nevertheless, there was a stateliness about the place. It had the careless generosity of the turn of the century, when the income tax was nonexistent, when there was steak for breakfast and lumber cost a few cents a foot, and no architect had to be bothered about size. It was good theatre, the dark walnut of the reception desk, the window seats, the convoluted columns by the fireplace; and the indestructible black walnut furniture was still there, its elaborateness now concealed, he was sorry to see, by slip covers. To his surprise, the lobby seemed as large as he remembered it. To the left, an old couple sat working over a communal jigsaw puzzle; in the center was the reception desk; and to the right, in a sort of fireplace nook, he saw Rhoda. If he had written the directions for his own entrance and for Rhoda's placing, he could not have done better. The unworldliness of that summer hotel lobby removed any sense of strangeness from their meeting. He had not seen Rhoda since he had left the apartment for North Africa, but now an elision of time made the length of separation unimportant.

Recently when he had met someone after a term of years, he had found himself acutely conscious of physical change, but Rhoda was just as he had expected her to be. In his thoughts she had been a timeless person because she had always disregarded

472

time. He was very used to the efforts made by women, and men too, in the acting profession, to combat approaching age. Massage, wheat germ, stretching, bending, to develop a posture more youthful than it would have been in one's teens — brisk, new-cut tweeds, and then the new horizons of hair styling, the comb that corrected the graying tendency — corrected, mind you, without coloration. In addition, new pills were just around the corner. Rats could be turned from gray back to brown again, and vice versa, if they were given or lacked the proper vitamins. It was said that no one had as yet properly worked out this problem with human beings, but a great many people, including hair stylists, were bringing some very important contributions toward its solution.

A few of these cosmetic thoughts passed through his mind in the first instant he saw Rhoda, and doubtless she must have thought of the same things, since everybody had an unpleasantly acute curiosity regarding geriatrics — but this was gone almost immediately. He knew at once that no one had needed to try to keep Rhoda's hair as it had been. It was lighter; the bronze quality that he had always loved was still there, though dimmer. Looking at her professionally, he could believe that the photogenic quality of her face had improved, giving it a more compelling character; and though she had not put on an ounce of weight, her face and figure gave no sign that abstinence had been an effort. She wore a severe gray tailored suit closely resembling the one he had first bought her. The only jewelry she wore was a diamond ring, not his diamond, and no wedding band. This last change amused him when he remembered her worrying about inadvertently keeping her glove on her left hand. He was aware of no effort in Rhoda's appearance, and his final thought was that she had got exactly what she wanted.

As she stood there, she was a perfect portrait of what she had wished to become, and the irony of it was that it was now a little out of date. She was too close to the Jamesian *Portrait of a Lady* or an Edith Wharton girl in *Hudson River Bracketed* to be wholly accepted in the present scene. There would be no one of her type this year at El Morocco or the Stork. There would have

473

been a hush of wonder if she had appeared in either of these places, but this would be exactly as she would have wished it. She was still the unattainable ideal, and she had attained it. He could not help thinking that the man whose opinion on such a subject he respected more highly than anyone else in the world — the hall porter at Claridge's — would have rated Rhoda very highly, and by God, he would have been exactly right. Rhoda had turned out to be the answer to her girlhood dreams. He could think to himself when he saw her that Rhoda, of all the people he had known, had finally made it, and he could even feel honestly proud that he had contributed toward her effort and proud that she had loved him once.

"Tom," she said, "you think I look all right, don't you?"

"You do, Rhoda," he said, "and I do hope you tried."

She smiled. It was one of her smiles that stopped just on the verge of a laugh.

"You know damn well I did," she said, and her voice was as young as it was when they met on Dock Street, "and you're the hardest man I've ever known to please in that way, except possibly Arthur Higgins."

"Thank you, dear," he said. "Linking Arthur and me together in that manner makes me very happy."

The speech was brittle and nervous, but he enjoyed the dialogue, and a quality behind the words made him think they were both behaving very well. He had been afraid that he might feel resentment, but he felt none at all now that he saw her. It was hard to know exactly what he felt. In spite of all there had been between them, he could partially believe that he was meeting Rhoda for the first time. He felt the old curiosity and quickened interest.

"As long as we're going to talk," she said, "we'd better go upstairs. We have one of those turret rooms and a sitting room. Do you remember — the one you wished we had?"

"Yes," he said, "I remember. I'm glad that you don't feel you're throwing your money away uselessly, Rhoda."

She smiled again, but her smile was different.

"Tom," she said, "it's awfully nice to see you again."

474

"Now that you mention it," he said, "the journey here has been worthwhile for me. I'm glad to see you, too, Rhoda, or as they say on the West Coast, the reaction is likewise."

"God, Tom," she said, "you still do brittle dialogue."

"Yes," he said, "brittle, but sometimes it isn't corny, Rhoda."

"Do you think anything I've said is corny?" Rhoda asked.

"No," he said, "not yet, Rhoda."

"I don't know why you still impress me," she said.

"I don't know why myself," he said, "but I'm delighted if I do."

She was right that the talk was brittle. It had a Pinero-Sheridan quality, but there still was something behind it.

"Because you're more intelligent than anyone else," she said, "at least for me."

"I may be," he said, "but I've never been smart, and really intelligent people ought to be smart, Rhoda."

"They don't go together very well," she said. "I've never known anyone who was both intelligent and smart."

The lapse of time momentarily was gone. He had not believed that this could have been so possible, but he knew the reason. He was living, as always, in two worlds at once and for once these worlds had coincided.

"You come pretty near to it," he said. "You're both intelligent and smart, my dear."

"Oh, Tom," she said, "please don't say that."

He was surprised that he had hurt her. He was even sorry that he was close to being right.

"Don't take it seriously," he said. "I'm sorry."

"Tom," she said, "let's not stay down here being sorry. Let's go upstairs where we can talk."

"I'd love to," he said, "as long as Mr. Brake won't mind. By the way, where is Mr. Brake?"

"Tom," she said, "do you still feel hurt?"

"No," he said, "not any more, not really, Rhoda."

"I know I was a bitch in certain ways," she said.

"Don't," he said. "Don't let's indulge in self-reproach. I had it coming to myself in certain ways."

475

"Presley knows you're coming," she said. "In fact, he wanted you to, and he won't be back for hours. Let's go upstairs. The bell captain is so interested."

"Only in a nice way, I'm sure," he said. "He seemed to me in the brief conversation I had with him like a clean, American boy."

"That's because you tipped him a dollar," she said. "I was looking out the window. Do you know they have the same elevator here?"

"You mean," he said, "the one with all the ropes and cables?"

"Yes," she said, "and it still goes up just as slowly. Do you remember what you said about it when it took us upstairs?"

He tried to think, but for once recall was gone.

"You said it was an elevator with a New England conscience," she said, "and it wasn't sure we were married."

He was touched that she had remembered, but women were more sentimental about small things than men; and then he recollected for a hideous, derisive moment that Emily had remembered that morning the bon mot about the Princess and the Crumb.

"If that's the way it still feels," he said, "maybe it will stall between floors this time."

"Darling," she said, "I wouldn't mind if it did, except for the boy who runs it."

"That's right," he said, "we do seem to be surrounded by clean American boys."

"You were one once yourself," she said, "and so is Harold."

"That's right," he said, "there's Harold."

"I'm glad there's Harold," she said. "I have been for years and years. Let's move out of here now. Everyone guesses at strange relationships in hotels, especially the room clerks."

"Why, Rhoda," he said, "in my experience everyone guesses at them anywhere."

In the end perhaps every human contact had its own extraneous quality, and all the qualities were different. He was the one who should have known, having stirred them in his imagination for more years than he cared to remember.

476

The bedroom-sitting room suites in the two ornate turrets that flanked the enormous building were, from their self-conscious decoration, obviously the most desirable in the house. The sitting room, with its arc of windows and its huge empty fireplace, still gave a hint of the pseudo-baronial atmosphere that its architect had obviously intended. There had once been a wealthy love for baronial halls and turrets, presumably a revolt from the Gothic that itself had been a revolt from the stern lines of Colonialism. At any rate, the room was highly suitable for their conversation.

"You have an imposing view," he said, "those young stands of spruce look as though Birnam Wood were moving toward Dunsinane."

He could not tell—she often could maintain a poker face—whether Rhoda had grasped his ponderously Boothlike allusion, but he was sorry that he had made it because he could now think of himself and Rhoda partially as a Mr. and Mrs. Macbeth, and that together they had murdered one or two things unintentionally, and that a regret still lingered of which neither of them would speak.

"Yes," she said, "all the pastures and everything have grown up since we were here. The jungle is closing in, but don't you have a feeling that everything else is closing in?"

An urgency in her question disturbed him without his being able to grasp exactly what she meant. Talking to her was like returning to another country whose language he had once spoken fluently but which he had not used recently.

"Maybe I have," he said, "but I don't know what you mean by everything else."

She smiled, and there was no change whatsoever in the quickness of her smile.

"The end of the show," she said. "You always used to say that in the third act that everything should be closing in."

"Oh, yes, the end of the show," he said. "I suppose it is getting to be about time when the exurbanites start wondering whether they can catch the last train to New Canaan, but I wouldn't say we were quite there yet."

"You'd like a drink, wouldn't you?" she asked. "Presley has some special Scotch and he'd feel hurt if you didn't try it."

There was one thing of which he was sure; he did not care in the least whether Presley was hurt or not.

"I'm of two minds," he said. "I've got to be driving back and I have an idea that I drank a good deal of Scotch last evening."

"I know," she said, "you had the Bramhalls up to dinner. Marion called me this morning."

"Yes," he said, "Emily asked them because she knew I wouldn't want to go up to their farm. It was like old times, partially."

It was only fair to mention Emily as long as she had mentioned Presley.

"I'll get the glasses and things," she said. "I've told the boy already to bring up ice."

"Oh," he said, "well, if he's bringing up the ice."

"And don't give him a dollar," she said. "I can't bear seeing you hand out dollars."

"Why can't you?" he asked. "I don't quite follow you."

"Oh, I don't know," she said. "I just know that I can't bear it. Here he comes now. Have him put it on the table by the window."

It was the bell captain again with a neat paper ice container and three tall glasses, two bottles of soda and one of quinine water. The three glasses, he thought, made a tactful implication, and as he put his hand in his pocket, he had a vision of platoons of bellboys through the years bringing ice and glasses—a restive vision, an overtone to a wasted life—but in America, if you wanted a drink, you had to have an ice cube.

"Shall I open the soda, sir?" the captain asked. "Or shall I leave the opener on the tray?"

"You'd better leave it in case Mrs. Harrow hasn't an opener with her," he said, and then immediately realized his mistake, and Rhoda was coming from the bedroom with a whiskey bottle.

"I beg everybody's pardon," he said. "It was a slip of the tongue. I meant Mrs. Brake, captain."

He pulled a dollar from his pocket and Rhoda spoke quickly.

478

"Mr. Harrow wants some silver if you have any," she said.

"Of course he hasn't any," Tom said. "Silver only wears out pockets. Stick to dollars, captain, and the quarters will take care of themselves."

"Oh, God," Rhoda said, "you haven't changed at all."

He was still laughing after the captain closed the door.

"It's unanticipated," he said, "isn't it? Yes, it's just the same. My weakness for you still persists. But then, I never did have a strong character. Never mind ice for me. To hell with ice."

"You've got to have ice if you paid a dollar for it," she said.

"You're wrong there," he said. "You don't necessarily get what you pay for, Rhoda."

"I wonder what he'll be saying to the clerk downstairs," she said.

"My dear," he said, "are you still worrying about what people say downstairs?"

He was glad when he sat down to see that Rhoda had not put ice in his glass. Although it was a very minor triumph, all success in life was the summation of such small things. He sat looking out of the window at the old fields covered by aggressive young spruce that stood with the military precision of wooden soldiers. Rhoda sat with her accurate untheatrical posture on the sofa with her back to the view. He had been careful not to sit beside her, not from a lack of desire, or because of fear of misinterpretation, but rather from a sense of something impending. The spruces made him think of what she had said about everything closing in. Birnam Wood was moving up to Dunsinane. Obviously things had always been moving from his earliest days, but he had not noticed the approach until lately. He was sorry to be confronted suddenly with the thought that the margin of life's possibilities had been narrowing rapidly for a long, long time until there no longer remained an adequate field for trial or error. He was glad to be in her company, because they had tried many of the same things together and now neither of them could erase the old mistakes. He had tossed away a great many things that were valuable as casually as he had tossed the dollar to the captain,

479

and now he was not sure that he cared. If you had tossed enough away, there was something gained in the sheer exercise of tossing.

"Tom," she asked, "what are you thinking about?"

"I'm thinking that I'm glad you asked me here," he said.

"You mean because you're glad to see me?" she asked.

"Yes," he said, "partially. Frankly, I thought it would be more of an emotional strain, and instead it isn't one. That's one peculiar thing about living, isn't it? You haven't the remotest idea what's going to be tough until you do it, and no one can tell you anything beforehand. At least no one ever told me."

In the silence that followed, he found himself smiling when he looked at her and he was thinking again that he was glad that she had asked him there. He had seldom felt so free to speak to anyone, so free that he had a fear of growing loquacious.

"Tom," she said, "are you sorry that you married me?"

"No dear," he said, "not at all. I wouldn't have missed a minute of it."

"You're not being nasty nice, are you?" she asked. "You're not thinking I caught you unawares because I was a designing little bitch?"

He took a sip of her husband's whiskey; it tasted exactly as he thought it would taste, too heavy, too rare, too redolent of heather, and to hell with heather and aroma. He was weary of aroma.

"Let's get this straight," he said, "and incidentally, I've been giving this matter quite a little thought lately. Don't give yourself any credit. No one gets into anything because someone makes him. The fault, dear Brutus, is not in our stars, but in ourselves, that we are underlings."

She gave the paper ice container an angry push and the ice made a complaining sound, not at all like the tinkle of ice on glass of which one read in childhood.

"I wish you'd stop quoting Shakespeare," she said. "You only do when you're difficult."

It was exactly like old times.

"At any rate, he's quotable," he said, "and it's remarkable

how few people nowadays are. For instance, I'm not quotable."

"No," she said, "at least not in polite society."

It was exactly like old times.

"Marion Bramhall said I'm quotable," he said, "last night."

"Marion's a fool," she said. "Not that I mean to be disagreeable, dear."

"I'm glad to hear you say so," he said. "It relieves me after all these years."

"All right," she said, "what did Marion think you said that she thought was quotable?"

The whiskey tasted of heather that was thicker than the songs of the late Sir Harry Lauder, and why was it that so much in life seemed to end in what resembled defunct Palace Theatre vaudeville?

"Well, it was this way," he said, "she was sitting next to me at dinner, and there had been a slight domestic upheaval before dinner — not over infidelity, but only over finances — and Marion Bramhall said something about casting bread upon the waters, and I said, quick as a flash — you know the way I am — I've always cast my bread upon the gals. Marion, not I, thought that this was quotable."

It was a long speech, but it had held her attention, and that was the main thing, to hold attention.

"Marion would have said it was quotable," she said, "and you've always been a bread thrower."

"Only on the gals," he said.

"Oh, no," she said, "you've thrown it everywhere."

It was not the Heather Dew, or whatever the whiskey was called, but her voice that made him feel happy again.

"It's sweet of you to say that," he said, "and to know that I'm consistent, and now we're on the subject, I want to tell you something else. Yesterday morning when I went to get the mail, a new, young minister in front of the Congregational Church asked me to step inside. Frankly, I'd never been there since we were married, Rhoda, although I've read a good deal of the Bible and I do believe in God — but that isn't the point I'm arriving at."

481

"Well," she said, "it ought to be."

"I know," he said, "that's a difficulty with everything. Everything ought to be, and very little is. I know it and I'm sure God knows it, but what I want to mention is a thought that came over me while I was there."

"What thought?" she asked.

"Well," he said, "it was a simple thought, and I'd be glad to tell you if you could get me some gin to mix with this tonic here, because I can't stand the skirl of the bagpipes in your husband's Scotch, Rhoda, and the bell captain has left me the opener in case I want to open the tonic bottle. I paid him a dollar for it. He didn't have any silver. How about some gin?"

She did not smile, but she still had a way of laughing when she did not laugh.

"It's a rare kind of gin," she said, "not ordinary gin."

"All right," he said, "even if it comes from the Tower of London."

"All right," she said, "but tell me first what you thought of in the church. I loved it, the church. I've always loved to think of it."

"Yes," he said, "brides are always beautiful. How about the gin?"

"You can have it," she said, "if you tell me what you thought of."

"All right," he said, "but artistically I've always tried to avoid corn, except occasionally in a movie. There wasn't any background music and the place was so dead-quiet Calvinist it startled me. I don't know why it is lately that quiet places do; maybe they make me feel afraid of God, not that I honestly feel afraid. It may be only the thought of an impending conversation."

"Go ahead," she said, "tell what you thought. You've always been afraid of telling what you think."

"I'm not afraid," he said. "Only when you tell what you think, it's so simple that there isn't much to say. All right, I thought I loved you when you were walking up the aisle, and I thought I loved you still. It's as simple as that, and don't let me ask you again — go out and get me the gin."

482

It only went to prove that unrehearsed lines in real life left a great deal to be desired. On the stage the mood could be perfect enough to give a writer and an audience artistic satisfaction; and he had written plenty of such scenes, so many that they confused themselves with everyday living. He knew that the things that he had said were artistically clumsy.

She stared at him and the lines of her face moved into a ludicrous, clumsy pattern, and then she sobbed discordantly.

"Darling," she said, "God, it's been dull without you. I don't know how I've stood it."

"Well, well," he said, but the pace was bad again, and she stopped him before he could make any obvious reply.

"Don't say what you're going to," she said, "because it might be true. Just stand here, don't say anything, and I'll go get your goddam gin."

"You don't have to," he said, "I can take it or leave it alone, Rhoda."

"Stop talking," she said, "until I come back, but I'll give you something to think about while I'm gone. I always loved you, too, only I didn't know it until he made an honest woman of me. Now don't ask me why. Please don't say anything."

Fortunately there was a moment's pause, while he listened to her unlocking her suitcase and blowing her nose and running water in the bathroom; and those offstage noises were intensely melancholy. He stood looking out the window at Birnam Wood and in those few minutes the trees seemed to have moved nearer. At least, he thought, the last thing he had said was both significant and terrible. It was true that he could take it or leave it alone, but instead of its being consoling, the fact was utter devastation.

"God," he said, without knowing he was speaking until he heard his voice, "it takes a lot of living before you can take it or leave it alone."

His awareness of what went on around him was disturbed by what had previously gone on. He did not know she was back in the room until he heard her voice near him.

"What's that you were saying?" she asked.

483

"Oh, nothing much," he said. "I was only quoting Edgar Guest, just saying I'd done a heap of living."

"I wish you wouldn't keep on quoting people," she said, "but maybe that's what God put us here to do."

"How's that again?" he asked. "Do what?"

"Live," she said, "live while you're alive."

"Well, if that's what He wants," he said, "He ought to be pretty proud of me."

"You'd better put some ice in that," she said. "You paid for it, you know."

"Don't be so obvious, my dear," he said. "Don't you know by this time, for heaven's sake, that you pay for everything?"

"Yes," she said, "I know by this time, I really do."

It occurred to him that in a surprisingly short time they had said nearly all they could ever say to each other, as things were now.

"Well, that's a real step forward," he said, and he sat down and picked up his glass. "The years we've wasted, the tears we've wasted."

"Please," she said, "stop quoting things. You and I don't have to quote."

"Well," he said, "all right. Instead I'll ask you a personal question. If you loved me in this way, why did you walk out on me?"

"I told you," she said. "I didn't know I loved you until I did it."

"Well, well," he said, "that's one way of reaching a conclusion."

"It was the uncertainty, Tom," she said. "I couldn't see what was going to happen to us."

"Well, we both know now," he said, "and this is very highly scented gin. Full many a cup of this aristocratic gin shall drown the memory of this insolence. Pardon me for quoting, Rhoda."

It was what he had always done, he was thinking. He had run around end and quoted, and now there was no end to run around. He was in the age of the atom bomb, with no place to hide. He was more at ease because he was sure that the most traumatic part of their meeting was nearly over, and she must

484

have felt it too, because when she sat down on the sofa with her back to the window, her hand and voice were steady.

"I hated it when you married Hopedale," she said.

"That makes me happy, my dear," he said, "it was an aggression, and now we're being frank, I hated it after I married Hopedale."

"Then why did you marry Emily?" she asked.

"Darling," he said, "that's a personal question and you're lucky that at the moment I'm tired of being a gentleman. Still, let's neither you nor me be too hard on Emily, because in many ways she has a heart of gold. I imagine I married her because Arthur Higgins hoped I would, and besides, she was a Hoosier girl at heart."

"Wasn't I ever a Hoosier girl?" she asked.

"No," he said, "and let's not get too personal or I'll ask you why you married Brake."

"You know why," she said, "but please don't use the word. Tom, it's like too much candy. Don't use the word, but I'll use it if you want me to. I'm awfully sick of security."

Unfortunately, he could take it or leave it now.

"For instance," she said, "Presley calls gin a charwoman's drink."

"Darling," he said, "I'm glad you told me, but let's not go any further."

"Tom, dear, I've missed you so," she said.

The danger in any sort of scene, he had always found, was that of repetition, which crept up insidiously when one least expected it, and now Rhoda had repeated herself. It was time to cut and move forward and no longer time to be bejaped by a never-never-land. It was a time to think of the grimness of the present. It was no time to be escaping from it into Bartlett's *Familiar Quotations* and no time to be speculating upon the tragedy of living. In the end there was nothing you could do except repent, and repentance in itself was usually untherapeutic and unacceptable to Providence. What surprised him was that he had forgotten for so long to ask her why she had wanted to see him.

It was possible that her real wish to see him lay in the scene they had acted, but there must have been an ostensible reason.

"Rhoda," he said, "I hope my reactions show, at least on paper, how glad I've been to see you. It has meant a great deal to me when combined with my other problems, but just why did you want to see me?"

He was delighted that he did not anticipate her answer.

"Tom," she said, "I completely forgot as soon as we started talking. Presley wanted me to see you."

The name made a disagreeable interruption which brought a mental picture of intimacies and banalities and finally frustration.

"I wouldn't say it's very bright of him," he said.

She shook her head in patient annoyance, showing he had not followed her train of thought.

"You don't know Presley," she said. "He doesn't worry about things like this. He doesn't worry any more about you in your way than you used to worry about him, but he wants to be fair. I must say I'm getting tired of men who always want to be fair. It's so male, if you know what I mean. It's so like *Tom Brown's School Days.*"

"Don't quote," he said. "Let's try to stop telling each other about the good books we've read. What does Tom Brown want to be fair about? Had he been having a good talk with Matthew Arnold?"

Rhoda shook her head patiently again.

"Not with Matthew Arnold, with the bank," she said, "and the Board, and it wasn't his business, but he heard they had called your loan."

When she had finished speaking, he had no idea exactly how he felt, except that the silence in the room kept him silent and motionless for a very appreciable time.

"It goes to show you shouldn't ever trust banks," he said. "Why the hell should he be concerned?"

"Tom," she said, and she moved her hand toward his, and he thought she was going to touch him, but she did not, "I was afraid you were going to act this way. You're always so queer

486

about common sense. He's worried about the separation settlement you made — you know, the securities you gave me. I really don't need them, Tom."

He did not answer because he could not think of any reply. The one thing that struck him was the incongruity of money with his mood, and he thought again that every individual differed from everyone else when it came to money.

"He wants me to give you the settlement back," she said. "I don't need it at all, you know."

He wished that he could analyze his feelings. It would have been better if she had made the suggestion herself, but not much better.

"Why, the son-of-a-bitch!" he said, and he found that he was on his feet when he said it, and now that the words were out and now that the impact of them made her draw her breath in sharply, he was sorry for his reaction, but not entirely sorry. One had to be consistent sometime and in the end pride and dignity had to exist occasionally; and for a moment, at any rate, he had forgotten conventional behavior and it was just as well to forget such things occasionally. He had taken her hands in his, and he had bent and kissed them. It was only immediately after he had done so that the thought came over him that he was never bad at kissing hands.

"Darling," he said, "forgive me. I'm sorry to strike an attitude. It's the rubbing shoulders with show business. Don't make me explain it. I'm sorry I reacted. Put it down as involuntary ingratitude and remember that I love you, dear."

He was not in control of his emotions. For the first time in years he realized that he was on the verge of weeping, and the realization shook him because he was able to ask himself the question: Just what in hell was he weeping about? Was it proximity to Rhoda? Was it regret for the past, or apprehension of the future? Or a feeling that the show was almost over, that the customers were fidgeting and coughing, and it was time to get them off to Grand Central? There was one thing certain: tears were useless, even in a confessional.

"Tom," she said, "I thought that was what you'd do."

487

"Well, thanks," he said. "I'm glad you thought it, Rhoda."

The clasp of her hands tightened over his for a moment, and she spoke very quickly, like a child at school, afraid she might forget a poem.

"Tom, how would it be if I left him, and we tried it all again?"

It was enough, when you came to balance it, and more than enough. He had been through enough thinking and through enough questions, and it was not fair to take on more without time for consideration. Ask a silly question, the saying was, and you get a silly answer.

"Rhoda, dear," he said, "that makes me very pleased because I know you mean it, dear, and I'm not dodging any issues. I'd enjoy it very much, but maybe it's time to take away the dancing girls, to quote the late Walter De la Mare, if you'll pardon me one more quote, darling, and if it was De la Mare. After all, Presley must be a good guy and he means well, even if he has a horrid taste in liquor. And Emily means well — and dammit all, it's our fault, not their fault, Rhoda — but again, thanks a lot."

"I wish you wouldn't always speak lines," she said, "but I suppose you can't help it. Anyway, under the circumstances, the least you can do is to kiss me good-by."

"Yes, Rhoda," he said. "I can't speak for Emily, but perhaps Presley wouldn't mind."

As he closed the door of the turret suite behind him, he realized he had never been so acutely aware before of the lateness of his time. In fact, it had never occurred to him that he would reach a stage of life at which he could no longer hopefully believe that a benevolent future could alter circumstances. Now he knew as sure as fate that never in this life would he encounter Rhoda Browne again.

XXX

The Right Thing Done and Over, and Night Was Drawing Nigh

It was later than he thought, and again he disliked reminding himself of lateness. Standing on the hotel veranda, he saw that the late May sun was close to setting — a serious matter, since this would mean that he would be late for dinner, and Emily, being invariably tardy about everything herself, was beginning to take a malicious comfort in expressing annoyance whenever he was late. The main dinner dishes would be dried in the oven and this would be annoying to Alfred and his wife, who might, in spite of the wages they received, give notice. They probably would in any event, as soon as the household furniture came up for auction. Fictional loyalty could not be expected from anyone in Alfred's position, but there was no use casting too far into the future. There was nothing over the horizon any longer to arouse the happy anticipations that had burgeoned in that region once. It was advisable to set one foot before the other, to live from day to day, or perhaps from hour to hour, or minute to minute. There was always happiness in strings of minutes, provided one had the sense to cut them into segments. And now the big dream motor car of wish-fulfillment was at the door. The moment the bell captain had seen him, that nice young man with his fresh crewcut had rushed out to fetch it.

That fin-tailed car of distinction, beloved by those who really cared, was awaiting him at the door, though in a day or two it would go out the window. It soothed him to view its overinflated pretentiousness. There was a futility in the spectacle, now that the sun was growing low, that emphasized his changing mood. There were meaningless spaces in the car, reminiscent of blanks in his own life . . . too many glove compartments, too many buttons on the panel, too many gadgets each cynically calculated to arouse in the bosom of a parvenu a desire to possess. It did not assist his mood to have the idea cross his mind that the whole streamlined, functional but overdeveloped body of the car was reminiscent of defects that existed in portions of his own dramatic work. In spite of his efforts at restraint, parts had been flamboyant and others had a tinny echo. He had always been tempted by the intellectual gadgets of technique and swayed by an inordinate, febrile desire to please — the affable Mr. Harrow. The phrase rang unpleasantly through his mind. The affable Mr. Harrow's affluent car was waiting at the door and his compulsive desire to appear well in the eyes of others was still active.

"Here, son," he said, "and thanks."

He gave the boy another dollar, and now as he moved behind the wheel, he adjusted his tweed golf cap. There had been no earthly reason to have handed out another dollar, and yet the gesture pleased him in that it was a minor aggression against almost everything, and also there was a possibility that Rhoda might be watching, not that he looked in that direction. If you made an exit, there was no harm in keeping it in character.

"Thank you, sir," the captain said, "come back soon."

Those were the last words spoken to him as he left the Wellington Manor House, sad words, because he knew he would never go there again. They rang like a coin on a counter, more insistent than the soothing sound of the motor's docilely alert cylinders. He had done the right thing and it would never be undone. This was the worst attribute of doing the right thing — one seldom, if ever, commented upon by Ralph Waldo Emerson.

Doing the right thing, he now realized, was enough of a novelty in his life to hold his interest and attention. Now that he faced the fact, he could understand why he had not done the right thing more often, but he had done it this time. He had turned down money and a further offer by a woman he still loved. He had done it, and he had no great wish to consider why he had, except to admit that pride and responsibility had obtruded themselves, unexpectedly. He was returning now rapidly, because of the lateness of the hour, to the third woman he had married, and that was the right thing. It was not a fair shake that, after behaving in what, according to convention, was an admirable manner, he should be able to derive no happiness or even smug satisfaction from the act. It may have been his aunt, he was thinking, and not his mother who had first told him that virtue was its own reward, and this had sounded well at the time. He had never expected to learn that this piece of wisdom, like many others, had its undertone of mockery and would take its own place in the procession of thoughts in which he could take no pleasure.

For purely dramatic reasons he had made many of his stage characters do the right thing, customarily in the third act, and the reason for this was obvious. When the right thing was achieved, it was time to drop the curtain because not much else could happen in the face of this accomplished fact.

Yet in the ending of a play he had seldom approved of a definite conclusion, but had preferred to leave the impression with his audience that only an episode was over when the curtain fell, and that the characters who had solved their problems by doing the right thing or the wrong thing would continue existing behind the curtain, still busy about their lives. That was approved technique in playwriting, but now it was not consoling. True, he himself was moving on after having done the right thing. The car was running perfectly, and he had always enjoyed driving an expensive motor car. But was all this haste or the journey itself worthwhile? After all, where would the car take him? Only into a highly foreseeable future in which there was nothing that he did not already know. There was nothing new in Emily, and nothing startling in the play that he had finished. It was competent and up to standard, but was there more? Doubtless he could write other plays and would be obliged to do so, but there would be no surprise about them except the possibility of a failure. The truth was that the time had nearly run from its inverted glass.

There it was, and there it wasn't. It was again like that persistent question of the shell-game operator at a half-forgotten county fair. Where was the little joker now?

He was on the main north-south highway, and the traffic was light so that he could step on the gas and move at sixty miles an hour back to everything that was waiting, but still he could not avoid the fact that there was nothing in front of him that mattered. He had in reality been traveling rapidly all his life over a shoddy road, decorated as meretriciously as the north-south highway, with its plastic refreshment booths and overnight motels . . . places of temporary respite for temporary indulgence, but no more. Still, once there had been something more, and once again, where was the little joker now? He had lost the little joker somewhere along the way.

He was back in the First Congregationalist Church again and Mr. Naughton, that vanished minister, was saying, "God bless you, Thomas." Those were days when he had everything without knowing it, youth, and Rhoda, and his untarnished talent. There was no reason to bolster his ego any longer now that he had done the right thing and was going home. There was no solace in being a psychopathic liar like Walter Price. He could face the truth without a tremor, now that he was going home. He was a mediocre playwright who was occasionally a good one, and he had failed in his human relationships besides. He had failed in ordinary consistency, and the worst of it was that the show was dragging on into a shocking anticlimax, with no way of ending it, no way of cutting short the script. At least he was sure there was no way until he found himself availing himself of one about ten miles down on the north-south highway where the road curved adequately, but still sharply, on a cliff that overlooked the sea.

He could tell himself that his action was not conscious. In fact, he was very sure of this, but when he faced what was happening nothing had been sheer accident. Granted that the car was at a high speed, it had the weight and balance to hold it on such a curve. It was his own impulse at the wheel that jerked it across the road toward the highway fence above the granite cliff by the sea. When he was aware of this, he was deeply shocked because he knew that he had deliberately intended it. In the instants that were left, there was time to recollect that there was always a pressure of self-destruction somewhere in any background. He saw the deep blue of the sea colored by the setting sun, and concrete posts with the cables between them; and obviously a heavy car like his could knock the structure down. He could see that he was facing an ending as surely as Ethan Frome had faced his on a wintry hill, and that the time was too short for successful countermeasures; but he had the sense not to step too hard on the power brakes or to turn the wheel too abruptly. Above all, it became clear in his mind that he did not want to die.

He could see and think so clearly that everything progressed in slow motion. The car was slowing down and its angle of impact had changed. He saw the left fender strike a post. He saw the fender crumple and heard the breaking of glass of a headlight. The impact threw him against the wheel, but the car was stopped. It had not broken through and still was on the road.

His being thrown against the wheel had knocked his wind out so that he found he was fighting to regain his breath and also against a wave of nausea. His hands shook as he put the car in reverse, and it moved back easily. The door was not jammed but his hands and knees still shook when he stepped out upon the road, and he was still fighting for his breath. When he moved to the front of the car, he saw that the fender was badly crumpled, but still free of the tire, and the radiator was not leaking. After all, it did pay perhaps to drive a high-priced car. He did not like to estimate what the repairs would cost, but the car could take him home.

The road had been clear, since it was the hour when the average motorist drew off to eat the home-cooked meals offered at the roadside, but nothing was empty for long on such a route. There was no reason for him to have been startled by the sound of a motorcycle behind him. It was a state trooper, of course, and all sorts of signs had told him that the road was carefully patrolled. The motorcycle came to a coughing stop behind the car and the trooper swung off it in a coordinated, single motion.

The appearance of the trooper had made him feel for the first time that he might have died without knowing it. The sunset, the sea, the roadside and the officer were all reminiscent of any of those tales or plays of death in which our hero does not know he has passed on until unlikely details dawn upon his consciousness. The trooper just then might readily have been a representative of the Power Above All Things, like the man with the account book in *Liliom* or the pilot in *Outward Bound*.

The trooper gave a worldly and unworldly illusion in the sunset because state troopers had always appeared to him like the chorus of a Viennese operetta. The man was dressed in light blue, a tightly buttoned tunic in the tradition of the Canadian Mounties. In the same tradition, he wore a ten-gallon hat whose stiff brim would protect him from sun and rain. He also wore flaring riding breeches with dark blue stripes and shiny black puttees, although it was doubtful whether he or anybody else in his barracks had ever been on horseback. Then there was his belt, with his efficient holster to round out the tableau. It was possible indeed to hold the thought that this lithe young man moving toward him briskly might have been an emissary of God, and the homeliness of his first question would have delighted Mr. Molnár.

"Just what do you think you're doing, Mac?" the trooper asked.

Tom Harrow had conversed with state troopers before, and it was an error to think that they all looked and thought alike, for once scrupulously observed, they became individuals. The man before him was in his middle thirties, with service in the last war stamped on him, conceivably military police. His face was sunburned. Though very closely shaven, his chin and jaw had a dark look and his eyebrows and hair were coal-black. "Black Irish" was probably the word for him, but second or third generation, judging from his speech. There was nothing in common between them except the crumpled car and the line of duty, until the officer had asked his question. He asked what he had been doing, and now it was time to answer.

"I'm not exactly sure what I was doing, officer," he said. "I'm still sorting it out in my mind."

494

It was probably necessary to maintain the dignity of the law by being arrogantly slow. The trooper walked to the fender and tapped it with his forefinger.

"Yeah," he said, "I was betting you'd break through. You got horseshoes in both pockets, Mac."

The shaking had gone from his hands, and except for a taste of bile in his mouth, his impulse to be sick was over, and it was the second time the officer had called him Mac.

"Trooper," he said, "from now on you call me 'mister,' or if you don't like that, call me 'sir.'"

He knew exactly the military way to say it, and the presence of the high bracket car was a help.

"I guess you've been an army officer," the trooper said.

"I was," he said, "not that the fact is germane, trooper."

He was talking in as dated a manner as someone out of the works of Richard Harding Davis. He had not intended to be patronizing, nor would he have been if he had not still been shaken; but the trooper's manner changed, and now he was curious rather than personal. Someone had said once that all cops were nice when you got to know them. He doubted it, and he had no desire to know the trooper, but the atmosphere was different.

"Didn't you see me in your rear-view mirror?" the trooper asked. "I'd been following you for the last five miles. You were over the speed limit, mister."

Tom was feeling better, but he still felt a sense of unreality. He had almost gone to some other place.

"I wasn't looking," he said. "I was thinking about other problems."

"Drivers shouldn't have problems," the trooper said.

The trooper unbuttoned his breast pocket, not the one with the whistle, and took out his book and pencil.

"Well," Tom Harrow said, and the sight of the book relieved him, "now it looks as though we're getting somewhere."

"Mister," the trooper said, "you were over the limit but you were driving good. What made you swerve over? Did you fall asleep?"

495

A truck passed them going north, oversized and overloaded, and its noise broke his thoughts.

"Perhaps I'd better move the car over into the right lane," Tom said.

"Never mind it now," the trooper said. "I asked: did you fall asleep, mister?"

"No, no, I wasn't asleep," Tom Harrow said. "I told you, my attention was off the road."

The trooper took a step nearer.

"How many drinks have you had, mister?"

Tom found himself wishing he had the money now that had gone for liquor bills. But, as it was, the officer would find nothing on his breath. If necessary he could walk a mile on a straight chalk line.

"That's a frank question; it deserves a frank answer," he said. "I was calling on someone and, yes, she did offer me a drink."

He felt his face redden because there was no reason for Rhoda or her memory to have entered the conversation, but now she was there, part of the sunset, part of the cold air that came off the ocean.

"To be more accurate," he said, "a lady offered me a drink of her husband's liquor. First some whiskey — Scotch — and it was so smoky that I couldn't get it down. Self-consciously smoky is what I mean. Then I asked her, how about some gin? And I couldn't take the gin either. It was too discriminating, intended solely for gentlemen of distinction, son; and, as it happened, I didn't feel I had any distinction at the time. No, I haven't been drinking lately, except for two swallows, son."

The eyes of the trooper were still on him, like eyes of justice.

"You don't look like you'd turn down smoky liquor," the trooper said.

Then Tom Harrow found that he was growing impatient.

"Suppose we leave my looks right here, officer," he said. "You can arrest me for speeding, or reckless driving — and here's my license — but suppose you do something. It's getting late."

The trooper made a notation in his book, but he was not writing a ticket.

496

"Oh," he said, "so you live right down the line?"

"Yes," Tom Harrow answered. "At least at the present time."

"Are you feeling all right, mister?" the trooper asked. "Not hurt or nervy or anything?"

"I'm feeling all right," Tom Harrow said. "In fact, I'm feeling fine."

"You wouldn't feel better if I was to drive you?"

"Why, no," he answered. "No, thanks. But it's kind of you to suggest it."

"You wouldn't like me to follow behind and see no one picks you up with that broken fender and only one good light?"

The trooper was letting Tom off and he appreciated it. He realized only later that his answer was, in its way, an answer to almost everything.

"Why, thanks," Tom said, "I can drive back alone all right."

In the end, no matter how many were in the car, you always drove alone.